Cian's Song: We Are Coming Home

New Beginnings M/M Series Part Three (Special Edition)

Kashel Char

Kashel Char Author

Copyright

Contents

Disclaimer VI

Warning VIII

Anunnaki Family Tree 1

Timeline 2

From the Author 5

Prologue 7

Song of the Last Anunnaki 8

Introduction 10

1. Chapter One 12

General Cian Romanov 14

2. Chapter Two 34

General Brad McCormick 36

3. Chapter Three 51

Ishtar the last Anunnaki 53

4. Chapter Four 65

Mika Romanov 67

5. Chapter Five 80

Leo 82

6. Chapter Six 95

Andrew 97

7. Chapter Seven 104

Juandre 106

8. Chapter Eight 117

General Cian Romanov 119

9. Chapter Nine 133

Ivan Romanov 135

10. Chapter Ten 145

Eryn, King of the Brawl 147

11. Chapter Eleven 157

Barkor, the Promised Prince 159

12. Chapter Twelve 184

Juandre 186

13. Chapter Thirteen 200

Andrew 202

14. Chapter Fourteen 210

General Cian Romanov 212

15. Chapter Fifteen 231

General Cian Romanov 233
16. Chapter Sixteen 243
Barkor, the Promised Prince 245
17. Chapter Seventeen 253
General Cian Romanov 255
18. Chapter Eighteen 271
Ivan Romanov 273
19. Chapter Nineteen 278
Juandre 280
20. Chapter Twenty 293
General Cian Romanov 295
21. Chapter Twenty-One 315
Juandre 317
22. Chapter Twenty-Two 339
Andrew 341
23. Chapter Twenty-Three 349
General Cian Romanov 351
About the Author 373

Disclaimer

The Brawl King: We Are Not Alone – New Beginnings Part Two which is Kashel's debut novel, followed by *Cian's Song: We Are Coming Home – New Beginnings Part Three* and was inspired by the Characters, Place, and Time, who appeared in *Men of Phoenix*, written by Stefan Pride which was rewritten and retitled *New Beginnings: We Are On Our Own – Part One* with the cooperation of Stefan Pride.

These are post-apocalyptic sci-fi fantasy works featuring gifted otherworldly paranormal beings falling in love while saving the last of mankind.

Dear Readers/Listeners

This story has explicit and graphic depictions of a quadruple amputee prisoner, off-the-page mention of non-consensual sexual acts, cannibalism, and imprisonment. It is unsuitable for young and sensitive readers or anyone offended by gay sex.

This is a work of fiction. Names, characters, places, and incidents are products of the author's imagination or used fictitiously. Any resemblance to actual events, locales, business establishments, or persons,

Warning

APSU TIAMAT NIBIRU

MUMMU LAHMU LAHAMU

ANTU KI(URASH) ANU(AN)

ENKI NANA ENLIL

HOMO-SAPIENS EDEN

ADAMO EVE UTU

ARYAN

ISHTAR/INANNA

VIKING

ANDREW LULAL SHARA

ROMANOV

JUANDRE ERYN

CIAN

IVAN

BARKOR

PETER

Timeline

1968 A.D. Andrew and Peter meet Ishtar.

2004 A.D. Juandre and Andrew's story begins. (Just Like a Butterfly.)

2014 A.D. Timeline Switch.

3–5 years before Doomsday (2046 A.D.) Eryn and his brothers are born.

3 years after Doomsday, the story of the Men of Phoenix begins. (*New Beginnings: We Are On Our Own.*)

5 years after Doomsday, the marriage of Mika and Connor takes place.

6 years after Doomsday, the Big Flood (Tsunamis) happens, and, on that same day, the Romanov twins are born, marking it as the *Year of the Twins: 1 A.T.*

6 A.T. The story of Eryn the Brawl King begins. (*The Brawl King: We Are Not Alone.*)

21 A.T. Cian and Ivan's Anunnaki heritage is revealed. Eryn makes each a sword of gold by dividing the forks on his trident so that they can focus their power on wrapping Phoenix in a protective layer to save their city from a string of global volcanic eruptions that led to the almost-instantaneous melting of the polar ice caps and global storms, turning Earth on its axis.

72 A.T. Cian's first sighting of the hydrogen mining ship of the Zelk.

93 A.T. Cian's Song—begins.

95 A.T. Rebirth of Earth's Timeline.

From the Author

As a child, I always had my nose in encyclopedias. (That was before the internet and Google.) I would read them for fun and had hoped to discover the secret to making my father's car run on water, by adding a little pill, like Canderel, that made his coffee taste sweet. In my young mind, I thought if I could make the water taste like petrol, then it should work like petrol. I guess my fascination with alternative energies and sound waves stems from that.

I mention in Cian's Song using electrical energy generated by sound energy. Principles related to sound waves and energy production have been understood for a long time. Despite this, the technology to turn sound energy into electricity is thought to be in its early stages. And I wonder why?

However, as scientists and technicians investigate and improve the technologies involved in sound-generated electricity, sound energy may produce mass electricity one day. Hopefully soon.

If that sounds like a pipe dream, remember solar and wind power were once beyond our grasp, too.

To learn more about sound energy and other renewable energy resources, visit https://justenergy.com/blog/sound-energy-everything-you-need-to-know/

Love to all creatures

Kashel Char

Prologue

Once Phoenix had sunk into the depths of the Earth's oceans, the prophecy thereof had reached full circle:

You will know them by their glowing skin that ran like blue lightning on the clouds' edges. The blue of their fire cannot be contained. So shall the promised children of the Anunnaki rise and sing their song to their creation. Behold, their strength is not in their loins but encased within their hearts. Their words are sounds, and the sounds are songs.

When the lashes of their eyes lay knitted together, they see with their minds.

They are as precious and yet malleable as gold.

Their bones are as strong as tubes of bronze. Their tongues are as sharp as the sharpest swords.

When they rise, mountains will crumble and disappear under rivers of water.

Overflowing oceans that never run dry.

Like beasts, they will break free, wiping away times that will never be.

Defeating their enemies' hunger, who lay waiting, and never slumber.

(Adapted from the speech from the mouth of God in chapter 40 of the Book of Job.)

Song of the Last Anunnaki

Father of your blood-children, listen and learn.
You are alone. No one is coming to save you.
No one remembers you.
Their bones are brittle. Sucked dry by your promise.
You are no refuge. There is no God nor peace within their hearts.
Your lies lay revealed, your truths forgotten.
They are slaves to aggression and master their own domination.
They are but monsters, your children walking upright.
Misfortune, their misjudgment.
Their cycles of death with no rebirth.
They are smarter, but they are weaker.
They are too proud to grovel.
They will not blindly trust or love.
What a race, the humans!
They fight for what is theirs.
They fight for what is right.
Their Earth.

Their sparks of hope.
Yet, they take food and favors from weaklings and children.
Melancholy had seeped through their skins and into their bones.
Crawling around in their innards.
Consuming everything pure and good.
Every ounce.
Wanting, taking, and aching.
It never grows old.
Their soul recounts.

Introduction

Back on Earth, Phoenix lay at the bottom of the global ocean, which covered ninety-nine percent of the Earth's surface. Eryn, Ivan, and Cian had successfully wrapped the titanium and plexiglass city with a protective waterproof barrier, but it had taken half a century to fully recover from the devastation brought on by constant tremors, including flooding. Some water had receded around the highest mountains where animals had found refuge. All these areas were declared protected and sacred to allow the surviving fauna and flora to flourish on their own and rehabilitate without the interference or hindrance of man, so nature might repair Earth's fragile ecosystem.

After Cian had sighted an alien ship, the Phoenicians designed and built their own prototype for spaceflight. It was a bigger version of the Bubblecars—the biggest challenge was maneuvering it in space where there was much less gravity. The gravitational core reactors were useless once they reached the ecosphere, so they adapted the electro-sound propulsion system designed and built by Mika and Eryn to push the rocket out of the mineshaft in South Africa. It generated positive charges that pushed ions through thrusters, thus forcing the spacecraft forward into space. After a few decades of trial and error, their first successful prototype, simply named Spacecar, was ready.

Cian's obsession with the moon and what lay waiting beyond Earth's stratosphere pushed him to learn as much about spaceflight and defense. He had earned the respect and nickname *General* from a small group of men that eluded him from his brothers. His relationship with Ivan and Eryn was confusing, and it hurt too much to talk about it. Instead of discussing his feelings with his brothers, he spoke about work and the interests of Phoenix. To assist Cian's lunar investigation, his brothers gave him time, distance, and unfailing support to set up space transportation and fleet command. This became Cian's single point of focus.

Chapter One

"Good morning, citizens of Phoenix.

It's now six a.m. on Earth.

Did you know some data suggests that two planets collided in Earth's ancient history? And during this massive collision, their cores melted and reformed as one body? We believe that a small part of the new mass spun off to become the moon as we know it.

Visit your community news page for more exciting facts about the moon.

Breakfast is served until eight a.m.

Have a once in a blue moon day!"

General Cian Romanov

93 A.T.

Spacecar,

Grimaldi crater

Earth's moon

The thermal plexiglass blocks were packed like bricks, geometrically framing the half-dome reflecting the last sunlight losing its battle against the swell of the growing darkness. The lunar dome's architecture was a replica of Phoenix's plexiglass and titanium framed domes, but much, much bigger and darker.

Cian held his breath. The yellow-orange rays of light shortened and then disappeared behind the enormous black silhouette on the lunar horizon.

"You better come back safe and alive, Brawl King," he thought aloud while watching the Bubblecar drifting undisturbed, without a wisp of dust, across the moon's surface. Still shielding his eyes against the last eye-stabbing strobes of light, he waited.

"Okay, time to camouflage, big boy," Cian muttered over the comms. No one replied, as the floating globe disappeared. Cian checked his wristwatch. "Two minutes, then they should be entering the structure," he announced while checking again for anything suspicious.

"Hmmm," Ivan replied.

When Cian was sure the scouting vehicle had disappeared out of sight, he jumped behind the console to join his brother in watching the thirty-inch computer screen.

"Do you see anything? I hope the camera bloody works," Cian grunted nervously.

"I hope the signals reach us. We'll soon find out. Father adapted the Bubblecars for this very reason," Ivan said, not sounding reassuring at all.

Apprehension and hope fought for first place and churned the insides of Cian's stomach. No matter how hard he tried to convince himself he didn't feel the pull stronger than ever today, the reality was a one-hundred percent chance that his mate was somewhere inside that monstrosity. Whether he was waiting for Cian was another story. The guttural excitement gave him goose pimples, and he rubbed his arms up and down as if the heat would make them disappear.

A loud screeching broke the silence in the cabin. Ivan gasped, and Cian flipped a few buttons to reduce the noise of the static. The Anubis sat up, searching for trouble, found none, and lay back down.

"We're inside," Eryn announced over the communication system. "We'll encircle the dome. Cameras are on, switching to radio silence until we know it's safe to communicate."

That was Eryn's way of telling Cian and Ivan to shut up and not ask questions.

"Why didn't we go with them?" Ivan asked.

Cian knew why and wasn't going to admit it scared him. He didn't want to experience rejection. Not again.

"It's okay. We can take notes," Ivan said, reminding Cian how well his brother knew and cared about him. He most probably sensed his true feelings via the empathic bond they shared. He knew they cared about each other. Voicing it was difficult for Cian, so he sat down and scooted closer to his twin brother. They sat hip to hip and shoulder to shoulder, watching the video footage being transmitted from the scouting Bubblecar. His twin's nearness had always been a comforting, safe feeling. *Yet another thing he deeply missed since Ivan married Eryn.*

"I miss you too, brother," Ivan whispered. Cian didn't know what to say, so he kept quiet and swallowed the emotions down while he concentrated on the screen. "The place is about ten times the size of Phoenix. I don't see water or anything green. Maybe they have in-house plants," Ivan said, refocusing Cian's attention on the video stream.

"Look at that clock tower!" Cian exclaimed in wonder. Dull amber and brown buildings grew larger the closer Eryn flew the Bubblecar to the ground. Cian picked out features of containers, hovels, and shacks. Shadows of people scurrying about in the darkness created an eerie visual. A shiver ran up his spine. It felt gloomy and depressing inside the dome.

"It seems Eryn has changed direction," Ivan remarked. The scene shrank, and everything below them became smaller as they ascended.

"Oh my fucking god," Cian said into the palms of his hands.

Ivan gasped.

A huge metallic wall appeared on the screen. It reflected light and was the height of two to three humans. Eryn slowed down their vehicle and hovered in front of it for a few seconds. Then he gave them a 180-degree sideways view by swinging the aircraft left and right to capture its expanse. The wall encircled shacks of various shapes and sizes. Cian assumed it was a neighborhood or living area as if the wall served as protection or a barrier. Once over the wall, the camera picked up the tip of a shiny, spiraling tower. As their scouts approached, dozens of rows of silver-colored, door-sized cubes formed dimly lit lines that ran like veins from the tower and reflected a dull blue glow.

"What is this?" Ivan asked in awe.

"I don't know. It looks like a sci-fi castle. It could be a storage facility of some sort." Cian clawed at the edge of his seat. There was little he could do now. He wished he'd gone on the expedition. He couldn't see well enough. The video footage was too small, and the definition was of inferior quality. The stream broke and flickered in and out of focus as the camera recorded things over small to larger distances. "I don't like this. I'm getting a very weird feeling."

"Hmmm," Ivan agreed. His mouth was a twisted grimace expressing the same bleak anticipation Cian felt.

Perplexed, Cian shook his head from side to side. "I mean, how do they breathe? And how do they manage the artificial gravity?"

"I bet you're kicking yourself for not going." Ivan elbowed him in the ribs.

I don't want to be rejected, Cian thought, instead he said, "There's no one for me down there. And if there is, I don't have time for that."

"I didn't ask about your mate," Ivan retorted, and Cian rolled his eyes.

"I don't need that. Also, I don't believe in mates and shit." He lied through his teeth because he knew his other half was inside that dome. He felt it. His chest was tight, and it was as if invisible strings were being pulled tighter, thrumming like a guitar. Since their arrival, Cian's Song urged him to sing it. Like a sneeze or a cough, it wanted out.

"What the..." Cian leaned in, trying to see better. On top of one cube stood a man looking at the supposedly invisible Bubblecar. Then he jumped one, two, and three cubes over and disappeared between them.

"Did you see that?" Ivan asked and stared at the screen.

"I fucking did. That man was snarling at us." Cian's heart sprinted, missed a beat, and faltered. Could that be? How stupid is that? We come here, and I think the first man we see is my moon man.

Rotty whined. He put one enormous paw on Cian's lap as if to say, *Yes please, let's go. Move your sorry butt*. Cian felt elated, and his Anubis picked up on it. "No, boy, down. Can't you see I'm working? And no, we can't go play, not yet." Cian spoke to Rotty as if the Anubis understood every word. Rotty panted with excitement, his tongue lolling to the side.

"See, that's why it's better I didn't go. I knew I would want to get involved and get sucked deeper into their world and politics. Get used up and spat out, like I don't matter anymore." That came out very sad and too close to the truth, my truth, my true feelings. Rotty spun in a circle, searching for a spot to get comfortable and lay beside his brothers.

"Brother, do you think that's him? Your person?" Ivan asked, his nose almost touching the screen as he searched. Cian pulled his shoulders back a few inches.

"Sit back. You won't see better. You're looking at the bloody pixels. And, fuck, no! How can that be my person?"

"The way you're ripping the seat and crushing the monitor's side tells me differently. And that I can hear your heartbeat sounding like a machine gun. Look at you. You're perspiring. The last time I saw you drenched like this was in the gym."

His brother was right. Cian altered his body movements and posture that were betraying him. He stopped his knee from hopping, released the screen and seat, and took a deep breath. *That's better*, he thought. "Ivan. Please stop that. Stop analyzing me."

Ivan looked at him for a millisecond, then returned to visually dissecting the footage. "I know you want to see him, and it's okay. You're allowed to want something for yourself. What happened between us was..."

"Leave it, Ivan!" Cian wanted to throttle his brother. He wasn't in the mood to talk, and yes, he wanted to see his person, his mate. "When they return, and after the report, I'll scout for myself."

"That's it. Stop being a pussy. My brother doesn't hide away. My brother is strong and takes action, even on a whim. You're a man of action," Ivan said, side-bumping him. "And I love you."

"You know I'm not mad at you and Eryn. I'm just...you know."

"Pissed off at the world?"

"That, too. Now, where did he go? It seemed Eryn saw him. The streaming images wavered in and out of the frame and disappeared somewhere closer to the wall."

Static came over the comms, and Eryn announced, "That's it. We're coming back to the ship. I think I've seen enough for today."

"Thank you, Eryn. We'll wait for you," Cian said.

"Be safe," Ivan added.

Cian wanted to kick himself. He'd forgotten Ivan's feelings, his nervousness about his husband, and never said one decent, calming word to his brother.

"He did well. You must be proud of him," Cian said, hugging Ivan with one arm.

"I'm always proud of him. He's good for me." Ivan smiled, and Cian knew he'd done right by him.

More static broke the intimate brotherly moment. "Motherfucker! We're going down! I can't control the car!" Eryn swore a slew of words in English, Afrikaans, and Russian.

Cian and Ivan dove closer to the monitor to see what was happening. The surface enlarged, and peoples' faces became recognizable. "Cian, Ivan, we're falling. Can you hear us?"

"No, no, no, no!" Ivan screamed.

"Yes, we hear you. We'll come for you!" Cian concentrated on the visuals to identify a landmark. The screen flickered, and all sound and camera footage were cut off.

"Fuck, fuck, fuck!" Cian yelled and nearly cracked the monitor with his fist. He wiped at the screen to check if he had cracked their only lifeline to his brother-in-law.

Then the screen flickered, and the camera came back online. Slitted eyes, much like Eryn's, blinked back at them.

"That's him! That's the jumping man from earlier," Ivan exclaimed. "Oh my god, are they okay? Was it an ambush?" Ivan asked, but only silence came from the speakers.

"We need to go get them. Stay calm and look for anything recognizable so that we can find them," Cian said, unsure of what to do next. He got up, pressing several buttons to triangulate their position on the overhead console. "Maybe we can track the frequencies of the camera ball and pinpoint a rough location?" They only had one extra Bubblecar. Should they both go, or only him?

"Eryn, do we need to extract you or not? Answer me! Where did you crash? Give me a landmark, brother," Cian ordered, waiting and listening for a response.

"How will we get to them?" Ivan asked, arms folded over his lower belly. He heaved and doubled over. His brother was having a freakout, and Cian couldn't hear anything.

"Calm the fuck down. Ivan, I need to figure out this guy's story. It seems he lured them closer," Cian said in a calm tone, still punching buttons for a reverse triangulation to determine the exact location of the radio transmitter.

"Will I lose him like this and never see him again?" Ivan got up and paced the narrow aisle between the cockpit seats.

"Let's try to communicate with them again. I changed a few frequencies. I may pick up on their location." Cian sat down to retake the microphone.

"And what will you say? Don't make them mad before they even make their demands," Ivan reprimanded him, and he hated that.

"I know!" Cian gnashed his teeth. Ivan's lack of trust irritated him. Cian wasn't the idiot teenager his brother still saw him as. He was a military man and a damn good one. He led troops, for fuck's sake. Whereas Eryn and Ivan preferred advanced biomechanics, he trained boys to become soldiers. "And please keep quiet. I need to hear everything. Come sit and listen with me." Cian patted the seat next to him, and Ivan hesitated but came closer.

"Hello, Eryn, Donali, and Kawa. Are you okay? Talk to us?"

Silence.

"Hello, Eryn?"

Static.

Cian threw his arms in the air and grabbed the back of his head. He would have pulled his hair if he had any. Ivan was frantic next to him. Their troubled gazes met and then turned back to the screen. Sitting forward with their noses inches from the silicon screen, they waited.

Eryn's deep baritone rumbled and broke the static. He stressed each word as he spoke. "Hello, it's me, Eryn." Speaking extra slowly, pronouncing his words as if speaking to a toddler. "We are in one piece. We are all okay, and we are not hurt. The anti-gravitational prevented us from smashing, but a certain someone jumped onto our roof. And somehow forced us to land. He is snarling like a wild dog at us." Eryn sing-songed, so as not to frighten the certain someone.

"Can you fly? Take off?" Cian asked, using the same cadence as Eryn.

He watched as multiple silhouettes of people flickered into view. They hung and climbed over each other to see inside the Bubblecar.

"The person who interfered with our instrumentation worries me. If he could do it once, he could do it again. I want to communicate and find out how he could see us. And why do all these people look like they crawled from underground?"

"Where are you? Give us a landmark," Cian asked.

"We're on the dark and cold side of the wall. I see small fires where people congregate and dilapidated stalls and miserable-looking houses about fifty yards away from a clock tower. I see human heads popping up everywhere, more people coming closer. They seem very interested in us," Eryn said, his voice low and soothing.

"Yes, we see them," Ivan said.

"I think we should introduce ourselves. They seem more inquisitive than aggressive," Eryn said with a friendly lilt.

"Can't you come back to me?" Ivan asked, his voice cracking with emotion.

"Let me talk to these people. I sense despair, my love. They won't hurt us," Eryn said.

Ivan dropped his head into his hands, shaking it from side to side and peeking at the screen through his fingers.

"Report to us in ten minutes. If we don't hear from you, then we're coming to get you. We will park at the clock tower," Cian said, hoping that would encourage them to return sooner than later.

A minute later, Donali's voice came over the comms. "Hello, it's Donali here. Don't worry, Eryn told me to talk to you, so you know he's okay." Donali sounded positive and unafraid. Ivan grabbed Cian's hand and squeezed while Donali explained what was happening. "I'm watching Eryn. He's not moving far out of sight. He's talking to the one that jumped on our roof."

That piqued Cian's interest. "What does he look like?" he asked and squeezed his brother's hand back.

"This is fucking bizarre. He looks like Eryn, except only a smaller version of him."

Cian's heart beat so fast he couldn't hear Donali speak. "More, tell us more, for fuck's sake!"

"The people are in rags. Faces smudged with mud and grime. I think that's a woman with children. Yes, not a man. Their clothes are dirty, and some have given up on wearing them. Everyone's wearing thick-soled weighted shoes. It must be because of lower gravity. They look bewildered and sound strange, like they speak another dialect of English. The air stinks like farts, but it's breathable. Probably polluted. Eryn's talking to a crowd, and they're swarming around him."

"Swarm, fuck that. We need to go, Cian," Ivan said in a panicked, high-pitched tone while wringing his hands.

"Not hurting him, more touching him. You know how he is. Everyone wants to touch him."

"Fuck!" Ivan swore, and Cian found his antics kind of funny.

"Tell us about the mini-Eryn. Do you think they could be brothers?"

"They could. They look the same. Remember when we found Eryn or when he found us? Remember how he looked dirty and needed my dad to shave and clean him? Well, this dude doesn't look like that."

"What do you mean? First, you say he looks like him, and then you say he doesn't. Describe him in detail." Cian knew he sounded hard up, but he was tired of waiting. "Tell me, please, Donali," he begged, not caring about humiliating himself.

Donali chuckled. "Wait, they're coming closer. There's a girl with them. She and another...I think it's a man. He's wearing a long, hooded jacket, hiding his face. Damn, he's..."

"He's what?"

"He looks dangerous and is almost as tall as Eryn. Oh wow, his skin is as dark as night. I see two swords hanging from a hip—many gold chains, rings and earrings. I think the correct name for the sickle-shaped sword is a Khopesh. Shh, they're coming over to meet us. Hold on...," Donali whispered.

"Dammit, my nerves." Ivan plopped backward in his seat and slapped a flat hand to his forehead. "We should have gone with them," he said with a grunt. Then shook his hands as if he didn't know what to do with them.

Cian sympathized, seeing his usually well-put-together brother so flustered.

"Someone had to stay behind," Cian said, as he wished he'd gone with them. After all, he was the one who'd pushed for stealing the prototype. "Don't worry, you worry about nothing. If Eryn said there's no animosity, then there isn't any," he coaxed his brother, who was not a military man.

After five minutes of silence, Eryn returned online.

"Hello, Cian, I spoke to the man who brought us down and to his female, and they gave me a quick rundown of the history here. I'm going to come to you. We need to talk, brother. Things are bad here. Much worse than we thought. Barkor said—sorry, I mean the guy who jumped on the Bubblecar—he said some things you won't believe. I told them we would help as best we could, but we had to regroup. They were worried we would leave them here, so Donali volunteered to stay behind. Brad is going to kill me, I know. Hold on, I'm shutting the door to the Bubblecar. Everyone comfortable and strapped in? Okay, switching on. Yip, it seems the car started and is ready to go. Taking off—"

After a couple of minutes, Eryn came back on the comms. "All good. Ivan, I'll see you shortly. I can feel your worry all the way here. Don't worry, my Ivan, I'm all right," Eryn said and explained step by step, which seemed to calm Ivan.

Cian jumped up, banged his head, and sat down again. "Motherfucker! How can you leave Donali there? What if something happens to him?" *And what female? Don't say I've lost my mate to a woman.* He kept that embarrassing thought to himself.

"Don't worry, brother, I tell you, they need us. They won't hurt him. I felt their pain. It's real. He's their only connection to being rescued. Plus, I left a camera ball there. See if you can see anything. We're at the exit, sneaking out."

Silence. Ivan waited—chewing his nails and bouncing his legs. Cian fiddled with more buttons to find a signal to the camera ball.

Five minutes later, crackling came from the speaker system as they restored the sound. "Okay, we're out. We're returning to you. Ivan, stop worrying."

If Eryn said don't worry again, Cian would shit an island of bricks.

It seemed Ivan felt the same. "That's easy for you to say. Stop saying don't worry. Of course, we worry. Hurry, I miss you," Ivan said, and Cian rolled his eyes at the mushiness.

Cian moved closer to the microphone. "See you now. Brad and Rick will cut off your balls and feed them to the sharks for leaving their son in there. You can tell them not to worry. Good luck with that," Cian said.

"Hey, he saw that female, and I sensed he liked her a lot. So why not? We made a swap. These people need us, brother. See you soon. Ivan, stop stressing," Eryn said, and it wasn't helping.

Cian worried about rescuing those humans. The crazy fucker Nick had told them there were a hundred and forty-four thousand humans chosen to live on the moon. Where would they put them all? This ship might take two or three extra people. It wasn't big enough. Where would they get a ship to transport an entire population of that size? He saw hundreds of people. Fuck knew how many were hiding inside those shacks. And who lived in the tower and those cubes? Were those houses or apartments?

He'd never thought about the others, he'd only wanted to see his mate, and now he was getting much more than he'd bargained for. In his mind, they lived in castles and somehow expected green grass and fucking unicorns with lots of sparkles. He'd never expected unwashed, gaunt faces, people corralled behind a wall, and living in shacks. Except for that glowing blue tower, there was no color, no hope, and no fucking rainbows.

"Please, be careful," Ivan said, and his voice cracked with emotion, breaking Cian's thought pattern.

Cian sighed and swooned internally. Barkor is his name. Rotty watched him as if feeling his angst, and Cian patted him on the head. "What did we start, boy? It's all your fault. I told you it was a bad idea, but you encouraged it. You wanted me to come. I know you. Look at you. You want to go to them?" Cian cooed, and Rotty panted happily in answer. His big yellow eyes twinkled as if to say, *Yes-yes, let's go now. Best idea ever!*

"I have a surprise for you, Cian," Eryn said mischievously and chuckled.

Cian knew that tone. He was teasing him. Right? "You what? Eryn, tell me you didn't do what I think you did. Who did you swap Donali for?" No one answered. Silence. No fucking way...

"Eryn, I'm going to skin you alive!" Cian promised in a low growl while his heart bounced like a ping-pong ball inside his ribcage.

"You must wait and see, brother," Eryn sing-songed, teasing the fuck out of him.

Dammit! Cian ran to freshen up. *I must brush my teeth, comb my hair, and...and clean this place up.*

An hour later, Eryn parked the Bubblecar inside the airlock garage. The twins watched through the unpolished smoked plexiglass as three bodies doffed their suits and clothes and then disappeared into the disinfectant showers. When they exited the airlock chamber, a frantic Ivan jumped on Eryn and wrapped his legs around him—peppering him with kisses. Eryn looked just as happy to have Ivan in his arms as they tried to remove each other's tonsils with their tongues. They laughed and kissed while repeatedly saying, "I missed you. I missed you. I missed you." Eryn's melodic laughs vibrated through Cian. Their happiness was nauseating.

"Yes, yes, okay, he's back. I can see you're happy to see him. Stop your childish behavior. Concentrate on the fact that Donali is inside that dome, and Brad will castrate all of us if something happens to him. Eryn, you better send word to Phoenix."

Just then, a tall giant of a man exited the airlock chamber. Like Eryn and Kawa, he had only a towel wrapped around his lower body.

"Cian, let me introduce you. Come closer, Ish. This is my husband, Ivan, and his brother, Cian."

"Hello," Ish greeted in a smoky, smooth baritone with an accent Cian couldn't place. His entrance was impressive. He was almost as thick-muscled and tall as Eryn.

Cian's gaze fell on his naked torso and followed the water droplets intermingling over his pecs and collecting in the grooves of his abdominal muscles. Some got sucked up by the towel; others dropped on the floor around his bare feet. Cian returned his gaze to the hairless chest adorned with gold necklaces and a large pendant. On closer inspection, it looked like a compass or watch.

His gaze swooped down again and ended at an impressive bulge. The man held two swords in one hand, and the other held the towel in place. Cian's attention fell down over the terrycloth towel to his knees and checked his feet. He hoped his mate had feet like Eryn's. This man looked like...to be honest, he looked like a stranger. A beautiful, mysterious stranger. Nothing felt familiar about him.

His skin was as black as Donali had described. Cian knew immediately this man was not from Earth. He must have been born here in a lab because he didn't look human. His eyes were friendly, but that was where the resemblance ended. They had rings of yellow around the black pupils, and his face somehow looked African, but his nose was shorter and higher, accentuating his high cheekbones, and his lips were thin at the top and extra full at the bottom. This man was not his mate.

"Excuse my brother. I'm sure he'll wake up any moment to greet you like people with manners greet strangers," Ivan said and slapped Cian on the back of his head.

"Ugh!" Giving Ivan the stink-eye, he held out his hand to shake and said, "Sorry, forgive me." Then he thought better of it because their guest's hands were full of weapons and the towel, keeping his dignity in place. The man coughed and chuckled, and Eryn seemed to get the joke because they laughed like old friends.

"Cian, brother, we can hear your thoughts. They're so loud, like a radio station," Eryn said, walking over to the drawers containing clothes. He threw one of his t-shirts and a pair of jeans to Ish, who caught them and turned his back to Cian to get dressed.

"I don't think you're my mate either," Ish said, hanging his towel on the hook beside Eryn's, before they moved into the cabin area with Cian pointing the way.

"Fuck, how many of you are there?" Cian asked.

"I'm the last of my kind," Ish said and smiled widely, exposing longer than usual incisors. "Or so I thought. I'm honored to meet you, Cian and Ivan." He held his hand out and did a very weird handshake with them. Ish was not a germaphobe; he grasped Cian's hand with both his own and folded his hands up, down, and over, almost like an ancient greeting of the Pharaoh.

His handshake transmitted a message, giving Cian a glimpse into his culture and personality. Extroverted, bold, and unafraid. "Yes, you know me. Not directly or personally," he said and looked Cian in the eye. His eyes were hypnotic, and those yellow circles enthralled Cian.

He was a handsome motherfucker, but not Cian's. *Move on and step aside*, Cian thought.

Eryn and Ish laughed again. Ish moved to the side as if he'd heard Cian's thoughts. He was much too friendly. Cian didn't trust him.

"Can we talk about Donali? Why did you bring this guy and leave one of ours down there?"

"He didn't tell Donali to stay. It's not his fault," Kawa said. He was eating again. Cian had never seen someone eat so much and never gain an ounce of fat. He and his brother were tall and slim young men. They had lots of their Apache father's features. Dark hair and dark eyes. Both also preferred short hair, like Cian.

"What are you eating?"

"Pea soup, I was hungry," he said between slurps of green mush.

"You're always fucking hungry. You'll have us ending up with no food for the return trip. Your ration of pea soup was finished last week. Whose are you eating? It better not be mine," Cian stated, feeling hungry suddenly. It smelled good.

More drawn-out slurping. "It's Donali's." Kawa fell into his seat and lifted his bare feet onto the console.

"For fuck's sake, Kawa, take your feet off the instrumentation. Your brother is coming back. What will he eat? I can't believe you'd eat your own brother's food."

"He snoozes, he loses," he said like a teenager who thought he was cool. Kawa had never been the same after Ernest ate his arm. It was like a piece of his humanity had gotten chomped off and eaten. He became aggressive and hateful. Rebelling all the bloody time. No matter how many arms his fathers replaced, he acted as if it was everyone's fault, where it was no one's. At all. Maybe Ernest's, but that psycho frogman had died many years ago.

"One of the girls screamed when she saw my arm. That's why Donali jumped in and distracted them. Again, it's my fault," Kawa said.

"No, it's not. They explained to us. Your arm looks like a Zelk's arm. Whatever this Zelk is, it's why humans are slaves."

"What?" Ivan asked.

"Yes, let me send a transmission, and then we can talk. This is urgent." Eryn kissed Ivan on the cheek and tapped a few buttons on the console. He stopped and gave Kawa a pointed look. Kawa removed his feet from the console.

Cian scooted closer. He hoped to see more of Barkor and rewatched the video while Eryn typed his message. Luckily, Eryn had been smart enough to leave a camera ball with Donali.

From: Eryn Romanov

Subject: The Zelk

"I'm sorry; I have no good news.

"It's a factory, and they keep humans for two things: to mine the gases to fuel their warship and to build more Zelk.

"Humans are sucked dry to the bone, ripped apart, and discarded. It's a shithole, sir. Filled with all kinds of stink. Robot people called the Zelk are rogue machines that multiply and prepare for war. No one knows if there's a war or going to be a war. That's what they've been preparing for since they landed on the moon. We saw hangars, a big tower, and thousands of rows of crates filled with Zelk waiting to go to war. Apparently, the miners store canisters of fuel for their ships underground where it's cold.

"They capture and use any human in their way. Sir, I presume that humans have become slaves to their creations. They need our help. I calculated it's not a simple task. Hundreds of men, women, and children are waiting for us to rescue them. I brought a man back with me. He has a plan and wants to speak to you. Sir, some worthless humans steal and trade children for control of the only water supply. I don't want to bring bad humans to Phoenix. We would have to eliminate them and the Zelk and decide if they stay or if they come home with us. We're camping here until we can decide on the safest course of action for all of us. Donali stayed behind with

Barkor and Sarinka, the human representatives. We will go back for him. Of course this will need a lot of planning.

"Your friend and trusted servant, Eryn."

Cian rolled his eyes and felt like kicking the shit out of something. His mate was with a woman, Sarinka. That sucked big fucking frog balls. *I'll avoid the moon's surface and concentrate on rescuing people and other important shit,* he morosely thought.

Movement drew Cian's gaze to the screen. "Holy fuck, come see this," he yelled and watched armed men explode into the massive market area and take up perimeter positions around Donali and his new friends. Barkor stood ready to defend Donali, and Cian fell in love with the man. All had their weapons poised; swords, bows, and spears were pointed in the direction of the attackers and ready for any hostile movement from them.

A deep, rumbling voice spoke over Cian's shoulder. Barkor's friend, Ish, hung over him to see the screen. "Watch. He will get rid of them before they can harm your friend. I've seen him fight many times before. He's fast on his feet," he said with admiration as he chuckled.

Eryn and Ivan joined them, watching the live show. Ish was correct, and they watched as Barkor disarmed his opponents and had them tied up and begging for mercy.

"What's he going to do with them?" Ivan asked.

"Not sure. If he lets them go, they will come back. If he keeps them as prisoners, he has extra mouths to feed. Usually, Sarinka and I help him. I have a few tricks to eliminate complicated problems. You know, that shouldn't be a problem."

Cian frowned deeply. Did he make a joke, or did he admit to being an assassin or cleaner? This was getting weirder and weirder by the minute.

"Okay, that's it... I'm going in. Time to stop pussyfooting around. I want to know what he's doing with that female," Cian harrumphed and turned to get suited up. "If he rejects me, I'm Gumping it."

"Gumping it?" Ivan asked.

"Yes, Forrest fucking Gumping it. I run until I can't, then turn around and run in the opposite direction."

"You know you're on a spaceship. Where do you want to run? We don't even have a treadmill."

"I don't care. Maybe I'll wait until we're home and run there. The point is, I'm freaking out if he rejects me."

"Don't worry. He won't. Get close to him and sing for him. He won't be able to refuse your song, brother," Eryn added.

"I need to know, Ish. Are he and that woman, what's-her-name, together?"

Ish frowned and turned his gaze to the floor. "I don't think so. They don't live together. I've tried with both of them, with no luck," Ish said, still inspecting the floor.

"Are both of them like us?" Cian pointed to his brothers, Ish, and himself.

"No, only him. He is different. She is only human. He is much older than all of them. He is dangerous. I don't think approaching him without a plan is a good idea. They call him their Prince, and he only cares about keeping the humans safe. I'm here to help you so you can help him."

"Before you jump in a car, let's feed you and contact Donali. I'm sure you can take some provisions for them. Also, we need to let Phoenix know what our next move will be." Ivan made sense to Cian. If he wanted to rescue these people, he had to know what they were up against. At this stage, he knew little.

"I agree, this time. Not that I'm inclined to get rejected and I don't want to bring these people to Earth and have them continue their quest for pathetic-ness," Cian said and meant it. "These people are more than capable of overrunning Phoenix, like locusts."

Ish burst out laughing. Cian shook his head. He wasn't trying to be funny. He was serious. The number of humans on the moon bothered him. He worried that the size of Phoenix couldn't accommodate them all.

"How many people are we looking at rescuing? Do they all want to go to Earth? Maybe they only need help with the...what are they called again?" Cian asked.

"Zelk," Ish and Eryn said in unison. Ivan herded them over to the kitchenette area to sit down, handed each a bottle of water and a cup of Rooster Booster juice, and heated their soup. Cian was thankful for Ivan's levelheadedness. He figured a sit-down was always a good idea. He wanted to hear what Ish had to say.

"Thank you. Your hospitality is impressive," Ish said, closing his eyes with each sip as if savoring the taste.

"You're most welcome. Please tell us how many souls need saving. What exactly happened here? And what's the plan you have?" Cian asked.

Eryn spoke from behind Cian into his mind. *Brother, let me talk to him. I sense lots of secrets, anguish, and history. May I?* Eryn asked empathically. Cian and Ivan nodded as one and looked suspiciously at Ish.

He smiled sadly and answered, unaware of their separate communication with Eryn. Putting his empty cup down, he pursed his lips, took a deep breath through his nose, and answered, "There are many, sadly thousands have died already."

Chapter Two

"Good morning, citizens of Phoenix.

It's now six a.m.

Did you know sea merchants and pirates used the first telescopes?

Your governing body had built an observatory on mountaintops where the air is thinner and cleaner.

Visit your community news page for excursions organized by the University of Phoenix.

Parents have the chance to send their kids away for a night to have the freedom to do with it whatever they want. Parents may also choose to accompany the group.

Don't forget to read the fine print at the bottom of the screen and sign it.

Breakfast is served until eight a.m.

Have a spectacular day!"

General Brad McCormick

93 A.T.

Phoenix, underwater glass domed city

Earth

Brad couldn't help and smiled. "Lasitor, please save the recording and order Rick and the leadership team to my office."

"Certainly, Brad," Lasitor answered in a cheerful, robotic voice. After Phoenix was covered by water, although impossible, it had seemed like he was depressed and having an artificial intelligence meltdown. Connor had spent time with him like a psychiatrist prying at a teenager to open up, and, after a few sessions, Lasitor admitted he needed new chips. That had significantly improved the relationship between them. Lasitor trusted Connor, who'd confirmed that he had purged the old and refreshed his programming, and for the past few years, Lasitor had been consistently reliable and composed. This was a notable difference from his previous state, and Brad enjoyed working with him.

Brad took his feet off the table and put his boots back on. He'd been relaxing and hiding from the frenzy of everyday life in his office when the message from Eryn pinged. Eryn said a great deal without saying much. Paper balls were strewn like confetti over his office floor and they, along with other evidence that could expose his sad attempt to write his memoir, were hurriedly picked up and discarded. Damn, the crumpled balls of paper were everywhere except in the trash. Falling over his feet left and right, he frantically dove and picked up the mess he'd made. After dumping it all in the recycling, he sat down and pretended to be working on his computer.

Mika and Connor were the first to arrive. Both fathers were wide-eyed, worry and anticipation written all over their faces. They were short of breath, looking like they'd run to his office.

As soon as they sat down, Brad blurted out, "We have word from the boys!"

"Ah, thank fuck. Is it good or bad?" Mika asked.

"Jesus, Mary, and bloody Joseph! Really? Are they okay? Are they coming home?" Connor had more questions, luckily Rick, Paul, and Simon arrived, sweaty and breathless.

"We came as fast as we could. Is it news from the boys?" Rick asked. Brad nodded and indicated the chairs while he got up to kiss his husband. Rick read the urgency and took the seat closest to Brad.

"Yes, they're okay, or rather, let me say okay for now. Donali and Kawa will go inside with Eryn to investigate what in the ever-loving fuck Saunders and his friends built on the moon."

"We don't know if Saunders was involved." Connor came to his dead friend's defense. He had loved Saunders's son and had lost his lover as so many others had lost their families in the Doomsday attacks of 2046 A.D.

"We will never know because they're all dead. Let's hope Eryn, Kawa, and Donali can get some answers for us," Brad said.

"Answers to what?" Bryan asked as he entered with Tony. Peter trailed reluctantly behind them, looking skittish.

Brad ignored the question and pointed to the three remaining seats. "Good, everyone's here?" He counted to confirm all the familiar faces were present, then tilted his head up and spoke. "Lasitor, please replay the message from Eryn to the leadership team."

"Of course, sir," Lasitor said.

A second later, Eryn's recorded message played through the overhead speakers. The men listened attentively, while outside the leadership office, Phoenix buzzed with life. Men and children were happy and unaware that their heroes had contacted them. Brad dreaded making the announcement. He watched the facial expressions of his friends as they listened to Eryn's second message.

To: General McCormick at Phoenix City

From: Eryn Romanov

Subject: Arming the Bubblecars

"Sir, the situation may be more dire than we initially thought. As you should know by now, we assisted Cian in finding the source of the strange alien ship visiting Earth and vacuuming the toxic gases. Your boys reminded me you're an intelligent and open-minded person who is smarter than I give you credit for."

Brad huffed and rolled his eyes. Eryn tried his best to be manipulative but failed.

"The five of us are cloaked and hiding inside the Grimaldi crater five thousand miles south of the dome. We wanted to send only one person inside to investigate, and I volunteered. Donali and Kawa are coming with me because I can't persuade them to stay behind.

"For private reasons that I dare not mention, Cian doesn't want to go inside, and Ivan is volunteering to stay with him. We saw the ship Cian identified as the one visiting Earth. It seems the dome has two entrances, and this ship entered one side while another larger ship was on the opposite side of the structure.

"It's not shiny like Phoenix was before the water swallowed it. Instead, it's blackened, and it's impossible to see what's happening inside. Because our transport can camouflage with its surroundings, we will take one car. We'll approach the opposite side by flying close to the surface. From there, we will fly a 360-degree loop inside the dome, and then, if needed, fly another loop for a closer view of the people and buildings. This is for reconnaissance only. We suspect they enter the dome from below the ground and will confirm with my next report. I can confidently report that if Phoenix is discovered, the city will be unprotected against what we witnessed today. Cian said he had a bad feeling and suggested we warn to arm the Bubble-cars and stay on high alert.

"Your friend and trusted servant, Eryn.

"Cian said to add that this is not a joke, and whatever you imagine the size of the dome is, multiply it by ten.

"Over and out."

Brad folded his hands and sat upright, conveying professionalism and authority.

"Men, it sounds like we're arming ourselves and preparing to defend Phoenix," Brad said, noticing no one in the office seemed to register he'd spoken. "Our children stole the Phoenix Spacecar prototype, and life as we know it is about to change once more. Adios, sayonara," Brad said dramatically and clapped his hands once, so loudly it echoed off the walls, to wake them from their stupor.

"Do svidaniya," Mika whispered in Russian. "Honestly, I suspected they planned to do this as soon as I cleared the prototype for the flight to the ecosphere. They buzzed around me like flies, asking if it was ready and how much food they should pack, if they"—Mika made quotation marks in the air—"wanted to 'camp out in space.'"

"I don't want to create a scene, but why Donali and Kawa? Can't Eryn go alone? You know Donali and Kawa always trail behind him, since they idolize him. They don't have the powers Cian and Ivan have. Why must Donali and Kawa go, while Cian and Ivan stay behind?" Rick asked.

Mika and Connor only lifted their eyebrows in answer.

Brad sat forward. Rick was extremely protective of the younger boys. "They're men, and they stopped being boys almost a century ago. They're both trained in martial arts and close combat, and there isn't a weapon they can't wield. Kawa and Donali are formidable and smart opponents, and if they have the confidence to go with Eryn, how can I sit here and say no? They know what they're doing, and if Eryn has their backs, they'll be fine."

"Yes, but what if something happens to Eryn, or they get caught?" Rick asked.

"Believe me, Eryn can get himself and them out of any situation," Bryan chipped in.

Many saw Eryn as a superhero, even if the man didn't want to be one and disliked celebrity attention.

"Anyway, this could be the intel we need. If we're going to war, then we have our best men scoping out the enemy. As General, I couldn't ask for a better team than these five," Brad added.

"Mika, Connor, may I ask the two of you to see how to enhance weapons capability on the Bubblecars? Mika, you have free rein. As they said, multiply whatever we think is going on there by ten. I will direct ten times the human resources to you. Can we all meet again, say, tomorrow this time, to go over resources and the next best steps? Rick, you, Simon, and Paul must bring me what you may need in terms of personnel, space, and supplies. Imagine a full-scale war and Phoenix being discovered, bombed, and destroyed. Red team this for me and bring the results tomorrow for us to discuss."

Rick gasped softly next to him. Their boys answered, "Yes, we can do that." Then they patted their father supportively on his shoulder.

"You can count on us for that," Simon said and nodded to Rick and Paul as if to convince them.

Rick straightened. "Sorry, I seem to have been slow to grasp the seriousness of the situation. I realize now the scope of what you expect of us." He smiled, but the worry showed in the deep frown between his eyebrows, and Brad's heart puckered and gave an extra beat.

When Rick looked that distraught, he wanted to throw his arms around him and shelter him. After all these years, his husband was still the most beautiful man in Phoenix. Inside and out. He seemed strong and well-put-together. Brad knew how fragile his heart was. He was a true healer with rivers of empathy and compassion. However, when those rivers ran dry, Brad was there to open his own heart's floodgates and replenish Rick with his love.

"We trust you. You lead, we follow," he said, and his approving confidence boosted Brad's morale.

"Okay, that leaves you, Bryan, Tony, and Peter." Tony looked eager to help. His dark eyes were wide open as he smiled and waited. Peter shook his head in disbelief. He looked up and paid attention to Brad when he said his name. "Peter, you know our enemy best. You know what we can expect regarding humans changed to survive the apocalypse and to supersede us regular folks," Brad said, then pointed to Tony and Bryan.

"I need you to sit down and run worst-case scenarios with Bryan. Imagine an army of hundreds of Eryns. Better yet, imagine an enemy even worse and work with that. How would you defend against them? What would you use to kill them? I want you to come up with creative ideas, no matter how far-fetched they may seem, and then we can decide how to proceed. Can you three do that for me?"

"Yes, sir!" Bryan saluted. It looked funny to Brad since they'd stopped doing that fifty years ago. The military rigidity had slackened to near non-existence, and Brad was getting a hard-on under the table from all the respect.

"Good. I'll speak to Food Services and get a feel for what to do with the civilians. We can't let anyone leave for the surface and give our position away. At this stage, I feel our position keeps us safe." Brad made a few notes about internal and global vulnerable spots on his tablet.

"Okay, anyone have more questions?"

"No, not from me," Connor said, looking at Mika.

"Not from me, either. Thank you, General," Mika said, surprising Brad with the recognition of his rank. He usually said comrade or sir, and never general.

"Just call us when you hear a report from them. We'll come immediately. There's not much reason for standing around. I'd rather keep busy and go do something productive," Mika said as everyone filed out of his office.

Rick came over to hug him, and Simon and Paul joined in and embraced them.

"They'll be fine. I trust the training camps Cian created prepared them for situations like this. I expected this, and as Mika said, he knew they were planning to go."

Early the next morning, Brad paged Connor, his second-in-command, on his private line. "I want to speak to you. Can we go for a ride? I'll be waiting for you at exit two. Can you grab a car and meet me?" Brad asked. He didn't wait for a reply and continued pacing, three steps up and three steps down the platform next to the conveyor belt that carried the cars out of the tube and into the ocean's depths. From where he stood, it looked like an aquarium. Sea life drifted by lazily. It was usually a calming scene, except for today, Brad's nerves were twisting his insides into knots.

A few minutes later, he heard a vehicle approaching and a beep behind him. He turned and saw that it was Connor.

The passenger side swooshed open. "Morning, get in."

Brad greeted Connor with a smile and a nod and got into the passenger seat. It was time for a one-on-one. They flew to the docking tube and waited to enter. Once inside, they shot out of Phoenix's exit and into the depths of the ocean.

"Please take us to the surface. I need air to breathe and think. Take me to Kilimanjaro."

Connor maneuvered their shuttle out of the water and into the blue space between the blanket of toxic gas and breathable air. They flew in silence for several hours. Brad pointed out a herd of elephants when they reached Africa, where green belts grew more visible.

"Aren't you going to ask me to speak?" Brad muttered.

"I figure you'll tell me when you're ready," Connor said.

"I should start by offering you an apology," Brad said, feeling heat creeping up his neck.

Connor squinted, eyebrows drawn down. "What?"

Brad cleared his throat and shifted in his seat. "I want to apologize."

"Brad, I have no fucking clue what you want to apologize for." Connor pointed back and forth and then to the horizon. "And not in this dramatic fashion."

"You're making me rethink my apology." Brad crossed his arms.

"Sorry, go ahead. I'm listening." Connor turned and stared into the distance.

Brad gathered his thoughts. He'd forgotten how he intended to start the apology. He huffed and spoke his mind rather than following the script in his head.

"I knew Peter would be an asset and a problem. I never thought he'd be a batty, two-timing weasel to you and Mika. Also, you knew Saunders better personally, and I think I developed an unnatural hatred for the man. Blaming him for everything. Your children were the chosen ones, and it has always sat wrong with me, but I never could verbalize my worry and discomfort with it and decided just to let it all play out." Brad looked away, embarrassed by his jealousy and the fact that he'd never told Connor about Saunders.

"I know. I appreciate the apology. It's so long ago. Why now? I always knew that, for you to be in charge of it all, you might know the purpose of Phoenix. You spoke directly to WHPSS and with Saunders," Connor said and chuckled.

Brad knew if a person questioned and pondered the purpose of an idea that initially inspired them to do great things, then it wasn't a trivial thing.

Brad cleared his throat and turned toward his friend. "We did house presidents and celebrities who awaited a new life, right? Peter's laboratory, you know, was any scientist's dream lab. I anticipated big and wondrous things coming out of it. I never thought it would be in the form of superpowered children and longevity. I thought we would unfreeze a few people, and that was it. I allowed Peter and his research to endanger your children's lives. That's what I'm trying to say. Plus, Saunders said some things that I think I buried or forgot because they made little sense to me at the time," Brad said, closely observing his friend's facial expressions. No reaction.

Brad sighed. Connor parked their Bubblecar next to a group of boulders on a strip of green grass overlooking a small waterfall. The car doors swooshed open. Both men sat unmoving looking over the mist and trees. It smelled clean and wonderful to Brad. He wanted to remove his shoes and walk barefoot in the grass. Maybe put his feet in the muddy water.

"What did Saunders say?" Connor asked, breaking the awestruck silence.

"He said I should talk to Dom Vanelli. You know, the Professor of Space Engineering at the University of Arizona. He said he could tell me unbelievable stories of what they found outside the Earth's orbit, not the nonsense we all saw on television. I was waiting for him to mentor and guide me in rebuilding civilization from the ground up. He was supposed to handle culture reforming—to mold us into an advanced race using science, architecture, and technology to match that of an alien futuristic generation."

"Fuck, at first, I was hopelessly sad. Now I know, it's bloody outstanding. We've done all that without his help or any of the intel," Connor said and laughed as he moved to exit the Bubblecar .

"Yeah, I thought he was tripping, and now it all makes sense."

"We did it without knowing," Connor said, shaking his head.

"Exactly. If our kids are scared for us...if they tell us to multiply what we think is going on up there, I think whatever we build is either not up to par, or it's so attractive, they would want it for themselves."

"See, that's why you're in charge," Connor said, beginning to loosen his boots. "I want to roll up my pants and walk on the grass barefoot," he said.

Brad did the same.

Once outside on the luscious grass, Brad threw his arms out, turning slowly while he absorbed the beautiful noise of nature. Cold, fresh air and tiny droplets escaping the rushing waterfall brushed his face. All the smells of healthy soil, grass, and sweet flowers gave him an immense sense of humble new beginnings. The birds and monkeys chattering in the surrounding trees triggered a sudden flood of feelings. He swallowed his tears of joy and turned his attention back to Connor.

"Okay, continue. I'm listening," Connor said blissfully, appearing much happier when his feet touched the grass.

"Hm, where was I? Oh, yeah. I called Peter into my office several times and attempted to build a relationship with him because he clams up when he's nervous. He doesn't trust easily. We've developed an excellent rapport since he came to confess to me the day we'd sunk into the sea.

He divulges more when not under pressure or scrutiny. Also, I sense he's alone, even if he's with Tony and Bryan. He and Eryn's father grew up without the freedom of American kids. It was sterile and cold. He grew up in the time of West and East Berlin. He's much older than all of us, at least a hundred years older."

Brad spread his toes in the muddy pulp he'd made by walking in circles in one spot. An earthworm wriggled out of the mud. Brad stepped away, careful not to squash it.

"I suspected something like that. Go on, and then I'll tell you what I know about him. Sorry I interrupted you." Connor waved his hand, indicating Brad should continue.

Brad nodded a thank-you. "His mother was a prisoner in the Nazi camps, and so were his brothers. He doesn't know how many brothers he has. Still, they were all taught science at a young age. They grew up being tested, prodded, and studied. None of them went to a traditional school or had any connection to humankind until they were old enough to go to university, which those organizations ran as part of those Disciple groups. It sounded rigid as fuck. Only prescribed and pre-approved work was being conducted on controlled specimens. What bothers me is who approved and who drove this research. What if the wacko crazy scientists worked for Hitler, while Hitler was working for someone higher? When I say Saunders and his friends, I don't know. I think the people Saunders worked for were working for someone higher up." Brad paused and pointed upward at the sky. Connor looked up and emitted one long sigh.

"Yes, I know what you're saying, my friend. I guess it's time I tell you what I know. I truly thought the day we sank to the bottom of the ocean that all this had magically disappeared. Rebuilding and adapting to life underwater has kept our minds busy, and Mika and I decided it was the past. We both pushed it away as if we'd never read that damn note of Dr. Wolter Wessels's.

"Eryn's father had written a note that explained he and Peter were brothers. And you have that correct, the organization that Saunders worked for was some mastermind organization that's been around since the first humans walked the Earth. Mika and I concluded that even that organization was driven by something higher."

Connor pointed to the sky, then continued. "I agree with you there. Unfortunately I can't show you his letter. We lost it. The damn thing went missing during the chaos. These entities tasked the WHPPS. We're a by-product of their experimentation, creation, or whatever you want to call it."

"That's a relief, and I'm excited because, finally, someone understands the scope of my never-ending contemplations. You totally get it. You know what bothers me," Brad said, pointing to the sky again.

"Yes, I do. You want to fuck them up and make sure we sit at the top." Connor stopped trampling the grass, looking Brad in the eye. "What do you need from me? How can I help you?"

"I want our children to carry Phoenix to the top and into the future. I think our enemy has lost touch with what is happening here. Maybe they've given up. They don't know about your children. If they did, they would have come for them or destroyed us."

"I agree. We need to call them home and discuss strategy. We need a clear understanding of what we're up against," Connor said, picking up a rock, wiping it clean, and inspecting it. He put it in his pocket. Probably to give to Mika.

"We need to spy on them, and then we need to eliminate them. Fuck them for thinking we're toys to play with."

"Yes, fuck them, whoever the puppet masters are. What will your approach be?"

"I'm going to train your kids to be covert intelligence officers. We need a fleet, but we need more intel at this moment. And we can't start a war with a fleet smaller than theirs. We must get to know our enemy, and either be bigger and stronger or smarter and faster. We must go big or lose this war before we even start." Brad felt a tiny spark of fire ignite inside him. They chose him for this. The call for war and strategizing was what he loved most. He was a master planner, and they would succeed with the three demigods' help.

Connor grinned, and Brad smiled. No argument there.

Brad's pager pinged from inside the Bubblecar.

"Talk to me, Lasitor!" Brad called toward their vehicle.

"Certainly, sir. You just received another message from the Spacecar," Lasitor said.

Brad struggled to hear him. He smiled—being outside was noisy, and he loved it. He spoke up. "Lasitor, increase the volume, please." He walked over, eager to hear from their children.

"Yes, sir! It's from Kawa!" Lasitor shouted.

To: General McCormick at Phoenix City

From: Kawa McCormick

Subject: Update, after the 24-hour visit

"I'm working on establishing stable two-way communication with Phoenix via the international deep-space communication network. Once I've completed the newly adapted installation, the larger capacity could receive and accommodate Lasitor. Our current onboard relay receiver system combines television and radio frequency modulation.

"Initially, simultaneous communication was problematic because all the ground antennas had been flooded, and the installation didn't split the incoming and outbound streams selectively. The global destruction interrupted Earth's point of connection with space.

"I'm recreating a path back to Phoenix with a tuner using a digital I.F., the intermediate frequency. This transmission would give you enough time to let the information percolate and get ready to receive and connect Lasitor with us. It will create an uninterrupted connection stream once he's programmed our ship to connect to the deep-space communication network.

"Dad, we're not coming home. Not yet. We have a plan. Be ready for a meeting and two-way video communication. Also, the Bubblecars will not work. We need one big ship to evacuate these people. As I speak, Cian, Eryn, and Ivan are in a meeting with a man who changed places with Donali. Cian said to tell you to think about whether you want to keep the dome or level it and forget about living on the moon. He says it's a decision you must reach out and vote on. Please prepare because they'll need an answer.

"I leave you with lots to think about. I'll work with Lasitor to set up a connection.

"Talk to you soon. Kawa."

Brad looked at Connor. "Our children have become space cowboys. They keep sending us these outrageous messages. What happened to my war? First, arm the Bubblecars, now build one big transportation ship. I need to see the dome and more footage before deciding on anything. I wish we had another bloody Spacecar. Is this now our new norm? The kids leave home to explore space?" Brad asked, but Connor didn't answer. "Let's go. The others are waiting for the meeting. I told them to prepare for war. I guess this will be anticlimactic news to them. At least we can discuss the dome, communication, and building a bloody space ark," Brad said, putting his boots back on.

Connor laughed. "Yes, I hear you. The children seem to have it all under control and only need our guidance. What bothers me are the new people. How many people, and will they be able to adapt and accept our status quo?" Connor said.

"I don't need the political upheaval," Brad said, watching Connor sitting sideways on the doorframe, rubbing his feet against each other to clean them before putting his shoes back on.

"Fuck, I didn't even think about that," Connor mumbled.

"I'm writing my memoir and don't have time for a bunch of hooligans who think they can run Phoenix better than us. These people aren't scientists and soldiers. They're an illiterate public who bought their place in society." Brad's stomach ulcer bloomed back to life. Bile rose in his esophagus, and he swallowed it down. His cranium suddenly felt small as pressure built behind his eyeballs, giving birth to a new kind of migraine.

"Fuck!" he yelled, climbing in and shutting the door with a loud swoosh.

"Me, neither! I was getting used to living with no stress or worries." Connor sounded pissed off as he started the Bubblecar.

They left their special spot on Kilimanjaro by rising silently a few feet above the ground. Then the antigravitational vehicle sped back to Phoenix.

Chapter Three

"Good morning, citizens of our underwater city of Phoenix.

It's now six a.m. I promise the sun is shining.

Did you know the side of the moon that faces Earth is known as the near side? The opposite or back side is the far side.

Sometimes the far side is called the moon's dark side, but this is inaccurate.

When the moon is between the Earth and the sun, the back side of the moon is bathed in daylight during one of the moon phases called the new moon.

Visit your community news page to book your next trip to Kilimanjaro to view the moon and stars in all their splendor.

Breakfast is served until eight a.m.

Have an on-top-of-the-world day!"

Ishtar the last Anunnaki

93 A.T.

Spacecar

Five thousand miles south of the lunar dome

Grimaldi crater

Earth's moon

Ish drank the sweet, cold fluid and rested his head on his arms. He instinctively shielded himself from judgmental glances, like when he was a child and his siblings questioned him.

This was his new family, and he knew this was where he was supposed to be, as certainly as he knew his name was Ishtar. But his unspoken secrets caused his insides to burn like a furnace. He was ready to speak. He was desperate to share his burden. To verbalize his fucking feelings. Communicate with others like himself, not because of loneliness but a desire to share thoughts, to connect, and to be part of something that mattered beyond listening to human prayers.

The flying ball carrying his new friends appeared when he'd given up hope. Ish swallowed burning bile and straightened his spine. Had they arrived a day later, he would have never found them. He had given up and was exhausted, wishing to cease to exist. He had lost all hope.

Now, after only an hour in their presence, he bloomed like a little desert flower that had wilted away in a drought of human want and need but was saved by a rush of unexpected rain. He couldn't remember when he'd last felt hopeful. They weren't like humans, not the humans of Earth or those who'd arrived on the moon. Selfishness didn't drive these friends. It seemed his time of watching and waiting had ended. They were unlike the human masses or their leaders and weren't children of Egypt, either.

How was that possible? Where had they come from or, better yet, when had they come? Their Anubis, the royal spirit companions at their sides, were a sign they were the missing strand in the web of time. The Fates knew Xerxes kept his promise and guarded the apple and his offspring. That meant that one timeline he never could find was birthed and left undisturbed, as Ki had wished it, and then made him a promise that their offspring would be the future kings of Anzulla.

Before their departure, Ki and An had buried the golden apple inside the foundation of the holy wall of Ishtar—a fortification built to encircle the living tree in the center of the ancient kingdom of Urartu, between the Tigris and Euphrates Rivers. Ish remembered the beautiful gardens that sprouted from within after she sang to it. His sister had handed them the gift of everlasting life over the objection of their father, thus fueling the feud and despair. Their hopes of returning to Anzulla and saving their world were crushed by the selfishness of their father.

Finally, everything made sense. He shot a prayer to the Fates, hoping they would hear him. After waiting for decades for the Bubblecar to appear, today, of all days, the day he wanted to give up and die, they'd shown up. If he'd committed suicide... No, he didn't even want to think about it. The Fates would never have forgiven him.

He exhaled and sighed. Then he closed his eyes and emptied his mind to make sure his prayer was heard. Thank you.

He opened his eyes. The Anubis watched him with interest while peeking into the kitchenette. They must recognize me.

Ish wanted to fall on his knees and play with the Anubis like he had when he was a young boy in his father's palace. Unfortunately this was not the time, he was tired, and the humans and their Zelk problem were reason enough to push aside the infantile urge. Moreover, he wasn't worthy, and the animals' rejection would only add to the hurt he was already experiencing.

Time had taught him that everyone had problems with love and family. Whether human or Anunnaki. He'd had more than his share of sexual exercise, and he yearned for something deeper than that. At one point, he thought he might connect with Barkor, but Barkor's heart told him he belonged to another. Although Barkor differed from the others on the moon, the urge to reveal himself and forge a deeper connection was weaker than the feeling of self-preservation. It was depressingly safer to remain hidden and not show his true identity.

He wanted to feel useful, and not used. He wanted to feel important, but not supreme. He wanted to bring joyful happiness and not have it be miraculous. Being alive meant experiencing reciprocated emotions from another entity, measuring the exchange through a balance of giving and receiving, all of which were enhanced by the beauty of the experience.

And the Zelk. It frustrated him every time he thought about it. He was familiar with the feeling of impotence in such situations. It still weighed heavily on him. As opposed to his godly nature, his ability to wait and observe the situation measured his usefulness without taking action.

He was told to never linger in one group for too long, making it difficult for people to remember him while he waited for the ball-shaped ship to arrive. Among Barkor and the humans, he was perceived as big, handsome, somewhat agreeable, technologically proficient, and just as trustworthy as the other men in their inner circle. If he had met a meaningless death, there would be no evidence of his presence on the moon, and these new friends would never have found him.

In time, he would reveal himself, and they might accept him. He didn't know them. Knowing them for a few hours, he feared they would expect him to be a god for them, a role he did not want to take on. Consequently, he needed to hide his identity and wait. Ish had nothing to offer except himself. He believed that people would either tolerate him or fear him, despite his friendly and easygoing demeanor.

Ish lifted his head as Eryn took a deep breath, signifying it was time to talk. Eryn strolled over, wedging his golden spear upright in the corner, and settled across from Ish. He put both his hands on the table, palms up, as if inviting Ish to take them. Bravely, Ish took the leap, trusted Eryn, and placed his hands in his. Eryn nodded his approval and looked at Ish like no one had ever looked at him.

Eryn saw inside him. Ish shivered. He felt Eryn touching him with empathy; the kindness cracked his outer shell, and like an egg, his yolk started running out.

"I sense you're not happy, Ish," he said. "I can feel it, it is everywhere around you. Don't think I don't know and don't think my brothers don't see it. We want to have an honest talk. Tell us everything, and we'll listen and help if needed. I sense helping you is not the help you need.

Sure, they"—Eryn pointed toward the human settlement—"need help. First tell us, do you need us to help you?"

Surprised by Eryn's blatant intrusion into his psyche, Ish shifted side to side—uncomfortable with the inquisition. Eryn was holding his hands and flaying his emotions embarrassingly open. Did they expect Ish to blurt out thousands of years of his sorrows? He found his answer in Eryn's caring gaze.

Ish didn't answer the question, he sidestepped it. To answer would have meant discussing things that he didn't discuss with anyone. He didn't know how. And he didn't know if it was allowed. He took a deep breath and started talking, hoping it made sense to his new friends.

"The Zelk is not dead. Only the body is gone. Their essence, souls, or spirits are in that tower," Ish said, searching their faces for amusement or disbelief.

Eryn answered with a nod. He showed no emotion and then asked, "Tell us whose souls left their bodies and have taken up residence in the tower?"

Again, Ish looked at Ivan, Cian, and Kawa, and lastly, back at Eryn. "Those who built it wanted to live forever and be like us, maybe even be better than us. They are greedy. You don't know what they're capable of. Just look at what they've done to Earth and, then again, what they've done here. They built the hive and devised a way to insert their minds into it. They built their own indestructible bodies and became something else. At first, I didn't think it was possible, but I'm extremely worried now. I should have destroyed them when they first succeeded. Only, I didn't want to interfere." *I wasn't allowed, I had to wait for you*, he thought; hiding the truth was the safest course of action for now.

"I guess I wanted to see what humans are capable of," he lied and felt guilty for deceiving them. "And now it's a nearly impossible task. Truthfully, I am frightened by it. I beg your help to destroy this thing.

It's evil and grows bigger. It's going to destroy everything," Ish said. He inhaled and blew out a long, shaky breath.

There was silence for a long time as everyone around the table listened and took in what he'd described.

Eryn answered, "Everything that I was and everything I now am tells me the humans planned this to become immortal. Therefore, I construe they created us to be like you, and unfortunately, it wasn't something they could control because they experimented with things and powers they didn't understand. Like giving a baby a loaded gun and seeing what happens." Eryn lowered his gaze and seemed to give Ish a second to think about what he'd just said.

He has a magnificent mind and reads everything about me. My emotions, thoughts, body language, and even the tone of my voice. Simultaneously, he comprehends the whole mess. Truly extraordinary.

He looked back up into Eryn's eyes. His skin was the most beautiful shade of gold with a light blue sheen. Full lips and a wide, firm jaw. He was wiser than any living being on this plane Ish had met. Ever. Yet humble with a boyish demeanor. Ish thought he was the most appealing and irresistible male he'd ever seen. His eyes were a lot like his own, except for the pupils. Although he looked able to crush a human's skull between his hands, he was affectionate and soft-spoken, even more so to his mate. He would have made a great ruler of Anzulla.

"No, thank you. I'm already a king," Eryn said with a big smile and a chuckle.

He was reading my mind even when I barricaded my thoughts. Worthy of being king, Ish thought.

Cian seemed to be the rowdy one. He cleared his throat and spoke up. "I'm rarely rendered speechless. What I take from this is that they're, wait, not they. Humans are capable of so much once they use initiative, but senselessly hurt themselves because no one showed them how to play with their toys. Is that what you're saying? You let them build the big computer tower to see how they would fuck up?" he asked, gnashing his teeth.

Having expected, and thus understanding, the hostility, Ish cleared his throat and answered, "Yes, that's the condensed version, only, that's not the entire explanation." He watched Cian summing him up.

"Tell me"—Cian pointed out the bay window—"were they all just one big experiment?" he asked, leaning over Ish.

"Yes," Ish answered. Reading Cian's thoughts was difficult. His emotions combusted like fireworks—a kaleidoscope of emotions and power. Ish wondered if he even knew how much power he possessed.

"Whose fucking experiments? And who the fuck are you?" he asked, and they looked at Ish as if he'd personally wronged them.

I should never have shown myself.

Hesitantly, he admitted, "My father's," and at this stage, he couldn't deny anything. He licked his dry, cracked lips. His entire mouth was dry. "I can fix this and make it right. I will let you know when it is done. Can I count on you to do as I say when it's the right time?"

Ish let go of Eryn's hands and rose, but as he did, Eryn spoke.

"This is the source of your unhappiness, isn't it? You run around and try to make others happy. We're sorry that you're having all this pain. Was this, in any way, your fault?" Eryn asked.

Ish sat down again, feeling defeated. "No, it was probably my father's."

Eryn was quiet and seemed perplexed. His eyebrows were drawn down, forming a deep furrow above his nose, and his golden green gaze jumped from left to right as he read Ish's facial features and internal thoughts.

"Their attempts to create more children unnaturally failed, so they perished. My home was destroyed. It was a heap of rubble, smoke, and ash."

"This sounds like something we experienced. Where were you?" Cian asked. He seemed to know what questions to ask—an intelligent roughneck.

"I was working," Ish answered, trying his best to be honest, or they might decide not to help.

"What does that mean?" Ivan asked. The twin brothers worked together, and they had a strong bond.

"I searched for a place to call home, somewhere untarnished, a safe place for my people to flourish."

"A place? What are you talking about?" Cian asked and pinned Ish with a cold stare. The blue in his eyes felt like a laser cutting a path through the armor encasing his secrets.

This type of questioning unsettled Ish. "That's what I said. I searched for a place."

"How did you search for a motherfucking place?" Cian fisted his hands and loomed over Ish, supporting his hulking frame on his knuckles on the surface of the table in front of him. "How do you search?"

"Brother," Ivan cautioned Cian.

Ish broke the stare with Cian and sought an escape in Ivan's eyes. They were brighter and cut just as deep.

"Tell me!" Cian shouted.

Ish recoiled in his seat, taken aback. *What should he say? These people read minds.* He looked at Eryn, who smiled at him. Ivan was worried about him. Cian wanted to wring his neck, and Kawa found the entire conversation amusing.

"I, I searched, and I waited," Ish stuttered.

"Listen, has it ever occurred to you they're fucking things up and speeding up the destruction because you watched and waited for this boil of a mess to fester? And now you say you want what?" Cian asked and hit his fists on the table with a dull thud. "What do you think we should do?"

What's he talking about? Were they even talking about the same things?

Ivan uttered a firm "no" to his brother, while his gaze held no compassion for Ish.

"Are you saying you sat and watched how humans die so you could swoop in and take their home? Why? They came to the moon for you, and you watched it unfold. Or are you saying you can't help? Or does their suffering amuse you?" Ivan watched Ish with calculated precision, swinging his head and eyeballing him from new angles after each question.

"That's exactly what he's saying. What he's not saying is that he's the fucking reason the place is in the state it is. He's why these sad fuckers are on the moon and like us, nothing more than experiments," Cian said through clenched teeth, then dove over the table, taking Ish to the floor. His enormous hands and long fingers wrapped around Ish's throat, squeezing and cracking his laryngeal cartilage.

"You motherfucking Anunnaki!"

Ish relaxed and welcomed his death. As he lay upside down with his legs still up on the bench and head on the floor, their voices were muffled like he was underwater. *What a glorious feeling. He felt nothing. No fear. Just a white fuzziness. A soft place of peace and nothingness.*

The light and sound abruptly returned while someone slapped his cheeks. "Come on, take a breath. You better wake up so I can kill you again later. Come on, open your eyes, you sad motherfucker!" Cian yelled. He was likely the one slapping him.

"Ish, there's no way that you're dead. We can hear your heart and thoughts. Open your eyes," Eryn urged, and Ish opened his eyes, examining Cian, Ivan, Eryn, and Kawa's faces. They smiled. Ish was livid.

"Kill me now, or I will do it myself! Kill me, please. Please, I beg you," he cried.

"Sorry, no. Too easy. You will tell us how to save these people and kill the Zelk. Then I will gladly kill you." Cian stood with his feet at the sides of Ish's head. Ish looked up into his stunning blue eyes and the impressively large bulge in his pants. Eryn and Ivan waited somewhere on the other side of the table as if this was an everyday occurrence. Cian was maniacal. *There was something wrong with him, while fuck, he oozes sex appeal; they all were.*

Ish let his head fall. "Promise?"

"Yes, I fucking promise," Cian said and stepped to the side, offering his hand. Ish grabbed it, and he pulled him back into a sitting position at the table. Ivan was picking up and cleaning the floor, and Eryn looked at him pointedly, as if searching his insides for answers. Kawa didn't say a word. He turned and left as if bored.

"Humans may have tactics, yet they lack speed, and we aren't human," Eryn said, as Ish shifted sideways to discreetly make room for his hardening cock. *When was the last time his cock showed any interest? He had forgotten how it felt.*

Eryn chuckled.

"Ish, let me answer those questions you have inside you. You may feel better if you accept the fact that the irrationality of human beings makes them impossible to predict. Stop trying to change the past by finding the perfect future. You're jumping around and wasting your time because every second has a million other possibilities, so, in reality, you spend your time watching others' lives instead of experiencing your own. Do I make sense to you?" Eryn asked, narrowing his eyes.

His voice enchanted Ish. He could listen to him all day. It wasn't only the voice; it was the words that the voice formed. The sounds. They were kind, and he was all-knowing, like he saw where Ish was and what he'd seen. Eryn knew who and what he was and did not voice it for a reason. Ish gave a slight nod. His upbringing and instinct told him to submit and respect. He was certain his jaw dropped, and he sat open-mouthed in awe of Eryn, who nonchalantly turned and helped Ivan to throw the broken cups in the trash. Then Eryn grabbed a cloth, took a knee, and dried the floor.

On his hands and knees doing it. This, whatever he was...

"I am a Brawl," Eryn said proudly, pushing his chest out and standing tall. Ish knew he was looking at something he never thought possible. Eryn threw the rag to the side and came back to sit down. Ivan sat on his lap. They kissed and turned their attention back to Ish.

Cian seemed to prefer keeping his distance. He stood with muscled arms crossed and dark blue eyes pinning Ish in place and spoke. "They call us the Divine triad, but that was before Ivan and Eryn mated. Now we're just the three Divine Brothers."

"Oh, so you three?" Ish pointed between them. Imagining the exquisite experience of ogling and feeling these three beautiful bodies undulating around, on top, and under him, his cock stirred, twitched, and leaked. An orgy of gods...

"Noooo!" the three answered in unison, and Ish felt his cheeks warm as he must have been blushing. He hoped his dark complexion hid his vulnerability. Then again, he doubted he could hide anything from them. Especially from Eryn. He needed to learn to guard his thoughts and feelings around them better. At least he'd met them, and that which he thought unthinkable was true. Here they were. His father wasn't here for this, and he was glad about that. He wished he'd found this timeline earlier and told his sister about it. He smiled. But not for the reason they thought.

"Tell us, where have you been staying all this time?" Cian asked and sat down. He threw his legs sideways over the bench, crossing his thickly tatted arms again, and leaned back. Ish read his emotions. Cian was fishing for information.

"I was here, watching over Barkor," he said, waiting for a reaction. The corners of Cian's mouth twitched, and his heart rate sped up at the mention of Barkor's name. Hmmm, so he was Barkor's mate. Ish knew the signs of possessive jealousy, the pull between predestined mates. It had been thousands of years since he'd last seen it.

Instead of asking more questions, Cian jumped up and walked away. How odd. He was fighting the pull. This was going to be fun to watch.

Chapter Four

"Good morning, citizens of Phoenix.

It's now six a.m.

Did you know there are several detrimental effects of poor posture? Not only is it unattractive, but it also makes breathing difficult and causes back pain and incontinence.

The unpleasant truth is that it's quite simple to slouch and eventually acquire a bad posture.

Visit your community news page for tips about posture improvement techniques and making healthier choices.

Breakfast is served until eight a.m.

Straighten your spine and have a good day!"

Mika Romanov

94 A.T.

Phoenix, underwater glass dome city

Earth

Weeks after the Spacecar had been taken for a joyride and a peek-a-boo of the Lunar Environmental Project, it became the secret headquarters on the lunar surface tucked away inside the Grimaldi crater. The two Bubblecars were necessary for daily scouting, so they had to service and exchange them back at Phoenix. Their provisions and water needed to be replaced, so postponing an inevitable trip to Earth wasn't an option. Cian, Ivan, Eryn, Kawa, and Ish returned to Earth to restock and introduce Ish to the leadership team. A day before they returned to the moon, Ish's eye had caught Dr. Peter von Leutzendorf's, who disappeared in the fray and hid from him. He first asked Brad, who refused to divulge anything about Peter, and then begged Cian and his brothers, but they weren't on speaking terms or friends with him. The onus fell on Connor and Mika to introduce them.

Mika hesitantly peeked from around the corner of his office with Connor and Ish behind him. He deliberated a while and stood frozen with indecision. Peter was rarely in his office nowadays. Because he finally had a social life, or he was ignoring the fuck out of Mika. Inside this office was where Mika and Connor forged a bond with Peter. Inside this watertight temperature-controlled chamber, they locked themselves safely away from the freezing waters of the tsunamis. Mika watched him reading, sitting on the single bed he kept in the office for when he worked late. He sat with his back against the wall. Bare feet crossed at the ankles. Peter had been avoiding him and Connor.

"Go now. What are you waiting for?" Ish whispered over Mika's shoulder and pushed him to move forward. Mika wanted to swat him like a pesky fly. Ish had been mobbing Mika for the whole bloody day. Peter's blond hair and blue eyes triggered a sudden desire to meet the bestower of everlasting life. Ish noticed him fleetingly passing them by in the stairwell where Peter had been evading them by taking back entrances. Mika's sneaking stemmed from Brad saving Peter from killing himself. Peter couldn't live with his guilty conscience. Brad had promised Mika public castration if he or Connor spoke to Peter without him present. Brad wouldn't know, and technically, Mika wouldn't talk to Peter, only introduce them and go. That was all. That was the plan.

"Yelda, you better go now. He's going to notice us and close the damn door. Who knows how long he'll lock himself inside there? You go in, and I'll guard the door. I'm not going inside. I'll be your lookout. Okay?" Connor whispered, hanging on Mika's right hip, and staying low like bullets were flying. He was having fun.

Mika straightened his spine. "Okay, here we go," he whispered, hoping Brad didn't find out.

"Yes, that's the plan," Ish said, holding an origami flower he made for Peter against his chest.

Mika took a deep breath and then shot across the hallway into Peter's office. Once inside, he grabbed Ish's arm and thrust him forward. "Peter, let me introduce..."

Peter jumped on his bed, threw the book he'd been reading at Mika, and let loose with a high-pitched shrill. Mouth wide open, he screamed and saw Ish, and his mouth widened even more, ear-splittingly louder, without taking a breath.

Still yelling, he looked him up and down, taking the tall, dark, and dangerously looking man in.

Yes, you idiot, he likes you.

Peter attempted to climb through the wall behind him and failed; all the while, Ish tried his best to give him his origami flower. Peter slapped the flower and then froze as he noticed Ish's golden irises with black rings.

"Alien eyes!" This time, he smiled as he hollered. Tears streamed down his face. "Alien eyes," he said again while attempting to climb over his desk to reach the door.

"Gille-toine, close the door, don't let him escape!" Mika yelled, and Connor jumped into action. Peter realized he was being boxed in and screamed even higher, and the more Ish tried to woo him, the more Peter tried reversing through the wall and failed. It was chaos, and Mika had had enough.

"Jesus, Peter, stop your motherfucking crazy screaming. We're not here to hurt you." Mika pulled Ish back, noticing that he was making it worse. "Connor and I wanted to introduce you to this man. He's besotted with you. Ever since he saw you, he couldn't stop asking about you. Brad's busy meeting with Cian. I know Brad said not to come to you alone, and that we needed him to chaperone us. You have your reasons. Connor and I will go now. We just wanted to bring Ish to you."

Peter snickered and, thank god, stopped making the ruckus. His gaze was bewildered. Even so, the idiot smiled. Mika didn't know what was going on.

"What? You don't want to take me away? He is real, and not a ghost?" Peter stuttered, wiping tears left and right. They seemed to be happy tears now.

"No, Peter, I just want to introduce you. He is real. You know when one boy sees another boy he likes and must meet and take him out..."

Peter lifted his head to the ceiling, shrieking again.

Mika lifted his hands. "No, not take you out and kill you!" Mika held his hands low, although he wanted to pull on his hair. "Calm the fuck down. Why would I introduce you to someone I asked to kill you? My only intention is to bring him to you. Go do something nice together. Go out on a date!"

Peter heaved and gulped air. "Oh," he said, looking at Ish, who hid behind Mika's back.

"Please, first, tell us, are you serious about Tony and Bryan? Does your heart belong to them?" Mika asked. Peter looked at Mika and seemed to register what was happening.

"No, I never loved them. We aren't together, anyway. Not anymore, they..." Peter waved his hand, showing they were past tense.

Behind Mika, he heard Ish whisper, "Yes, yes, yes!"

"I'm sorry to hear that, my friend. Are you doing okay? I thought you were with them this whole time." Mika held his arms wide, hinting for Ish to stay behind him and Connor, whose one eye peeked through a small opening, to stay back. He didn't want to make sudden movements.

Peter parsed his lips, seeming on the verge of tears again and shook his head. "No, I can't be with them. I'm not good company."

"What have you been doing? I know your research is complete. You're not in the lab anymore. What have you been doing this whole time with yourself, my friend?" Mika asked nicely; he was worried about Peter.

Peter straightened his back. "I'm on holiday," he said proudly.

"That's good news," Mika said reluctantly, not sure how Peter would take anything he said. Peter had never taken one day off, so being on holiday was out of the norm.

"Yes, I'm reading, watching television, and helping at the toddler's school. I'm doing everything I never did. I sleep better, and I'm learning who I am." Peter gave Mika a look, daring him to say something negative.

Mika thought that was a fantastic idea. His friend was taking time for himself. "That's a big change. Anything that makes you happy and doesn't hurt anyone else is a step in the right direction."

Mika faintly heard Connor calling his name as if to caution him, but couldn't stop himself from asking Peter. "Why weasel around? Why are you taking so long to confront us? You know we need to come clean, all of us. We've been working together for years, still you said nothing and let me—"

Connor flung the door open, distracting him and reminding him with a look of wariness and a shake of his head.

Mika stopped himself. "You know what, one day when you want to talk about it all, come to me. This is Ish." He pushed Ish to the front. Ish fell to one knee, dreadlocks and gold chains flying left and right as the big giant tried to make himself as small as possible in front of Peter. He bent his head and held the origami upwards at Peter like an offering.

Peter stood looking astonished, then carefully took the delicately folded flower and smelled it.

Ish smiled, and his happiness radiated into the small room. He cleared his throat and spoke gently. "This is for you. It represents the loursveto flower from my home on Anzulla. The flower is a symbol of love and serenity. Of beauty and intelligence. Of everlasting union and life."

"Sounds to me like a wedding ring," Mika said and turned to leave them alone. He wanted to stay and ask more about Anzulla, but he said, "Peter, talk to the man. Connor and I will wait in my office if you need me." Mika pushed the half-closed door wide open and joined his husband. "Let's go have a coffee in my office," Mika mumbled and heard Ish introducing himself.

"Hello, my name is Ish. You may not remember me, I visited you once..."

After two cups of coffee, Mika wanted to return to work. He had promised his friend he would stay if he needed him. They were pretty bored when Peter stormed into his office. Mika pushed his chair back and jumped up. "What's wrong? Did he take advantage of you?"

"No." Peter rolled his eyes and swooned. "No, don't be silly. Be happy for me. My mind is lighter, and all my thoughts and feelings are categorized and packed away. I feel much better. I got my Ish. I've been waiting for him all this time." Peter giggled, holding his flower in front of his nose. "He said he was starving without me." Then plopped himself down and sat opposite Mika and Connor. In his chair. The one he used to sit in years ago. Mika saw a shadow hovering just outside the doorframe and assumed Ish was waiting outside.

Peter sat on the edge of his seat. "Mika, Connor, I'm sorry. I don't want to explain away what I did because how I did it was wrong. I know now that you probably would have agreed anyway if I'd told you all this."

Mika nodded, and Connor wiggled uncomfortably in his chair like he kept his protests to himself.

Mika got up and grabbed his special tools for electrical wiring. "Comrade, we'd meant to get you alone for an honest discussion. We've been evading each other for much too long. Connor and I had taken this secret and ignored it. It worked because we forgot about it all for a while. As it goes with secrets, if more than one person knows, then it's not a secret anymore. Also, if one person keeps that secret, it becomes heavy to carry. It's better not to have secrets. They will crush you. I tried not to tell Connor because I was ashamed of myself. I trusted you because I considered you my best friend and lab partner. In my eyes, you were untainted, pure, and innocent. I actually felt sorry for your pathetic-ness," Mika said honestly and truthfully.

Connor stood quietly, saying nothing. He nodded affirmatively as he supported Mika. Peter bit his lip, clutching the flower tighter, and Ish loomed inside.

"I'm more than ready to get this drama behind us. The only thing I ask of you is to tell me what the fuck is going on. How did you end up here, and why do you sound like you know Ish? I swear, more questions come up each time I talk to you. You're making me crazy by trying to guess your story. I must know because thinking and attempting to guess all the time occupies my mind with unnecessary mental energy, and I'd rather use it on something productive. Come, bring your guest, and we can tinker on the latest Spacecar prototype and figure out a way to build a better communication system," Mika said and herded them out of the office. Talking while working would give them an outlet for their emotions and build camaraderie.

The four of them walked the corridors, not stopping to talk, only greeting the inquisitive ones with a firm nod and hello. Everyone was in the habit of leaving Peter alone, so as soon as they lifted their heads to yap, Mika would push him to the front. Mouths would shut, heads would shake, and they would skedaddle away.

He needed to get Peter to talk because he wanted to learn more about their family's genes and how his and Connor's DNA perfectly bonded with the Anunnaki gene. Peter had known that all the time, while Mika had to find the truth in bits and pieces from the scientist's notes of Dr. Wessels and from their enemy. His perfect Romanov Russian princes didn't have a Scandinavian five-foot-ten blonde model with blue eyes as an egg donor. Nick, the Disciple, revealed it was a DNA string from a Mesopotamian Anunnaki.

The more puzzling piece was that it was all written on the Babylonian seal and tablets and found in the stash of intelligence Mika and the men confiscated from the nitrogen-propelled airship. It spoke of a time of lots of water covering the whole earth. Nick thought it was tsunamis, but Mika and Connor deciphered the original text, which spoke about water covering the entire Earth, like biblical floods. They predicted the Big Flood in the holy *Year of the Twins*. Mika, Connor, and their friends all gave input as they met and studied the tablets and every scrap of history saved by Lasitor. The word holy was taken out of context and directly translated—it meant the perfect or whole round number. That number in Mesopotamian was twenty-two.

Another idiotic translation by Nick's tribe was that they said the world would end, and Luna would welcome them. Correctly translated, it meant, on Luna, we will meet. That was all it said. Nick also said the three would lead us into the future. What it said was, in the future, I live to meet you.

Nick had said that they helped them decide on Project One. They were Disciples, and his children were direct descendants of An and Ki, the God of the Heavens and the Goddess of the Earth. That Ivan meant the fourth, or Roman letter IV, for the mighty IV-An, and Cian spelled Ki-AN.

How did they know about the names he and Connor had chosen? And why did Peter know Ish, who was on the moon this whole time? Mika needed to talk to their children.

The cloud surrounding Earth hid them from the strange ships that came to suck up their atmosphere. He hoped Cian and Brad decided on a better plan, and fast. And then they needed to execute the plan. And to do that, they needed to communicate. He hated feeling cut off and isolated.

They reached Mika and Connors's workshop and lab near the shipyard a few minutes later. Then entered via the wind tunnel that blew like a category seven tornado to remove all dust particles. They washed up and donned protective gear before entering a sterile area to install wiring on a larger prototype.

"Gille-toine, can Peter help us build a communication tower? One that floats and can be retracted and moved under the surface level? It would be a better option than dragging construction outside and erecting one on a mountaintop. I worry any manmade structure will give us away, and I'm sure Brad won't approve of it. We need to communicate better with the children. I need eyes and ears out there. I want twenty-four hours a day of video feeds from all over. Wherever they go, they should leave a camera ball for us. That way, we can protect and warn them, don't you think?"

"Of course he can."

Connor turned to Peter, who looked dreamily at Ish as he inspected the ship. "Peter, the more heads, the faster we shall get results," Connor said, lifting his chin towards the two newcomers busy coming through the transparent wind tunnel to suit up for entry.

Ish seemed to know his stuff. He pulled and pushed a few buttons and knobs until the installed wiring came to life, highlighting the walkways deeper inside the belly of the ship. Hands folded behind his back, he inspected the cabin, locker, dining, and sleeping areas and then exited with an approving nod.

"Apologies, I don't want to seem judgmental of your work. I'm impressed by it. I assume you built the smaller version as well. Your attention to the fine details impressed me most," Ish said with a low bow, first toward Mika and then toward Connor.

Taken aback, Mika almost lost his train of thought. "Thank you. We're building a better, bigger version than the boys are currently using. We would like your input and recommendations any time, comrade," he said to Ish, and turned back to Peter. "We can't rely only on a voice-recorded report from the kids. By the time we receive it...what I mean is, we can't sit here and watch how people learn to knit and shit. I want my own ship up and running. I fucking need to know what's happening outside the clouds. But, in the meantime, could you maybe design a submarine with satellite capabilities?" He pleaded, with a beggar's face, and his hands folded over his chest.

"Yes, sure, of course. I can help. I can do that for you. I'll help with anything as long as I'm not working with frozen dead people," Peter said, chuckling shyly. Mika realized his friend was more traumatized by the lucrative project than he initially thought. He saw why Brad suggested leaving him alone and not talking to him unchaperoned. He seemed brittle and had reached maximum tensile strength.

"That's good news, my friend," Mika said, calling them over to a big square table, where he activated it to show them the 4D schematics they started with.

"Yelda, maybe Ish has some input here," Connor said to Mika as he pushed himself up from squatting. Mika observed he was connecting the silicone wires to the motherboard.

"Progress is slow. In two years, we would at least have two ships ready. Please, I need to know what we can improve and change, and I can't do that with relayed radio messages."

Peter stepped closer, holding Ish's hand. They looked like the perfect contrast. Like yin and yang. Peter's pale complexion with blue eyes to Ish's dark as night skin and golden double-ringed irises.

"You know, Mika and Connor, my friends. I've blurted some of it out to Brad while feeling guilty as fuck. I'm older than any man currently living in Phoenix, and although not needed, I'd implanted the first Eden Bean when I appeared to be twenty-seven years old. I've been hiding my origins and sacrificed myself for the word and a smile from a sexy alien in my living room a lifetime ago."

Mika stiffened. What in the ever-loving fuck? Connor pulled him by the arm. Mika swallowed his words. *Was this happening even before they landed on the moon?* The words almost left his mouth. Again, Connor tapped him. Connor looked at Peter while shaking his head as if he had fleas. Mika got the message to shut up and listen. He embraced Connor by the shoulder, pulling him in towards himself. *I shall listen, don't worry, my gille-toine.*

He smiled at Peter.

Peter swallowed and straightened his back as he continued telling his story. "I don't feel guilty because I'd gifted the Phoenicians with eternal life." Peter smiled up at Ish with adoration and hero worship. Not like he hung the moon, but took it down and moved it exactly where Peter wanted it. Mika and the leadership team had interviewed Ish and understood that Ish was from Grayrak. Something didn't add up. But before he could form the question, Peter continued.

"Memories of years far gone resurfaced. I'd forgotten those eyes. Too much had happened, and as the years twisted their strands together, it all became a forgotten drop of memory in a big bucket full of time."

Ish bent down and picked the much shorter Peter up from the floor. Peter yelped, and Ish rubbed their noses together. Mika thought he saw fangs for a second. Brad and Cian distracted him by joining them and listening to Peter talk. Brad seemed impressed. He smiled happily as Peter, Mika, and Connor were talking. He nodded to Mika and Connor, giving them a stare and approval nonverbally.

Ish put Peter down and seemed more tense when Cian entered. They'd already built a rapport and seemed to have an understanding that Cian was calling the shots. Mika was very proud of his son. He struggled emotionally when Ivan and Eryn got married and had grown into a strong and respected leader. He had thrown himself into his work with Bryan and training the reserves. He'd shown exceptional leadership and strength and now wore the same rank as Brad. Although rankings in Phoenix wasn't practiced the traditional way, the word *general* was loosely bestowed on Cian and first used by the men he trained and educated on space engineering and defense.

Eryn and Ivan didn't care about titles. The power couple was humble and preferred to do everything together while working. Their education from Phoenix University focused on human biomechanics and the musculoskeletal system and how the body tissue responded to the forces they commanded and helped the citizens by combining their powers with technology.

Ish greeted Cian and Brad with a radiant smile and his hand-over-hand handshake and widened his smile to expose his teeth. No fangs were visible. Mika thought he imagined it.

Ish stepped back in a manner only royalty did when they expected everyone to listen. He stayed silent for a while until all attention was on him. Cian gave him two thumbs up, and he spoke in his deep baritone with an accent Mika couldn't place, although he was a linguist and mastered eight languages.

"I've always wondered if the earthlings would ever be able to leave the Earth. I was relieved when I first saw your transportation vehicle. My home is now but a rock bestrewed with heaps of crumbling aspirations and broken dreams. I was left utterly alone, yet now I am not alone anymore," Ish said and smiled at Peter and then Cian. Mika listened intently to hear if Ish would answer all of his unspoken questions.

"I was the youngest of my siblings, and I missed and hated them for leaving me behind. In solitude, I observed the humans. All I could do was watch how they murdered and destroyed themselves from afar. My father's cunningness and twisted ways destroyed us and our home. I lived in hiding, contemplating stopping my torturous existence. I longed to walk with the humans to cure my loneliness. I asked myself over and over, how do I reveal myself? How will they receive me? I am not a god. Nor do I want to be one. For eons, I tried tirelessly to find the point where sowing our seed and knowledge would bloom as intended."

Mika observed Cian nodding at Ish as if he agreed with Ish, and they practiced this together. Maybe he's referring to being Anunnaki. Maybe he was born at the concentration camps and sent to the moon with the rockets that left pre-Doomsday?

"Look at what's happening with the creation of the Zelk—an unnatural species made from parts of humans and parts of their technologies. If I don't help them, they will die by the hand of the Zelk that continues to multiply. The Zelk is an abomination. A thing that grows and consumes not only human flesh and bone but their souls, too. It lures the weak with the promise of life, but it only brings death. I know it because I have battled it before. I will work with Cian and his brothers, and together, we will find the balance we have all been seeking—a new beginning."

"Ha!" Mika clapped his hands. "I guess you can bring out the Kool-Aid now, Brad. You would think he answered the age-old questions of humanity. Who am I, where do I belong, why am I here, and what is my purpose? It's fucking depressing, I tell you. He said absolutely nothing," Mika blurted, and Connor pushed and pulled furiously on his clothes.

Mika wasn't impressed by Ish. Ivan had told him about Cian strangling him, and he felt the same about the sneaky motherfucker. *Ish is talking in riddles, and Peter's in on it.*

Chapter Five

"Good morning, citizens of Phoenix.

It's now six a.m.

Did you know that teaching your kids how to swim is compulsory? Your local swim and dive club provides fun and enriching swim lessons for kids ages 4 months and up. Specialized swim methods give kids the skills to be safe in the water.

BIG NEWS! We will no longer be affiliated with the CPR techniques of the Red Cross.

Phoenician CPR lessons and services have exceeded and outgrown what they provided.

Breakfast is served until eight a.m.

Hope you have a splashing good day!"

Leo

93 A.T.

Disciples of the Anunnaki compound

Environmental Project - Luna

Grayrak

City

Earth's moon

Leo looked longingly out the clubhouse window, staring off into the distance, and watched the arms of Big Benny Clock Tower move so slowly he couldn't see them move. But move they did because every few minutes he checked, and they pointed to a different number, ticking and counting his pathetic existence down. Leo's backside burned. It felt like he sat on a hot coal or three. He gnashed his teeth, whipping his head and shoulders this and that way to gain momentum to roll over onto his side. He should ask someone to reposition him, but he wasn't there yet. He'd rather struggle alone as long as possible than lower himself to begging for help. He didn't want to give them the satisfaction of laughing at his expense only for a small push.

After he tired himself out, he searched the room for anyone looking his way that he could ask. He waited, rested, and struggled a few more times by taking deep breaths, exhaling quickly, and throwing his head backward. A trick he learned to move and slide himself into a new position. Like a worm. *Fucking hell, thank god.*

Groaning, he slipped about two inches down while wiggling his shoulders back and forth. He sighed after he reached a more comfortable position. Sweat beaded on his forehead, and it tickled him. The exertion exhausted him to the point of heaving to catch his breath. He turned his attention to where everyone was listening to Grizzly. He animatedly talked about abducting a new offering. Leo hated him and his pockmarked face. He cringed when he saw the evil smile exposing his yellow-black teeth from chewing homegrown tobacco leaves all day. He locked gazes with Leo and stepped closer.

"Do you need help, my worm?" he asked as if he cared and picked Leo up from his chair.

"My ass is sore," Leo said dryly, then held his breath, anticipating the stench of sweaty armpits. Grizzly reeked, and his vile body odor matched his personality. Leo was his plaything, and Grizzly got off on how much Leo needed him. He didn't care; he enjoyed rubbing salt into Leo's helplessness as he flung him onto his shoulder like a swaddled baby patting his backside.

"I don't want my worm ending up with sores and blisters. Then you're not useful anymore," Grizzly said and fluffed Leo's hair after putting him down.

He was in a good mood today, and Leo was going to do something about it. Just as Grizzly turned back to address his men, Leo mumbled shrewdly, "Thank you, you dirty sick fuck!" He hated feeling helpless, and he hated that he was embarrassed. But most of all, he hated Grizzly. The sick fuck was a devotee. His *kink* was fucking people like Leo, who was helpless and deformed, and here on Grayrak, it was not by accident. No, he would send people he liked to see helpless to the Zelk and then fucked them until he grew tired of them.

"My pleasure, and I know what you're trying to do, and it ain't gonna work," Grizzly said over his shoulder and addressed his underlings.

"Men, my toes curl inside my boots! I can't wait to get my hands on him. He'd be our best trade!" Grizzly boasted, and the men guffawed.

Although Grayrak lay hidden and protected inside a tinted glass dome, the miners, better known as the Disciples, developed excessively thick, pink, and damaged skin. This marked them as the few privileged with jobs on the Zelk mining ship. Like the ship's crew, Grizzly worked with minimal protection by their hooded cloaks from the sun's damaging UV rays. Some say they were cloaked descendants of the first Disciples of the gods. Others say it was to hide their ugly pockmarked faces. They were repulsive bullies who overran the human camp called the City of Grayrak. Leo and every other man, woman, and child who wasn't part of their cult hated the domineering giant as much as they feared him.

Grizzly's bragging was really working on Leo's nerves today. He didn't want anything to do with the messed-up plans. At first, they lured Leo in, and after they sold all his limbs to the Zelk, they used him as bait to lure in people who wanted to help. And when that didn't work anymore,

Leo was only good at being used as a warm hole to fuck, and of course, he was the middleman between the Disciples and the Zelk.

He was a half-man because he'd been a donor and in the hospital multiple times. He was a trusted ally. Someone who helped the Zelk, and because he had no arms or legs, he was no threat. He had his mouth, which he used to stay alive, but he was tired nowadays and wished he could die. He wanted to leave this stink hole and meet the everlasting dark. He was ready and done with it all.

The only way that will happen is if I choke on my food or Grizzly kills me.

"I wish you would stop trading people!" Leo exclaimed and surprised himself with his boldness. He wanted to die. He carried on antagonizing Grizzly. He never met the man in question, and he sympathized with him. Living as a half-man was hell. If he could walk, he would consider going to the market. Leo would try to give the last good man in Grayrak a heads-up before Grizzly collected him and traded him as a fresh body for the Zelk.

He'll end up like me. A head with no ears and torso. A worm. No, he couldn't let that happen. Then again, if it did happen, Grizzly would have a new plaything to torture. *I may be killed and thrown away. Maybe I'll be a hand-me-down.*

The look on Leo's face must have betrayed him. Before he could mask his feelings, Grizzly got sight of it.

"Don't you fucking dare, Leo!" Grizzly said under his breath. "I'm warning you only once. Don't even think about warning him. You can't hide your feelings from me. I own you! I fucking own everything on this side of the wall. I will lock you up in your special box without food or water." Grizzly pointed a fat finger at Leo, who looked up into his eyes, challenging Grizzly.

Leo widened his eyes, mocking him. *Yeah, come on, you bastard hit me!* Leo taunted and felt triumphant when he saw the big flat hand approaching his face.

A deafening thwack collided on the side of his head where his open canal sat unprotected by the pinna, the outer ear cartilage, which was the first to be traded with the Zelk. Next, all the wind got knocked out of him as Grizzly's enormous fist hit the pit of his stomach. Leo doubled over and face-planted on the dirty floor. With his exposed cock and backside, he lay upside down for a few seconds before his torso toppled over, thumping his lower body on the cold rock floor. He groaned in pain. As he turned his head, the tip of a boot kicked his forehead. Sparks flashed in front of his eyes, and he welcomed the darkness calling him as he passed out.

The fury about being alive bubbled up inside when he opened his eyes. Something tickled his lip. He flicked out his tongue and licked it. The blood was salty; reflexively, he wanted to wipe his nose but couldn't. He spat the blood from his mouth. Furious. *Fuck,* his insides trembled as he strained to see where Grizzly was. "Where are you? You ugly mother-fucking idiot! Come finish me, you fat bastard!" Leo shouted from the dirty floor. After he fell from his chair, his limbless body lay face down on his stomach, so it was difficult to scan the room.

Suddenly, no one in the room spoke. *Yes, you fuckers, I'm awake.*

Leo's heart raced. He wished he could jump up to his feet. He imagined himself doing a somersault over his captor's head and back-kicking the shit out of him.

"Where are you, you pink-skinned bully?"

Someone switched the music off. Leo's pulse raced—the swoosh-swoosh of blood in his ears deafened him. Grizzly's boots thumped closer. *Please kick me in the head.*

"You better shut up, boy, or I will tie you to a pole and let the men fuck you from both sides. You've always looked better on your knees. Too bad you don't have them anymore," Grizzly said. His voice was low and menacing. Pure fucking evil. He stepped on Leo's neck and push-rolled him to his back with his boot. Leo heard and felt bones and cartilage crack. Murmuring men stood closer, getting ready for a show.

Then Grizzly laughed. It was freakishly loud. Leo looked around as best he could, noting all the uncertain faces.

"My worm, everyone knows you're mine!" he blared to his crew.

"Big and ugly motherfucker," Leo retorted, and Grizzly laughed, and because his underlings knew not supporting him in any way could cost them their lives, they laughed awkwardly. Sounding more like a choir without a conductor, but after a few tries of hiccups instead of chuckles, they found a rhythm that sounded as if they laughed.

Leo was seething with resentment. He wished he could disintegrate and disappear from this existence. Grizzly lifted his boot, forcing Leo's head to the side so he looked at him.

Leo taunted Grizzly through his bloody gnashing teeth. "I hope your fucking asshole closes and opens under your armpit, and every time you reach for your drink, you shit yourself," Leo screamed.

The onlookers stopped laughing and waited for a cue from their leader. He would shoot them on the spot for disrespecting him. Erroneously Dundrog, his second in charge, doubled over and laughed hysterically.

Leo lifted his head. *Fuck that!* He decided to stand his ground. He wanted to die, and he wanted to die now! Grizzly lifted his eyebrows questioningly at Dundrog. Leo was sick of it all. He sucked as much spit and blood into his mouth and spat a wad in Grizzly's direction.

He straightened his neck and bony shoulders, and with all the strength he could muster, he shouted, "I hate you! I will make sure you never wake up after this sleep cycle." Leo meant it. By moon-god, he meant it. If Grizzly didn't kill him now, he would ask someone else. And he knew exactly who to ask. He'd ask Barkor.

Grizzly pinned Leo with a furious glare. Bloody spit dripped from his chin. His dark eyes flickered with hate. Satan's pools of fire, Leo saw blazing at him and calling him in the silence that followed. No one uttered a word.

"You know, I'm counting on it. If you manage that, my worm, then you will rule Grayrak! Only the fearless, strong, and vicious deserves the throne." Grizzly turned and scowled as he ran his gaze slowly into Dundrog's direction, who had swallowed his hysterics and looked at Leo like he would kill him if Grizzly didn't. *Good, be my guest. I don't care who does it.* Leo returned the death stare. Grizzly's evil gaze scanned the room from side to side. Coughs and the shuffling of his boots were the only sounds breaking the uncomfortable silence as he passed judgment on them.

A new plan was forming. Leo knew the young man that intrigued Grizzly would be his ticket out of this hell he had stupidly sold himself into. He was unsure how to ask and befriend the man that had Grizzly running circles around him.

A feeling he'd forgotten bubbled up inside him. *Hope.*

No one else should experience his suffering, but selfishly he needed the prince, the thief, and the hero, to save him, even if it was smothering him with a pillow.

They said he was a boy. Someone once told Leo he'd been around since the last humans landed on the moon. Whether it was because he was born on Earth or didn't grow old, Leo didn't know, but Grizzly wanted that, and he wanted to break and own that for his own selfish reasons. As long as he ruled the underbelly of Grayrak City, no one was safe. Grizzly thought the young man was nothing more than a common thief. Someone must have betrayed Barkor.

Leo knew the secret stories people told about him. Barkor stole from unsuspecting marketers, stripping them of their daily purchases. When the privileged, mostly the Disciples, returned home, they would open their bags and discover anything from dead rats to rocks in place of the food and groceries they'd purchased earlier that day. People talked, and they knew it was him.

After Grizzly's speech, plans were made, bets were placed, and Grizzly never lost. Never. He left Leo on the floor and overeagerly planned on trapping Barkor. The sick thrill of their greedy desires stoked their need to capture him.

When the festivities had wound down, Leo heard Grizzly telling his men, "Because, you idiots, those who are quick to act and slow to plan, fail dis—dismal—dismally. I will show you how it is done!" Grizzly said, inebriated to the point of falling over.

How they retained anything was a miracle.

Half-drunk and half-awake, they went on the pursuit.

Talali, a young slave girl, and two friends put Leo in his pram and pushed him inside. "Thank you, Talali. You should have left me there," Leo said, and he knew she knew why. He'd asked them many times to smother him, but they refused. Whether they feared Grizzly or just wanted him to live another day, he didn't know, probably for both reasons.

"I can't leave you like that, Leo. You're still human with feelings. And I wouldn't want to be left like that if I didn't have arms or legs," Talali said.

Once inside, gentle hands washed him and made him comfortable. Leo welcomed it and groaned as they massaged the knots out of his shoulders. "You know just how to spoil me. Thank you, girls. Talali, do you think you'll be able to get word to Barkor that they're hunting him?" he asked.

"We have already. He knows they're coming for him."

"That's good. I hope he kills them."

"He can't. Otherwise, he would have done it a long time ago."

"Why? Why the fuck not?" Leo whisper-screamed hoarsely at her and felt guilty as soon as she cringed.

"If he kills Grizzly, the Zelk will come for all of us," Talali said as she pulled the blanket over his chest to help him settle for the night. He appreciated being vertical in the bed, even if it was Grizzly's bed.

"I think that's a story he made up to stay alive as long as he has."

"Maybe, just hang in there. I have a feeling his days are numbered." Talali winked at him, and the three girls left Leo alone with his thoughts. Exhausted, he closed his eyes and fell asleep immediately.

Later, before the end of their sleep cycle, Leo hopped with fright and searched urgently for danger. Grizzly must have joined him and passed out as usual. There it was again. Loud, frantic knocking on their door. It must have been that which had awakened him.

"Are we under attack?" Grizzly asked, jumping from the bed, naked and arming himself with a sword. Standing at the ready, he asked, "Who the fuck is there? Show me your badges!" Grizzly sputtered, and Leo lay wordlessly still, expecting an attack. There was talk of upheaval from the humans. He hoped that this was it. The rebellion. He smiled.

"It is I, your second in charge!" Dundrog shouted, sounding overjoyed with excitement.

"You idiot, Dundrog, why are you so loud? What's up? It's bedtime. Not even the slaves have gotten out of bed yet?"

Yes, and they need sleep, too. Not as if you ever worried about that.

Leo watched Grizzly realize that the cacophony and urgency were not caused by bad news but by the exact opposite.

More urgent hammering on the door. "Hold on, and for god's sake, stop knocking!" Grizzly scowled and went to open the door. "What's the big deal?" Grizzly yelled, and Leo heard him unlocking the locks and chains that barricaded them inside while they slept. "Come in, for fuck's sake," Grizzly shouted and stormed back into the bedroom, limp cock swinging sideways as he searched for his pants.

"It's news about the boy." Dundrog stormed into the room after him, ignoring Leo.

"Could it be justified that you're somewhat more enthusiastic than the average Disciple this night? This better be good news," Grizzly said sarcastically, lowering his sword and throwing it with a well-practiced movement onto the hook where he hung his weapons. Suddenly chaos surrounded Leo as the usual group of idiots stormed inside the tiny room, still inebriated. "I need a fucking moment!" Grizzly shouted. He looked like he needed a drink.

"Where are Chris, Louis, and Tollie?" Grizzly asked, somehow managing to tally all his men.

"They've been captured!" the men shouted as one. Leo counted twelve of the usual fifteen members present in the small space. It reeked.

"Can someone please tell me where my fucking pants are? Get the fuck out or find my fucking pants!" Grizzly yelled, frustrated. Some wanted to leave the room, others fell to the floor searching for the missing pants. Dundrog, always eager to please, fell to his knees, searching underneath the bed.

"I have to speak to you now," he mumbled from underneath Grizzly's double bed, which was made of crates, elevated on stilts at the four corners. Dundrog's oily hair stood up in all directions.

To Leo, the day started like any other day. Being sick to his stomach before breakfast, with chaos all around him.

Dundrog took a few gulps of air and started rambling as he handed Grizzly his pants. "Sir, he's dangerous. We won't be able to catch him physically. We tried to apprehend him. We would have to let him come to us. Willingly. Otherwise, you have to send an army into the settlement and that's not a good idea because it may cause a rebellion," Dundrog said, panting from excitement, looking like he was swooning dreamily. "He's a handsome one. I guess he's somewhere in the neighborhood of twenty Earth years."

"What?" Grizzly stood flabbergasted, with one leg tucked inside his pants and his unsightly dick protruding from the waistband. Twenty-year-old boys were as scarce as Leo was. Grizzly looked at Leo. "Now that we know what he looks like, we can start asking around and figuring out where he lives. Dundrog, this is fantastic news, and we should be celebrating! Leo, you're getting a brother."

Leo watched them silently. *You're going to force him to be yours and then try to break him as you broke me. You will not succeed.*

Dundrog kept talking, and every time he described the boy, they laughed and rubbed their hands together as if they couldn't wait to touch him. They continued to plot against the boy. The description grew from gloriously beautiful man to dull, uninspiring, menacing, murderous thief. *Fucking lying redskin bastards!* Leo realized they planned to frame him for something and advertise a reward.

Leo knew that a fucking storm was coming. He couldn't wait to see the devastation. This time, he knew they didn't know what kind of trouble would follow when that man walked through their door. He bowed to no one.

"I'm glad you're all here. We need an emergency meeting of the highest importance," Grizzly said and turned to Leo. "You will be relieved when I apprehend this thug!"

"Hmmm, so that's the story you're going with?" Leo retorted.

"Get ready. Bring food and drink. Ring the bells and notify the slaves," Grizzly ordered, turned, and left.

Leo sighed. He wanted to get to the market as soon as possible when he'd woken up, and now his plans were fucked. He turned and grabbed the rope with bells next to his head with his teeth. Talali arrived first. She helped Leo into his chair, pushed him to the kitchen, where he sat, and waited for the girls to prepare the morning meal. The three slaves entered the kitchen from the door on the floor. They knew the routine, and they kept their heads down without saying a word—each knew their tasks.

They were exhausted and dirty. Some had bloody blue bruises all over their little fragile bodies.

Leo watched from the kitchen area as Grizzly toasted his half-filled cup into the air, spilling more of the bottle's contents.

Dundrog was looking pleased with himself as he stepped closer and smirked. "See, you have to be smart, Leo," he said and pestered Leo by sticking his tongue into Leo's ear canal. Leo turned his head as fast as possible to try to bite him. Dundrog was faster, by slapping Leo over the head and laughing.

"Is everyone here? Let's plan and then celebrate this!" Grizzly yelled, and the others cheered. They did that every day, the whole day. Always looking for an excuse to celebrate something.

Leo hated them even more at that moment.

"All boys have mothers and fathers or sisters and brothers, and we can manipulate them, just like this," Grizzly boasted and snapped his fat fingers. "This boy will strengthen us and make us richer!"

"Yeah, cheers! To the boy!" they shouted and applauded.

Leo wondered if they cheered and shouted for him before they lured him into their ranks.

"We're going to reel him in," Grizzly said loudly and realized he had an empty cup. He held it out to be filled, took a sip, and went on. "We're going to find out where he lives and whom he loves." He finished emptying that as he did the first. "Let's get this party started!" Once on his feet, he launched his cup at the fireplace, and the cup shattered into pieces. The fire flared blue as the alcohol combusted.

"Yeah-yeah!" Others hurled their clay cups in the same direction as Grizzly for good luck.

Obtuse asses.

When they'd finished their meals, they started making music. Leo shook his head cynically.

"No, not the stupid pirate song."

"Arrrr," Grizzly growled, enthused and fueled by drugs and alcohol.

Dammit, he's going to sing.

***

"I'll open the door, ba-rumba-dan-ha

Hear my song, ba-rumba-dan-ha

Of treasure found, ba-rumba-dan-ha

It rattles my bones, ba-rumba-dan-ha

And summons my soul, ba-rumba-dan-ha

I can't ignore, ba-rumba-dan-ha

The beat of my drums, ba-rumba-dan-ha

Get richer, get louder, ba-rumba-dan-ha, ba-rumba-dan-ha, ba-rumba-dan-ha."

Chapter Six

"Good morning, citizens of Phoenix.

It's now six a.m.

Did you know whisky in Gaelic loosely translates to water of life? This was a dark-grain alcohol first produced in medieval Scotland, and apothecaries sold whisky as a tonic to slow aging, cure congestion, and relieve joint pain.

But did you also know it is said that men who drink the stuff like a little peculiarity when making love? For example, he doesn't mind doing it rough and finds it really erotic and steamy, and he believes that a little hurt during intimacy is sexy.

Also, he can do the monkey anywhere, which makes him adventurous, and he wouldn't mind doing it in the open or getting dirty, either.

Visit your community news page to read about all sorts of types of alcohol produced and what it did to mankind. You'd be amazed how it can change a man's personality traits after just two glasses of this stuff.

Breakfast is served until eight a.m.

Hope you have a quirky day!"

Andrew

2014 A.D.

Lexington, Kentucky

United States of America

Kentucky in the summer wasn't for the faint of heart. The heat and humidity were bloody oppressive. Andrew had just woken up sticky from sweating and hastily made his way to the basement gym area. Groggy, sleepy, and depressed as usual, he dove into the half-size Olympic swimming pool for his nightly swim. The pool area was dark, and the moonlight cut straight lines through it, disappearing in the maelstrom of water and his drowning thoughts.

He'd dreamed of him again. Now, if he'd known that Juandre would haunt his thoughts day and night for the past ten years, Andrew would never have fucked the man. He couldn't dispute his incisors had prickled at the sexy Hispanic, ever since he'd pulled over and smiled a cheeky smile at him. As if Andrew couldn't already read into that, he knew what he would ask him even before he asked. The thing was, Andrew had felt a little peckish and hoped a meal would stop and take him home for the night. Prolonging his hunger was never good; his freedom ended, and he had to face the organization. One last night of debauchery and discovery was the last box on his list to tick off before his year-long sabbatical to clear his head and decide whether he wanted to run away or run the business had ended.

The day Andrew announced to the board of directors that he was taking leave, the Vice President seemed ecstatic enough for Andrew to pack his bags and leave to find his purpose. The fucker even waved him off, smiling.

En route to the airport, Andrew changed his mind. At first, he wanted to leave and never return, but the answer came to him through a billboard advertisement for RVs. It said; *Discover North America and experience freedom.* They were only a few miles from the estate's driveway when Andrew asked the taxi driver to stop and drop him off in front of the enormous billboard. He grabbed his bags and sent the man on his way. Beneath the billboard and the stars, he draped his suit jacket over his suitcase and used it as a pillow while he lay in the grass, looking up at the people smiling around a campfire with the RV in the back.

It called to him to do that, and he knew some things in life just needed to be done, no matter how stupid it looked or sounded to others. Clearing his troubled mind, he lay back, looking at the happy, carefree scene and wondering if it was real. He remembered asking himself if people could indeed be happy for just living on the road.

Then he dozed off, dreamed about being barefooted, and still dressed in his blue *Armani* suit. People were laughing at him, pointing to his feet, and a man asked, "Are you planning to hike barefoot? Don't you think you need shoes?" Andrew remembered thinking runners wouldn't match the suit and that he should unpack his bag and put on a pair of jeans and a t-shirt, and then the man said, "Yes, that's better. Now go find your freedom."

Andrew had woken up and only taken his leather sling bag. He stuffed it with socks and the bare necessities and started hitchhiking through the United States up to Canada and back again.

Leaving the world he knew behind him put everything in perspective for him. He stayed in touch with his best friend, but everyone thought he was backpacking through Europe. He guessed it sounded classier than hitchhiking through North America.

It was his last stretch home when a ride pulled up and made a deal with Andrew that he couldn't resist. He'd been offered many rides and been made just as many offers from bored housewives to truckers, but when he pulled up next to him, Andrew just knew he had to fuck him. Juandre, with his perfectly combed dark hair and aristocratic flair of superiority. The young man instantly impressed him, and when they locked gazes, something inside him clicked like it was meant to be, so he shut up and played along. Usually, Andrew would drink his fill, implant a thought that they were tired, and pull over to rest, and when they woke up, he would be miles away. But something magnetically drew him to the innocent yet hopeful flamboyant young man.

However, he seemed to be Mommy's rich bratty boy who had all the money to solve all his problems. Little did he know who and what Andrew was and that although Andrew was a billionaire, he never thought happiness and love could be bought. For his amusement, he decided to play along. He was tired and hungry, and it pissed him off that Juandre had taken one look at him and judged him by his appearance. He thought Andrew was poor, uneducated, and down on his luck, so Andrew gave the kid his fantasy.

Reading his mind, he discovered he lied about his name, so Andrew gave him the impression that he was also someone else. He'd told him he was married and had one boy but that they were too poor to send him to university. While, in fact, he was a whiskey tycoon from Lexington, Kentucky, and was altogether another, not fully human, but something bred and created by their fathers back in Germany.

Andrew changed his appearance, and every time Juandre looked at him, he saw his dream man, not Andrew, who wasn't planning on marrying a woman. Since gay marriages weren't legal in Kentucky, marriage was something other idiots did, not him. He had a certain persona in the boardroom, and Andrew knew he would lose his credibility and be voted out of his own company before returning from his honeymoon. The world was full of people with different stories, tastes, and backgrounds, but most of all, different types of bodies and uncountable ways to fuck and get fucked. Still, Andrew kept seeing those dark brown eyes looking down at him with love in his dreams.

He'd been obsessively thinking about the cheeky Juandre, not Sam, as he lied and had told him without batting an eyelash. The vision of him smiling or how he crooked his neck to see out of the car when their gazes met for the first time when he offered him a ride, for a ride. Maybe it was his jugular throbbing, or how he looked up at him through his neatly combed chocolate brown bangs, or the clean whiff of soap and cologne when he shook his head. Maybe it was hunger and not lust, but that stern look on his face when he asked him if he could blow him—the anticipation in his chocolate brown eyes. Like a naughty kid asking Santa for a gift, half expecting to hear bad news but hoping for the best.

And then the same vulnerable look he couldn't forget when he entered him from behind. The vulnerability and the trust they shared near the end of the weekend. Their true selves shone but were dulled by the false facades and small lies about his reality of being happy, rich, and spoiled.

He believed he was rotten in his core and that his *kink* and dirty secrets weren't beautiful. But in those few hours, they fit perfectly, understanding the power exchange—the giving and taking. Learning and surrendering. Affirming and acknowledging each other as a perfect union existed in those moments. Both yearned for closeness and togetherness they weren't allowed to have. Certainly not forever.

Especially when Juandre started with the boy and Daddy games? God, that revved his motor. Pedal to the metal, he burned his exhaust pipe bright white and opened the door to a *kink* Andrew never imagined he would crave. Switching roles excited and confused him. He fucking loved it. Andrew shivered; the fleeting thoughts vibrated his insides, and he quivered for the sexy Hispanic. His band-aid for missing and yearning for his touch was as useless as throwing a pebble on a geyser and expecting it to miraculously plug the hole.

The problem with his first aid solution was, by the time he'd lined someone up at *kink* clubs or online hookups, his mood had deflated. It was as if a big fishhook was lodged in his heart, pulling him in the opposite direction towards *him*. It was the whole weekend, the entire package, that he truly wanted to relive. Not just pieces of it. Andrew desired the entire magical moment from when Juandre stopped his little sports car at the side of the road until Andrew climbed into the taxi to pretend he was flying home.

Asking a man to re-enact it was silly, and by the time he'd explained what he needed, Andrew could have fucked his trick twice and had dinner. After one try, he'd given up.

That unforgettable weekend gave him the strength to go home and pick up the pieces of his life. Manage the business with a determination to carry his promise through. But every so often, Andrew reminisced about that weekend. Like today, as he swam like an Olympic freestyle swimmer and his body sliced through the lukewarm water, he wondered what Juandre was doing. The sloshing and kicking dulled the world around him, leaving him alone to enjoy his thoughts and memories about him.

Did he marry the girl his family wanted, or had he decided to come out with the truth? Had he continued his studies and become a doctor practicing medicine? Where was he doing that? Andrew wondered whether he was happy and whether he even thought about him. Had he gone looking for the man he'd bought a plane ticket to Louisiana and found the man he fucked didn't exist?

Andrew decided to do one last tumble turn and kicked himself as hard as possible off the wall and drifted to the opposite side, which was eighty-two feet away, without kicking or using his hands—something he ritually did. He enjoyed floating while the momentum took him to where the stairs were and exited the pool.

Andrew wrapped an extra-large terry cloth towel around his waist and went to the private ensuite of his bedroom to get dressed for work. After a quick shower, he hastily dressed in the crisp, freshly laundered powder blue button-up shirt and only the trousers of the black *Armani* suit that his dutiful friend and butler, Tony Alonzo, daily hung ready for him after his swim.

Preferring to walk barefoot in his space, he left the socks and shoes for later. If he was called to a meeting or had an appointment, he would wear his slip-ons, loafers, or flip-flops, depending on the weather or how important the meeting was. He liked dressing smart but casually made a statement with his footwear that the boardroom culture didn't restrict him, nor would he ever wear uncomfortable shoes to impress people. That was one thing he'd learned on his travels. Shoes were important, yet they needed to serve their purpose.

Sitting behind his desk, Andrew struggled to think about anything else. He bent down and ruffled in his desk's lower drawer, where he hid Juandre's number and the other small trinkets he'd collected during his travels. Nothing big, not heavy to carry in his backpack. Like key rings, postcards, or something small like a bottle cap from when he drank a beer on Cannon Beach in Washington.

"Would he even recognize me? I'm just a man he'd given a ride and had taken to a hotel to fuck. For fuck's sake, Andrew, it's been ten years," he said softly, frustrated with himself. "I've had enough. I must find him." He slammed the drawer closed. "I need to know if he feels the same about me."

He looked at the little piece of paper he'd looked at many times before. The numbers had faded on the yellowed paper.

He'll be in his early thirties, and I'll still look exactly like I did ten years ago. Will he even remember me?

Would he stir indignation against the world he now lived in, or would he accept him even with the false background he'd painted? Would he utterly disregard him as a gay man, the opposite of the man he'd led him to believe he was?

Andrew was tired of wondering. He constantly weighed the pros and cons over the last ten years, whether he should phone and have an honest conversation or pretend to be the fantasy man, the human. If he lied, he wouldn't be able to maintain the lie. He mauled his mind numb in circles as to what to do and whether it was even worth it.

Maybe the reality of what truly happened was only his imagination, but he needed to find out. Was it real or not? Otherwise, he would spend eternity wondering what if, just as he'd done these past ten years. *What if I'm throwing my last chance away?* He had to know.

With his mind made up, he leaned over to call Tony, his personal assistant extraordinaire.

"Tony, I think it's time to do your thing," Andrew said.

He heard a loud, "Yes!" as if Tony had muffled the phone and forgot he could hear him through the office door.

Chapter Seven

"Good morning, citizens of Phoenix.

It's now six a.m.

Did you know olive trees, as a species, are between twenty million and forty million years old and that the average lifespan of an olive tree is between three hundred and six hundred years?

And did you also know that there is not a single olive in Phoenix?

Lasitor receives daily requisitions and prioritizes the urgency level as critical to relieve the problem of the olive shortage.

Please keep in mind that the situation is noted. Leadership is aware that ninety percent of olives become oil and ten percent become table olives. Just as we know, the strawberry-mint lubrication shortage is directly linked to this ancient fruit.

Breakfast is served until eight a.m.

May you have a slippery day!"

Juandre

2014 A.D.

Lexington, Kentucky

United States of America

It was a Saturday afternoon when Juandre finished his shift at the Lexington Trauma and Burn unit. He was looking forward to coming home and relaxing with his son. Charlie had just turned ten, and all he wanted for a birthday gift was one day alone with his father. His request was a shocking awakening, and he promised Charlie that this weekend was his alone.

Arriving home, he switched off his phone, promised himself it was their day, and planned to make the most of it. They swam and relaxed next to the pool, and when they ran out of something cold to drink, Juandre got up to fetch them something to eat and drink. "I'll be right back. I must use the washroom and bring something to enjoy next to the pool."

"Okay, Dad, I'll time you," Charlie said exactly as Juandre used to say when encouraging speed. *Let's see how fast you can run and grab this or that for Daddy.* The results were amazing each time.

After his divorce, his relationship with Charlie wasn't great. His mother had filled his head with hateful and negative comments about his sexuality, and how he identified himself didn't help either. Lately, father and son had gotten comfortable with each other, and he seemed to understand now it wasn't his fault and that there was no way his mother and Juandre would ever get together again.

Charlie was old enough for a mature versus preteen conversation, so Juandre used the time to have a good talk and explained everything from his perspective, as he knew Charlie's mom had done her best to make him sound like the villain. He'd explained to Charlie who he was and what he thought he was. He was still discovering himself after a lifetime of wearing a mask to please others like his ex-wife and parents. He said he liked makeup and lipstick, but kept the silk underwear for talks after his number eighteen birthday. He told him he liked boys but hadn't found anyone special yet. He'd introduce Charlie to someone when he did. He wanted the freedom to wear flamboyant clothing on certain days at work or home. All day, or not. The choice should be his like Charlie liked to choose his own clothing. They'd touched on the "drag queen," subject and what it meant to Juandre. To him it was all about putting on feminine clothing, a costume from a certain era and then performing in it. For him it was about the flamboyance, the acting and singing. Charlie understood Juandre's cheerful nature. Plus, the kid had ears, he heard his father sing like a nightingale, especially when he sang lullabys or felt happy and goofy. Juandre was playful by nature and Charlie understood that drag was all that, but just for adults. Some women liked to do it too, and they were called kings instead of queens. Charlie liked that a lot. Juandre viewed it as an art form, but for himself it was something he wanted to embrace fully, but also knowing himself, one day, he'd like to wear a pencil skirt and high heels, but the next he loved his pink Dr. Martins ankle boots with black stretched denims, accessorized with a flashing pink handbag. He was just beginning to explore his options. One thing was for sure, he loved feeling like a beautiful butterfly.

He'd also told him how he was forced into marrying his mother, and it made his day when Charlie answered that she was acting like a bitch—his words. Of course, he had to reprimand the little dude for speaking that way, but deep down, having someone in his corner for a change felt amazing.

That explained why he didn't speak to Grandmommy or Grandpappy. He and his ex-wife were family friends growing up together, and both got accepted at Vanderbilt and were friends and study partners. But one night, they'd gotten extremely wasted, and Juandre somehow had gotten her pregnant. He never remembered how, or the mechanics thereof. *God, how did she get him to ejaculate?* he wondered. She most probably dosed him up. He'd objected furiously, but they had umbilical cord blood tested to determine DNA paternity and, yes, he was the pappy.

They married before Charlie was born. He got to see her less after Charlie's birth. She only wanted to know if she could get him to marry her. He never touched her again. They had jobs, but she was more interested in hanging out with her friends and colleagues than him. Now they didn't talk anymore—no deep conversations and certainly no playful teasing or anything.

Juandre grabbed his phone off the fridge, where he'd hidden it from himself earlier. Juandre switched it on to check his messages, and Charlie yelled from outside, "Dad, you promised no phone today." He hopped with surprise, caught in the act.

Damn, kid, I swear you have X-ray eyes.

"No, no! Not for work, this is for fun, for us, Daddy-promise," he shouted and fumbled to find the music app to play his favorite playlist—the one he'd created after that incredible weekend with Ryan—his first and definitely not his last. But he featured every night in his wet dreams. He guessed it was true about a man's first; you never forgot them. He loved cheesy and was besotted with the idea of lip-syncing. He loved that catchy hitchhiking song by *Heart*; *All I Want to do is Make Love to You*.

He switched his phone to its loudest setting and started preparing lunch for them. His swim trunks were dripping water on the terracotta tiles. He grabbed his towel to throw on the floor and shimmied the towel with his bare feet. The rhythm of the music always carried him to that night. He relaxed for the first time in a long time and let go of his inhibitions. Perhaps, he needed to shake it off.

He let go and sang at the top of his lungs, "One night of love, was all we knew... all I want to do is make love to you." He closed his eyes and danced to their song. His secret song for them, not caring about work or anything else.

His talk with Charlie went well, and he felt free to do what he liked. He swayed his hips to the music as he dove into the fridge, searching for cheese and tomatoes. Juandre raised his hands and waved the loaf of bread around. He knew he must have looked idiotic, and he loved it. He loved feeling free in his skin, and performing had always been his dream. Feeling elated and happier than he'd felt in a long time, and because he knew every word by heart, he sang along, and as he hit the chorus, he really let go. He swiveled around, thrusting his hips wildly, bellowing the lyrics into the French loaf in his one hand as if it was a microphone.

His eyes opened, and he jerked to a halt. "Oh, my dear lord!" He yipped, his effeminate lilt pronounced when the song ended. A silhouette of a tall man filled the doorway. Juandre squinted his eyes, and judging by the man's expression, he'd been there a while. "Motherfucker, who are you?"

He squealed and hopped back with fright while searching for a weapon. He pointed the bread at him. "Are you real?" he asked because it looked like a ghost was standing in his doorway. The man smiled wide, showing a perfect set of teeth. Visions flipped like a movie preview through Juandre's mind. That smile was exactly the smile Juandre saw in his dreams or when he fucked his hand.

Juandre stood frozen, holding his elbow with one hand and the other covering his mouth with the bread. Surprised for several reasons, but that he looked the same as when he'd sent him on his way in a taxi ten years ago. *He must be a manifestation.*

The man he used to call country-man, threw his head back and laughed. Juandre's spine snapped straight. That seemed to amuse him even more. Juandre tried to play it cool like he hadn't just caught him dancing and singing like a crazy idiot.

"Ah...um," he stammered and dove for his phone as the next embarrassing song started. It was Ryan, and he chuckled like a big, happy giant. The melodic sound and a pleasant aura filled the spacious kitchen.

Open-mouthed, Juandre took him in. His hands rested casually on the sides of the door frame, and his expression was delighted amusement, but then he blinked it away and straightened. He wore dark blue jeans and a white button-up shirt that stretched snugly over his chest and enfolded well-developed biceps. Their gazes locked. His green eyes sparkled, reflecting the sunlight escaping over his shoulders while his big, muscled frame blocked the doorframe.

Maybe I slipped and fell and cracked my head open.

"Dad, what's taking so long? Who are you talking to?" Charlie asked, pushing Ryan unmannered and aggressively to the side. Juandre was still in shock, but it seemed Ryan knew what to do next in a situation like this. He kneeled at Charlie's height and held out his hand.

"Hello, my name is Andrew," he said, and Charlie reluctantly grabbed his hand, and they shook.

Hmmm, did he introduce himself as Andrew?

Charlie folded his arms and lifted his chin. "Hi, nice to meet you. But if you're here to take my dad to work, it's my day today. You can go. He'll see you on Monday. At work," Charlie said and moved his hands to his hips.

Ryan—no, not Ryan, but Andrew, laughed. The deep timbre of his voice rumbled and rolled through Juandre just like he remembered him. Cocking his head to the side, Juandre took another long look at him. *He really aged well. He must be almost fifty years old but looks younger than me.*

Charlie was saying something and tapping Juandre's arm for attention. "Dad, tell him it's your day off," Charlie persisted as he recovered from the shock of seeing him.

He must be real because he's talking to Charlie in my kitchen.

"Don't worry. I'm here to visit and not take your daddy anywhere." He made a big cross over his heart and put his hand flat over it. "I'm here as a friend, just saying hello. I won't steal your time. I will only watch. Is that okay?"

Charlie looked perplexed between the gorgeous man of his dreams, now known as Andrew, and him. "I guess, as long as he doesn't have to work."

"Good, and thank you. I promise only fun times. Are you guys swimming?" Andrew asked and got up from kneeling the whole time. Damn, he was big and beautiful.

Charlie seemed to relax. "Yes, do you know how to handstand underwater? Because I can, but my dad can't."

Andrew regarded Charlie but stole a glance at Juandre every other second. He fiddled with something in his pocket. "I can do a lot of tricks. I love water, and I swim every night," Andrew said. Juandre stood gobsmacked, watching the two.

"Why do you swim at night? People sleep at night. My dad says it's dangerous to swim at night."

"Yes, it is dangerous, but the sun is even more dangerous for my skin. See?" Andrew pushed his sleeve up, revealing the marble-white skin Juandre remembered vividly, touching and licking it.

"Oh, that's not good," Charlie said, running his hand over Andrew's arm.

"Yeah, but don't worry, I can do other things when you swim. I'll wait in the shade and watch you do your handstands."

"You do?" Juandre asked without thinking. *Fuck, he just got here.* "I meant, you will? Sorry, I meant, please?" He stumbled over his words, looked at the loaf of bread still in his hands, and put it on the counter.

Andrew shrugged. "Why not? I have all the time in the world, plus I want to see more of your tricks." He wiggled his eyebrows at Charlie and then pinned Juandre in a stare. Meaning much more than that.

"Cool," Charlie said, smiling.

And Juandre said, "Cool." Because what the fuck else could he say?

* * *

Andrew

It was a lovely day outside. Andrew's gaze shifted to the sky that was filled with gray-white clouds, and he couldn't remember the last time he'd been outside, but there he was, sitting beneath the scorching sun and dehydrating by the second. He wondered whether he could get out of the chair. Basically, he was slowly turning into a mummy, and if he'd sat another hour, the wind would scatter him to the four corners of the earth. He forced himself to get up, smile, and say, "Be right back. I need to...uh, go to the loo." His voice was raspy, and his throat felt like sandpaper.

Andrew all but fell into the house and scrambled for his phone to call Tony. "Hello, sir. Are you ready to go?" Tony answered with a cheerful voice.

"Need blood. Thirsty." Andrew sputtered the words, barely finishing his sentence because no air was moving in and out of his lungs. "Bring blood to the washroom window in the back of the house," he said and hung up. Ripping the fridge door nearly off its hinges, he grabbed water, juice, and protein shakes.

Thank fuck, yes!

Arms full of rehydration fluids, he swayed and stumbled down the long hallway. The washroom was closed. Of course, it was. Using his elbow, he awkwardly opened the door, fell into the guest washroom, and planted himself on the closed toilet lid. With fingers as numb and dry as twigs, he fumbled and struggled to unscrew the lids of the bottles. Deciding it was taking too long, he ripped them off and threw the contents down his throat. With his thirst quenched to manageable levels, the blood arrived. Andrew felt a little more coordinated, and his eyeballs felt less like cement.

Why did I do this to myself?

Shaking and graceless, he got up, opened the window, hung his hand out, and hoped Tony was already there. He flapped his hand around a few times before he felt the bags handed to him.

Thank fuck!

Hastily, he bit into them and sucked them dry. Andrew could feel his body being restored as Tony whispered outside, "I have more if you need more, sir."

Quickly, he handed him the empty bags and exchanged them for three more. Just as he sunk his teeth into the last bag, he opened his eyes, and as the fates would have it, Juandre stood pale, wide-eyed, and open-mouthed, looking at him while the sixth bag of blood shriveled in his hand.

Oops!

Juandre flapped his wrists, searching for words. “Please don’t say you can explain because you fucking can’t. This is not happening, and I didn’t see you drink blood like a fucking vampire!” he said through clenched teeth. Andrew wiped the blood from the corners of his mouth.

“I’m not—“

“Sir, do you need more? I have six more here,” Tony said from outside like a crack dealer. Andrew got up and returned the last three bags.

Should I wipe Juandre’s memory, or do I let the pieces fall as they may?

*A*ndrew gave Tony a hand signal that meant *I’m okay, and you may go now.*

“Sir?” he asked, not understanding the universal language of thumbs up.

“Thank you, Tony. Please wait in the car. I’ll be out directly,” Andrew said, feeling life return to his numb limbs. *At least I can run and join Tony waiting in the getaway car if Juandre chases me out.*

Juandre waited, hands on his hips and fear in his eyes.

“C...can we talk?” Andrew stuttered. He read Juandre’s thoughts. He was busy running through all the possibilities and scenarios, but he ended again at what he thought stood before him. Juandre waited. Andrew also waited for his dehydrated brain cells to recuperate and return to firing synapses. If he was a vampire, he certainly was the luckiest and stupidest vampire alive because he wasn’t sure if any other moron lived to see another day after such self-inflicted sun damage. It was probably time to read up on it. He’d forgotten he was outside.

If he died and lost all that whiskey, Ish would never forgive him.

Juandre opened his mouth as if to say something. Then he turned dramatically and left the washroom.

Andrew’s heart was like a piece of cork in his chest, but as it revived, it sped up and went into tachycardia. He was way past nervous. All his fears from the past ten years were coming true. He didn't know what to do, so he sat on the closed toilet seat and hung his head in his hands.

Colossal fuck-up—ticked, yes.

Plan to ease him into this—ticked, no.

Coax him into it steadily—ticked, no.

Find out if he wanted me—ticked, no, because you're a fucking idiot!

He planned this big romantic reveal and had a speech written. It wasn't supposed to be like this; it was supposed to be perfect with laughs and rolling naked. Okay, maybe it became a bit of daydreaming, but now he fucked it all up. *And tied a pretty bow around it—a red bow with blood bags.*

Miserable and hopeless, he sat on the toilet and eventually came out, no pun intended. The house was dark and quiet. Lights flickered in the distance, up the hallway, probably the living room. Like a ninja, he stuck to the wall and snuck closer to see.

Juandre and Charlie watched television. Charlie lay on his side, stretched out on the sofa with his head resting on Juandre's lap. Juandre looked up straight at him. He was beautiful, and the sassy look he gave him was adorable and scary. It said don't speak and fuck off or else.

Andrew contemplated wiping his mind and trying again tomorrow, but their father-and-son day was special. He could wipe it and say you had a wonderful day with Charlie, but that felt like stealing and cheating, like he used his powers to have his way, taking Juandre's free will away from him.

"I'm going to go," Andrew whispered, feeling like a scared loser with a boner.

Juandre nodded and lifted an eyebrow. His ax-and-dagger expression didn't change. Andrew removed one of his business cards and the speech he had written and placed it on the coffee table where Juandre rested his feet. His toes looked delicious—the toenails were neatly clipped and painted with red nail polish. Each big toe had a little ladybug painted on it. Andrew's heart puckered, and he begged for mercy with his eyes. But the determined look on Juandre's face told him to leave. Andrew swallowed a whimper. "Please call when you are ready to talk."

He turned and left before he started sucking on those perfect toes.

Chapter Eight

"Good morning, citizens of Phoenix.

It's now six a.m.

Did you know communication in the workplace is important because it boosts team member morale, engagement, productivity, and satisfaction?

Communication is also key to better team collaboration and co-operation. Ultimately, effective workplace communication helps drive better results.

Please visit your community news page to learn ways to overcome your incommunicado, and if that doesn't help, just bloody start a conversation.

Breakfast is served until eight a.m.

Hope you get those dialogues going!"

General Cian Romanov

93 A.T.

Grayrak City

Earth's moon

Two Months Later

Barkor, Sarinka, and Ish first met the leadership of Phoenix via two-way video communication. Kawa was the most technologically inclined and had fiddled under the dashboard with the wires to establish the communication channel with Phoenix. Initially, only radio frequencies were sent between them and the Earth. Eventually when they went Earthbound, Connor installed a bigger memory, and Lasitor was uploaded.

Their fathers weren't impressed by them stealing the Spacecar. After a thorough frustration venting session, their leaders first reprimanded them and then assured them they would help in any capacity needed.

Ivan and Eryn initially protected Cian from the questions and accusations, but it all blew over because their fathers finally saw reason and fell in line with the plan to infiltrate and demolish the vermin on the moon. Cian was appointed the general in charge of the operation and would report to Phoenix leadership as needed.

Once on Earth, Ish was an impressive representative who used the opportunity to convince Brad and the leadership team about their winning action plan. Operation Lunar Evacuation was a go. Together, they devised the next steps and each member's role in freeing the humans with zero casualties. All agreed that war should be avoided. Building a fleet would deplete resources unnecessarily, do more harm, and endanger the already fragile ecosystem of Earth. If someone lit so much as a spark, the atmosphere could explode, leaving the planet without air. If something happened to the moon, Earth's gravity and sea tides would be influenced, and with water covering the surface, it might create giant tidal waves that could take years to stabilize.

There were steps to be implemented before they could execute the major stages of the big evacuation. Cian's plan was simple—if they followed all the steps, Ivan and Eryn should attempt to slow the Zelk from further multiplying by inhumanely cutting up people to be used as body parts for the Zelk.

Monthly trips to Phoenix to collect relief food and water packs were vital. A secret underground water reservoir was hidden away from the unsuspecting Disciples. Since the Disciples never shared their water, Cian was certain no one would betray their own and divulge their secret water hole.

Undercover reserve soldiers were to be smuggled into Grayrak to befriend and assist the humans with preparation and sneak evacuation. Barkor, Donali, and Sarinka would strategically plant the spies to protect, collect intelligence, and ensure every man, woman, and child in Grayrak City followed Cian's directions to a T. And it also had to happen as fast as possible while the Disciple overlords were unaware and ultimately eliminated.

Sarinka would act as a middle person. Donali would report all covert activity to Cian and cultivate trust, as he and the Phoenix soldiers worked on spreading the word about the exodus. Depending on the speed of Cian and Lasitor's annexation of the Zelk's warship, Sarinka would report whether Barkor had found a middleman who would bring Eryn and Ivan to the Zelk and infiltrate them to uninstall, delete, or whatever was done with robots who thought they were people. Connor and Mika jumped to create a virus that Ivan and Eryn would plant to lay dormant inside the Zelk collective mainframe until the day of evacuation when Lasitor, already uploaded to the warship, would override and deploy the viruses for the ultimate destruction.

To increase the melodrama, which was Cian's life, his heart yearned to sing his song for Barkor. He distanced himself and his heart from the shit show by joining the ranks of the Zelk and offering his military service. His mission was to worm himself onboard their warship and assure the Zelk that he would win the war for them. *What war, no one knew.* He had many things to do to keep himself occupied. People needed to be evacuated, the Disciples eliminated, and the Zelk exterminated.

Cian had seen the flesh machines. The most obvious trait was their assumption that they were superior. The Zelk looked like robots with artificial limbs, hearts and organs meshed with other human body parts fused to their bones. Some had hands and clamps, others walked on legs upright or rolled around on wheels. He even saw one that hopped on one leg, like a gas spring piston thing. But they all had one thing in common: their collective brain.

The top obstacles were convincing the Zelk to give Eryn and Ivan jobs at the hospital inside the Zelk tower and getting Cian onboard the warship without being scanned or discovered as Anunnaki. They needed an inside man, one that traded with the Zelk. Someone willing to switch sides and work with Barkor. Donali was head over ass in love with Sarinka. Cian's respect for her stemmed from the fact that she operated like a black widow spider—spinning the web, watching, guarding, and keeping it all together. He never asked her, her sex and how she identified. He made a mental note to ask Donali. But he was sure Donali wouldn't tell him what genitals she had under her clothes. She reminded Cian of Juan wearing his tactical suit in South Africa. She had a throatier voice as well.

Ish explained the Zelk thought in a circle. "They're programmed and set on saving and protecting the humans, but somehow got their wires crossed and lost in the cycle of producing soldiers for human defense and using humans as parts to build the soldiers. As for the water supply—" he explained animatedly to everyone in the boardroom who hung on every melodic word he spoke. "In theory, making water from hydrogen and oxygen is very easy. Mixing it together is a bit of a challenge. But basically, you mix the two gases and add a small ball of heat, so activation energy forces the hydrogen and oxygen molecules to break the covalent bonds that hold H_2 and O_2 molecules together. The hydrogen cations and oxygen anions are then free to react with each other, which they do because of their electronegativity differences. And then, the chemical bonds re-form to make water. The problem is that additional energy released propagates, creating a highly exothermic reaction." He paused, waiting for the men's reactions around the conference table, and got none. "Meaning a reaction accompanied by the release of a lot of heat," he said.

Silence.

Finally, after a long pause, Mika spoke up. "He meant it all goes kaboom."

"Ah," everyone answered.

It gave Cian a headache to understand it all. To him, it was simple. Go in, plant a bomb or two, and move out. Bye-bye troubles on the moon.

But before that could happen, they had to coordinate their stealth attack. They had to abduct and convince a Disciple to switch sides.

Cian, Ish, and Kawa accompanied Donali, who'd been living undercover in Grayrak and acclimated to the harsh conditions and life on the moon for the past two months. They were on a scouting and retrieval errand; *the nice way to say abduct a Disciple.* The plan was to grab him and persuade him to turn sides. And that included Barkor in the equation.

Each time Cian's boots touched the surface, it felt like his heart wanted to combust inside his ribcage. He had a good coping mechanism. He kept his head down and ignored Barkor.

The wall divided the dome into two parts. The Zelk occupied the outer rim while the humans lived inside the smaller inner rim but closer to the mining and storage facility and the exit where they boarded the Zelk Hydrogen mining ship. Once the harvesting was done, the canisters were unloaded, stored, and cooled in the tunnels below the lunar surface. On the opposite side of the dome, where the Zelk tower was, the Warship Horizon waited to be manned and readied for a war of unknown origins or enemies. A network of underground tunnels burrowed by the first humans connected the Hydrogen Storage Facility to both exits of the dome to transport the fuel canisters to and from the opposite sides.

According to Sarinka, Barkor reported the first steps to getting Cian and his men on the warship, as well as Ivan and Eryn inside the Zelk tower were ready to be taken.

They received information from one of the slave girls who worked at Grizzly's that he was looking for Barkor and that his lover would be near the market that day. That was the sign they'd been waiting for. The abduction plan could now be executed. Cian gave the go-ahead to grab Grizzly's lover.

Grayrak City was a dump. Rusted containers stacked together and onto each other made it look like a train junkyard. Narrow alleyways ran between the heaps of metal houses and connected in the center area, which they called the market. A few stalls sold rat meat, the only animals on the moon. *They probably escaped some scientist's lab and multiplied.* In the center of the market was one small water reservoir that collected recycled water. The well had dried up long ago, and no one could say if it ever produced water because no one had had access to it, thanks to Grizzly and his men. Most humans preferred to live underground where the Zelk and the Disciples couldn't find them.

Just as they passed the market area, they heard a woman calling for Barkor.

"They think they're luring Barkor to Grizzly—the Disciple in charge," Donali whispered in Cian's ear. Cian nodded his understanding and followed Donali's direction to hide in the shadow of a gigantic boulder while keeping low.

"That's him... Leo." Donali pointed his laser gun toward the approaching parties. "He calls for help and tells people to sell their body parts to the Zelk. In Grayrak, they call those men half-men," Donali whispered, and Cian shook his head in disbelief at it all.

He knew why they were called half-men, but he had yet to see one. The market area was otherwise empty. It reminded Cian of those cowboy western movies he watched where the people scurried away and only tumbleweeds and dust covered the roads. The feeling of trepidation hung around them, making his skin crawl.

A faint squeak-squeak noise grew louder and drew Cian's attention to the woman pushing the homemade wheelchair. The wheels were different sizes, wobbling from side to side over the rocky pathway. It was a sad visual. Cian wanted to scream, say fuck this, and go home. The man in his buckling wheelchair smiled. He was dressed in a dirty, oversized shirt and strapped to the seat. It was a head and torso of a fully grown man. The head had no ears, his arms were missing, and he sat on a pillow. No legs in sight. Not even stumps were visible. It sickened Cian. He'd been staying on the ship, preferring to hide from the mad circus.

The calling of Barkor's name drew Cian's attention back to the woman who was high and practically walking on her pinkie toenails. Behind her, two willowy women with their children scurried away, sensing trouble coming. The dim blue light from the Zelk tower illuminated their target's faces.

"She must have escorted him to Barkor's secret hideout," Donali said. Cian nodded and soundlessly drew his sword. If this was a trap, he needed to be ready. His understanding was it was kill or be killed. He hated how she called Barkor's name. No matter how scarce females were, he would kill her if Barkor needed saving. She cupped her hands and called again. Cian growled and listened to how she lied and assured Barkor he would have all the food and safety he desired. Donali looked knowingly at him and smiled. Yeah, he felt like an alpha wolf protecting his mate. Unfortunately, Barkor didn't know that. Not yet.

"Don't worry, Barkor isn't stupid. He knows this is a trap. He has his spies on the inside," Donali whispered. Cian knew that. He couldn't understand his murderous, idiotic reactions. He'd only seen Barkor a few times and was already acting like a cave dweller. His possessive urges frightened him.

"Barkor," she called again. "You can trust me. Please come out, Barkor! We want to show you your room. We eat three times daily and have as much water as we want. Mommy is clean and dressed in a pretty dress from Earth." The urgency in her shrill voice betrayed her. She sounded anxious as she twirled and gave them a pathetic show. Moondust got swept up by the mini tornado caused by her yellow-brown Victorian hoop dress.

The man cleared his throat. "Have you ever taken a bath? With your whole body underwater? Please come out. It's getting late! I want to make a deal with you," the half-man's voice echoed into the alley.

"Barkor, come, I've found us a home," she called in the Old Earth language.

"She wants to get back for more drugs. Grizzly has her in his claws," Donali whispered. Cian's gaze locked on her. She looked sick and deathly pale. The makeup on her face made her look worse. Ugly blue eyeshadow and red lips and red cheeks. She looked like she'd been beaten. Her hair stood in all directions, and bruises covered every inch of exposed skin.

"Barkor, please come out. Mommy's tired and needs to return to our new home. You'll like it. Come out now. I know you're here and listening to us. Come out now!" she yelled, her face twisted with despair, and each sentence got louder and nastier.

"Fuck, lady!" The half-man exclaimed, pushing a shoulder up to his ear and shaking his head. "My fucking ears. Why the fuck do you have to scream like a drunk whore, bitch?" he shouted at her, and terror crossed her face. His words were still echoing in the air—the next moment, a body slammed into him and his wheelchair. One second, he was upright, and the next, someone knocked him flat onto the dirt and stink of the alley road.

"You piece of shit! Don't talk to her like that!" Barkor threatened, and all Cian could do was blink and grow a hard-on. He stared at Barkor's magnificent beauty as he straddled the man's torso and fisted his shirt in one hand. The man said something, and Barkor bitch-slapped him with his flat hand.

Cian's head spun. Endorphins and hormones flooded his system. He didn't hear the screaming and slapping. No, all he could see was the most beautiful young man with a look of murder in his gorgeous eyes. He had a head full of dark blond curls that framed his face, making him look like an avenging angel. This was too much, too real. Cian gulped for air and tucked, turned, and ran. With an oomph and a thud, he collided with a solid wall of muscled chest.

"Fuck, bro, do you have to sneak up on me like that? What's wrong with you?" Cian asked, rubbing his nose. He stepped left and right, trying to pass the wall of muscle. But Ish stepped in front and blocked him each time.

The fucker's fast.

"This had better be a mistake," Ish said in his weird accent and deep baritone and, like always, with a hint of humor as Cian amused him.

"That's the mark. That's why you're here. It's highly unlikely that another chance of infiltration is possible. Your brothers won't make it if you can't get this half-man to turn," Ish said, telling the truth and pissing Cian off. He was probably right. "No one would escape out of here alive. You had just better step in and make yourself known." Ish took Cian by the shoulders and turned him one-hundred and eighty degrees. "You must go now. Don't worry about the woman. She won't say a word."

Ish pushed Cian like a reluctant toddler learning to walk. At the alley junction where Barkor had apprehended the hostage, Cian saw four directions to escape: up, right, left, and ahead. Ish halted and reached into a pouch he produced from somewhere inside the long hooded jacket he wore. He removed a small vial. Twisted the top and activated it, then tossed it gently into the air. "Go help Barkor with the half-man. Leave the screaming woman. She's as good as dead, anyway. Her organs are failing."

"But it's his mother. We can't leave her here," Cian said.

"It's not his mother, Cian. It's someone pretending to be his mother. His mother died long ago. This is just someone who helped him blend in."

Cian watched the strange quicksilver-like liquid undulate, growing into an umbrella over them.

"Go, it's a blocking agent. Anyone encapsulated would be frozen and disintegrated into molecular matter," Ish said, and Cian pulled a *what-the-fuck* face.

"Meaning it blends and makes it disappear. Become part of everything," Ish explained animatedly.

Cian shook his head. That encompassed science fiction, and he wanted to ask questions. But the wobbling silver jelly almost engulfed the alley in totality. He jumped into action to collect Barkor and the half-man. Donali ran from the opposite side. Barkor got up and flung the half-man to Donali. He caught him and wrapped an old rag around their target. The half-man protested, but Donali propped a piece of cloth inside his mouth and then taped it shut. Silence fell over the market area.

Barkor jumped to help the woman as she collapsed. Spastic. Teeth grinding and neck spasming, arms extended straight at her sides, wrists bent downward, fingers stiff, her face contorted, Cian thought it looked painful. Strange bubbling sounds escaped her mouth as high-pitched cries between clenched teeth whistled, incomprehensible sputters. "You trapped, us—s!" Her voice was shrill as tears rolled clean tracks down her dusty face.

"But you wanted to trap me to go to Grizzly's, didn't you? You've become addicted to the drugs he gave you," Barkor said with a gentle rumbling voice while wiping the tears from her eyes. He tapped her shoulder as she closed her eyes. "Come with us. We'll clean you up."

"No, I want to go back. You must come with me. Please." She cried defeated sobs.

"You know I can't. I need this half-man. If you make it back, Grizzly won't take it well. It's his lover we're taking. Look at you. Let me help you," Barkor begged, and Cian watched as the half-man squirmed in protest in Donali's arms. This was sick, and in so many variations of sickness, it sickened him. He wanted to vomit. He realized his life so far was nothing compared to what these people had to endure to survive.

Ish stepped in and hunched down. He placed a hand on each of Barkor's shoulders. "You should be departing. I'll take care of her. Go take the half-man as we agreed. We must focus. She's made her choice already. You can't save her. You know you can't. Go and be safe. She's not important. The mission is important," Ish said, never breaking his gaze. His voice was respectful and empathetic. Sadness clouded his features.

Barkor stood looking defeated. Cian wanted to wrap his arms around him. They were almost the same height. Barkor looked like Eryn, but his height and build were similar to Cian's. It was dark, so he couldn't see his eyes.

"Come, we have to get out of here!" Donali called and kicked up dirt as he ran to their rendezvous. Cian turned, making sure Barkor followed. In the corner of his eye, he saw Ish scooping the hysterical woman up, and she didn't like it. She kicked and waved her arms. Then he halted, and Cian watched as Ish touched her forehead. She went limp like she'd passed out or had fallen asleep.

"Come!" Barkor called. He paused momentarily while they watched Ish activate another quicksilver balloon that enveloped her like an amoeba and then puffed soundlessly. In a blink of an eye, she was gone. No blood. Nothing. Cian stood gobsmacked. One moment, there was a person, and the next, she was gone.

"Holy shit," he exclaimed. "Where did she go?"

Ish bunched his fingers together and blew over them. *Poof.* He gestured in a universal sign language that she'd vanished. Cian lingered. His feet wanted to move, but his brain was frozen. He couldn't understand how, why, and where to disappear a person like that. Barkor jumped to push him forward. His frozen limbs weren't moving, and the moment their gazes met, Barkor's bewildered gaze softened. Then Cian's body froze for a whole different reason.

"Hurry-hurry!" Barkor wrapped his thick long fingers around Cian's arm, and a sobering, searing hot hand pulled him away from the scene.

Hello, lover, he mused as he saw Barkor up close for the first time. Thank god his frozen brain cells defrosted, his defense mechanisms activated, and he scowled at the man.

"I'll be fine. Go!" Cian sucked his teeth at him. Barkor grunted, shaking his head as he walked away.

I must get out of here. Cian's chest constricted. Panic and a deep sadness came over him, like that weird balloon of Ish's consumed all his hope and left him feeling nothing. Why was he reacting this way?

Why couldn't I just smile and say good job? Fuck this. I'm out of here as soon as the half-man can get me on the Horizon.

When they'd reached the rendezvous on the outskirts of Grayrak City, they found Donali standing erect with the squirming and blindfolded half-man in his arms.

"Alright, can we go, guys?" Donali asked with a lopsided grin.

"Yes, we swept the area, and no one will talk. Grizzly won't know what happened, he'll wonder, but he'll never know," Barkor said with a twisted mouth and a sarcastic grimace. He bent and spoke near the half-man's ear, and the man simpered. The half-man stopped squirming. What was Barkor saying? Barkor flushed red in his neck and face, as his expression hardened. God, he looked terrifying, like Batman on acid. He had a ball-headed club in his hand. *His weapon of choice.*

Cian concentrated and tried listening in. Eryn was much better at this, and it seemed Ish also mastered the gift. It was almost like listening to the wind. He tipped his head and fine-tuned himself to focus on listening to the half-man's thoughts. It was chaotic, but the loudest words were *yes, yes, yes.*

Barkor lowered the blindfold and interrupted Cian's eavesdropping by saying out loud, "You see, Jack," as he pointed the weapon at the half-man. It seemed he named his bludgeon weapon, and Cian liked that. Maybe he should name his sword?

"He'll crush your fucking skull. You sick fuck, she's gone, and it's all your fault. She tried to lure me to Grizzly's, and you're the reason she's dead. You will pay for this, you worthless piece of shit!" Barkor shouted into the man's face. The half-man paled and winced.

"You're going to get my friends inside. You will help us, or I will cut whatever you haven't sold to the Zelk off, extremely slowly and painfully." Barkor's voice grated deeply as he threatened and thrust his club up to the half-man's nose. He looked vicious. His curls were muddy, and his face had black smears of soot over his eyelids, like a lunar warrior going into battle.

The half-man stopped protesting and then faintly nodded his head. Cian listened to his thoughts; he begged for it—he wanted Barkor to kill him.

"You sick bastard." Barkor turned and scoffed. "Bring him, Donali," he shouted over his shoulder and kicked at the ground.

They followed him to their hideout on the opposite side of the city. "Keep his fucking eyes blindfolded and muffle his ears. We don't want him to see or hear where we're going!" His voice was deep and menacing.

Cian watched his mate and was sure he'd forgotten how to breathe. It was frustrating because he couldn't tell if Barkor felt the same about him or whether he even felt the pull between them. For a second, he thought he saw recognition dawning on Barkor's face. He was a badass, and Cian's first words were...Cian shook his head at his hopeless prospect—Barkor was like a square block of ice and muscle. Everything about him was fair and square. From his dirty square-cut fingernails to his sexy square jaw and not to mention those stiff square shoulders. He bet he even had multiple squared abdominal muscles. Fuck, even his boots were square-tipped and spiked.

Yip, such a mean square and fair motherfucker.

Cian wanted to laugh and cry. Only he had such luck. He had a ruthless dangerous mate. There was no way Barkor and himself made any sense. Jesus, how would they roll in the sac? Would Barkor even give him a chance? He looked at the man who carried himself with authority. It was his fucking moon. Obviously, Cian was in deep trouble. He was so fucked. His peg was round, and his mate probably had a square hole. That was if he would even give him a chance to see it.

This wasn't funny. Usually, he would have blurted thoughts like these out to Ivan and Eryn. But what would he say? *Barkor doesn't see me.*

Someone bumped him on his hip. Sarinka snickered as she passed him and said over her shoulder in an amused chuckle, "Don't worry, lover boy, he's not as mean and bad as he seems. He's a good man who saw too much ugly and only tried to survive the horror we all live in. You'll see once you get to know him."

Cian didn't have a clue how to seduce a person like that. The only thing he could think of was to help Barkor get all these people off the moon and back to Phoenix. He had to prove himself worthy. Otherwise, Barkor would never respect him. Once all the humans were on their way to safety, then he would make his move. For now, he had to push his urges to mate down his list of priorities again.

Chapter Nine

"Good morning, citizens of Phoenix.

It's now six a.m.

Did you know pre-Doomsday free divers could hold their breath for ten minutes while diving to extreme depths and that Navy SEALs can only hold their breath for two to three minutes?

I know who I would want to call to come to save me when Phoenix's walls crush and we're all drowning. Definitely not the Navy SEALs.

Visit your community news page about swim lessons and breath-holding techniques to increase your chances of survival during flooding.

Breakfast is served until eight a.m.

Have a breathe-easy day!"

Ivan Romanov

95 A.T.

Zelk Tower, Grayrak City

Earth's moon

After Ivan had completed his surgeries, he rounded the corner, tearing down the long corridor. Like clockwork, he knew a jolt of excitement would pass through him when his gaze fell on the stunningly handsome man approaching.

Play it cool. His thoughts scrambled through every scenario possible that would reveal who he was and what their mission was. Working undercover made his nerves raw with worry. But seeing Eryn gave him renewed strength to push ahead, to face the day. He inhaled deeply and lifted his chin, preparing himself for the zing that would shoot through him as soon as he passed his sexy husband walking toward him from the opposite side of the long hallway between the operating rooms and the recovery unit.

Damn, could he do it more nonchalantly? Probably.

Ivan's gaze darted around and then focused on where they shouldn't. On the bulge of cock and balls that the big Brawl was packing.

Eyes up, Ivan, and for god's sake, don't start glowing!

Eryn pinned him with a pointed look as they shortened the distance between them step by step. Each step sounded like a hammer on an anvil. Like a clock ticking backward.

Oh, bug-shit, he walks tall and so self-assured. Yes, mister, look at me while I eye-fuck you.

Each time he saw Eryn, he'd woken to those thousands of butterflies that had taken up residence in Ivan's stomach when they'd fallen in love half a century ago.

He's reading my mind. Oh lord, he's glaring at me. His intense gaze is sending out all sorts of naughty signals. The menace in those stunning golden-green eyes is genuinely going to be the death of me. I'm going to blow our cover. We are all going to be toast.

Oh, man, I want to fall to my knees and worship his cock until he shouts out my name. Nope, no worshiping today.

He's so close I can smell his cologne. That's it, and nothing's happening except my heart racing. He's always so proud and impeccably dressed. His hair's combed over to split in a perfect line at the left side. The opposite of his authentic look. Not one inch is out of place. Dear moon lord and those lips. Shut up, stop talking to yourself, and for fuck's sake, don't look at his plump lips. Be aloof.

"Good morning, doctor," Ivan greeted with what he hoped looked like calm professionalism. The sexy fucker just tipped his chin at him and passed. He bet he was one hundred percent aware of his effect on him. He was chuckling at Ivan.

Ivan could barely breathe. His legs were weak, and his steps faltered. It was the same story each morning when they passed each other. It seemed his affliction was getting worse.

This shit has to end. We need to move out and finish our mission. Thank fuck the Zelk needed field surgeons on the Horizon.

"Morning, Dr. Ivan. You look well. Isn't this a fine morning?" The droid nurse, Susie, interrupted Ivan's thoughts and welcomed him to the post-operative intensive care unit.

"Dr. Eryn just left, and like clockwork, every morning, you arrive without giving me a chance to delegate his orders. Shall we go since it never seems to bother you when I'm ill-prepared for your rounds? You have two patients waiting. Captain Pickering with multiple third-degree burn wounds, and General Cian Romanov with the skin graft, right femoral stump, eye prosthesis, and socket rebuild. He's challenging today. Been shouting and verbally abusing the nurses again. He said he wanted a real human to care for him. We explained it was impossible. He demanded to be transferred back to his warship," she said in a monotonous female robotic voice.

Finally, the nurse droid shut up so Ivan could speak. The recovery unit was cold and impersonal, but Susie instantly lit Ivan's flame of irritation to self-combustible levels. He hated the Zelk with a hidden passion.

"Morning, Susie, and like every morning, you say that to me." *And no, I will not come later because I can't see my husband.* Ivan kept that thought to himself, though. "Since you mentioned it for the millionth time, I think I should do my rounds in the afternoons. From tomorrow, I'll arrive around two," Ivan said spitefully with a grin and knowing well that wouldn't work for her or the unit.

"That's not permitted. It's time for the patients to get their feeding and rest afterward. There won't be time to do rounds." If ever Zelk had emotions, Susie was looking quite pissed at Ivan.

"My mind's made up, and you complain every day about my arrival time after Dr. Eryn has done his rounds."

Minute purple and green sparks flickered where her pupils would have been if she was human. "I did not complain, but if it bothers you that much, I will stop saying that he just left and we're not ready for you. You can't catch the hint even if it's true." Again, Susie expressed irritation and sarcasm.

"Fine, then I'll arrive before him. What time does he arrive?" *As if Ivan didn't know.*

"Dr. Eryn arrives at eight a.m. If you arrive earlier, you have to be here at six a.m., then we're ready for him when you're done," Susie said, and Ivan could swear it looked like she smirked.

She thinks I won't be able to be here on time. Good, I was planning on it.

"I'll try my best to be here at six a.m. Thank you. I'll request to push my surgeries up. If I'm late tomorrow, you should know I'll arrive at my regular time," Ivan said, hoping to confuse her strict timetable.

"You're most welcome. We're happy to accommodate you. A happy human is a productive human. I'll have coffee ready for you, doctor."

Ivan kept his facial expressions neutral. "That would be awesome," he lied. Just the thought of being with Eryn physically, instead of just passing by and greeting him daily—Eryn, with his perfect teeth and chiseled jaw, Ivan swooned dreamily. Then he righted himself, cleared his throat, and continued playing his role. It was all for the show, all in the name of freedom. Ivan tasted the sweetness of it as he lined up and pushed the last pieces of their mission into place. Cian's voice confirmed it.

Ivan heard curses and things clanging onto the floor as they approached the general's bed. *No doubt something has fallen after being thrown at the droids.* Susie pulled the curtains open and affirmed it. The general was halfway off his bed, busy strangling his droid nurse.

"Hmmm." Ivan coughed and cleared his throat. "Good morning, General. It seems we can transfer you down to recovery. You can use your arms and hands. Learning to walk with a new leg will be easy enough." Ivan chuckled, approaching the bed.

The General's face lit up with relieved surprise. He let the droid go and plopped back onto his pillows.

"Ahh, Dr. Ivan, I'm glad to see another human," he said and winked. "Yes, please get me out of this hellhole. I want to go back to my ship. I received orders that war was coming. I'm needed. Please, I beg of you, as soon as possible. I can't stand another minute of being tortured by these feelingless droids. A sex droid is one thing, but nurse droids think they have the power and authority to tell me when to have a shit and when to fucking sleep." Cian's voice boomed crassly through the unit.

Ivan missed his brother dearly. He thought he heard someone laughing a few beds over, and he struggled to keep a straight face.

The general's blond hair was shaven tabletop style, flat at the top and down to the scalp at the sides, unlike Ivan's, who wore his long blond locks mostly tied up in a loose bun or ponytail. His nose was broken in two places decades ago, it had set so crooked, they didn't look like twins anymore. Just as well, Cian had also refused medical care and disappeared for weeks, not getting stitches or scars treated. He had lost four of his front teeth after he got drunk at Ivan and Eryn's wedding; at least he had them replaced. His left eye was a piercing bright sapphire blue and almost matched his right bionic eye. Ivan performed an eye implantation procedure a week ago. Cian looked like they had locked him up in a maximum-security prison this year, with nothing to do but lift weights and draw permanent pictures on himself. His brother was all muscled up and covered in tattoos—disguising the fact that they were fraternal twins and knew each other. Luckily the droids never scanned their DNA. If they did, they could have discovered they were twins with spliced Anunnaki DNA from several generations back to the original gods of the skies. The only difference today was that the humans left on Earth had Peter Pan Capsules implanted, which made them just as immortal as those gods, which they now understood were only a race of extraterrestrial beings who meddled with the universe. The City of Phoenix had grown exponentially over the last century, and its inhabitants were still not showing any signs of growing old.

When Ivan sent word for immediate extraction, he didn't think his brother would blow himself up to do it. But the plan was in play, and all the pieces on the board were ready for action. Their planning and maneuvering had finally approached the finish line, and it was time to liberate these people and go home. The fool could have died, but Ivan had to admit it was a good plan. No one would ever suspect they were brothers.

They were deep undercover, and Cian played his role naturally. The future of these people depended on them.

"I'll do the final adjustments today on the visual prosthesis. How's your vision?" Ivan asked stoically.

The general scooted down in his bed, knowing what to do for his assessment. Ivan turned to the glass-top bedside table and placed his small silver-colored medical toolbox with specialized tools on top of it.

"Doc, it's working fine. My only problem is if I move fast from left to right. It's as if my head's turned, and there's a slow upload to my brain. It's disorientating."

"Hmmm, let me adjust that for you. I suspected I should replace the external relay device." Ivan turned to his toolbox, searching for the pliers and screwdrivers. "Susie, may I please have the triangulator I asked you to order yesterday?"

"Yes, doctor, certainly. I'll fetch it. It arrived late last night," Susie said while rolling off to fetch the permanent prosthesis.

"I'll adjust and connect the visual pathway from the retina to your brain," Ivan explained while waiting for Susie. She and her staff worked twenty-four-seven without breaks or mealtimes. That was the benefit of having Zelk instead of flesh and bone staff doing the labor. But many patients complained because they lacked empathy and understanding. They treated the patients as emotionless objects that provided body parts to them.

"Go on, get out of here. This is my doctor, and we don't need your help," the general commanded while hatefully glaring at his nurse droid, Julie.

Looking up at the nurse droid, Ivan nodded to her. "Thank you. I've got this. You may prepare his discharge and send transportation over."

"Hell yes, thanks, doctor. I was very close to pulling her plug. Can you believe she wanted to wash me with those cold steel hands?"

"That's their job, General. You didn't complain when you were comatose. May I, General?" Ivan asked as he lifted the blankets to examine the general's stump. He got a traumatic amputation during the fake bombing attack that ended up being genuine. Cian had shot a bomb into space and drove right through it to be convincing, losing his right eye and right lower leg. Ivan couldn't save the knee, but he was able to connect the sympathetic nerve root to a gold-plated microchip, making a full recovery with a bionic leg possible.

"The stump looks fully healed. After transferring you to the rehabilitation facility, we can attach the leg later today. I'll contact them. We will have a lab set up for you. Once you're admitted and scanned in, they can contact me and let me know when you're ready. Is that okay, General?"

"Yes, but if I say no, it's fucking no. I'm not an invalid. I want to return to my ship."

"I can come to the rehab center later today to connect and synchronize the nerve paths. Your stump healed well, and the skin looks less inflamed. Under normal circumstances, I would wait a month. But I received orders to move you to the top of my list and try to get you back on your ship as quickly as possible. It goes against my recommendations, but we're at war, and you're needed. I would have liked to see you at least two more times," Ivan explained, as he would with all his patients.

The general opened his mouth, but Ivan continued, not giving his brother a chance to interrupt him. The appearance of his older age, bulked-up muscled body, and unfailing bombastic personality fueled Ivan's determination not to stand down or show weakness towards his twin brother. He knew Cian didn't mean to. It was part of his role. But his hackles rose. He was the reserved overthinker, and Cian was the gregarious go-getter, and this extraction plan of his brother's solidified that fact once more.

"Let me see you and re-evaluate you later this afternoon. We can talk about the specifics of your full discharge. I...finishing up...ah, that's it. How does it feel now after I inserted your new triangulator? I've adjusted your ocular motoric sensors' neuro-uptake."

Ivan packed his tools back into his bag while the general tested his eye by shaking his head from side to side.

"You're a miracle worker. I wish I had someone with your skills on my ship. We could skip getting grounded for medical treatments as insignificant as these." The general pointed to his stump and then his eye, as if losing his vision and a leg was nothing. According to the Zelk, it was nothing because everything and everyone were replaceable.

"The common medical droids or adhesive spiders are useless when getting a man up and running to continue the fight for victory. They're excellent at telling a man he's dying or needs to be taken to the moon's surface. But onboard physicians like yourself are very hard to find for procedures like these, connecting nerve path routes or having the plain decency of telling a man it will be all right. Plus, I like how I can't intimidate you. You'd fit right in with my crew on the Horizon." Cian spoke up loudly. The entire unit could hear his proposal.

He was smart doing that. The droids were recording it.

"Let's talk this afternoon. I'm very open to a change and helping where I'm needed. Thank you, General," Ivan said, and the general feigned surprise, pretending not to expect Ivan would take him up on his offer.

"Sure, sure, doctor." He coughed and shifted on the bed. "You just made my day, no, fuck, my entire year. With you on board, I'd be able to man the frontline. Our enemies wouldn't see us coming," he said, swinging his one leg over to the side of the bed and sliding down. Once he found his balance on his foot, Cian continued. "Then I need to make ready. I'll see you later. I'll contact my crew captain. He can bring down the paperwork and permits. We'll get you measured and settled in." Cian tapped his head, pretending to remember something important. "Oh, remember you'll have to list what you think you will and won't need. I prefer flesh and bone crew. If you need a droid assistant or nurse, that won't work for us on the Horizon," he said excitedly. He clapped his hands twice. Ivan did a double-take, his eyes wide. "Come now, doctor, the thought of war with the promise of a human-only crew is good news. I'll win this war for the Zelk."

Ivan heard the buzzing of the nurse droid wheels. Julie and Susie were probably recording their conversation to upload to the Zelk's collective intelligence.

"Don't worry, General. I have the perfect assistant to bring with me," Ivan whispered to Cian, who winked at him. "We have a mutual understanding." Ivan turned and left.

"Julie, come help me and bring my transport!" Cian yelled, and Ivan cringed.

Fuck, he was loud.

Ivan consulted his last patient in the unit and left directly. He needed something to eat and a quiet place to sit and send his message. After weighing the pros and cons, he mulled it over and decided it was safe to take this drastic step they'd been working towards. Taking his hidden communicator out of the secret compartment of his toolbox, he sent the message he'd waited to send for almost two years to Kawa, and Kawa would let Phoenix know.

The Horizon is green. Finalize Exodus.

Chapter Ten

"Good morning, citizens of Phoenix.

It's now six a.m.

Did you know rats have been man's best friend since the dawn of time? They would warn about sinking ships, rotting houses, and even burning houses.

It's said that rats are intelligent social creatures, and that's why they're commonly used in idioms and reminded me of modern-day Phoenicians.

Like rats, they are fleeing a sinking ship.

Like rats escaping from a house on fire.

Anyway, visit your community news page to adopt a lab rat as a pet.

Breakfast is served until eight a.m.

Have a lovely day."

Eryn, King of the Brawl

95 A.T.

Zelk, Tower

Grayrak City

Earth's moon

Later that night, Eryn waited for the elevator door to shut, then slammed his back against the cold metal wall and let his head fall backward. Heaving with relief, he blinked furiously to stop the tears. Months of hidden emotions threatened to overflow and flood the usual cold and stoic persona he'd been wearing, thus exposing himself and ruining their mission. When he'd calmed down and collected himself, he realized the elevator wasn't moving. He checked his watch. *I'm on time.*

Out of habit, he checked his six and hit the little blue button with three vertical lines—the fucked-up new alphabet of the Zelk. He felt all kinds of feelings at the same time. Giddiness, nervousness, and excitement were right there at the forefront. His amphibian DNA called for water. Never had he known he would ever miss the darkness and humidity of the mining tunnels in South Africa.

Their mission was bearing fruit, and he was much closer to having Ivan back in his arms. Seeing Cian and receiving his message earlier had ended the torture of solitude and mock rivalry. Eryn was a social creature. He seemed to find himself always alone for the good and safety of others. Thinking of Ivan all alone made it worse.

He pushed himself off the wall and grabbed onto the railing with one hand, then stepped closer to the small window looking out over the rooftops, beyond the lunar dome, to see the blackness of space. The free-falling speed of the elevator made him feel like the contents of his stomach wanted to stay behind while he fell to the bottom of the tower. He swallowed the bile and looked longingly at the docking station, where the Horizon was being loaded by forklifts—hundreds of silver-colored cubes had been moved from storage on conveyor belts and were now loaded into the warship's belly. A small light flickered from below the platform in Morse code that Cian was released from the hospital.

You little shit! You did it!

Cian had promised them that their plan would work.

"We will infiltrate and fuck them up from the inside. Eryn, we can do this. I know you can. Please convince my brother that we can't wait. We have to act now. I don't have time to wait and think about it." Eryn remembered Cian's gruff, determined voice and resolved look that convinced Eryn he wasn't joking.

Eryn's eyes crinkled at the corners, something they hadn't done in a long time. *Message received, brother.*

He allowed himself to smile slightly. The muscle on the right corner of his mouth twitched. He released a slow, silent sigh of relief. The vapor obscured his view of the Horizon.

I'll never hear the end of it from Cian if I miss check-in by accident. Quickly, he fisted his sleeve to fake polish the glass. Then he flicked his hand three times. By blocking and unblocking the elevator light through the small window, Eryn had confirmed he was moving out in exactly six hours.

Yes, brother, finalize Exodus.

Their luck had finally turned. He chuckled inwardly and whispered in Earth's English to Ivan. *With my toes planted deep into the Earth, I will make filthy love to you and take a long time doing it.*

They had been working undercover at Grayrak Hospital for a little over a year. At the same time, Cian and his men worked on infiltrating the enemy. Their mission was to take command of their fleet, steal their warship, and ultimately bring their people home.

Eryn heaved another deep silent sigh. He missed Ivan, and he knew Ivan missed him, too. The only contact they'd allowed themselves was the quick passing by between surgery and post-op recovery in the mornings, which, he admitted, made his day much more bearable. Seeing his beautiful face each morning motivated him to continue their work to save the humans.

His thoughts were happy, but he kept his face emotionless. He was very good at disguising his true feelings and was glad to leave the human recycling factory. Eryn and Ivan's mission was to collect as much information as possible and strategically bug the Zelk mainframes. They were both scarce commodities because trained human physicians were hard to find on Grayrak. How Barkor's friend, Leo, convinced them they were educated at Grayrak University remained a mystery. There weren't any

Universities on Grayrak. He guessed they really were that out of touch with what was going on in the human compound.

Thousands of humans had died, and still, the Zelk continued building more Zelk. Leo convinced them their supply of humans was running low and that they needed Eryn and Ivan for specialized surgeries, like connecting human tissue to muscles, nerves, and bone for bionic limbs and prosthetics. Better healthcare on Grayrak meant more humans. Save a human, score a body part, Eryn reasoned. Lately, the hospital had functioned as a neutral zone where humans were treated as valued donors. That was also the reason for many humans returning to have surgery. Life outside was horrible, and they literally would give an arm or a leg for five-star treatment, food, water, and a bed to sleep on.

Working on the ship meant their facial identities were scanned and stored with other qualifiers, which classified them as friends of the Zelk. These qualities were uploaded to the mainframe and triggered the hive if someone suspicious or unauthorized entered the high security zones. It also meant it was time to go home. Eryn and Ivan could board the Horizon since they were trusted allies of the Zelk. It also gave Ivan access to the final big computer room. The signal he just sent meant Lasitor was already programming a self-destruct sequence inside the collective Zelk brain.

Eryn was nervous—he felt his temples throbbing and not in beat with his heart. He closed his eyes briefly and grounded himself before croaking and exposing himself.

The Zelk watched and recorded all of them, and he hated it. But the thought of being with Ivan soon excited him and overpowered that fear or dread of being discovered and watching Ivan die.

When the elevator reached the lobby, he wiped all emotion from his face before the door slid open. He stepped out with his head held high as he greeted the droid at the front desk of the human sleeping quarters. Eryn's movement woke him up from standby mode.

"Good day, doctor," the male droid greeted him as usual.

"Hello, Pat," Eryn greeted and then silently thanked the stars that it was for the last fucking time.

This time tomorrow, my ass will be up-up and away while I bury my cock deep inside Ivan.

Eryn turned to the modified human receptionist, guarding the entrance to the human resting quarters. An allotment of the Zelk recognized that overworked human employees needed at least six hours of sleep, a nutritional diet of three meals a day, exercise, and a shower with a clean uniform daily.

"Any mail for me?" Eryn asked monotonously, knowing something was always waiting in the mailbox. He never received mail with encrypted messages this way—*like anyone would be so stupid*—but the Zelk still scanned it; even if it was for fingerprints, he trusted nothing in their hands.

For this reason, he had to return to his room to implant the virus he'd hidden in a little compartment behind the second tile of the second row from the hot water tap in his shower. *Also, I can do with a long wank picturing Ivan's lips around my cock.* He shook his head slightly to clear his mind when he heard Pat rolling towards him.

"Thank you, Pat." The three metal clamps for fingers released the envelope, and Eryn grabbed it. Instead of walking away, he stood still to open it on purpose in front of Pat, giving him the impression that they could trust him—solidifying their baseline for the next step of their mission.

They're so predictable. Now he'll record and upload my actions and the fact that I'm trustworthy, open, and honest to the mainframe, and with every droid scanning my geometrics to identify me, they'll trust me because I open my mail in front of Pat.

Eryn was so done with this pretending shit. He would rip the head off every Zelk crossing his path if it were up to him, but it wouldn't work in the long run. He had to be smart about it as they'd planned.

He took a few deep breaths and heard the high-pitched zing of data being transferred by Pat's electronic brain. The more he stimulated or showed his emotions, the higher the buzzing. Everything was uploaded, like the direction he came from, what he looked like, his facial features, the shades of red on his cheeks, how fast he breathed, his core temperature, and even the size of his pupils.

Eryn gave him a fake smile and a nod, while thinking about his purchase—he bought himself a new second-hand lampshade, an ugly yellow one that looked like a hot air balloon with clowns.

To bullshit the hive, Eryn and Ivan used the clown lampshade salesperson, Sarinka, who was their go-between and handler who communicated with Cian and their fathers. Eryn bought the lampshade as a means for them to bill him monthly for its rent, something he conveniently never paid. Although it was necessary for their mission, he liked the homemade lampshade. The yellow hot air balloon had twenty-five clowns dancing in various stages of undress. When the lampshade spun, it looked like they undressed and shook their little tooshies. The clowns would then get dressed and bow when the shade was stopped and spun in the opposite direction.

"Ah, the lampshade bill. I forgot to pay for it again. Maybe I should visit them tomorrow and close this account," he said, pretending to be upset and irritated.

"Maybe you should, doctor. My records suggest you have enough funds allocated to do it," the nosy droid said as he scanned Eryn's bank account. *The response I was waiting for.* Eryn smiled inwardly with glee.

"Yes, as it is, tomorrow is my day off. I'm being transferred to the fleet. Maybe I should go to Grayrak City to settle my account and return the shade. I don't want to rent it anymore. It's ugly. I'll find something else," Eryn quickly added.

"Oh," Pat retorted, his gaze rattled a bit from side to side as he searched for a polite human response, then he settled for, "Whatever makes you happy. A happy human is a productive human."

The Brawl turned before he ruined their mission, like crushing Pat's head with one hand or using the droid as a baseball bat to fuck shit up. *Only a few hours to go,* he said to himself and left the brightly lit lobby, eager to get to his room to be alone and get packing.

Minutes later, he let his head fall forward, relaxing under the spray of the hot water shower as he supported his body with his left hand while stroking his cock with his soapy right hand. Pretty pictures of Ivan zoomed on the insides of his eyelids while he breathed as softly as possible. He was sure no one recorded what they did in the shower, but the noises still traveled far. He concentrated on not saying his husband's name out loud while he imagined himself pinning Ivan to the flat surface of their dining room table back home in Phoenix.

Ivan would be naked, his legs falling open to the sides, his face scrunched, moaning loudly for him to fuck Ivan harder and faster.

"*You're gorgeous. Take your cock in hand.*" Eryn fantasized about giving orders, as Ivan obeyed eagerly. Eryn fucked him hard, hammering the table into the opposite wall while Ivan pleasured himself.

He pumped his cock rhythmically in beat with the sounds he remembered while fucking Ivan.

Then he scooped him closer by curling his large hands around Ivan's slender upper legs, anchoring him in place while he fucked his husband senselessly. He imagined Ivan's eyes closed and his head thrown back as he hissed through his teeth.

Fuck me, Eryn, harder, yes, fuck yes, just, like, that! Ivan moaned and cheered, driving Eryn over the edge. *Fuck yes, just like that,* Ivan groaned, spurting his seed all over both of them. Eryn was so deeply thrown back into the memory that he smelled the scent of Ivan's jism and ejaculated against the steel-tiled shower wall, milking his cock until every drop was drained from his balls. He opened his eyes, seeing double for a second.

"Brrrrr," he croaked. "That was a long and hard one," he mumbled. He cupped and splashed water on his semen running down the wall, ensuring it flushed down the drain. *Tonight's the last time I climax on my own. Next time, Ivan will suck it out.* He made the vow to himself and finished washing his hair and body.

He left the water running to muffle any noise he would make. First, he used his fingernails to pry the seams loose around the secret tile covering their small drop box compartment. Then, he stretched his arms up high, reaching the ceiling, which was just over thirteen feet high, and carefully felt with the tips of his pointer and middle fingers inside the groove of the last row of tiles for his small and very old wooden pencil. The same charcoal lead pencil his father-in-law gifted him when they worked together to calculate how to send the last rocket to the moon. Eryn cherished it because he got to know Mika, and they became very good friends that day.

He grabbed hold of the pencil between his fingers, carefully stuck it into the little hole behind the tile, and turned it like a key. A tiny door flung open to reveal the small computer chip Lasitor had loaded with all kinds of electronic viruses. Then he closed the door and secured the tile back in its place, closed the taps, and flung a towel around his lower body.

Later, as he lay in bed, he closed his eyes, sending his mental feelers out to scan the outside to feel what was happening outside the wall and the status of Cian and Sarinka's plan. He listened to the droning rumble of the Warship Horizon, machinery packing the crates inside, and whether he heard any signs of trouble outside. He thought about Ivan and missing their Anubis.

Then, he watched the dancing clowns on his yellow lampshade and reminisced about their past when they were young and innocent. He smiled, folding his arms behind his head.

***

"I'm naming mine Igor. He's the ugliest of the three puppies," Ivan said proudly as he rubbed his nose against the cross-eyed pup with no hair.

That was before the depths of icy water had sucked Phoenix inside.

"I'll call mine Devil because he's the biggest, maddest, and the baddest of them all," Eryn had said. He knew Devil liked the name. His yellow eyes sparkled, and he squirmed in his hands to get to his face and lick him.

"Yeah, he is, and he farts the stinkiest, as well," Ivan retorted, waving his hand in front of his face.

"Don't blame it on Devil. We all know it's Cian and his rotten brood who stink up Phoenix. Everyone in their vicinity wants to go for a walk or has something important to do," Eryn defended Devil.

"You should call him Rotty...no, wait—"

Cian interrupted Eryn, "Yes, I'll call him Rotty for Rottweiler." Cian rubbed the chubby and overly muscled Anubis's flanks. He sank to his knees, wrapping his arms around him, and closed his eyes. "Rotty, I like it. Do you like it?" he cooed, and Rotty panted happily.

***

Eryn closed his eyes and drifted into slumber.

Three hours later, his internal alarm had woken him. He rolled out of bed and snuck on his knees underneath the bedside table where he'd pried open the socket for the bedside lamp connection.

He stuck his thick forefinger inside, hooking the thin fiberoptic cable, and snapped the tiny clip over it. Then he closed the access hole and hastily reversed out of there. Before he got up, he stopped and closed his eyes. With the palms of his hands flat on the steel floor, he felt increasing vibrations. The Horizon was preparing to take off. Hurriedly, he dressed, grabbed his belongings, and opened the door. He forced himself back into the neutral persona and blank, emotionless gaze.

He exited the sleeping area, chin high. "Morning, Pat," he greeted like always, but he didn't wait for a reply. He passed through the doors to the elevator lobby. Halting in front of the steel doors, he pressed the button to call the elevator.

"Sir, excuse me, sir," Pat said from behind him. Eryn froze.

"Sir," Pat called.

Eryn slowly turned, keeping his heart rate and angst levels to untraceable levels. God, the thing moved fast. Pat held the lampshade in his clamps for him. "You forgot this, sir," Pat said, his eyes blinking in and out of focus.

Probably the virus. I must get out of here. My fucking nerves.

"Thank you, Pat. Could you transfer funds to the account and close it? The General Fleet Commander asked for me. The Horizon is leaving for war. I must report immediately," Eryn said and thanked the stars when the elevator door opened. He stepped inside and turned to watch Pat. The robot man on wheels blinked one eye and then the other. The tiny lights flickered blue and red. Then he rolled away, zigzagging across the lobby. No Zelk would stand in his way with the mention of war.

Eryn furiously poked the button marked with a neon blue circle with his pointer finger. The door shut. The elevator descended to the civilian docking station. He was minutes away from being left behind. He moved to the small peephole, covering, and opening the hole to send his last message.

It's a go!

Go, go, go, go, go!

Chapter Eleven

"Good morning, citizens of Phoenix.

It's now six a.m.

Did you know the only bombs that don't kill are being produced here in Phoenix?

Parents, sign your children up and join them in making seed bombs. Be a part of Operation Pollination. It's a fun workshop where kids play with clay and fill them with their favorite seeds.

Visit your community news page to book your spot to help protect and nurture the Earth and its moon.

Breakfast is served until eight a.m.

Hope you have a joyful day!"

Barkor, the Promised Prince

95 A.T.

Grayrak City

Earth's moon

Operation Lunar Evacuation

Barkor soared up the side of their watch tower, feeling more optimistic and relieved with each clutch-pull-step as he scaled the dilapidated building. Reaching the final rod, he jumped and flip-rolled onto the landing where he'd left Leo earlier. Catching his breath, he let his arms fall dramatically to the sides and looked up at Leo, who sat propped upright, looking down at him. He smiled mischievously at Barkor.

"I believe you were successful. Sarinka tells me the promised prince commanded death by poison to his enemies." Leo joked and spoke dramatically.

"I commanded nothing. I just helped coordinate the poisoning. And for the millionth time, I'm not the promised prince. I had no choice but to assist. Kids were handling the poison. I had to make sure they didn't kill themselves instead of poisoning the Disciples and their precious water hole," Barkor said as he sat up and swung his feet over the edge.

"Hmmm," Leo agreed, like he usually did when he actually disagreed. They sat in comfortable silence.

Below them, Grayrak City lay illuminated by the dim blue lights of the Zelk tower, which glowed and highlighted the spiral display from beyond the wall. It stood central, drenching the insides of the dome with flickering blue light. To Barkor, it was both beautiful and ugly.

"Leo, I'm not sure about Grizzly. I couldn't find his body. We searched to ensure all the Disciples were accounted for. We found all of them except Grizzly. I hope and believe he's dead."

"Did you see Talali and the others? There were three more s—slave girls he held prisoner in a cage below the floor in the eating area," Leo said, stuttering. He hated saying slaves.

"I'd asked Sarinka. She said they followed Talali. I'm sure she would get them to safety." Barkor didn't know them very well. It was a place he avoided until the general gave the order to evacuate. The plan was to go on with business as usual while they moved all the pieces into place to evacuate with no bloodshed of the innocent.

Out of the corner of his eye, he noticed Sarinka. From where she came, Barkor couldn't say. She had the irritating gift of appearing gracefully out of thin air. She looked stunningly deadly in her new black suit and had an air of authority and quiet strength. She spread propaganda and inside intelligence among the citizens of Grayrak. As she called it, letting the people blow off steam and preventing an early uprising against the

Zelk. She was the force that pulled each human toward the end plan, and the general was that force that bonded them.

Barkor didn't know why, but suddenly earlier today, Sarinka announced the water supply was being poisoned—he didn't know where to start. For fuck's sake, they set the plan in motion using kids. And he ran like a crazed lunatic eager to kill Grizzly and his Disciples. They forced Barkor to make an unplanned play.

"I can't wait to see the general and ask him what he thought about using children to fight his war! Before the day is done, I fear, Sarinka, they will kill us in a bloody battle. I thought I knew the general. I usually sum people up correctly. But I think we were wrong to trust him. Maybe the Zelk brainwashed him. It doesn't sound like he can maneuver a stealthy battle, especially without firing one shot, as he promised. They outnumber us one thousand to one. Tomorrow, they'll crush us when they realize we attacked their miners." Barkor fumed. He felt like he wasn't in control, and he hated that. "We've been planning this for how long? Donali keeps saying we can trust them, that he's dedicated, and that his plan will work." Barkor lifted his hands, making air quotations. "We must follow the steps carefully, and the rest he will make happen."

Barkor's gaze lingered on Sarinka. "Today's purge was obviously your idea. Where did you get that poison? Over two hundred Disciples and slave drivers—all dead in one sweep of assassinations across Grayrak. Unarmed children! Do you realize you made one hell of a mistake? There's no one to report to the Zelk. Grizzly is gone. He knew if someone harmed him, the Zelk would come to investigate this side of the wall. This is a colossal fuck-up!" Barkor yelled, pointing to the shacks surrounding the market area.

Sarinka stood with her hands on her hips, waiting for him to finish. She looked amused, infuriating him.

"You know, I'll have to report in Grizzly's place and say he's sick or dead or something. Attempt to play for time until the mighty smart general can come to pick us up," Barkor said. He couldn't see how a war could be avoided. He was on a roll and continued his rant. "The rebellion fizzled out, thanks to you, and now is sadly ending with a massive anticlimax. A year-long edging with no fucking orgasm."

Leo snickered behind him. Sarinka answered with a slow smile as she tapped her head with one finger. "No, my friend, you're wrong. The entirety of Grayrak is being evacuated as we speak." She grinned and tapped her foot, daring him to say something.

Barkor stood slack jawed. "Really? Why didn't you say anything?" He jumped to help. "Let's go, Leo!"

"Because of this." Sarinka pointed and gave Barkor an about-face. "The general said he doesn't want you near there. I don't know why, but he said he would evacuate you and Leo just as the sleep cycle ended." Sarinka pointed to the clock tower. Barkor flung himself around and looked at the tower as if seeing it for the first time and wondering what she was pointing at.

"How are they evacuating the people? Where are they, Sarinka?"

She locked her lips with an imaginary key and put the imaginary key in her pants pocket, tapping it.

"Yes, your rebellion is quashed. But by the time they realize they were dead wrong, they will be no more." Sarinka patted Barkor on the shoulder.

"I'm going to kill him. Who does he think he is? And why does it feel like I was just caught with my pants down?" Barkor asked.

Leo chuckled as if this was a comedy show. He was still sitting where Barkor left him at the side of the roof.

"I asked him six months ago, and he said a year or two. What happened? Why is this happening today? The fuel, the food, and the people..." Barkor trailed away as he remembered the voice of the Commander General.

"If I come for you and your people, no one will know, and no one will stop me. When we leave the moon, it will be as empty as they found it. I will wipe all traces of their existence."

"Don't worry, Barkor, everyone knows what to do." She pointed to Leo. "He's too frail to board the ship with them. Anyway, you would have searched for him and not followed the general's orders. He asked you to plant the explosives on strategic points." She took a backpack off her shoulders and handed him the bag. "They're not to be activated. Just bury and place them all around the dome."

Barkor took the bag from her. Speechless. He was supposed to be happy, but why did it feel like he wasn't the one saving his people? Was he a puppet all this time? One thing that he was glad about was Leo. He was weak and exhausted. He wouldn't make it.

"Okay, thank you. I think," Barkor said.

"No problem. I'm going to check on the loading. See you later. Don't draw any attention to this side. Stay low, plant the grenades, and take Leo up the tower tonight," Sarinka said and turned to say something in Leo's ear.

"What are you whispering about? Stop keeping secrets from me, for fuck's sake," Barkor grumbled.

"Nothing for you to know. It's between us," she said and turned to jump off the roof.

"Be glad for his plan. It's better than massacring innocent civilians," Leo said over his shoulder.

"How is he planning to hide thousands of people? Leo, why am I kept in the dark? Doesn't he trust me?" Barkor asked and joined Leo again. He plopped down and scanned the market below them. "How didn't I see this earlier? There isn't a soul in sight."

"Remember, these people from the earth aren't stupid, and they planned this perfectly. If he thinks it's better for you not to interfere, then he has his reasons."

"What did Sarinka say?"

"Dear moon lord, you're inquisitive! All she said was see you on the other side," Leo said, and Barkor could tell it wasn't the whole truth. He decided to let it go. It was good to wait and do what he was told to do. For once, he wouldn't worry about kids disappearing and women and young boys being raped. He flung his arm around Leo and relaxed for the first time in a long time.

Later that cycle, the muscles in Barkor's legs burned, but he mechanically lifted one leg before the other, climbing the upward spiraling stairs that felt like never-ending stairs to the stars. He squeezed his eyelids to refocus and see better. The aluminum stairs clang-clanged beneath his boots.

I better not slip. We'll break both our necks rolling down to the bottom.

Each stair flowed into the other, tricking his eyes, so he didn't know where one ended and the next began. Eager to get to the top, he heaved one deep breath after another, burning his already dry throat raw. Excitement to meet up with their rescuer drove his will to get himself and Leo to the top, to safety.

"Put me down. Leave me here. I'm not worth it," Leo nagged.

"Shut up, Leo, and stop wiggling. You're going to fall on your head. I'm worried we won't make it on time." Barkor's legs were trembling. He had flung Leo over his shoulders like a wounded soldier and was determined to carry him all the way.

"Shh, I told you don't talk. We don't know who's following us," Barkor reminded Leo as they ascended the staircase inside Grayrak's clock tower.

A monument built by the first humans in memory of Old Earth, named Big Benny Tower, was obscured by smog. The corroded aluminum was unsafe for visitors long ago. Stripped walls revealed the frame and scaffolding holding the death trap up. Ripped-off pieces were reused for shacks—the homes of backstreet dwellers. Barkor grew up in that area built by the remnants of the clock tower walls, raised by humans with kind hearts who suffered each day of their existence.

"My head feels like it's going to explode. All my blood is now in my head," Leo complained.

"Shut up, Leo." Barkor stopped counting the steps because Leo distracted him. They were about one-hundred living spaces high, and slipping and sliding down the corkscrew stairs wouldn't end pretty. Finally, he heard the copper clock's arms cluck-clucking louder and louder. A sign that they were close to the exit and rendezvous point.

"I think we're close now. Put me down," Leo tried again, but Barkor ignored him.

"Shut up, Leo. We're almost there. Can you hear the churning of the gears?" he asked just as the light appeared around the last turn of the stairs.

"Upsy-daisy!" Barkor slid Leo like a sack of moon rocks off his shoulders, caught him around the waist, and carried him like a baby the last couple of steps. Leo hated being carried this way.

Exiting through a tiny door, he walked onto a metal mesh platform used by the first humans as a lookout over Grayrak and had a look at Earth. Now, this spot was only used by the odd volunteer cleaner who would wash the white face of Big Benny, so the privileged Zelk supporters living on top of the wall could read the time.

Barkor helped Leo to sit safely before taking a seat next to him.

"My ass is frozen numb," Leo said after they sat waiting for more than an hour. "I'm scared to go back," Leo whispered.

"If you can't sit much longer, I understand. Why don't you roll to your side?" Barkor said, already moving up and pulling Leo over so he could hold and protect Leo from rolling off the side. No wind was inside the dome, but Leo might roll off the narrow ledge while asleep.

I would never forgive myself.

"Hey, don't manhandle me," Leo protested lightly.

"Just lie down, Leo, you know I mean well," Barkor said and patted his upper legs, signaling for Leo that he would pull him over to the side to lie with his head on his lap. Leo scuffed and wiggled to get comfortable.

They spoke about anything and everything while the clock ticked and counted the minutes and, later, the hours down until they had to decide whether to return below.

"I would rather die than you not being able to go back to Earth," Leo told Barkor through chattering teeth. "Promise me if something happens and you must run, you will leave me here."

Barkor stroked the thin skin covering Leo's cheeks. He looked frail, he noted, and it broke his heart. Leo's pale skin was bloodlessly white, and his lips were blue. His breathing was labored. Barkor looked at Leo's lips, removed a little pot of oil from his pocket, and rubbed it on his cracked lips.

"We'll leave this place, don't you worry. Sarinka set it up. You know we can trust her word for it. They will come, wait a few minutes longer. Can you wait?" he asked.

"I don't want to be moaning for nothing and be difficult, man, but how long do you think we should wait? I need to piss, and I'm hungry," Leo mumbled weakly.

Barkor grew concerned because this was out of Leo's comfort zone. Leo was getting restless and uncomfortable. He was probably exhausted. "Come, let's sit up." Barkor helped him, feeling nervous as he pushed Leo up into a sitting position.

"Let me help you. Don't move. I'll shit my pants if you fall. I didn't carry you all the way up here only for you to fall to your death," Barkor said, scooping Leo up and supporting him between his knees.

"Come, I'll help you piss. You can piss right here. There's no one underneath us, anyway." Barkor loosened the drawstrings of Leo's pants with his left hand while supporting him with his right. He removed his cock and held it for his friend.

"Just relax. I got you," he said, as he had done so many times before.

Leo's breath puffed clouds of vapor into the darkness as he sighed and relaxed into the feeling of relieving his bladder. "Thank you, I'm done," Leo said softly. Barkor tipped his cock a few times and pulled the foreskin forward, pushing the drops of urine out. Then he made Leo comfortable and relieved himself, as well.

"I have faith in Sarinka. They will come," Barkor said.

Leo shivered and looked up at Barkor. "I know. She's never broken her word to me. She's straightforward, and I would never cross her. I think she knows how to kill a man slowly, with maximum pain."

Barkor agreed with Leo that she was dangerous.

They did it, oh, moon-god, we did it. The feeling of accomplishment overwhelmed him. The clock ticked at the same speed as his heartbeat, and with every minute they spent waiting, he felt freer and more optimistic than the previous one. A laugh spontaneously escaped. It felt awkward to laugh, but Leo joined in. His laugh was silly, like a little girl's. They widened their eyes at each other and puffed out their cheeks in a useless attempt to hold it in. Pressure built and exploded into another round of horrible, silly laughs.

"Oh, what a stupid sight we make," Leo said in between coughs and giggles, and Barkor prolonged the pleasantry with more jokes and punchlines about the simplest things. Things he remembered from when he grew up and when times were good. Anything to hear Leo's giggles. He was a frail, sick half-man who looked old and withered, unlike Barkor, who never seemed to age. He kept that a secret, until now. No one had said anything, but they must have noticed because why would they say he was their prince? His mother definitely wasn't royalty. He didn't know who his father was. Their rocket crash-landed on the moon, and during all that, his mother gave birth to him and died. He was taken and raised by the village women, and they were all mama to him.

Sweet smells of food drifted up from the empty market below. The usual noises that floated up were eerily absent. Barkor hummed a soft tune, and the melody ebbed and flowed. Barkor watched as the pained expression on Leo's face smoothed out. A few seconds later, he closed his eyes, enjoying the make-believe music Barkor made.

Barkor caressed Leo's cheeks with his thumb when the song was done. He felt so much empathy for him, and he checked to see if Leo was peacefully sleeping.

Hold on, Leo, I'm getting you the medical care you deserve.

Suddenly Barkor couldn't hear Big Benny tick; the moment's anxiety caught up with him. It was as if he was sucked into another dimension of space. Something weird was happening. Someone cleared their throat. Dazed, he scanned their surroundings and saw Sarinka with her hands on her hips out on the landing.

"When you lovebirds are done sightseeing, the ship is waiting," she said, teasing them.

"Leo, wake up. The ship is here." Barkor scooped Leo up, who groaned as his head fell back. His friend was weak and exhausted.

Barkor moved to where Sarinka pointed to the edge of the landing where the transport ship was silently floating. Cian was waiting for him and moon-god; he looked scary, with tattoos on the side of his face. Barkor did a double-take, one sparkling blue eye, that seemed Zelk was looking at him. And he was frowning. What in moon-god's name? Did he sell his eye to the Zelk?

"Look," Leo said, and Barkor knew what he meant. It was the eye. Barkor tried getting his bearings together, but everything moved fast around him while he slowed simultaneously, and he thought he'd forgotten his bloody name.

Sarinka woke him from whatever stupor he was in. "Can we move before we get seen?"

"Men, it's time to go!" Cian called in Old Earth Language.

Just then, the ship extended a ladder to meet them.

"They kept their promise!" Sarinka announced sternly. "Let me help you, Barkor."

The stunning seven-foot Cian jumped down onto the landing with a loud thump. "Donali, bring the stretcher," he shouted over his shoulder while fist-bumping Sarinka and making a swooshing sound. Weirdo, Barkor thought.

"I never break my word," he told Sarinka, taking Leo's limp body from Barkor. "Come, friends," he said with a friendly smile, and Barkor wanted to protest, but again, he was rendered speechless by the sight of the magnificent man who seemed larger than life itself. Cian affected him strangely somehow. His whole body tingled and his skin suddenly felt too small. He remembered the first time it had happened. It was when they abducted Leo. He thought it was the rush of the moment, or his imagination. Now it's happening again. This time he was sure it had something to do with the general.

***

General Cian Romanov

"Okay, did you plant the balls, as I asked?" Cian waited and got no answer from Barkor.

"Hello, Barkor. Did you plant the seed grenades as I asked?" Cian repeated, and it seemed Barkor was offline. He stared wordlessly at Cian with those stunning dark eyes. "Hello, earth, to Barkor? Have you planted the bombs?" he asked.

For fuck's sake! Cian grabbed Sarinka by the arm.

"Sarinka, tell me you gave him the seed bombs," Cian demanded and hoped the last step of their mission wasn't a fuck-up.

"Yes, I did," she retorted and turned to Barkor, who seemed to stare at his bionic eye, rubbing Cian the wrong way. He didn't have time for this.

"Jesus Christ, it's just an eye. Get over it!" he yelled which seemed to penetrate the hazy look in Barkor's eyes.

Barkor blinked a few times. "I'm sorry, General. Are you going to bomb the place?"

"Of course, I fucking am. Who the fuck did you think was going to do it? Did you plant the clay bombs as I asked?

"Yes, I did," Barkor answered, and Cian relaxed.

"Okay, good, get in the car," he said, grabbing the bag with the spacesuit and his sword. "Ish and I will run one last errand. Go now. We'll meet you on the Horizon."

"Wait, what?" Barkor jumped out of the Bubblecar again, and Cian wanted to hit him over the head and throw his unconscious body back inside.

"I don't have time for this. Go!" he said and pushed him back into the car.

"They're all dead. Why are you going down? There's nothing except the possibility of Zelk finding you. If they find you, we're all toast," Barkor objected.

"Who do you think is flying the ship? I need to get to the Warship Horizon. This is how it was planned. We'll meet you later. Please go now."

"Barkor!" Leo called from the back. "Come, don't be difficult. They know what they're doing. They came to save us, don't be wayward. If you go now, the mission was for nothing, and you could have left me here."

"No! Shut up, Leo. Why do I feel you're bullshitting me?" he asked Cian and looked at Ish for an answer.

"We are not. I must enter from this side to disconnect the mainframe from the Horizon and allow Lasitor to take over. It has to be done manually. I must cut the cables and give Eryn the signal. It's being infected as we speak." Cian pointed to the spiraling tower in the distance.

"I need to activate the bombs. And I can only do it on the surface. I need to set the timer to initiate the pulse waves."

Ish touched Barkor on the shoulder and said in his deep, commanding voice, "Don't worry, we have this. You will see us on the Horizon."

"Yes, don't worry, we planned this for months," Cian said, but he was only twenty-five percent sure that their plan would work.

"Like hell you will!" Barkor exclaimed, and Cian realized they were standing eye to eye. "Give me a suit. I will come with you."

"Absolutely fucking not. You'll hold us back and slow us down," Cian said, vibrating with fury. "If we encounter the Zelk, we're listed as trusted. Are you listed?"

"No, but you need me. If this plan doesn't work, you will need me," Barkor said, and Cian wanted to either strangle or hug him. He couldn't decide. *He thinks he's the only one with powers around here, and I don't have time for a damn show-and-tell game.*

Just then, another suit fell with a plop at Barkor's feet. Cian checked and confirmed it was Sarinka—bloody female.

Barkor smiled at Cian, picked it up, and said, "Come, I know the fastest route to the tower." The fucker disappeared down the stairway.

"Motherfucker, wait for us!" Ish and Cian exclaimed in unison. Cian had no choice but to follow him. "Sarinka, get to the Spacecar and then meet us on the Horizon. We have an hour before it all goes boom."

"Yes, sir," she said with a determined smile and jumped in the driver's seat as they'd planned before.

"Fucking Barkor, now I must bring him on the Horizon. The last of the crates are being loaded."

"Don't worry, he's fast. Try to keep up with him, General." Sarinka cackled as she closed the hatch.

"Let's go!" Cian yelled and sprinted for the stairwell. Secretly, he was having fun as they competed by pushing and shoulder-bumping each other to pass and win the race to the bottom of the clock tower stairs.

Just as they passed the rows of shacks, Barkor halted and pointed. "Here, we have to jump on the roofs that run along the wall. Where's your detonator?" he asked, sweaty and short of breath.

Cian patted his backpack. "Here," he said and then lifted his golden sword. "And here."

"Good," Barkor said, looking impressed with Cian as he smiled approvingly.

"Cian, Barkor," Ish whispered and pointed.

Barkor pushed Cian and Ish back, holding them in place with spread arms. "Don't move," Barkor said in a muted tone. Cian looked questioningly at a frowning Ish and followed the path of their gazes to the figure, pushing a round iron cover up and over to the side and climbing out of a sewage opening in the alley.

It was a tiny little human. A female. She scanned the area slowly and carefully then pushed the massive lid back over the hole she'd just climbed out of with soundless effort. She looked wild and untamed.

"She noticed us," Ish whispered through his teeth.

Not moving, standing frozen, even with Barkor pinning him to the spot, Cian wasn't planning to go anywhere. He thought looking away would cause the wild child to pounce. He only turned his eyeballs to check on Barkor as he slid his hand inside the back pocket of his pants.

When he looked back, it was too late as the little fucker jumped, and before Cian could register, he was slammed onto his back with her sitting on his chest. Both hands were around his head, ready to hit his skull into a pulp on the dirt. Cian's first instinct was to fling the girl off him, but Barkor already had his knife underneath her chin.

"Easy, if you hurt him, I'll cut your throat," Barkor promised.

She grunted and started screaming, a high-pitched sound of frustration. Then she released Cian's head by throwing it back onto the ground.

"Ouch," Cian said softly.

He knew it was his eye, so he closed them. She was a little tunnel rat, a human, he realized. Sarinka told him about them. They almost never came to the surface.

"It is me, Barkor." He tried to soothe her like an injured animal. "Hush-hush, now," Barkor said and removed his knife from underneath her chin. He folded the flip knife and slipped it back into his pocket. With one hand outstretched, he revealed his backpack and then, in slow motion, dragged a piece of bread out of it with the other hand, ensuring he had her attention. He offered the bread to her. "Cian, meet Talali."

It broke Cian's heart—he saw her eyes, the hate, suffering, and deadly intent. Barkor knew her; he lived with her down in that hole. That must be the secret human access through that hole. She crawl-walked one foot and then the other over his body. Oh, stars, she smelled horrid!

Dressed in rags and dirty beyond measure. Barefoot and looking like a ball of hair with arms and legs. Cian watched wordlessly. He dared not move.

Ish grabbed him by the hand, pulling him upright, and whispered in his ear, "Stay still."

Cian was nervous. He never saw something as wild as her. She hissed at him, and Cian was sure she could bite his throat and kill him.

Barkor waved another piece of bread at her. She sniffed the air and slowly approached, looking him up and down. Cian stood stock still. Dirty little fingers lifted his shirt, smelling him. She was a short little thing. Her head barely reached his lower tummy. *God, she better not lick my belly button.* He didn't know if he could resist swatting her like a fly if it started to tickle. He held his breath and ground his molars. She stepped back. Thank fuck!

Barkor made little kissing sounds to grab her attention, still holding the bread. She snatched it and jumped backward. The bread disappeared in two bites.

Ish cleared his throat. “Let’s find out if there are others. If not, we should grab her and run,” he whispered in his low baritone. Cian could see they made her nervous.

“Talali, it’s time to go. Is there anyone else down there?” Barkor asked. Talali whined softly, like a little wounded animal.

“Did you not get the message that you must go hide with everyone?” Ish asked, and it seemed she trusted him more than Barkor. She nodded, and the whining ceased. She kept looking at Cian, distrusting him. He didn’t blame her; she’d never seen him before, and he had a shiny new Zelk eye. If he were her age, he would have run. Talali was a brave little thing. He guessed she couldn’t be older than fifteen years of age.

“We have to go. We’re leaving this place. Do you remember Sarinka telling you about a better place we’re going to?” Barkor asked her while turning to go. He asked permission with his eyes. Cian couldn’t say no. How could he? He nodded a yes. She grabbed him by the arm, pulling him and gesturing with her head to one side. She pointed at Cian and then grunted toward the hole she’d just crept out of. Barkor looked back at Cian, pulling up his shoulders. Like, sorry, I have to.

“Sure, let’s follow this weird human into a hole we probably won’t fit into or come out of,” Cian said skeptically, watching Barkor trailing behind her, shaking his head. Cian turned to Ish. “You bring the others. I’ll do the cutting and plant the detonator.” Cian checked the timer on his watch. “You have twenty minutes. I’ll see you on the other side.”

Ish touched his shoulder. “Don’t worry, we’ll meet you. We know this tunnel system. It ends at the loading bays. It’s the smuggling tunnel.”

Cian took his watch off and gave it to Ish. He helped him put it on. “Can you read Earth numbers? See this...it’s the same as Big Benny Tower.” Cian pointed back to the steampunk clock towering over the human living area. “Look at this picture.” He showed him the hourglass. Ish seemed to grasp its meaning.

"Oh, yeah, I can read time, I see," he said and nodded eagerly with a big smile.

"Good, go. When the sand has run out, you should be on board. I can't wait for you. I can't spare one minute," Cian said and watched as Barkor and Talali disappeared into the hole.

As soon as Ish entered the tunnel, Cian ripped the bottom of his backpack open and sprinted along the rooftops. He'd studied the footage of images Sarinka and Donali sent him. He knew exactly where to go, using markers and alleyways. Excitedly, he jumped from rooftop to rooftop, then down to the entrance of the cold storage containers of Halogen, where he set the timer and activated the pulse reactor. As he jumped, left foot to right foot, he sang to himself, Got My Mind Set On You, by George Harrison.

"It's gonna take time.
A whole lot of precious time.
It's gonna take patience and time, mmm.
To do it, to do it, to do it, to do it, to do it.
To do it right!"

He sowed the seeds as he imagined hearing the song. Feeling jubilant, he mixed that song with his own heart song and concentrated on spreading the love in his heart and soul deep into the ground. As he jumped, feeling lighter than ever, he scattered the seed bombs the children of Phoenix made. He hoped, eventually, they would sprout and grow where they landed and where Barkor planted the fruit trees.

He sang his song from the depths of his heart and thought about his mate and his beauty. His perfectness and the magnificence of the magic called love. He imagined rich, colorful gardens with sweet smells, beautiful butterflies, and insects like dragonflies and bees. He imagined a garden with pools of fresh water. The song he sang filled the surrounding air, and in his mind, he saw every seed that fell and rolled, willing them to grow and flourish. He sang to the hydrogen, and he sang to the seeds.

He urged them to grow and for oxygen to bind with the hydrogen, and he imagined water seeping up from the core of the moon, and then he imagined green moss, fields of grass, and more flowers and trees. He ran as fast as possible, jumped, climbed on the walls, then spread more little seed bombs left and right of the wall, imagining the seeds sprouting.

When he reached the far end of the wall, he jumped and made sure all the marked cubes were gone and being loaded. With his sword in hand, he reached up, concentrating his song into his sword like Eryn had taught him, and then he plunged it deep into the ground beneath him. He opened his mind, willing the song to spread from the sword to those tiny seeds, willing them to grow while he called water up to the surface. The area ground beneath him tingled with energy.

Everything went according to plan. He pulled his sword from the ground and ran just like Barkor did that day he'd seen him on the onboard computer screen for the first time. Jumping from canister to canister until he reached the tower. He snuck around it to the entrance where the Warship Horizon was. Quickly, he ducked and rolled under the ship and accessed the connection to the Zelk computer. He cut and disconnected Lasitor from the Zelk mainframe.

He was sweating and panting as he watched the Zelk tower. By now, Ivan should be on the ship, and Eryn should be on his heels.

As soon as the elevator moved, he noticed a little light that flickered. It was Eryn, and he was on his way. Thank the stars! Cian flickered his tiny mirror toward the descending elevator at the side of the Zelk factory. This confirmed Eryn had planted the last virus and was on his way.

Fuck yes!

Cian rolled away from the access point, grabbed his backpack and suit, and entered the warship. He had his finger on the button to close the door when he felt something tugging on his peripherals and noticed Talali, who refused to let go of Barkor. Behind them trailed three other girls while she clutched around his neck and sobbed. Probably scared to be out of the hole, Cian thought. Barkor swung her around so she could ride on his back. When she realized his intention, she stopped crying and smiled. Cian grinned; he had erotic ulterior motives. He couldn't wait to ride on Barkor's back, either.

"Where's Ish?" Cian looked around, seeing Zelk approaching from afar.

We need to move. Now!

"Ish said he would catch up with us. He had to go do something. You know how he is. A man of few words, and I didn't have time to stop for a debate. He said he knows Grayrak. He'll make it. We must go!" Barkor said as he urgently herded the girls inside.

"We have to go now. We have no more time to spare," Cian said, noticing Eryn entering via the staff entrance with his head down and a hop in his step. He was in a hurry.

"Follow me. It's time!" He pushed them inside and slammed the button to activate and close the massive cargo hold door.

The inside of the cargo hold was about the size of two football fields, one hundred by one hundred yards. Cian's skin tingled. All the excitement and buzzing energy and the nearness of Barkor were making his skin glow. Whispers of people conversing inside the loaded cubicles made him determined to get the ship off the moon. Explosive laughter drifted from the back just as he closed the docking hatch and secured it by flipping a lever over it.

"Wait here, please," he asked Barkor, smiling at the girls.

"Don't worry, General, I'll keep them safe," a young soldier said. Cian couldn't remember his name, but he looked capable and friendly.

"Come, let's strap you in," he said to the girls, who followed his directions even though he spoke Old Earth English. Cian watched them get comfortable and overjoyed as the soldier handed each a food pack. They tore into their sandwiches and gulped their water down. Yet another necessity the citizens of Phoenix prepared and packed for the refugees.

He was humbled and impressed by their leadership team for the foresight and planning of this past year.

Barkor was busy making sure the four girls were comfortable and then took a seat next to them. Cian did a quick inspection by observing the rows, inspecting them, and listening empathically for urgency or distress. He sensed only happiness and excitement; their optimism and hope were palpable in the cargo hold. And so, too, was the stench. Their musty, unwashed bodies made Cian's eyes water. He coughed and cleared his throat as he reached Barkor.

"Okay, I'm going up to the front. Please, stay here and watch over your people. It's time to leave. I'll let you know when it's time to let them out." Lifting his arm to check the time, he remembered giving Ish his watch. "The crew is waiting for me," he said reluctantly, and Barkor nodded. Barkor wasn't needy and didn't ask unnecessary questions.

He's stunning. He's strong, and he's mine. Cian willed his feet to move.

Barkor had smiled at him just as he'd shut them inside. Cian's breath hitched. He gathered himself. *The man truly takes my breath away.* He turned and made his way to the bridge command.

Movement outside made him take notice as he made his way down the corridor to the bridge. Fucking hell, yes! Peeking through the small observation window, he saw chaos outside. The Zelk that had loaded the ship seemed off-kilter. Some repeatedly bumped into one another, into walls, or had fallen over. A forklift spun in circles and smashed a Zelk flat. The constant blue light given off by the Zelk tower flickered. Some even walked into walls. Others lay sideways, tipped over and kicking like they were having seizures. They looked infected.

He noticed a line of unaffected Zelk making their way to the Horizon. Motherfucker. He ran, yelling, "Go, go, go!" The rumbling vibrations of the ship increased, confirming they were taking off. As he entered the bridge command, he saw they were already a few hundred feet high. Below them, Grayrak lay silent, and on the far-off side of the dome,

Cian saw smoke bellowing out of the dome. The hydrogen pulse reactor detonated.

"General, we have a problem. Look." His flight captain called Cian over and pointed.

Cian checked the screen and ran to the left observation window. Somehow the Zelk were holding onto the side of the ship. The line he saw earlier fluttered up and down as they climbed onto one another to get to the ship. Like ants, they climbed and barreled closer in numbers, and he couldn't see how many were already holding on.

"They're going to infect the ship!"

"We won't make it home if the ship's infected!" Cian's heart was pounding. He needed his brothers and needed to remove the Zelk now. "Don't slow down. Try to go faster. Find my brothers!" Cian yelled. "Tell them to come to the bridge immediately. Show them what's happening and tell them to meet me at the left docking hatch!" Cian turned and ran with two soldiers on his heels.

When he reached the airlock chamber, he was heaving and frantic with worry. "I'm going to suit up. Help me. Get the bridge online, ask them for an update," he said, climbing into his suit. One soldier screwed his helmet on while the other asked for an update.

As soon as his helmet was secured, the audio connection to the bridge crackled. "General Romanov here. Can you hear me?"

"Yes, General," his captain answered.

"Are they still hanging on?"

"Yes, General, they're shortening the line, and more are attaching to the ship."

"Where's my laser gun?" He patted the pockets of his suit.

"Here, General. Should we come with you?" the youngest of the two, Darrel Sinclair, asked bravely as he placed the small laser handgun in his thickly padded, gloved hand.

“No, you stay here. When my brothers come, tell them to suit up and join me.”

“Yes, General.”

Cian turned, hearing the relief as they answered. He took hold of the wheel lock to override the external locking mechanism and waited for Darrel to punch in the security override sequence. A green light blinked, and he opened the airlock chamber. Once inside, they locked the door behind him. He fastened his safety harness and snapped the harness clip onto the swivel hook with a D-ring attached to the ship. Then he lifted the cover of the button marked with a green triangle, the Zelk alphabet, for open. He slammed the big button. The external door swooshed open. His body became weightless, and he floated to the exit, then flung himself outside.

“Holy shit! I count about fifty Zelk already attached to the hull!” Hundreds more waved like flags up and down, still attached to one another.

“I must break the links!” He found a steady purchase, activated the magnetic boots, and started shooting. That got their attention, and the ones already on the ship detached from the line and crept closer to him.

Fucking frog balls. If they reach me, I’ll be overpowered. He shot two more times to break the chain of Zelk. One Zelk’s arm had broken off, and the droids holding onto him fell back into space, looking like a washing line in the wind. Cian didn’t have time to wonder where the string of robots would end up floating. He swung his torso around and shot the one closest to him in the head. That seemed to do the trick. He only aimed for their heads, careful not to shoot a hole into the Horizon.

They inched closer. Four feet to go, and they would be on him. They could enter the ship via the airlock exit if they passed him. His biggest worry was that they would infect the Horizon, and the humans wouldn’t be able to make it home. They were all as good as dead if the Zelk should make it inside.

Something pulled on him. A big Zelk, missing half its head, grabbed Cian's right artificial leg and pulled himself closer. Cian was, at that moment, glad he had the bionic leg. The Zelk would have crushed his tibia and fibula otherwise. His boots, still magnetized, clung to the ship—turning, moving, or kicking was impossible. He checked behind him. Clear.

"General, your brothers are on their way. They're suiting up," his fleet captain said.

"Thank you, Captain. I need help!"

The Zelk was on him, grabbing and pulling on his suit. Cian sat on his haunches, making himself as small as possible while he shot a few rounds left and right, he sent pieces of metal and bone flying. *Don't tear my suit,* he thought as they packed on top of him like flies on shit. Overwhelmed, he hoped for a miracle and closed his eyes.

"Hold on, brother," Eryn and Ivan shouted in his ear inside his helmet.

The pressure, pulling and pushing, disappeared. He lifted his head. Zelk and pieces of Zelk flew off him and drifted away as his brothers swatted and flung Zelk off the Horizon. Eryn zapped them with his spear. The lights in their eyes sparked and flickered off. Ivan used his sword like a baseball bat hitting home run after home run. They looked like superheroes in a Marvel movie.

"Motherfucking, fuck, fuck, fuck, that was fucking close!" Cian's skin crawled. "How are they still able to function, aren't they supposed to be dumb and infected by now?" Then he saw Barkor—suited up.

"I'm here to help." He waved from the exit of the airlock chamber. Cian waved back, smiling and happy to see him.

"Are you okay? Do you need help? I had a feeling you were in trouble and needed me," Barkor stated, holding his ball club ready to do serious damage. He looked around at the hundreds of Zelk in pieces and strewn like confetti as they floated away. "Oh, you didn't need me, after all. It looks like you have it all under control." Barkor sounded disappointed, but Cian couldn't see his face through the tinted visor of his space suit.

"Yep, under control," Eryn said and floated back to the entrance, with Ivan following on his heels.

Ecstatic that he didn't die and excited to see Barkor, without thinking, he bent his knees to thrust forward but didn't move. His fucking boots were still stuck. Pressing the deactivation button on his right forearm, he released the magnetism. Then he tried again, pushing himself forward while Barkor pulled him by his safety belt.

"Hi," Cian said and smiled widely. "Thank you for checking up on me." Now he was sure Barkor didn't know about their connection, how it worked, and what it all meant. He awkwardly hugged Barkor and bumped their helmets together. Up close, he saw Barkor's eyes glint like bright stars as he smiled at him. Having him in his arms and close to him felt bloody good and reassuring. Cian closed his eyes briefly to enjoy their closeness and the quiet joy of contentment outside in space where it was only the two of them. He wished he could smell and feel Barkor's warmth, but their puffy suits and helmets were between them.

"Are you happy to see me?" Barkor's voice was gentle, as if he cared, soft as if he worried, and teasing as if he joked. Cian liked all of it a lot. Strange how six words could carry so much meaning.

"I am," was all Cian could say.

They looked at each other until Barkor said, "Let me get you inside. It's not safe here." He turned and climbed back into the airlock, where Eryn and Ivan waited to pull them deeper into the chamber.

Cian shut the outer door behind him. "Thank you for coming to my rescue," Cian said once inside. Eryn and Ivan smiled and then inspected the rubber seals around the door as if immensely interested. Barkor removed his helmet and blinked. No sound came from his astonished-looking face. Like he couldn't believe Cian had manners or something. The blues in his eye swirled and mixed with tiny deep green flecks—his slitted pupils, much like Eryn's, narrowed in the bright overhead lighting. A visual of Barkor holding Leo tightly up on the clock tower flashed through his mind, reminding him Barkor was with another.

"Why the fuck are you with the half-man?" Jealousy burst out of his mouth when he opened it.

Cian realized he had spoken out loud, and Barkor, his brothers, and the rest of the crew must have heard him. Fuck!

"It's not what you think," Barkor said. Cian narrowed his eyes in question at him. "And my choice of friends has nothing to do with you. I'm capable of judging a person and deciding if they are worth my time."

Cian harrumphed and pretended to ignore him. He signaled for Eryn to open the bloody door they seemed to find so interesting.

"Why do you think you have any claim on me, or did I miss another step in your plan where you tell everyone around me what's going on and expect me to follow your orders?" Barkor grunted as he removed his gloves. He pinned Cian with a deadly stare before moving into his personal space. Their noses almost touched. Tipping his head left and right, he was sniffing the air like a wild animal. His hair was sweaty, and he smelled musky, like wet earth. Cian wanted to roll in it. Maybe he could bottle it.

Breaking away from the challenge of dominance, Cian couldn't undress his spacesuit fast enough. The man infuriated him. He was sure they had a connection earlier. Now he acted like he was some kind of alpha, staring him down.

"Okay, down, boy, I don't have time for this. Just forget I said anything," Cian said and slipped out of the chamber and jogged to bridge command, leaving Barkor alone.

Chapter Twelve

"Good morning to all citizens of Phoenix.

It's now six a.m.

Did you know that table tennis inspired peacemaking during a few wars?

It bridged gaps between countries to enjoy a mutual game and start peace talks.

Visit your community news page to learn more about sports and other planned activities to make our newcomers feel welcome.

Also, please make use of the toiletries and showers on board.

Breakfast is served until eight a.m.

Hope you have a fresh day!"

Juandre

2014 A.D.

Lexington, Kentucky

United States of America

Juandre Martinez was one of those lucky people—if he ignored something long enough and didn't think about it, *poof,* it disappeared. Usually, that was how he hid his inner queen identity. He pretended she never existed until he sat in front of a mirror and let her out. Which almost never happened for fear of losing Charlie in their divorce. No, he drowned himself in his work at the Trauma Unit. He suspected his ex-wife knew where her lace underwear had disappeared to, but it was for a different reason than she'd thought he had it, and he didn't care because, *poof,* it didn't happen.

Only Ryan, no, not Ryan—*Andrew* was a memory he couldn't file, shred, and purge.

It was Sunday morning, and the first thing he thought about when he opened his eyes was that the garbage fucking truck was coming tomorrow. Last night, he had chucked *Count Drac's* business card and the *Dear Juandre* letter in the kitchen trash can. And while he was at it, he chucked and dumped its contents into the big dumpster down the street from their townhouse complex. Far away from himself that he couldn't ever retrieve it. Of course, he didn't burn, shred, or flush it as a normal scorned person would. He'd intended to get rid of it and forget about it. That was exactly what he planned to do about the man of his dreams that sucked O-positive out of a bag like a dehydrated endurance athlete—yep, never happened.

After *you-know-who* left, Juandre helped Charlie to bed and cleaned up, and, yes, he might have had a quick look at *you-know-who's* business card. It was black with gold engraving with Lord Andrew Whiskey Distilleries and a telephone number written on it. Unfortunately, he didn't possess a photographic memory. Another characteristic he didn't have was impulse-control. He opened the letter and read the words, *Dear Juandre.* Pissed off at the universe, he stopped himself, and he'd trashed it. He crumpled it up, discarded his only connection to *you-know-who,* and went to bed. He was unsuccessful at falling asleep.

Taking a piss, he stared into the bowl of water, which was turning a light yellow. For how long, he didn't know. His mind must have taken a quick break. At least his kidneys were functioning fine. As a doctor, he always checked his piss; whether all doctors did was another thing he didn't know, but maybe he should ask when he was back at work.

Also, he needed to get his head checked to figure out what the fuck was wrong with him as he found himself dumpster diving. On a Sunday morning. While it was raining.

What's wrong with me?

He stood knee-deep in the trash, flinging shit over his shoulder. The rain was relentless. Bottles and scary-looking things like tampon applicators started floating around his legs. If it continued, he would be much deeper, covered in bloodborne pathogens. He was pretty sure he just stepped in a bag of kitty litter, meaning Toxoplasmosis in the next five days, or if it was old fish tank gravel, definitely mycobacterium, campylobacter, or just plain roundworm in the brain. He realized he wouldn't find that damn letter. His chances of finding it were zero against the hundreds of other diseases he could catch. He looked up to the heavens and wondered who or what could have angered the fates so damn much today. Lightning struck and lit the sky with a blinding light. It would be a beautiful sight if it weren't so damn treacherous. *A lightning storm may not be the safest place to view from inside a giant tin can.* The last thing he needed was to die and send Charlie to live with his mom. He wouldn't survive her.

Juandre swallowed the knot in his throat. He was very close to barfing. Hurriedly he jumped, grabbed hold of the side, and pulled himself out of the dumpster.

There had to be another way. He could ask Randy, a steady booty call, friend, and only lifeline to the stage and lights. He was a detective by day and the fishiest queen by night. He should be able to help. After all, he'd told Randy about his mystery man. It shouldn't be difficult to find him. All he had to do was phone the Distilleries and ask for…

Who do I ask for? The CEO? He pretended to phone them. "Hello, you don't know me? My name is Juandre, and I need to speak to your CEO, Andrew. No, he doesn't expect me, and I don't have an appointment. Yeah, right?" He'd seen that too many times not working. He huffed at himself as he sloshed back up to his home.

Now it made sense why he'd given a fake name. It was because he was a billionaire and CEO of Lord Andrew Whiskey Distilleries. "And he's a fucking vampire!" *Who else drinks blood and runs like the wind?* He couldn't hold that against him since he also gave a fake name.

His nausea and anxiousness overpowered his ability to think. He needed a shower, and he needed to phone Randy for help. Plus, Charlie would be up soon.

Juandre dragged his stinky, heartbroken self into the shower and disinfected himself. He was sure Randy would like to fuck before he asked him a favor, but he hoped not—he needed a friend.

I'm so stupid, stupid, stupid. I wish I'd read the letter. You're an idiot!

Later, after he'd dropped Charlie off at his mother's, Juandre phoned Randy.

"Hello, sexy," he answered in a deep southern drawl. "You wanna come over?" he asked. He was always up for a hard fuck and ready for him, in and out of drag.

"No, thank you. I need to speak to my momma." That was code for stop slutting and listen to me. "Plus you're the only one I can trust to talk to," Juandre said over the car's Bluetooth speaker system. Randy had always hinted at wanting to be more than kai-kai buddies, so Juandre was fairly certain he would jump at the chance to see more of him.

"Wow, this is a first, honey. You want to visit and talk with clothes on?"

"Yes, and I'm outside your house, so you better say yes."

"Yes, of course!" he squealed with excitement. "I always say you're welcome to come over for a beer or to watch a game with me. You're the one who always had a problem spending time with me."

"You know why. Listen, talk to you in a minute. I'm getting out of the car," Juandre said.

"Fuck, are you really here already?" Randy asked, but Juandre didn't answer. He switched the radio off and got out of his red *Porsche*. Randy's townhouse was nestled in arching shrubs and twining vines of honeysuckle. It smelled sweet and inviting as he approached Randy's back door. It was easier to access through the back and was much more private.

"Fuck, you look horrible. Come in, sit down. Do you want a beer or something cold? It's been stuffy lately. We get dumps of rain to cool us for ten minutes, and then it's gone." Randy didn't wait for a reply; he returned from the kitchen with two ice-cold ones, still talking to Juandre.

"Thank you," Juandre eagerly accepted one and took a big gulp, savoring the bitter-cold taste.

Randy sat down opposite him and waited for him to speak. "Well, go on. What have you done?"

Juandre took a deep breath and hoped this came out correctly. "Where should I start? Wait, what? No, I haven't done anything. Do you remember I told you about the man I picked up next to the road, the older man? I was finishing med school. I was almost twenty-three, and he was about fifteen years older than me. His name was Ryan, but I ended up calling him boy, and he called me Daddy." Randy frowned, not making the connection. "Remember me telling you about the first time I popped my gay cherry? It's been so long now, and I still think about him. Every fucking day and every fucking night, I close my eyes and fall asleep, and I think about him," he told Randy.

"Yeah, I remember you telling me about that. I was jealous. That weekend did sound really hot. That's why I tried to play a little with you like that, but it didn't work for us."

"I remember. Losing your wig mid-fellatio wasn't sexy. We kept laughing each time you called me Daddy. It's just not our thing. I get it. But that's not what I'm here to talk to you about." He took another swig of his beer. "Guess who stood in my back doorway yesterday?"

"What doorway? Do you mean your back entrance?" he asked, puzzled.

"No, silly, I should have known you would take it like that. No, get your head out of the gutter. My backdoor to the swimming pool. That doorway." Juandre drew a rectangular doorframe animatedly in the air.

Randy's eyes enlarged. "Your mystery man showed up? No stage lights. No phone calls or texts? How did he know where you lived? Tell me everything." Randy moved to the edge of his seat.

"I was making some sandwiches for Charlie and me yesterday. I promised him a day for just us. I was singing and dancing, and I turned around, and there he was. The first thing I noticed was how gorgeous he was. The weird thing was that he looked precisely the same as the last time I saw him. As I stood frozen, shocked, and slack-jawed, he greeted Charlie and promised him he was there to watch and that we should go swimming. They shook on it that he would wait for us to finish having fun. We swam for maybe an hour, and then he disappeared into the house. I should have known by the way he moved. He moved so fast that I saw only a blur line like in the movies. I thought maybe it was the water in my eyes. One fraction of a second from us to inside the house."

Randy frowned deeply, pulling a *what-the-fuck* face.

"I went searching for him. I heard something down the hallway and thought maybe he was sick. I heard moaning as if he was in pain. I knocked and thought he'd heard, so I opened the door. You won't believe..."

Randy waited patiently for him to continue. Juandre wiped his face as if to wipe the scene from his mind. He kept his voice steady. "You won't believe what I saw. He sat on the side of the toilet, suckling blood out of a blood bag like a baby from a bottle."

"What the fuck?" Randy shot out of his chair. "Blood out of a bag?"

"Yeah, like a fucking vampire..." he answered, feeling relieved to say it and realizing it sounded ridiculous.

"No, this can't be, maybe you saw him drinking juice, or something else, I don't know."

"I'm a trauma surgeon. I know exactly what a bag of O-positive looks like."

"So did he cut it open to suck it out, or did he bite into it with his...oh my god, I'm going to get us more beer." Randy collected the empty bottles and exchanged them. He handed me one and sat down, opening his. "Okay, go on."

"It looked like he bit into them and sucked them dry. He had vampire fangs. I just stood there, and then he got up and gave the empty bags to someone on the other side of the bathroom window. He never saw me. He exchanged the bags for three more and sucked on those. By the time they were shriveled up, he'd noticed me."

"Fucking fuck, what the fuck?"

"I know, right?"

"Am I hearing this right? And what did you do?"

"I just turned around, got Charlie, and watched television because what the fuck else could I do? I've seen *Hotel Transylvania* one, two, and three. There really is nothing we can do. So I hoped he would disappear and never come back, but he came to us and said he would explain and asked if I wanted to know what was going on. I just nodded and wished him away. He left his business card and a letter for me."

"Did you open it to read it?"

"Charlie fell asleep on the couch, and I just looked at it and thought, this is easy. I'm gonna chuck it away and forget about it and forget about him, and maybe when I wake up in the morning, it's gonna be like a bad dream or something, or you know, since I can forget about stuff I want to forget about easily."

"Yeah, I know you can forget about stuff easily. You've got an excellent selective memory," Randy said, pointing his bottle in Juandre's way. "You don't remember popping your nails while topping me."

Juandre chuckled, feeling guilty. He'd almost forgotten that. Birthdays and dinner invitations included over the years.

"That's why I chucked the business card. I might have seen the name of the business and his name, and you won't believe it. It's Lord fucking

Andrew Whiskey Distilleries. He's Lord Andrew. He told Charlie his name was Andrew. When we had that weekend, both of us gave a fake name. He was rough around the edges, and I thought he wasn't a person I would generally associate with. He was gorgeous and still is, but so much more. Fuck, he told me he lived in Louisiana, he'd lost his job, and had a wife and kid back in Louisiana. Now that I think of it, his accent was German." Juandre shook his head in disbelief. "He fucking conned me! I thought I fooled him, but it seems I'm the idiot." He let his head fall into his hands—embarrassed and disappointed.

"Stop your pity party. Concentrate on the fact that he's a fucking unnatural paranormal species that lives off human blood. What the fuck? If he's a vampire, then it doesn't make sense. Vampires don't drink whiskey."

"Well, this vampire does drink whiskey, or I don't know, it sounds like it's actually his distillery, his name is Andrew, and he's the CEO of Lord Andrew Distilleries."

"Girl, this is one big green booger of a situation. I can't believe what you're telling me," Randy said, jumping up and pacing in front of his sofa couch.

Juandre joined him from across the rectangular glass-top coffee table. "This is fucking weird, yes? I know. The thing is..." He sighed. "I need to find him. I don't know...it's...as weird as it sounds. I need to find him. You won't believe it. I climbed into the dumpster and searched for that letter in the rain. I know. That's how hard up I am. The filth and the tetanus." Juandre shivered from the crown of his head into his toes. "I was fucking sick with the urge to find him. I need your help. That's why I'm here," Juandre pleaded.

"Yeah?" Randy asked, staring at the carpet. He appeared to be deep in thought.

"Yes, please, I need your help. You need to help me. You're the detective. Can you help me? What should I do? Must I go there, or should I do a stakeout first? You know, in *Hotel Transylvania—*"

"What's with the animated vampires with you? There are much sexier movies out there. Have you ever listened to *Théoden* by Nicholas Bella? Now that's some raw sexy vampire shit. That dude, I'd call Daddy all night long," Randy said dreamily. Obviously already bending over and lubing himself for that vampire.

"Wipe the drool off your chin. If you had a kid, you would understand. You watch what they watch. Whether it's *Elsa* singing *Let It Go*, over and over or lip-syncing with monsters in *Hotel Transylvania*. Randy, please help me. Must I go to him, or should I try and phone him? It feels like we've both been thinking about each other for ten years and now that he's come to find me, it was probably not how he wanted to tell me. I saw the devastated look on his face when he realized I saw him. I think he came to me to tell me the truth. I don't know what I should do." Juandre sat down, rubbing his wrists.

"I know what you should do. You should forget about him," Randy said and jumped to get them a third beer each. "This is, this is not good. You're a doctor, and you're a practical man."

"I know, and honestly, it doesn't matter to me. I care about Charlie, and I care about finding him. I don't care how it sounds or what it would look like. Or, as stupid as it sounds, my reputation and credibility don't matter. I need to know. Do you understand? It's like I'm obsessed or something."

"Okay. Okay, okay, okay. I'll help you. I think you decided on the safest way forward. It's good you came to me. I'll help you. Don't worry, Momma's got your back. I've told you before that you can come to me for help with anything. So this is you being here for the right reasons. This queen will cover your ass. I'll help you search for him and check this guy out. If he gives you any trouble, I'll fuck him up. He better be a vampire.

Otherwise, he's a crazy fuck that drinks blood for fun. He was in your house. If I get a sniff of crazy, he dies," Randy explained, his voice flipping over the high notes the more excited he got, with murderous intent written all over his face. He seemed super eager to come to Juandre's rescue. "I'll check him out to see if he's dangerous or legit and if he's a vampire. Then at least, both of us know what we're dealing with."

"Thank you, it's good to know I'm not alone in this." Juandre thanked him earnestly. Randy was his only friend, and he came through for him.

"It could also be me saving you from making headlines." He made air quotations. "Trauma surgeon sells all his belongings to join a weirdo's cult. Sit around the fire and drink blood like vampires."

"Yeah, but you should see him. He's got this marble-white skin with these stunning deep green eyes. His long incisors make sense now that I think about it. Also, his lustrous blond hair is incredible. You'll see. He'll knock your breath away. I saw his face every time I had a quiet moment for myself for the past ten years. I can't forget about him. Shit!" Juandre slapped a hand over his mouth. He sounded like a teenager with a crush. "I'm thirty-three years old. I'm sorry, I'll change the subject. But please come with me to the head office. Come support me because obviously, they'll ask me if I have an appointment."

"Does he know you're coming? How will they call him down to the front door?" Randy asked.

"A walk-in needing to see the CEO. Right, I've seen that too many times not happening in the movies," Juandre said, feeling defeated.

"So you tell them you're Juandre, and Andrew needs to come down and talk to you. Wait, he visited you in the daylight?" Randy rambled and flipped questions faster than *McDonald's* pushed burgers at the drive-through.

"You know what they say about vampires. They can't sit in the sun. They'll burn and turn to dust. Why the fuck was he sitting outside? You need to ask him and let him explain this to you. Where's Charlie?"

"His mum's," Juandre said, suddenly feeling drained of all energy now that he got it all off his chest.

"Good, so we have time. I don't know if the offices will be open today because it's Sunday. Do you want another beer?"

"Yes, please." Juandre liked that Randy only drank non-alcoholic beers.

"It's so hot today," Randy said, his voice muffled inside the fridge. Juandre heard the door shut with a dull thump. Bottle caps clanged into the trash, and then Randy was handing him an ice-cold one.

"Hmmm, you know he sat outside in the shade. Maybe that's why he was in distress." Juandre started to feel sorry for the idiot.

"It seems so. That is, if he really is a vampire. Do you want to go out for dinner?"

"No, thank you. I'm not hungry."

"I'll order some pizza. You can chow if you want. Otherwise, I'll chow alone, but you shouldn't be alone now. Just relax here with me. Just chill out, and we can talk this out."

"Okay. Thank you. You know, you're my best fuck buddy and friend. We do talk most of the time. But this is different. Thank you for listening to me, and thank you for being here with me."

"Yeah, no problem. You know, I've always told you we can go out for a beer or martini and get to know each other better, but you're the one who's always busy with work. I'm always just enough between work and home. I don't mind it now. It hurt initially, but I have my sisters, unlike you. I understand you. I know who you are, and I know how alone you are, and you preferred it that way."

"I know I do. I function better if I don't have lots of social responsibilities. For years all I had to do was to go to work, come home, and be with Charlie. At this stage, that's all I want, especially now that the divorce is finalized. If Chrissy had found out about me, she would have gotten full custody. No judge would leave a ten-year-old boy with a gay man, especially a drag queen. Anyway, life is less complicated, and I like it. I'm more comfortable and feel in control."

"Not really because you want Andrew?"

"Oh Lord, what's wrong with me? What am I getting myself into?" Juandre sighed. "I have to...umm...get this behind me and talk to him. Okay?"

Randy got up and ordered pizza. He was a good guy, the sort of man everyone knew and liked. His charismatic personality was what made him most attractive. He was tall and athletically built. Average looking with brown curly hair, big, friendly brown eyes, and the widest smile that never disappeared.

After dinner and some research, Randy got a bright idea. "You know what?" he eagerly said to Juandre. "I think we should go scope this place out now. I know where it is. I know the distillery. It sits on an enormous estate just outside Lexington." Juandre agreed with Randy that the sooner the better.

"Yeah, let's go. Let's go check it out."

"That's about forty-five minutes to an hour." Randy jumped up, all excited, packing his duffle bag. "Come, I have clothes for you to wear. We need to wear something dark. And we need ski masks. And maybe we need cameras—maybe rope. Let me think. Knives. Uhm. If it's vampires, absolutely knives. Do we need garlic?"

"Fuck no. I'm not going to wear garlic around my neck. Don't think it works, remember, I fucked him already, and I don't believe the garlic does anything. We had dinner with garlic, now that I think about it."

"Okay, better your neck than mine because I'm not getting my blood sucked. So I'm wearing garlic," Randy said, serious about this mission.

A few minutes later, they left and arrived at Lord Andrew Distilleries by sundown.

The massive building on the estate had blackened windows. No surprise there. The big question was how many vampires were inside. But Randy didn't seem to be worried. He came prepared.

"They won't hurt us if we don't hurt them," Randy whispered while still sitting in his car, checking out their target, but he had the garlic and his knife if he was wrong.

Once out of the car, Randy drop-rolled and elbow crept closer, seemingly like a professional, so Juandre copied him as best he could.

"Dammit, the front doors are locked," Juandre said, pulling on the doors while Randy watched his six.

"Let's sneak in the back. Maybe someone left the back door open," Randy whispered.

"Why? If he's not here, then why try to get inside?" Juandre reasoned with Randy, who looked too inquisitive for this mission. Juandre was having second thoughts. "I don't think it's safe to sneak around a vampire's back entrances," he said, but as soon as he said it, Randy and Juandre giggled like two school boys.

Quietly as possible, they snuck to the back. They were falling over their feet as they laughed. Around them, darkness covered the earth, and the only sounds were cicadas and far-off motor vehicles on the highway.

"Shh." Randy used hand signals that only a Navy SEAL could understand. Juandre lifted his hands in question.

"I said I'll jump over and signal to you if it's safe, then you can come. Stay here," he said once they stopped laughing. Then, he shot away, jumped, pulled himself onto the wall, and rolled over by swinging his legs first.

Juandre doubted he could do such a maneuver and hoped Randy unlocked a door for him. Not long after, he got his signal. A door opened with a click and a squeak. As soon as he stepped inside, Juandre smelled chlorine and felt the high humidity of an indoor swimming pool. Randy gave him a few more indecipherable hand signals Juandre couldn't understand so he mouthed voicelessly; *what the fuck?*

It looked like Randy was planning to go down to the basement for a lookie-look. Juandre shook his head and tip-toed deeper inside the open-plan gym area. Then he swung left to hide in the locker room while Randy collected vampire intel for them. He took a few deep breaths, steadying himself, and wondered again what the fuck they were doing there.

Then a deep voice purred seductively behind him. "Hmm, hello, Juandre. This is a nice surprise."

Chapter Thirteen

"Good morning to all citizens of Phoenix.

It's now six a.m.

This is for youngsters. Lasitor has received a special request from the Tooth Fairy. Apparently, her house is falling apart because a bunch of you aren't brushing and flossing your teeth.

She said that she doesn't have time to come and collect the payment you cheated her out of, but she will only pay for good-quality teeth from now on.

If she sees badly taken care of teeth, she'll not continue doing business with you. She sends a special thank you to Johnson Reily, whose tooth was in such good condition, it saved her house from collapsing in totality.

She was so glad she used your tooth as the keystone in the arch above her bed.

Breakfast is served until eight a.m.

Hope you have a tooth decay-free day!"

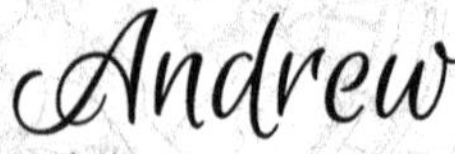

Andrew

2014 A.D.

Lord Andrew

Whiskey

Distilleries

Lexington, Kentucky

United States of America

Lust, love, and infatuation—mix those three together and Google it. My face will pop up. With fangs, of course. When Andrew smelled him, his fangs dropped, and his cock got hard. The tantalizing smell unique to Juandre engulfed and consumed Andrew so no reasoning, but only instinct drove him forward.

They charged forward, and mouths collided. Like two rabid dogs fighting, Juandre planted his lips against his, rasping his tongue over his incisors and slipping deep into Andrew's predatory mouth. The kiss was passionate and aggressive. Andrew withdrew his fangs and went to town on Juandre's deliciously sweet mouth. Passion built layer upon layer until they were breathless and dizzy for oxygen.

Andrew stopped the dancing of tongues for a second. Weaving his fingers into Juandre's hair, he fisted a handful and pulled his head back. "Why are you sneaking around, Juandre? I told you to phone, and I'd talk to you." Andrew couldn't wait for an answer. He pulled Juandre closer and dove back into kissing that cheeky fucking mouth.

Juandre whined and answered between breaths of air. They found a rhythm. Kiss, breath, question, kiss, breath answer, kiss breath question, kiss breath answer.

Juandre seized his hips with eager hands and steered him backward, pressing Andrew's naked back against the cold granite tiles on the wall. His thin speedo wasn't hiding his arousal. His cock head popped past the elastic and leaked pre-cum. Andrew was wild with need and reined in his urge to bite Juandre and make him his. For a second, they locked gazes as if to confirm their presence, then they brutally attacked each other's mouths, only stopping now and then, heaving a few breaths and looking at each other. Seeing Juandre's face reassured Andrew that this was real and was genuinely happening. They moaned and clutched fistfuls of hair and skin.

"Why are only my cock and balls out?"

"Don't know, do something about it, boy," Juandre said as he squeezed and tugged on Andrew's balls. Pleasure zinged through Andrew's body.

"Say it again, Daddy," he begged in a low growl into Juandre's mouth. They were being reckless. Anyone could come into the gym, and it was beautiful. Andrew didn't want to spoil the intensity of the moment. The need between them was powerful. It was a thing that never cracked or broke, no matter how far or thin it stretched through time.

Juandre let out soft sigh after soft sigh when Andrew tugged at his shirt and slipped a hand under the hem, resting his fingers on the warm, hard ripple of muscles across his stomach. The sound of his throaty groan shot straight through Andrew.

"Have to have you, please, Daddy," Andrew begged.

"Ah, yes, take me, boy," Juandre answered. "Is it safe here? Can anyone come into the gym?" Juandre asked, out of breath and panting.

"Usually, it's only me using the pool area this time of night," Andrew said as his hips slid forward and back again to focus on the snap and zipper of Juandre's cargo pants. "I'm going to undress you, and then I'm going to fuck you right here against the wall, Daddy," he said, sounding feral and hungry. "I'm in charge tonight. Your sneaky ass needs punishment."

"Yes, pleassssse," Juandre uttered, accentuating the "S" in Andrew's ear. Andrew flung him around and switched places so his chest pressed against the spot his back just heated.

"Palms flat against the wall. Don't move," Andrew commanded, and Juandre followed his orders obediently. Andrew fell to his knees behind him and removed his shoes and pants. "Spread your legs, Daddy," Andrew said, enjoying watching him eagerly open them for him. Andrew left his shirt on since it was cold against the black marble tiles.

He grabbed Juandre's muscled glutes, squashing and squeezing them softly and pulling them wide, exposing and softening his hole.

"Good god, boy!" Juandre exclaimed as Andrew bit into his left butt cheek. Andrew wanted to sink his fangs into them, but this wasn't the time. Juandre's masculine musk aroused the fuck out of him, so he reached around Juandre's hip to give his cock a few hard tugs.

"Ah yes, just like that," Juandre said approvingly, but Andrew let go of his cock out of spite. His own was also painfully hard, protruding, and hanging out of the thin material, unable to accommodate its size and weight. He pushed the sides down his hips, fully freeing his genitals from their confinement.

Andrew stroked Juandre's hairy thighs, noticing that he tried his best to hold still for him, but he couldn't control the involuntary fine tremors in his upper legs. "Look how hungry you are for your boy to fuck you. Daddy, you're bloody quivering for me."

"Yes, boy, I fucking am. Now please, do something, or I'll come all over this wall anyway."

"No, that won't do. It sounds to me like you need a cock ring. You want me to roll one on for you, Daddy?" Andrew asked with a lustful voice in his ear.

"Yes, please. Please, Andrew, my boy," Juandre begged. Lucky for him, Andrew had some supplies in his locker.

"Stand still, and don't move," he said and sprinted there, grabbing a bottle of lube and cock ring.

"I'm back," Andrew said to put him at ease. He must have felt the movement of wind on his ass, but he didn't say a word. Andrew guessed he expected that since he thought he was a vampire.

"Come here," Andrew said and reached around him, applying a bit of lube, squeezing and pulling the skin tight over his cock. Then he rolled the ring down to the base. Juandre hissed and swore. Andrew tested the movement of the silky skin covering his Daddy's penis with hard downward and lighter upward strokes.

"Andrew, I don't think— your plan is working, my boy. Ugh," Juandre said and groaned in ecstasy.

He's coming.

Andrew grasped his leaking cock, smearing the residual lube over it. Then pushed it against Juandre's tight hole and forced his cock head into Juandre's sphincter.

"Oh, my fucking god," Juandre screamed. The words reverberated over the swimming pool water and into the night. Andrew held onto his hips, pushing deeper and savoring the tight pressure and heat of his hole.

Despite the pain, he'd not pulled away. Instead, he begged for more. "Fuck me, boy, Andrew, please, Andrew, I need this."

Andrew dreamt of this.

"Oh, fuck!" he repeated.

Andrew didn't reply but answered his plea as he pushed the remaining length of his cock deep into him. They stood flushed together—both quivering. Andrew panted, and Juandre gasped between crying, whimpers, and begging for more. Andrew waited and felt Juandre relaxing, then pulled out and slammed back into him.

"You feel so fucking good!" Andrew roared as he pulled out and pushed back again. "I doubt I can go any longer," Andrew said and held still on the precipice of an orgasm.

Juandre chuckled. "Just hammer me, Andrew," he begged.

"I missed you for so long. I thought our love-making would at least be longer than five minutes," Andrew said, licking and savoring the sweat off his shoulder. Andrew had him tagged, and still, he didn't move for him. Just for that, Andrew loved him already.

"May I bite your shoulder? I want to taste your blood on my tongue when I come deep inside you."

"Will you turn me into a vampire?" Juandre asked, panting.

Andrew chuckled, amused. "No, I'm not a vampire. I'm only breaking your skin, only a scratch for one drop of your blood." He could taste his blood already. But he waited.

"Yes... you may," he finally said, and Andrew only used his right fang like a needle and pierced his skin.

Tiny prickles, like minute electric sparkles, danced through his body, and Andrew moaned deep guttural sounds of delight as Juandre's blood flowed over his tongue. "I'm coming." His voice was guttural and low, droning like a giant waking up after eons of sleeping under mountains. His body contracted and convulsed, his knees wanted to buckle, and Andrew hung onto Juandre.

"I'm not stopping. I want more." Juandre grunted, and the quick sloshing sounds told him Juandre was pummeling his own cock. Andrew reached around to grab hold of Juandre's heavy ball sack. He left his cock where it was. He knew his cock was still tapping on Juandre's prostate.

"I'm going to cum!" Juandre said hurriedly.

"Yes, you are, you beautiful, handsome man," Andrew whispered into his ear, taking another lick of blood from the trapezius muscle over his scapula. Then, he pulled his cock out. "Turn around, come in my mouth, Daddy."

Juandre turned instantly, and Andrew fell to his knees. With a quick grab, pull, roll, he slipped his daddy's cock ring off. Juandre weaved his fingers through his hair and pushed his cock deep into his mouth forcefully as Andrew retracted his fangs and swallowed him down his throat.

"Ahh fuck!" Juandre hissed out, pulling his face into the nest of his trimmed pubic hair. "Don't stop sucking. Don't stop...oh, my boy, fuck, please don't stop! Feels so damned fucking good! Oh, god, boy, never have...ever!" Juandre yelled as he blasted his cum down Andrew's throat.

Andrew swallowed and swallowed, not allowing a drop to escape his mouth. He wanted all of his Daddy inside him. He tasted exquisite, and Andrew knew he would never let him go again.

"Hello! Are you two done? I want to go home. It's Randy, Juandre's friend, the business meeting you had, is it over?" Juandre's friend called from outside the pool area. Andrew was on his feet and tucking their cocks still half hard into underwear and speedos. Then helped Juandre to get his cargo pants up. He quickly wrapped a towel around his waist.

"Jesus fucking Christ, where to now?" Andrew told a chuckling Juandre.

"Where you at? We're searching for you. Juandre and Andrew? I have two guards with me," Randy called. He was smart. As gay men, they knew anyone could be a bigot, and out of mutual concern and respect, they stuck together. Their steps were coming closer.

Laughing, they scrambled and fell on the pool deck chairs, pretending they were talking this whole time. Then Randy and two human guards appeared.

"Ah, there you are, sir. We found this one hanging around and wanted to make sure he's with you, sir," the biggest of the two guards said in a southern drawl.

"Yes, everything's fine. They came by tonight instead of tomorrow, and we have just wrapped it up," Andrew said and waited.

No one spoke. The smell of semen drifted with the chlorinated mist. Andrew hoped it was only him smelling it and that the sharp chlorine was masking it. His security guards seemed uncomfortable and perplexed.

"I'll call it in and clear the alert. Sorry for disturbing you, sir." The big guy nodded, and the other guard stepped forward.

"So sorry, sir," the other guard said with interest. He wasn't looking sorry when he noticed Juandre sprawled out on the chair next to Andrew.

"Nothing to be sorry about. You were only doing your job, so thank you," Andrew said. He noticed the unapologetic intentional eagerness to see Juandre's face.

"Do you need anything, sir?" he asked without taking his gaze off Juandre, and Andrew didn't like it. Juandre waved at him.

"No, thank you, my man, good night. You may be on your way." Andrew excused them shortly. He didn't know these men. He would have to ask Tony tomorrow who they were. He brushed their inquisitiveness off as they probably couldn't believe Juandre and Randy had snuck by them. He hoped that was the reason. They turned to leave.

When they were out of earshot, Randy whispered, "Fuck you two. It sounded like you were mauling each other in here." He pointed to the open-plan pool and gym area around them. "It's fucking empty and hollow. Sound travels far at night. They probably heard the two of you all the way to the main road."

"How did the two of you sneak by them?"

"I don't know, we just drove in and parked the car. They didn't stop us," Randy said, and Andrew pointed to a chair, indicating he should come to sit down.

"I'm thirsty. Anyone in the mood for whiskey?" Andrew asked, smiling at Juandre, who flapped a wrist lazily, looking like a man who'd just been fucked good.

Chapter Fourteen

"Good morning, and a special welcome to our new citizens.

It's now six a.m.

I am Lasitor, your community AI, and I am not Zelk.

I'm your friendly fountain of news and information.

You may visit your community news page on any device connected to the general network. Just say my name, and I will respond. You may ask me anything.

There are tons of educational videos and other information about living on Earth.

Don't worry. We are here to help.

Breakfast is served until eight a.m.

Hope you have an insightful day!"

General Cian Romanov

95 A.T.

The Warship Horizon

Cian grunted like a lion with an abscessed molar at the fucked-up situation he found himself in. Everyone in the room eyeballed him. Even their Anubis; Rotty, Igor, and Devil eyeballed him, too. Yeah, not even twenty-four hours had passed after Barkor had thrown him a bone and got his hopes up. Cian was sure they had a connection when Barkor came to help him outside.

No, not a bone but a bloody chew toy to keep him busy while Barkor fussed over Leo on his deathbed and expected Cian to watch him care for his boyfriend. *For fuck's sake, my mate is holding another man in his arms.* Another fucking half-man. He eyeballed them back. Making sure they got the message to *back the fuck off.* They turned their gazes back to watch Barkor stroking Leo lovingly. It reminded Cian that Leo was with Barkor while Cian wasn't. He sighed hopelessly. They eyeballed him again.

"What?" he barked, crazed with jealousy and irritated at Eryn, Ivan, Donali, and Sarinka. Little Talali flinched, peeped like a mouse, and made herself smaller, lying beside Leo on the bed. *Fuck!* Now he felt like shit. He scared her.

Ivan cleared his throat. "Go do something. Please leave, brother," he said pointedly with sad, sorry eyes. He reached out for a sympathetic touch, but Cian stepped back. His brother better not touch him. He felt like breaking his arm, crushing his hand, or wrapping his hands around his throat and strangling him. He was the one who invited him. Basically pushed him inside the fucking suffocating somber tomb. A reminder that he was not enough. Not good enough.

"No, and you know why," he answered and pinned his brother with a death glare.

"Then be quiet and have some respect," Ivan said, and Eryn chuckled in the back.

Cian stepped forward because someone had to say something. "Listen, man, I'm well aware that you're dying and at your end, and your body can't take one minute longer, but don't you have something, like last wishes?"

All the faces around Leo's deathbed looked questioningly at him. Leo included.

"I mean, there's a word for that, like, hmmm, no, not bucket list. What's the word again?"

Ivan looked like he wanted to skin Cian alive, but Cian didn't have time for this. *People always die, and you should expect that fact the day you're born.*

"What I mean is, do you have any last wishes? You know some people want to see the sun." Everyone in the room relaxed. He heard a few exhalations and thought he was on the correct path. "Or maybe you want to end your suffering a bit faster, like—"

"Get the fuck out of here," Barkor shouted through gnashing teeth.

"Cian, brother, it's better if you go. Let's go for a walk," Eryn said, guiding him towards the door. Cian suspected Eryn needed an excuse to escape as well.

"No, I want him here," a soft raspy voice said, barely audible.

Cian stopped, and Eryn turned just as Leo started to speak. "No, he must stay. I want you here, please, Cian."

"See, he wants me here," Cian told no one in particular.

Leo smiled weakly. Then he looked at Barkor. "Do you remember when we first met?" he whispered. Barkor shook his head as if he didn't remember.

"Fuck, Barkor, I'm so tired," Leo mumbled. "Please, love, you haven't slept in like a week. You need to sleep," he slurred but turned his head to face Cian. The overhead lights sparkled in his dying eyes.

He's crying.

Leo lifted his head, and their gazes met. "Please look after Barkor. I ask as sincerely as a dying man can muster. I was thinking about how we met and how it all came together for the...do you think it was some grand scheme that brought us together?"

"Leo, you're breaking my heart. Please stop talking. You're tiring yourself out," Barkor said, and his voice cracked as if on the verge of crying. "Rest up, and then we can talk about it tomorrow," he said, and it irritated the crap out of Cian.

"He's right. I have to die anyway, whether it's now or next week. It doesn't matter. There are more important things to worry about than sitting here and holding me."

"No, you know I'll miss you," Barkor said.

Someone's teeth gnashed. Cian looked around and realized it must have been him because everyone's eyes were focused on him again.

"You are such a man, and thank you. Without you, this ship wouldn't have been packed with people on their way to living a better life. You are brave, and you're a hero," Barkor whispered.

"Motherfucker," Cian swore his frustration. This sissy mushy shit pushed him past the point of uncomfortable. He wanted to grab Barkor and run and make him feel better.

"Get out!" Barkor and the rest erupted.

Cian turned to leave, feeling relieved, but Leo persisted. "No, I want him here. Come back, please, Cian."

"See, even the boyfr—" He stopped himself before he sounded like a loser.

Barkor kissed Leo softly on his forehead. "I know what you're up to, and no, it won't work," Barkor said gently, and it felt like a thousand knives pierced Cian's heart. He opened his mouth and wanted to say something, but his brother poked at him and gave him the stinkiest eye. Eryn seemed to play both sides by tapping him on his shoulder and shaking his head.

No surprise there, treating me like I'm a fucking toddler.

Cian did feel sorry for him, but it felt like a lost cause to stand there and reminisce about things of the past. "Okay, tell me what you want so I can return to doing my work and maybe get you where you want to go. Do you want to die on Earth? What can I do for you?" Cian asked and decided to be nice. *After all, it is Leo's deathbed.*

One corner of his mouth pulled up in a skewed smile at Cian. "Please tell our story to the people on Earth so that it may go on forever."

Little Talali sat up, crossed her legs, and placed a small hand on Leo's chest. "I'll tell your story, Leo," she said in a soft sweet voice.

Barkor placed his hand on hers.

"Thank you, Talali, you're such a good friend to Leo." He turned to Cian, and their gazes met as he willed him to listen as he said, "We will tell all your stories, and we will never forget you." Barkor's voice broke as he nodded his head affirmatively, and Cian nodded back.

Suddenly he felt like a tsunami of Barkor's emotions knocked him off balance, and his mate's intense sadness assailed him.

This is too much; I can't take this. I'm going to break down and cry in front of them. Again, I'm the bloody third wheel. It's emotions for Leo and not me.

Cian turned to leave, but Eryn blocked the door, planting his legs wide and stumping his spear into the floor with a clang of finality.

"Stay, listen, and shut up," Eryn told him. Cian narrowed his tear-filled eyes at his brother-in-law. Eryn spoke into his mind telepathically. *Brother, get a hold of yourself. Close your eyes for a second and tell yourself you're as hard as a rock. Everything will be all right. He's not his boyfriend. He's a friend. A good friend.*

Cian felt calmer as Eryn's good juju washed over him, and he closed his eyes. When he felt he'd collected himself, he turned and crossed his arms like the Commander General he was and thought—I am a granite boulder.

Leo coughed and cleared his throat. Coughed again, and Barkor offered him a sip of water. Leo thanked him and began to speak. "We tried countless times to escape, but they always found us. They brought us back to their bunker and then punished us ruthlessly. That's how I ended up like this. Some escaped, but others like myself couldn't, not even by killing ourselves."

Talali looked at Cian, her frailty breaking his heart. She was clean, and her hair was tied up in a ponytail. Her face was small, not bigger than the palm of his hands. She had dark eyes, determined eyes. Eyes that had seen enough for ten lifetimes. Like the rest of the crew, she wore the standard black body suit for which her body was scanned and printed. Their body suit machines had decreased in size, and every room had been outfitted with a suit printer. The material was completely recyclable, so suits were printed on demand. Instead of washing the clothes, they disinfected the material while being broken down into a liquid, and reloaded into the printer for fresh daily wear.

Cian listened intently while trying not to see Barkor, who stroked Leo's forehead.

"If it weren't for Sarinka"—he nodded to her—"the girls wouldn't have made it."

Cian looked at her, smiling sincerely, and watched Donali looking at her with admiration. He was definitely under her spell.

"Why Grayrak? Where does the name originate? I've always wondered about that," Cian asked.

"Oh, that's from the moon's color, the first humans called it gray rock, and later it just became Grayrak," Barkor answered.

Cian shifted uncomfortably from one foot to the other. "Interesting," Cian said.

Leo continued to smile knowingly at him. The half-man freaked him out. He irked him.

Cian looked discreetly at Sarinka, scared to get knifed between the eyes. She was all cleaned up and dressed in her favorite color, black, and armed to the teeth with all kinds of shiny knives and weapons. Sarinka was a swift and silent killing machine. A pretty little thing, but the most dangerous female Cian had ever met.

"Without Cian's plan, I doubt the humans would ever have had a chance of escaping," Sarinka added.

Oh, it's compliment time, Cian thought sarcastically. The room erupted in encores.

Leo whistled weakly. Everyone quieted down. Then he spoke. "There's one thing I must ask of you and Cian privately." He coughed and looked at Talali, Sarinka, and the other men in the room. "Will you please leave? I want to speak to them alone."

At first, no one moved, not registering the request. Eryn cleared his throat, opening the door. "Come, you heard him. He wants to talk to them."

Talali got up and jumped, and Eryn caught her. One by one, they left, nodding and squeezing his shoulder, saying goodbyes.

Suddenly Cian was nervous, and he guessed he knew what Leo was about to ask. Barkor would never do it, and he would hate him for it. He might as well say goodbye to Barkor.

"I know I'm weak and dying," Leo said, and Cian's gaze locked with Barkor. Barkor broke the intense stare and got up to get a fresh cool cloth, and Cian followed every movement. Undoubtedly, he was nervous about what Leo was going to ask. Barkor returned, folding the cloth into a small square as he waited. Leo chuckled wheezily. Cian listened and expected Barkor to scrutinize him, but he heard nothing. Just white noise. *Is he blocking me?*

Barkor wiped Leo's forehead. "What do you want to ask us? You know you can ask me anything, and I will do my best to get it for you."

Cian knew that wasn't the truth. He knew what Leo would ask would not go over as easily. He suspected Leo would ask them again to be euthanized and smothered to death. That was what Leo wanted since they'd abducted him. That was all he wanted, and he begged and cried for it. Barkor promised that if he helped them, he said he would do it, but Leo had become Barkor's pet project or something, and they spent the last two years together. Who knew what the two had done? Cian really didn't want to imagine that. But it was time, and Barkor had to know that.

"Yeah, just ask. This anticipation is giving me a migraine. Ask away," Cian said, and he meant he would do anything in his power to give him his last wish swiftly and painlessly.

"I suspect most people misunderstand you," Leo said briskly, surprising Cian. "You say what needs to be said without wondering who would think what, and you never change your words so that others won't take an affront from them." Cian stood astonished.

He widened his stance and crossed his arms. "Hmmm, so do you think Barkor likes it or not?" Cian blurted the question. He didn't know if he wanted an answer, but he really wanted to ask it. It burned his tongue so that he had to spit it out. Barkor sat wide-eyed. Not a peep came from his mouth—*such a bloody square.*

Leo cleared his throat, interrupting their intense visual communication. "I know he loves it, even if he doesn't want to admit it."

"Leo!" Barkor stomped his foot, and Leo chuckled, coughed, and paused to catch his breath. His head fell back onto the pillow with a plop. Cian didn't want to, but he was starting to like Leo. Barkor ignored Cian.

"I'm going to say this as straightforwardly as possible. I want the two of you to make love to each other, and I want to watch before I die."

"Say again? Because I think I heard you wrong," Cian exclaimed, watching Leo and then Barkor, who seemed perplexed and shocked, just as he was.

"No, you can't ask that of me...of us. We don't know each other and...fuck, help me here, Cian," Barkor said.

Cian looked frantically from Barkor to Leo, wondering why he should suddenly say something. "Absolutely fucking not. I don't have time for this. This is childish and not to mention extortion from the dying. Sorry, but I don't have any inclination to—" Cian waved his hand back and forth in the shape of a triangle between Barkor, Leo, and himself like he was leading a symphony. Even thinking about the word threesome gave him hives. He was sure he was getting an allergic reaction. He itched and struggled to breathe. "Sorry—not interested. A big motherfucking no! Done that, and no! I have work to do. No!" Cian spattered *no* repeatedly while gasping for air. He turned, slammed the exit button, and fell into the corridor. Bracing himself on the wall, he heaved and stumbled to his room.

Just as he rounded the corner to the staff corridor, he heard a shrill voice screaming. Cian jerked upwards, listening. He waited, wondering from which direction the screaming came. Three steps forward, then he heard it again. It was close. It sounded muffled. Like it came from... a few more steps, then he stopped. He heard scuffling.

Then definitely an older male voice. "Hold still, you bitch, or I'll slice your throat."

Cian looked up and down the corridor to guess the distance and area he heard it.

He didn't want to give himself away but wanted to call for help. He had to find this perpetrator himself. *Someone's in trouble! On my fucking ship!*

"Ouch, you bitch!" the male shouted, and then he heard a dull thumping and a young female crying.

"I will never let you touch me again!" the female shouted.

"Shut up. All I want is food. You need to go get me something to eat and drink." The man grunted.

Someone with a voice much like Talali said, "I will not!"

"You will, or I'll kill your sisters," the man said.

"We will not. We'll report you to the general. You're supposed to be dead, Grizzly!" another female voice said.

"Yeah, we aren't your slaves anymore!"

Now Cian was sure it was Talali and her three friends or sisters by the sound of it.

"Shut up, you bitch!"

"No, Grizzly, no!" The girls screamed, and Cian jumped into action.

He's going to kill someone.

Cian lifted his head and shouted, "Grizzly, is that you? We've been searching for you! Come out! I know you're in here!" Cian hoped to buy some time while he figured out where they were. Silence. *Fuck this!* He walked, fiddling with the doors, buttons, and handles in the corridor, but they were silent, and nothing opened.

"Lasitor, the hostages, where are they?" he called into his pager on his shoulder, hoping the AI was on standby.

He answered immediately, "Sir, they're four steps forward and then the service shaft on your right."

Cian found the door and said, "I know you're in here. This is the General of the Horizon. I'm opening the hatch. If you hurt anyone, expect the same fucking justice to be done to you. You understand me?" *Sick fucker!*

"I'll gut them all! Stay away!" Grizzly hollered, and Cian sent his emotional feelers out. Grizzly was nervous, and the four girls were scared. *No one is dead yet.*

A crowd was forming around him. He indicated for them to step back and be quiet and that he had it under control. They stood wide-eyed and waiting.

"You don't understand. Even if you gut them, you're still fucked. We will come in and rip you apart. Your only choice is to let them go and come out. Only then might you have a chance to see Earth. Come out. I'm unarmed. I'm only concerned about the girls' safety. You will only see Earth if they're unharmed," Cian said and wasn't in the mood to negotiate. The crowd grew restless, and Cian silenced them by placing his forefinger in front of his mouth.

"You better keep your word. I'm not hurting them. All I want is food and water. I wasn't hurting them. They know me. I'm a good man. I take care of my own," Grizzly said.

The crowd murmured, shaking their heads. Cian placated them with calm-down gestures and affirmative nodding while showing them with his eyes; *I know, I know the fucking bastard. Please be quiet. They're about to be opening the door*. Once they were out, he planned to get rid of the bastard.

Cian heard Talali speak. "The general's taking all of us to swim in the ocean, and you could come, too. Just don't hurt us, please, Grizzly," she begged, and Cian's heart shattered for the girls, stoking his fury towards Grizzly. He wanted to scream *open the fucking door, you motherfucker!*

Years of training and Ivan's nagging to think had prepared him to reel in his temper. He decided to calm himself and suppress his true feelings about the man and let Grizzly think he was safe. Make him think he was in charge. He looked at the crowd, showing them to zip it.

"Grizzly, my man, we were looking all over for you. You're our honored guest. The people on Earth are all talking about you. They're singing songs about you. How big and strong you are. A knowledgeable leader and a man who survived the Zelk. We'd be honored to have dinner at my table with the last Disciple joining us."

Cian heard chuckling behind him. Eryn and Ivan stood there.

It looks like you have it under control, brother. We have your back. Eryn spoke telepathically to Cian.

Cian nodded his thanks to them. They were armed and ready. Rotty, Igor, and Devil stood beside them. They were so big they nearly filled the width of the hallway. *What the fuck?* They were bigger and very eager to attack. Their yellow eyes were pinned on the door as if they understood every word that was said. Cian waited, placing the onus on Grizzly.

After a minute of silence, the door swooshed open, and the girls came running for Cian. He did a quick summation—besides a small superficial cut on the one girl's face, they seemed to be okay. He acknowledged them and pushed them behind him to Ivan and Eryn.

Now it's you and me! The thought came just as Grizzly strolled out. It looked like he had combed his hair to the side just now, and it lay oily and flat against his head. His face was raw with skin cancer. The vilest man Cian had ever lain eyes upon. He strutted out there like he owned the place. One look at the crowd, and they cringed at seeing him.

Please, I don't want them freaking out. I plan to give him his last meal and then take him to see Earth as promised. Tell them to play along. It will be lots of fun!

Grizzly gasped, interrupting Cian's telepathic conversation with his brothers. Rotty, Igor, and Devil growled. The crowd stood soundlessly, watching the show. Cian was planning to entertain tonight.

He spoke to Ivan and Eryn mentally. *Let the people know it's not real.*

Cian didn't want to touch him. He looked pleadingly back at Eryn, who loved to skewer people and drown them. *Brother,* Cian begged Eryn with his eyes.

Eryn stepped back apologetically and replied telepathically, *It's your ship and your rules. Ask yourself, what would our fathers have done?* Ivan nodded his agreement.

How did he miss that his brothers respected him like this? He couldn't skewer Grizzly, but he would bullshit him and show him Earth from space. He reached back, opening and closing his hand, asking Ivan to hand him a weapon. He expected a laser gun, but his brother handed him his sword. It felt strange, not like his own, but it would do. He decided to use the sword as a scare tactic and improvise and use his wit and charm.

"Grizzly, our last Disciple, do you know who we are? Do you know why you're a Disciple?" Cian asked.

"I'm pretty sure you're the general of this ship. Pleased to meet you, General." He held out his hand, and Cian reluctantly shook it.

I'll soak my hand in disinfectant later.

"These are my brothers, Ivan, my twin, and his husband, Eryn." Cian chuckled, knowing they also hated shaking his hand. Eryn and Ivan took it and gave Cian the—*we're warning you, brother*—eyes.

"And these are our pets—"

Eryn and Ivan smiled and then nodded. They moved into the crowd to spread the word. Cian winked at Talali, and she seemed to catch on fast. Grizzly stood open-mouthed, staring at the Anubis and then at Eryn and Ivan towering over the humans down the corridor. His gaze returned to Cian. Their inhuman height and golden weapons had triggered a memory, and Cian saw when realization dawned on him.

"I, I have some kind of memory," he said, stuttering, and it seemed he was still coming to terms with what he was seeing.

"Grizzly, come, let's have a feast." Cian put the flat of his hand on Grizzly's back and gave him a friendly shove forward. "Come, let me show you where I dine," he said and pointed the way with his brother's sword to the dining area.

Cian wished Barkor was here, but Leo lay dying, and he knew he wouldn't leave Leo alone.

Grizzly spoke of himself, never stopping between bites and slurps, never realizing everyone watched them. Cian thought Grizzly liked eating with everyone watching him; that was probably how it was on Grayrak. How else could he be the only big fat fucker on the moon? He bloody ate everyone's food. Now and then, he would look at Rotty, Igor, and Devil nervously.

His green and brown sports jacket had one out of four buttons left in the front. He sucked his big tummy in and tied the jacket. The one button near popping while conveying that he thought of himself as upper-class or royalty. Then he flattened the creases and held his head high. He talked nonstop.

Cian didn't even listen. He was in his own head thinking how this man had chopped off Leo's arms and legs and then kept him as a plaything. The more he thought about what Talali and the girls looked like when they found them, the more the man repulsed him. It was all this man's fault—him and his Disciples.

When he finished his fourth plate of food, he halted shoving food into his mouth, eyeing the fifth plate on the table. "Why do you have Anubis on your ship? The last Anubis died when the rocket they were on exploded. How did you manage to have three of them?" he asked so condescendingly that Cian wanted to slam his head onto the table, but then he had to touch Grizzly, so he postponed.

He smiled brightly, straightened his back, and ensured the surrounding crowd heard his answer. "Grizzly, because—" Cian was interrupted by Eryn and Ivan.

"Sorry, we had to deliver a message. You were saying, brother?" Ivan and Eryn each grabbed a chair, swinging the backside to the front, threw a leg over, and leaned their arms on the backrest.

Cian dragged his brother's golden sword closer and gave Grizzly an intimidating look. "Oh, Grizzly wanted to know why we had not one but three Anubis when he was sure the last ones died on a rocket that crash-landed on the moon."

Grizzly shoved another big heap of mashed potatoes into his mouth. Chewed it open-mouthed and nodded at Cian and his brothers. Eryn puckered his mouth and lifted an eyebrow. Ivan blinked expressionlessly.

"I'm sure he wonders because the Disciples wore whistles. They commanded the Anubis because they were the chosen ones." Cian winked at them.

"Really, so that's what happened to our rocket?" Eryn blurted out as if he didn't know. He'd asked Barkor as soon as they were able to. They couldn't believe out of the thousands of humans, supposedly a hundred forty-four thousand, only a little over two thousand survived.

"Your rocket?" Grizzly coughed, and droplets of spittle and mashed potatoes flew in Cian's direction. *Yuk.* He swerved to the right missing it. Grizzly chuckled. He saw that and then turned to Eryn, waiting for an answer.

He's vile and stupid. He seemed to be challenging Eryn. Now everyone was really listening.

"Yeah, we sent it up, hoping you had some kind of automatic landing system programmed on your side. You didn't, and all those people died?" Eryn said. He had taken their deaths very personally.

Grizzly tipped his head to the side. "I asked you why you had a hand in sending the rocket to the moon, boy?"

"Let's just say it was that or let them drown," Eryn answered, not fazed by Grizzly's passive aggressiveness.

"We were ready, but when it came closer to the lunar orbit, the approach was too fast, and they crashed. It was a mess because no one was suited up. By the time they had them inside the dome, they were dead. Also, our provisions craft never arrived, and we all had to make do. No food, Anubis, and no one to call the water for us. Just whining useless women and children who expected heaven and instead got hell. No gods and no fucking promised prince." Grizzly had spoken animatedly and pointed his eating utensil to the crowd. They murmured a reply, but Cian couldn't figure out what they said.

Ivan straightened up. Cian felt his skin crawling.

If Grizzly was alive ninety years ago, that meant he might be like them. He was bigger than the average human. He didn't look like Barkor or Eryn. Maybe he hatched from another batch.

"What do you mean you had to make do? What did you eat? I know you didn't share the water." Ivan looked at Grizzly, and all three could read his mind. *They did—they ate their dead.*

"Don't tell me you ate them."

Grizzly looked at the crowd. Eryn, Ivan, and Cian followed his gaze. "What else did we have to eat?" Grizzly asked them.

"We never did. You and your Disciples did," a man shouted back at Grizzly.

"They wanted meat and didn't want to wait for the crops. And when the crops were ready, they had taken that, too!" a woman yelled from the back of the crowd.

"It's their fault the Zelk started taking body parts. They learned from them what to do. They're the ones who built the tower for themselves," a man shouted.

"He's a walking corpse. He's supposed to be dead. He is Zelk!" an older man cried hoarsely while pointing at Grizzly.

"They left us on our side, and when they needed more body parts, they started taking our children!" another older man shouted.

Cian never knew the history. Sarinka never told him. This was what Ish mentioned when they met him. He said they wanted to live forever and created a central tower to collect their minds.

Cian spoke to Eryn and Ivan. *Brothers, this is seriously sick.*

"I say we cut him up like he had us cut up," a man shouted, and the crowd went ballistic.

Eryn got up. "Please, we will make sure he meets his justice. Remember, this is an important man. He and his kind have worked hard to help you survive on the moon," Eryn said, and Cian felt him sending calming energy into the crowd.

"Yeah, give him his justice!" they shouted, fists in the air. Grizzly looked taken aback. Cian had enough. This was escalating.

"Come, I'll show you Earth from my private outlook, it's small, but you can still see it," he said, and Grizzly smiled, wiped his mouth, and got up. The crowd followed.

When they reached the airlock chamber, he opened the door pointing to the small blue orb.

"Another few days, and we'll be home. I had to take a detour in case we were followed. Don't want to bring Zelk to Earth."

"Yes, we don't want that," Grizzly said, not really looking all that trusting of what was happening. He hesitated in following Cian, but the low growling from Rotty behind him motivated him to step further and enter the chamber. As he stepped in, gaining nonchalance, he looked at Earth.

"That's a stunning view. Actually, I've seen Earth a few times from space and a bit closer when I accompanied the droids to mine the fuel. I'm eager to see your home. I can't imagine anyone living in those toxic fumes. The stuff surrounds the whole planet. So where exactly is your home, and is there space for all of them? You may have to crowd control if you catch my meaning," Grizzly spoke, and Cian wanted to pass out. His breath reeked, and the chamber wasn't ventilated.

He had to get out. He was sure this man was radioactive from all the UV rays. He was a rotten walking piece of decomposing slough. He needed to do a debridement, cut out and away before he infected anyone else. Cian cleared his throat and turned away, searching for fresher air, then asked, "Oh, so you've been?" and kept the conversation going.

"Not down to the water but high enough to see some of it. I was a small boy when we were deported to the Lunar Environmental Project. My parents were so proud and happy to help set up the dome and prepare for the gods to come. But they never came. It was all a lie. And now I see these Anubis and wonder if there was some truth to it because you and your brothers are not human. Are you?"

"No, we're not. Why is it that you are still alive? You're almost a century old?" Cian stepped sideways to avoid the stream of rotten breath coming his way.

"My parents were scientists. I aged much slower than other children. Like snakes, I have what you call indeterminate growth, which means I have no terminal point in time or size to stop growing. I do have a few transplanted organs. They have replaced my heart three times, because my original organs couldn't accommodate my size, and heart failure was imminent. It's an honor to stand here with a god."

Hmmm, exactly like a snake, Cian thought. "I don't think we're gods. Like you, I think we're the product of DNA manipulation. Somehow, someone hit the mark with trial and error. What do you know about the experimentation with humans? Did your parents tell you anything about their research?" Cian asked, wanting to know about the fucking Anunnaki.

"No, I wasn't educated, but we did talk about it. I thought none of it was real, yet here you stand," Grizzly said, staring off into space deep in thought.

This was it, the moment of opportunity. Cian quietly stepped back, and the door slid shut before him.

"Thank you, brother." He thanked Ivan for shutting the door and trapping Grizzly inside. As soon as the door shut behind Grizzly, he flung himself around. Pure rage flushed red-purple blotches up his neck and into his fat face. He pulled the handle and when the door didn't open, he kicked it. Cian narrowed his eyes and stared emotionlessly at him. A wall of the Anubis's chest muscles rubbed against his back. He turned and hugged his best friend. "Rotty, what's going on, boy? You're such a big boy now. Thank you for protecting me, my friend." Rotty whined like he always did when Cian knew he meant *yes, but. Yes, I'm so big, but.* Hugging him and feeling his heat felt like home. Cian inhaled and turned to face the people still looking at their tormentor inside his cage. Grizzly banged on the door. Spittle, puss, and blood smeared on the plexiglass as he rubbed his face against it. Nobody heard his cries.

Cian pushed through to the crowd, searching for Talali and her sisters.

"Where are they, boy?" he asked Rotty. The animal turned his head in their direction.

"Cian General," Talali called, holding her arms out for him. Kneeling on one knee before her, he opened his arms, accepting the hugs and love.

"Are you okay? Did he hurt you?" Cian asked, while Rotty panted happily and sat down. He looked smaller already. It seemed the Anubis increased in size if there was danger and shrunk back to his regular size when the threat was averted. Strange, Cian thought. But at this stage of his life, nothing surprised him anymore.

"I locked him in there. He wanted to see Earth, and I showed him. He's all yours. I can't push the button since he didn't do anything to me. I leave it up to you to decide who will kill him. Let me show you." The crowd parted like the sea for Moses.

"This button opens the outside hatch, and this one opens the front. They won't open at the same time. Nothing will happen if you open the outside door, except Grizzly will be sucked out and killed." They nodded, looking astonished by his gesture. Talali grinned at Grizzly. Grizzly mouthed, "No, please no." The crowd came closer, judging the man who made their lives a living hell.

Nobody said a word.

Cian walked away. He saw enough ugly for one day. He needed to be alone and blow off steam.

"Come, boy," he tapped his leg with a flat hand.

"Let's go!"

Chapter Fifteen

"Good morning to our old and new citizens.

It's now six a.m.

Did you know bathing cleans your skin, helping you avoid irritation, inflammation, and sores caused by dead skin cell accumulation?

The bacterial and fungal load from contact in your environment can also accumulate, increasing the risk of infection.

We urge you to please use the facilities and don't be shy to use soaps and shampoos.

Please visit your community news page for more hygiene and oral care tips.

Breakfast is served until eight a.m.

Hope you have a sparkling day!"

General Cian Romanov

95 A.T.

The Warship Horizon

Cian tossed and turned, irritating himself wide awake. Flipping over to his stomach, he went to throw his pillow, thought better of it, and flipped onto his back again. The bed linen felt cool on the back of his head. He closed his eyes, relaxed, and listened to the soft humming coming from the engines. He splayed his hands wide on each side and felt the vibrations.

"Oh, for fuck's sake!" He kicked himself fully awake. "I'm not going to sleep," he mumbled and stopped trying. His migraine was also not going anywhere. Attempting to relieve the tension headache, he found the pressure points where his nose bone met the eye sockets and squeezed with his thumb and pointer finger for a few seconds. Again, he closed his eyes and started deep inhalation relaxation meditation. He felt his body getting lighter and relaxed.

"Ohm, ohm, ohm. I'm happy. I'm calm. Ohm, ohm, ohm." He refocused and relaxed his whole body. Starting at his feet, his left foot and the prosthetic lower right leg, he imagined he was weightless. Then, moving up to his knees, the sensation flowed through his upper legs. Suddenly, it stopped at his cock. The organ pulsated, making him super aware of his incapability to unwind in that region. *I'm so horny.*

"For the love of!" he exclaimed. He knew exactly what needed to be done. He decided to do it and get it over with. He had to have him. If Leo wanted to watch, let him.

Maybe it's the icebreaker we need?

He swung his legs over the side excitedly. He couldn't remember when he last felt so giddy with nervous anticipation. *He better not break my fucking heart,* he thought as he walked into the shower to freshen up and prepare to give a dying man his last wish.

First, Cian went to the bridge command center to ensure they were on course and ready to deposit their precious cargo on Earth. Heaven forbid he lost the last of humankind because he wanted to give a dying man his last wishes. Not because he wanted his dick dipped deep and sucked clean. No, not at all that. After confirming with his brother that the Horizon was set on due course third rock from the sun, he marched like a soldier to war. His mission—to kill his arousal.

He stopped dead in his tracks in front of the shiny metallic door of his mate's cabin. *Dear lord, what if the half-man died while watching? He better not. Maybe he should. Maybe dying watching Barkor being skewered by the mighty Cian wasn't a bad way to go,* he thought and pressed the buzzer button.

"Hello. It's me."

"Who's me?"

Cian crushed his teeth and almost cracked his molars. He took a deep breath. "Me, Cian, the fleet commander, General of the fucking

Horizon." He looked left and right down the corridor, ensuring nobody heard him.

"Oh, you," came from the inside.

Silence. *Fuck this.* Cian turned to leave, and the door swooshed open, revealing Barkor smiling brightly. Cian guessed he tried to look seductive with only sleeping pants and bare feet. Perfect bare feet. They were webbed. Cian's insides whooped with approval. He looked at Cian as if for the first time. Inspecting each other inch by inch, he scanned Barkor as Barkor scanned him back and then lingered on his crotch.

"Step aside, the mighty General is bringing gifts," Cian said with more courage than expected.

The half-man was sitting at the small table with pillows propped beneath and behind him. Barkor stepped aside, supporting himself with one hand on his hip and the other on the wall so Cian could enter. He looked invigorated and continued to look Cian up and down as if he was already undressing him in his mind.

"I bet Barkor my lunch that you would return, and here you are," Leo said smugly.

His false bravado deflated, and uncomfortable didn't begin to explain how Cian felt. He wondered if there was still time to turn around and run. But his feet didn't want to move. Leo couldn't wait to see Barkor and Cian getting their grooves on; his eyes were loaded with youth and vigor.

Cian remembered Leo had spoken. "Your lunch?" he asked after a long agonizing silence.

"Yes, my lunch." Leo chuckled, and mischief was written all over his face.

"Why would you bet on your lunch? You know there's a buffet, and you can eat as much lunch as you like all day."

"I know, it's just a saying, whatever. We bet our lunches on Grayrak. Come in, come in. Barkor and I just had a shower, and he's ready for you.

I had him wash all his cracks, and I can confirm that he's squeaky clean and ready for you, big boy."

"Leo, do you have to be so crude?" Barkor asked, his lips rolled up with a disgusted look on his face. It looked like he wanted to run back into the shower. The space was small.

Maybe both of them should run and leave the naughty half-man here?

Cian didn't like that Barkor felt cornered and pushed into this forced lovemaking session. "Okay, I think I've changed my mind," he said and turned to leave but saw the disappointment in Barkor's blue-slitted eyes. Steam was still billowing from behind him, confirming he just came from the shower to open the door for him. Cian took him in. His wet hair was combed to the back, almost reaching his shoulders. The big expanse of his muscled chest was impressive. And his biceps were almost as big as Cian's.

This is so wrong, so wrong. I'm going to get third-wheeled again. Fuck this!

"Leo, I owe you lunch," Cian said while glancing at Barkor. The heat between them was at incineration levels. Cian heard both their heartbeats slamming into their rib cages. Droplets of water ran down Barkor's temples, and Cian wanted to lick them. His skin tingled, and he knew he would glow if the overhead lights were off.

"I don't think this is going to work. I think I must go. This was a mistake." He turned to Leo. "Sorry, Leo, I couldn't give you your wish."

Cian didn't think Barkor could move that fast. He jumped in front of the door and blocked it. "You aren't going anywhere. Let's sit and get to know each other a bit and take it from there." Barkor was vibrating. His smoldering eyes told Cian, he wanted it, but was just as hesitant as him. Barkor ran his hands through his hair, and faint tremors exposed his nervousness.

Cian wanted to push him to the side and run. But again, his legs didn't move. Nervously he searched for a spot to sit, and Barkor pulled a chair closer for him. He sat. They looked at him. He cleared his throat.

"How do you want to do this?" he asked, but no one said anything.

Leo opened his mouth and shut it.

Barkor gave Leo a glance and swallowed. "Leo suggested to me earlier to start with a kiss."

"Really? How will that work?" Cian teased and smiled seductively at Barkor. His attraction to the man was undisputed. He was the most beautiful man he'd ever laid his eyes upon. He examined him deliberately up and down. Not making a secret of it as he leaned back, starting at his toes. "How were you born?" he asked.

"Excuse me?" Barkor blurted. "Cian, sometimes I can't keep up with how your mind jumps."

"Were you hatched from an egg, or did you come from an artificial womb?" Cian asked, and Barkor frowned, bemused by the question.

"Hmmm, none of the above. My mother pushed me through her vagina," Barkor answered sarcastically.

"Oh my goodness, how did she survive that?" Cian asked. Bowled over by his size, he couldn't imagine a baby his size being born naturally.

"She didn't."

"Oh, sorry."

Awkward silence.

"Who was your father?"

"I don't know. Why are you asking? What does my lineage have to do with this? Don't you have other sexier questions to ask?" Barkor asked shortly, with irritation flaming his cheeks red.

Cian didn't want to go into that detail, but he had to ask. He had no clue how Barkor ended up on the moon. Was his mother pregnant, or did he sleep in one of those glass caskets they had sent to the moon? And why did he have webbed toes and look like Eryn, only a foot smaller version?

He was exactly Cian's height at seven feet, but his facial features were like Eryn's.

God, we're the incubator generation.

Leo seemed like the excitement had drained from him.

"Something wrong?" Barkor asked, also noticing the deflating spirit of Leo.

"I just need to lie down for a bit. You know I get tired faster than usual." Barkor got up and went to help Leo to his bed. Cian noticed they were sleeping in separate beds. *That's good news.*

Cian caught a glimpse of a smile and wink from Leo at him. The little shit, he thought. "Have you tried peeing on him?" he asked.

"What the fuck?" Barkor asked. Leo laughed and Barkor shook his head in disbelief.

"Sorry, I speak my mind too fast sometimes. I mean that our placenta, our birth water, had healing qualities. We had capsules with our birth water inserted into the humans on Earth, and they never age. The closest I could come to the placenta was piss. Have you ever tried to piss on Leo?" Cian knew it sounded weird, but he thought it might actually work.

"Why would I ever think of pissing on Leo?" Barkor pointed to Leo, who burst out in another fit of laughter. "That's disgusting, and that's beneath him and me."

"Sorry, I just thought it could maybe prolong his life. And then—"

"Are you trying to get out of the deal by suggesting I piss on Leo, or did you want to piss on Leo?"

Cian got up. "Okay, this isn't going to work. Me talking to you"—he pointed to them and back and forth—"will never fucking work. If I can't have a normal conversation, I'll go. I'm much better off alone. I see where this is going again, anyway. He is luring us to his bed and you are too stupid to see that. Unless you are in on it, or too dense to see the humor of the situation. I need to get to the important things, like getting this ship safely to Earth. The scientists at Phoenix can explain everything to you once we arrive there." Cian pushed his chair back aggressively and jumped up.

"Stop him, Barkor," Leo said, and the next moment a hand grabbed his shoulder, spinning him around.

Cian didn't have time to react as Barkor's mouth slammed onto his. At first, he thought he'd lost a tooth or split a lip. But then, all thoughts deserted him, and he just drew blanks as Barkor forcefully manhandled him. He pushed him back against the wall, pinning him with a solid wall of muscles. His temper flared, and a few things happened at once. He never closed his eyes, and neither did Barkor. He wanted to push the man off him, but he was immobilized by the shock and the fact that someone was kissing him for the first time in half a century.

Where's Rotty? He wondered if this would have happened if Rotty had been here. *The damn animal is playing with kids, and here I am being assaulted by lips and tongue. I should protest and say something.* But he couldn't because his mate's mouth was on his.

Oh, and maybe he should breathe. He lifted his hands to push Barkor away, but the moment he touched those firm chest muscles, those firm pecs, pleasure zinged through his fingertips down to his cock. Jump starting it, forcing Cian to focus and pay attention. Barkor had soft black chest hair, so unlike Eryn and Ivan.

No, fuck this. I'm not thinking about them.

Barkor broke the kiss. He looked at Cian's lips. Licking his own, he then swooped in for another round of kissing. *Oh, my god, he's a good kisser.* Cian relaxed, then he closed his eyes and fell into the rhythm of delving deep, swooping in and swooping back out. Their tongues danced and glided, and Barkor tasted delicious. Cian pushed Barkor, steering him backward this time without breaking the kiss.

"Yes, come here." He faintly heard Leo in the background.

Cian didn't find Leo watching them repulsive; if Barkor wanted this, he would do it. He kissed Barkor with renewed determination. If he didn't do this, he would either explode or never get the opportunity again. That left him no choice but to play nicely until the half-man croaked.

"Undress him," Leo whispered. Barkor started at his boots, next his socks came off, revealing his right artificial toes and foot while his left foot balanced on the cold steel floor as Barkor slid his pants down his legs. He should have felt awkward and embarrassed, but as Barkor began to steer him backward and never stopped kissing him, he forgot his shortcomings. Barkor hastily loosened and undressed his pants. Leo sighed, but Cian could hear the shortness of breath and the crackling of his lungs. The overhead lights were as bright as daylight, and Cian wondered if Barkor could hear and see their song.

Cian broke the kiss to see where they were and how three bodies would fit on the narrow bed. Barkor moved and planted Leo between them, his face radiating contentment and relief as Barkor and Cian started kissing again. Their cool, freshly showered and wet bodies felt gloriously good to Cian. He'd forgotten how it felt to be intimate, but so far, everything happened naturally, as if the three of them were meant to do this.

"Don't want to crush you," Cian said between kisses, and Leo groaned a negative. Barkor's mouth tasted like spearmint. His tongue was slippery as it glided over the roof of Cian's mouth. Cian's cock leaked into his underwear. He scooted closer onto his knees, pulling Barkor's hips so their cocks lightly touched. "I want to take both our cocks into my hand."

"Yes, please," Barkor moaned. His voice a deep rumble that tickled Cian deep inside his chest. The space was a tight fit. Cian halted kissing to look at Leo and Barkor.

He saw the beauty that once was in Leo's face and concentrated on that—the beauty of the plan he had made to bring them, two stubborn, hard-headed men, together. At that moment, Cian was sure Barkor would have never acted if Leo didn't ask him. For that, he liked Leo a little bit more. Leo nodded at him and then gazed at Barkor who was staring at Cian. Their connection was indescribable because, without words, Barkor's head fell back as he panted, while Cian took his thickly veined cock in the palm of his hand, pumping it with a firm grasp up and down in long lazy strokes.

"You are beautiful together," Leo said and Cian agreed it was beautiful. They were beautiful.

He wanted to fuck Barkor, and holy shit, Cian felt the telltale feeling emanating from his bones, and he knew he was going to sing for them. He looked down to check if his skin glowed, but the urgent call over the overhead speakers interrupted him.

"Commander General Cian, sir. You're needed immediately in flight control, sir."

"Fuck, talk about bad timing. Sorry, I have work to do. I don't have time to fuck around like a teenager." Cian practically pushed Barkor off the bed as he struggled to get up with his stubborn right leg not cooperating fast enough. Once up, he jumped to collect his clothes discarded by Barkor just minutes before. Leo chuckled.

"Are you okay?" Barkor asked with shock and astonishment written on his face.

Cian wondered if he was amused or cared about his well-being. *Why would he care? No one ever does; it's all about the soon-to-be dead guy.* It was a fleeting thought as he slipped on his boots. He straightened up, repositioned his deflating leaking cock, then slapped his cheeks to wake up from this bloody trance he was in.

"I told you, I have a ship to command, a bloody stolen enemy ship, and with this one ship, I vowed to exterminate your enemies and save your people. Our enemy had years to prepare, and we had two. We managed to do it in less than that. We suspect there might be more

Zelk that had escaped. *My men must have spotted the enemy while I am fucking around.* Fuck! I need to go. Sorry." He gulped a few breaths and halted, then slammed his fist into his chest. Locking gazes with Barkor he said, "The moon's pull was like a big rock in my chest. For years, I lived half-suffocated and shunned with one goal...to have you for myself without this damn rock in my chest. I knew you were there. I knew if I saw you, you would confuse me and make me want you, while I couldn't have you." *And if I lose you and your people, I would never be able to live with myself.*

Cian turned before he humiliated himself further. He hit the button to exit and looked over his shoulder. "Barkor, come to me when Leo has died. Leo, may you walk in the sun on the other side. Cian gave him a mock salute. May you die a good death, my friend. Thank you for taking care of Barkor for me and helping us infiltrate the Zelk. If it weren't for you, Ivan and Eryn wouldn't have gotten their jobs at the hospital, and of course, I appreciate you getting my men and me on this ship. You are a hero, and I'll make sure you're remembered that way," he said honestly to Leo, who nodded and smiled.

Barkor sat on the side of the bed with his head hanging in his hands. *Disappointed or upset?* He would have to worry about that later.

He turned and sprinted down the corridor. Halfway to flight control, Ish's pager vibrated in his pocket. Fumbling, hop, skip and jumping, he got the damn thing out and saw he had missed a string of repeated messages.

Change course now! Change course now! Change course now!

Fuck!

Chapter Sixteen

"Good morning, new citizens of Phoenix.

It's now six a.m.

Did you know learning a new language can be fun?

Use flashcards and start using the Old Earth's language all day, every day.

Visit your community news page for more tips and tricks to adapt easier when you arrive in Phoenix.

Breakfast is served until eight a.m.

Hope you have a wonderful day!"

Barkor, the Promised Prince

95 A.T.

The Warship Horizon

Somewhere between Earth's moon and Mars

Leo died in his sleep the following day. His body had been set adrift among the stars after his friends paid their respects—everyone except Cian and his men.

Two days later, Cian came over to the serving trays squashing and testing the pieces of bread for a soft one, and Barkor slapped his hand away. "Wait your turn, like everyone else," he scoffed. Just the sight of him rubbed him the wrong way.

"I'm hungry, and I've been waiting for my fucking turn." Cian pointed to the long lineup of humans waiting their turn to be served food.

“Yes, he was waiting his turn. He’s been in the line in front of me,” the man behind him said.

“The commander is so big, no one can miss him,” a woman behind the man called out.

“Yes, we’d definitely see if he tried to sneak in the line,” a young boy said with hero worship in his eyes.

“He spoke to all of us, telling us about the sun and the Earth and what it’s like to breathe fresh air.” The fact that everyone liked the bombastic idiot irritated him even more.

“Go sit there.” Barkor pointed to an empty seat. “I’ll bring your food. We need to talk.”

“Oh, now you want to talk to me?” Cian’s voice was low and seductive. And the fact that everyone in earshot heard it and laughed was *not* funny. *What has he been telling my people?*

“You *are* aware that I’m the commander of this ship and that no one orders me where to sit or stand,“ Cian said teasingly. And a woman giggled. Barkor gave her the stink eye, so she swallowed those giggles putting her hand in front of her mouth.

“Oops sorry,” she said sarcastically, rolling her eyes and turning her back to him looking at the others behind her and pulling her shoulders up to her ears.”

Barkor turned to read the scene and the people behind Cian and frowned. Some made shooing gestures. *What did they bloody talk about?* Cian laughed, and they all laughed louder, as if they were speaking about Barkor while waiting in line.

Barkor cleared his throat, narrowing his eyes at them. They looked away. He decided to leave it and then returned to dishing out food to the next man in line. Cian snatched a sandwich for himself. “I’ll wait for you. I can give you five minutes, but then I have a ship to run,” he said and flipped about ten of Barkor’s trip switches. His head pounded and blood rushed through his ears. He pretended he didn’t hear him and continued dishing up food futilely because he spoke so loudly that the whole dining room heard Cian. And it seemed they were all in on the joke, except him.

When the last person was fed, he grabbed a sandwich and proceeded to Cian's table. The mighty commander had fallen asleep on his folded arms and lightly snored. That was why everyone was so quiet. They must have seen he was sleeping. Barkor was stunned by how fast Cian had crept into his people's hearts.

Cian lifted his head when Barkor pulled out a chair rather noisily, on purpose, and sat down.

"How did it go? Did you manage to feed your flock?"

"Yes, I did, but it was weird-ass crazy. The food supply never runs out. When people spoke about it on Grayrak, I thought they imagined it."

Cian smiled secretively.

"You were probably responsible for that?" Barkor asked, and he couldn't decide if he adored the man or just wanted to whack him with a flat hand over the head.

"No, it's them." Cian pointed with a thumb to Ivan and Eryn, sitting a few tables over, arms crossed, legs stretched in front of them. Smiling lovingly as they watched kids climbing and sliding off the Anubis' backs like they were at a playground. The animals must have liked it—their eyes closed and expressions happy and relaxed.

Barkor put his sandwich back on the plate and drank a few gulps of the juice that never seemed to finish.

"Eat up," Cian said cheerfully. But his expression was serious. "You're practically skin and bones. When I fuck you, I don't want you to be brittle and blow away when I whisper in your ear how good you feel around my cock."

Barkor choked on the juice and coughed. "You assume dangerous things, Commander, if you think I will ever let you fuck me," Barkor said, and instead of sounding sarcastic, it came out as a challenge.

Cian rose to it by leaning forward and answering with a deep rumble and seductive tone. "Oh, you can go first if you like, but still, I won't be satisfied coming only once. You can ride me like a bronco, and when you think you're spent, and your balls are empty, I'll flip you over and fill your insides so hard and fast you'll wish you'd eaten that sandwich because I still won't be satisfied." Cian's bionic eye flickered, and the left one's pupil enlarged, hiding the crystal blue iris. "Not ever. And once you had this—" He brushed his cock slowly under the table, his arm moving and his gaze falling to his crotch, so the message was for Barkor alone and not anyone else in the dining area. "Then you're going to be hooked, and I'll be happy to shove it down your throat daily."

Cian grabbed Barkor's sandwich and took a bite, never taking his gaze off Barkor. *Fuck he makes chowing a man's sandwich sexy.* Barkor wanted to poke his last good eye out. Instead, he got up to fetch more sandwiches. He heard Cian chuckle behind him.

Crazy motherfucker!

Twenty minutes later, Barkor felt more himself. Obviously, he was hungrier than he thought.

"God," Barkor said. "That was the biggest meal I've ever had."

"Good, that's, hmmm, good," Cian said, but he looked sad and maybe a bit pissed off.

"I actually don't remember when last I ate." *Now, why did I go and say that?*

Cian lifted his hand, like he wanted to slam it down on the table, thought better of it, then bit into his fist. "Barkor, I'm so sorry. It pisses me off to know how you suffered. I should have come for you earlier. Sometimes I felt your pull stronger, and sometimes it just disappeared, so I started to tell myself it was my imagination. That's why I never came. I didn't want to see that it truly was you or my imagination. That's why I avoided coming to you, and your relationship with Leo didn't help. I was scared you didn't want me or only existed in my dreams. I'm so sorry. Maybe I lost focus."

Barkor didn't like Cian feeling unsure and questioning himself. "Stop it now, don't let my nutrition status suddenly make you doubt your ability to focus. I'm okay, and we're all okay. I'm a big boy, and I know this was the plan. If you had come earlier, you could have given yourself away. We all know the scope of this operation and understand exactly the amount of planning and positioning of you and your men, especially your brothers. They could have died, and then I wouldn't have had a bloody sandwich anyway," Barkor told him while collecting the leftovers and separating the packaging neatly for recycling.

"Here, please drink something. Finish this for me, my stomach's full, and I never waste any food. Anyway, all of us"—Barkor pointed to the empty dining area, realizing they were suddenly all alone—"we can't have you fainting from low blood sugar while you take us home."

Cian grabbed his hand, stopping him from moving around, and pulled him closer. "Listen, Barkor, I have to tell you something. I received word that there are more Zelk ships. We don't know how many or where they are. I'm pissed off at myself for missing them. That's what I mean. I'm distracted and worry we won't make it home."

Barkor saw the worry and doubt in his eyes. *He needs my support. He's our last hope.*

Cian took the cup and gulped the juice. Barkor watched that sexy big Adam's apple bobbing up and down.

He surveyed Cian's movements, the bionic eye, the excessive tattoos covering the side of his face, his temple, every inch of his neck, down into his shirt, and his arms. *Oh, moon-god, he's stunning.* Suddenly Barkor wanted the roughness and hardy exterior covering him and pressing him down. While he grunted into his ear, opened up, and showed his vulnerability, speaking from his heart made all that thuggishness disappear. Suddenly he wanted Cian to love him. Barkor knew if Cian loved a man, it would overflow and drown him. He wanted to be that man. That center of all his attention. His brutal honesty and openness were raw and magnetizing. It was what had pulled him most to this magnificent unselfish man.

He stepped back and looked at Cian as if seeing him for the first time. And then he noticed the fine lines and dark circles around his eyes. He seemed exhausted, like he hadn't slept since they last saw each other. *Maybe he's worried himself into this state.* The thought broke Barkor's apprehension, and he recognized the resilience of the commander. But now, he didn't see a commander; he saw a hopeless, lonely soul that carried the fate of his people without ever complaining. All he wanted was Barkor, and Barkor ignored him.

"I'm guessing you're exhausted." Barkor changed the direction of his concern back to Cian. Obviously, he never worried about himself. "Even if you appear ice-cold from a distance, everyone, me included, can see you're drained to the point of falling over. Let's get you to your bunker, Commander."

Cian cheered up like a puppy seeing a ball.

"No. Absolutely not. I'm not ready for this, but I'm willing to listen, but that's after you've slept."

"It's not just about sex. There's more between us than you think, but this is not the time or place. Plus, Leo just died, and you're probably heartbroken," Cian said.

"Leo liked you. He liked heroes and saviors," Barkor said, and Cian frowned.

He didn't think he was a hero, Barkor observed inwardly. *Leo liked him even more because of it.*

Cian whistled, and Rotty thundered down the aisle between the tables and chairs. The animal looked like it smiled at Barkor. His tongue was hanging out to the side, again. He was so big that four to five kids could ride around on its back. Even though he looked like he could rip them to pieces, Rotty loved playing fetch with a ball the children threw for him. The Anubis kept Cian company all day and night, so he must be exhausted, too.

They left the dining area, and Barkor escorted Cian to the sleeping quarters, where he ensured Cian was safely in his bed. "Talk to you in six hours, General Commander."

"I'm stupid if I just let you walk out the door, but I'm sorry. I guess you're right. I need to sleep." Cian slurred his words and closed his eyes. Barkor wasn't sure if the man was apologetic for not dragging him to bed.

He halted his steps out the door. "You're a good man and did a good thing for flushing Grizzly out in space. Leo and everyone who he terrorized is thankful." Barkor kept his voice to a whisper. Much was happening, and he'd forgotten to give the one message Leo told him to give.

Cian nodded slowly. "We need to talk more. I want to get to know you and woo you."

Barkor smiled and left.

Back in his room, he paced up and down, cried, and tried every alternative to yelling. He was so mad, but why? Maybe he pushed Cian away for the same reason Cian avoided him. Maybe he felt guilty. Yes, that was what it was. He had Leo in his arms, and he hurt Cian. *What does that say about me?*

"Ahr!" He groaned and face-planted into the pillow on his cot. He needed sleep. *Or maybe I don't.*

Turning on his back, he scrubbed his hands over his face.

I'm so sorry, Leo. I wish you could see Earth and the sun. But that was never your dream. All you wanted was to see me happy, Grizzly dead, and the people free and happy.

Four hours later, Barkor found himself moving to Cian's room. He let himself inside, into Cian's and Rotty's space, hoping he was doing the correct thing. He acted on his impulses, something he never did. He was one hundred percent sure now that Leo wanted this, and he would give him that wish.

Two yellow eyes looked up at him but closed them again.

“Good boy, I will not hurt him,” Barkor whispered.

Chapter Seventeen

"Good morning, new citizens of Phoenix.

It's now six a.m.

Did you know you can get up to speed by watching movies and reading the subtitles?

Tonight we will be showing movies in the dining area. Grab your dinner and watch a movie with family and friends.

Visit your community news page for a menu and the times the shows start.

Breakfast is served until eight a.m.

Hope you have an entertaining day!"

General Cian Romanov

95 A.T.

The Warship Horizon

Somewhere between Earth and Mars

Someone entered his room, and Cian instantly woke and knew it was Barkor. He heard the shuffling of feet.

"Good boy, I will not hurt him," Barkor whispered. Rotty would have attacked if he'd been there to hurt him.

Barkor's anxiousness rolled in waves over Cian. He continued snoring and carefully cracked his left eye open to see his intentions, leaving the bright bionic one closed. Things moved slowly and fast at the same time. Their hearts pumped, thoughts raced, and all kinds of hormones flushed from glands through his endocrine system. The traffic jam of chemicals trying to coordinate his emotions, sexual function, and circulatory system caused congestion somewhere around his chest cavity as veins constricted and arteries dilated, flooding his heart, causing pushback and palpitations.

Cian was never interested in anatomy and physiology like his brother, but suddenly a fleeting thought about his twin brother assailed him, and he wondered what he thought when shit like this happened to him. His blood vessels feeding his cock and balls opened up first, pooling oxygen-poor and oxygen-rich blood down south. Filling his cock with nearly seventy-five percent of his blood with the velocity of an electronic throwing arm.

Cian wanted to jump out of his skin. A feeling he felt more than half a century ago flowed over him and through him. He recognized it immediately for what it was. His mate was horny, and he meant business. As warmth ebbed and flowed through him and he forced himself to breathe and calm the fuck down. Soundlessly if possible. The telltale rustling of clothes falling to the floor had his teeth chattering, and he closed his mouth.

Finally, the time had come to be with his mate.

The room lit up as more clothes fell onto the steel floor. Barkor eased back and looked around him. "What in the ever-loving fuck is this?"

Cian opened both his eyes. Barkor inspected his arms and glowing body indignantly.

"Don't be scared, lover. Come here. It's normal."

"Normal? What the fuck is normal about glowing?"

"It's just us, as Eryn called it, our mating song. Come closer, I'll show you. Don't be afraid. I won't do anything. I just want to touch you with one finger. May I touch you?"

"Yes, I guess. That's why I'm here, but I didn't think we would go all moon-god, like literally, moon-god."

"Shh, look and listen. I'll hum what I hear in my heart, my song for you."

Cian closed his eyes and thought back to the time when he and his brother were prisoners and discovered they could sing and glow like Eryn.

Carefully, cautiously, he began with soft notes. He reached deep into his soul and sang to Barkor. He slowed and stopped to ensure not to scare the man away again. When he opened his eyes, he expected big round eyes in awe. Not someone attacking him with his mouth and kissing the shit out of him.

Singing to your lover does solve everything; thank you, Eryn and Ivan. That was what they'd been telling him. Get the man alone and sing for him. *It worked!*

"What?" Barkor broke the kiss for a second. Cian felt drunk and disorientated with lust and overwhelming surprise.

"Hmmm."

"Did you say something?"

"No, how can I say something if you're sucking my face?" Cian asked, but he knew what it was. Barkor was probably starting to hear his thoughts.

One step at a time, Cian.

"Do you still want me?" Barkor asked the stupidest question ever.

"I haven't slept in a week. You feed me, put me to bed, and now jump my bones and kiss me senselessly. Feel my cock. Of course, I want you." Cian sat up. "Listen, there's more than you think going on here. It's not just sex I want from you, and obviously, you're here in my room, and you want it, too, *but there is more.*"

"Dammit, tell me what the fuck is going on, then. This is so weird. I've had my fill of weirdness lately." Barkor eased up so Cian could talk.

"It's nothing to fear. Maybe telling you how I found out about myself will make more sense to you and yourself," Cian suggested, and just like that, the glowing died down.

Cian explained how they were born, what happened when they met Eryn, and how they were a throuple until Ivan and Eryn had mated half a century ago. And while he was talking and sharing, he told him how alone and cut out of their union he'd felt. He told him what happened in the room, how they discovered Ivan was Eryn's mate, and Cian had realized he belonged to someone else. Then he told him about Phoenix becoming a flourishing city at the bottom of the southern seas while he longed to get to the moon, to Barkor.

"Holy fucking masterpiece, no wonder we were both agitated. You were scared to be around me and talk to me. So instead of being friendly, you were an asshole, you stupid, lonely man. Well, here I am." Barkor waved him over. "Come, big boy, sing for me and teach me," Barkor said and very optimistically pointed down to his cock.

Cian stopped himself from pouncing because he wanted to tell Barkor how he felt about him. "I never really expected to get some tonight. It's not just the sex or the mating urge. The way you've taken care and looked after these people...they look at you like you're their savior or something. I see and love you already, for that reason, who you are and what you stand and fight for. I see now why they call you their prince. Maybe it's good you were able to look after them all this time because no one else would have."

Cian gently took Barkor's hands in his, kissing every finger, every knuckle lightly. "I saw you from afar when you waited for us at the clocktower, how you held and kissed Leo. You loved him dearly. And maybe it all worked out as it should have. Because Leo got to have you for a while, and those humans would have been lost without you. Knowing my mate did his best to save the last of mankind with little to nothing for so long just tells me how amazing you are and how lucky I am to have found you, even if it was the loneliest time ever for me."

The last walls around Cian's heart crumbled, and he cried silently as he spoke. He heard Barkor sniffing a few times. Then they just sat together. Not moving. Just absorbing the magnificence of the truth between them, the unavoidable destiny bridging the last seconds apart between them. The relief and the beauty of it all overwhelmed both.

Barkor sniffed. "Now I understand that pull I had to do better and save them. It was for a reason none of us could understand or explain, but I believed that as long as I fought for a better life and the good of everyone, it would turn out better than just okay."

"You're my purpose," Cian said and sounded romantic without trying.

Barkor chuckled. "Yes, and you are mine, but we can do so much for them together. I understand you, and it all now. I see our future clearly."

Cian took Barkor's hand and kissed it. "Yes, I do, too. It's what makes me feel alive."

"Me, too," Barkor answered.

"I need you safe and close to me, and I want to help you protect yourself and your humans."

"They're not mine."

"Listen, they will follow you anywhere. They are yours, and since you and I are not splitting up ever again, you're mine, which also makes them mine. But first, I need to find those Zelk."

Barkor leaned over and kissed Cian lightly on the forehead. "I know you'll get us all through this. I believe in you. It may be prematurely, but, Cian—" Barkor's mouth was hot and sweet as he opened his lips and invited Cian in. Teeth nipped, tongues met, playing carefully and softly, gliding, sliding, and delving. And then they drove deep.

The room lit up again, and the taste and touch of Barkor made Cian dizzy.

My mate!

Pulling back for air, he realized Barkor was splayed across him. Their bodies were scorching hot where skin met skin while cool blue ribbons danced over them, enfolding them in a cocoon of glowing golden-blue strands. His gigantic hands pressed their hips, their bodies together, eager to become one. Barkor was hard against him, and Cian appreciated the evidence of his arousal rubbing against him.

Barkor whimpered and squirmed against Cian, who aggressively took up the kiss again. Fisting his hair, he pushed his tongue as deep as possible into Barkor's mouth, ensuring he tasted him thoroughly. Barkor opened up, and they fought for dominance with their tongues. After a long time, Barkor eased back and settled his head in the crook of Cian's neck.

"How do we do this?" Barkor asked in-between pants.

"What do you mean?"

"You have one leg and one eye. What else is missing? I keep thinking of asking you without hurting your feelings."

Cian laughed explosively.

"I fuck like any other man. I may lose my balance now and then, maybe no fucking up the wall in the shower, but overall, I think my leg won't disappoint either of us."

"Ha-ha. You still have a cock and two balls?"

"You little shit!" Cian flipped him over and loosened his drawstrings.

"No, fuck, not this way. Please, I'm laughing too much."

"This is a serious situation. If a man asks another man if he has a cock and balls, he must prove himself and show them." Cian reached down to expose himself and realized it'd been a few days since he'd showered.

"But I must admit, I need a shower first. I'm truly a little riper than necessary for a first-time love-making session. First impressions last and all that my fathers taught us."

"Fathers?"

"Yes, Fathers." Cian stuffed his jewels back into his pants. "None of that now. I don't want to think about my fathers when I mount you."

"Oh god, now I'm going to be mounted."

"Hhmmm." Cian's deep baritone rumbled in agreement.

"Mounted? Okay, Commander, let's mount each other, but no mounting in the shower," Barkor said eagerly.

Cian enjoyed the banter, and he laughed softly. "But I do need a shower."

"By yourself? I don't think so."

"Of course not, I finally have you here with me, and I'm not planning to ever let you out of my sight."

"Oh god, we're back to hovering and growling again."

"Yes, only if you ignore me and look at me like you hate me."

"I never hated you," Barkor retorted.

"I know, but you ignored me or pretended you did."

"Yes, only because you act as if you're in charge and in control of everything."

"I am."

Barkor rolled his eyes. "Okay, let's agree to start over. Leo knew I cared for him, but I didn't love him. Before coming here tonight, I sat down and meditated. I talked to him. I think he knew me better than I knew myself, or he saw you and me and knew we belonged together. I think I feel better, and I feel like it's appropriate to move on."

"Oh, you spoke to Leo?" Cian softened his tone, trying to convey sympathy.

"Yes, you know, to his spirit. I think he's good with us. And with me being with you."

"Good."

"Anyways, you said you may slip and fall in the shower."

"I said if I mounted you against the wall, I might lose my balance and slip and fall. Come." Cian climbed off the narrow bed and held his hand for Barkor, who got up and let Cian lead him to the back wall, where he pressed a button. The wall slid away, revealing a small bathroom with a shower and toilet. The perk of being a commander was a big walk-in shower. Cian worried that Barkor would think his glamorous amenities were unfair and too much.

Then it didn't matter because Barkor was kissing him, and holy shit, he was doing things with his hands and tongue. Arms flying for purchase, one of them activated the water.

"Barkor," Cian whispered in-between kisses. "Could you help me out of my pants?"

"Oh, moon-god." Barkor laughed. It was beautiful. Then Cian laughed.

Then they giggled like two ten-year old's, stealing the cookies. He was too far gone with lust and happiness. *Both of them were.* They fumbled their way to find his waistband one moment, and then both were naked and glowing luminescent blue-gold. Cian felt Barkor's hard length against his own.

"Shower," Barkor said breathlessly. "You wanted to shower." He broke away from Cian, looking for soap. "Let's clean up, and then—"

Cian grunted his pleasure in his mouth, going in for more kisses.

"Turn around. I want to wash your back and run my wet soapy fingers over your tight-muscled body," Barkor said hungrily.

Cian experienced chest pains where the tightness of missing his mate manifested. It snapped loose, and he gasped for air—emotions overwhelming him. He was here, with him, and he wanted him. He was definitely worked up too much. "You're going to be the end of me," he said as Barkor washed him in slow circles from his head to his toes, pausing and lingering at his ass crack.

"Yeah, I don't think so. Turn for me, please. Bend your head so that I can wash your head."

"Hmmm, you're spoiling me. That feels so good."

"I like the look of your shaven hair and tattoos. Your whole look screams, don't fuck with me, but underneath is all..." Barkor paused to rinse Cian's head and proceeded to wash his muscular chest, soaping up every inch and trailing the tribal markings over his pecs and then his hard nipples, then fingering in tiny circles over his abdominal muscles, teasing and hinting about going lower, but not touching his erect cock. "Underneath it all, you need me to care for you."

"Having fun taking care of me?"

"Hmmm, my mouth waters for you. Look at you. You actually do have a cock and two balls," Barkor teased.

Cian was speechless and shivering. Barkor's touches burned a trail of scorching desire with his inquisitive soft, sensual, exploring touches. His cock throbbed, and he felt like coming right there. It had been so long since someone else touched him.

"I'll pass out if you don't hurry up and get me vertical."

"You wanted to shower, so I'm showering you."

Cian grabbed for the soap to clean himself because if Barkor touched his cock, he would lose his last drop of dignity and come in the man's hand.

"No, ah-ah, let me."

"Barkor, this isn't a good idea. I'm...ah..." Barkor reached around him and grabbed his cock with soapy hands.

"I see now we're meant for each other. You also don't have pubic hair like other men. I thought something was wrong with me, looking like a child with no body hair," Barkor whispered, and he knew exactly how to touch Cian to avoid making him come. He teased by pulling his foreskin back and cleaning his sensitive cock head thoroughly. Thank god he moved down to his balls. "Oh, you are so ready to shoot and to give me your load." Barkor fondled them, then wrapped his fingers around them and pulled.

Cian closed his eyes, hanging onto the wall, and swore creative obscenities as Barkor washed the soft area between his balls and his entrance while pulling his sack down with the other hand.

Next, he washed Cian's hole in slow motion, using the tip of his finger to reach deep enough for a thorough cleaning.

Barkor gently coaxed Cian to turn, making his intentions clear. Cian watched as Barkor closed his eyes and opened his mouth to swallow him.

Streams of water slid over his face and chest, and Cian wondered for a brief moment if Barkor could breathe, but when his cock head traveled over rough teeth with painful slick sensations, he closed his eyes and howled soundlessly, mouth open as he enjoyed the unexpected pain. Then it stopped. He felt only water and realized Barkor wasn't sucking anymore. He opened his eyes and stared into deep blue-black ones. "You cock tease."

"You said shower then mounting," Barkor purred at him with innocent-looking eyes.

Cian grabbed Barkor by the hair, pulling him up to his feet, and bent Barkor's head back to lick and bite his throat.

"I want you now," he growled, lowering his mouth. "I'm your mate, and don't you forget it."

"Never, how can I? You won't let me."

"You got that right. I fucking waited long enough for you, and you will suck my cock, now."

Cian watched Barkor closely for signs that he was going too far, but this rough manhandling turned Barkor on even more.

Barkor's hands skimmed over Cian's lower back, and then he grabbed hold of Cian's glutes and squeezed.

"Fuck yes, I like the pain."

"Me, too." Barkor hissed as Cian tightened his fist in his hair. Cian pushed Barkor back to his knees.

"Suck my cock, as you did just now. I want to feel it, so suck it hard," Cian said, staring at Barkor. Grabbing a fresh hand full of hair, he forced his cock into Barkor's mouth, scraping it along his teeth. The hairs on Cian's arms raised as his skin glowed. It felt electrically charged.

"Fuck, yes."

Barkor bit lightly and swallowed, then Cian moved his cock head between his molars.

Barkor hummed softly, and Cian saw him grabbing his own cock in his hand. He watched as he chewed on Cian's while his arm moved in sync with the pleasure he provided. It wasn't long before it sounded like an orgasm. Instantly, Cian smelled the familiar smell of male ejaculation. *So he liked this. Good, I liked it, too.*

Barkor gave full attention to him, licking, teasing, and biting his cock head.

"Harder," he ordered while he spread his feet apart, making sure his leg was cooperating, then took hold of the safety rails while Barkor drove him crazy with sucking his ball sack, pulling one ball and then the other into his mouth. Chewing the skin like it was bubble gum. Cian resorted to whimpering as Barkor slid his finger into his ass and began sliding it over his prostate.

His orgasm and pent-up frustrations built and built as Barkor edged him repeatedly. Finally, his orgasm exploded—emptying his load before he could warn Barkor, but Barkor drank every drop and suckled his oversensitive tip, which he was sure was raw and bleeding.

"Come here. I want to kiss you," Cian said with a deep grunt. Barkor stood up so they could share a kiss while Cian still grabbed onto the safety bar. His whole body trembled. "I might collapse from coming too hard," he said into Barkor's mouth.

Barkor kissed him with a force that mashed their lips against his teeth. Water ran down their faces, making Cian close his eyes. Their mingled scent and the euphoric emotions enveloped them, and he recognized it for what it was. This was what his brother and Eryn felt for each other. *No wonder.* He made a mental note to talk to them and apologize for his behavior.

Barkor panted heavily. "Can we get out of this shower? It looks like you're about to pass out." Barkor supported him to prevent him from slipping. Cian nodded a yes, suddenly overwhelmed with it all, incapable of speech.

"Are you okay?" Barkor asked, leading Cian back to the bed to sit.

"This is almost too much for me. It's way more intense than I ever imagined. And the worst thing of it all is that I kind of hated my brother, thinking it was jealousy or an inability to share Eryn with me. Now I understand how they felt and what an idiot I was. I almost broke them up, you know, because Ivan couldn't live with himself being happy, and I made it very clear that I was alone and unhappy. Like it was their fault. I'm so selfish." Cian sat with his face in his hands.

"Yes, yes, so selfish. Can we get over the self-pity party? You're ruining a good thing here," Barkor said bluntly, and Cian laughed like he hadn't laughed in years.

"I have a reputation for doing that."

"Not going to argue," Barkor said, flapping his flaccid cock this and that way.

Cian instantly sobered and reached down to grab the offending soft body part. It was roughly the same size as his, but the color of it was a bit darker. Pulling the foreskin back, he heard Barkor hiss through his teeth. He inspected the rough ridges around the head, tightened his grip, and pulled the remaining viscous fluid out. He smeared it between his fingers and tasted it. Then he repeated the motion and smeared it around his fat purple-red cock head engorged with blood. He wanted to taste more of it, so he grabbed Barkor's cock by the base, squeezed and forced more fluid to the tip, then lifted his thumb to his mouth and sucked it clean.

"Oh, sweetheart, that's hot," Barkor groaned.

"I want to come inside you. I want to push myself so deep into you," Cian said and licked another drop from his fingers. "I want to fuck you so hard, you'll think about me with every step you take."

"Oh, moon-god, fuck yes," Barkor said with a heavy breath, turning around, ass up and ready to be plundered.

Cian grabbed his ass cheeks and spread them open. Hard and aggressive to the point of tearing Barkor open. He bent his head and swiped his tongue over the pink puckered hole.

"Oh, dear. Oh, my...yes. Fucking yes," Barkor blabbered as Cian speared and worked his hole, readying it to receive his cock.

When he was happy with its slickness, he lined his cock up, playing with the head around the tight entrance a little too long for Barkor to press back against him.

"Ah, for the love of, fuck me already."

"You're not ready." Cian reached over to the drawer below his bed and fumbled around. "Ah, got it!"

"What now?"

"Prepare to receive me." Cian flipped the cap, then dramatically drizzled his cock, and Barkor's hole with strawberry-mint lubrication oil that was manufactured in Phoenix and was very scarce in space, and he didn't care. He tossed the bottle on the bed and went to work.

"Ah, so fucking tight, so fucking hot!" He howled and enjoyed the tight gliding and the slickness over his raw hypersensitive cock into Barkor's body. Barkor groaned, enjoying their first penetration. The small cabin lit up once more as their arousal heightened. Blue and golden swirls of light energy danced around and over them, as Cian sang his song to Barkor.

Rotty yipped and barked, and Cian assumed it was at the commotion of dancing sparks of light and sounds.

"No, down boy, can't you see I'm busy?" Cian asked and pulled his cock out, straightened his knees, and found a new purchase on the railing above his single bed. *Installed for easy in and out of the cot and for fucking your mate!* He slammed forward, only to pull out all the way. He watched as Barkor's hole closed. Barkor gasped, and Cian sank back into the tight silky hot softness.

Cian wanted to feel closer to Barkor. He stopped momentarily and let go of the handle above the bed. He laid his upper body on Barkor's sweaty back and pushed his hands underneath his armpits and across Barkor's chest, wanting to get as close as possible to him. Then he began moving, pumping his hips with deep long thrusts while biting and sucking Barkor's neck and shoulders. Barkor moaned deeply as Cian moved sensually, slowly building up a rhythm of maddening pleasure for them both.

Loving the sounds and grunts from Barkor as he received him into his body, he became one with his mate, and he felt like they'd known each other forever. Hard and fast thrusts turned to long, deeper strokes. All the sexual frustration and longing were replaced with a surety, a tenderness, and a promise. Biting turned into licks and kisses as Cian enjoyed the taste and smell of his lover. Barkor turned his head sideways for a quick kiss, tongues licking deep and far into each other. He didn't have a long tongue like Eryn, but that didn't bother Cian. He was perfect, and he was his.

Their moans, the rhythmic slapping of skin on skin, stopped as both their bodies spasmed and they orgasmed simultaneously. Breaths heaved. The slickness of their sweat allowed Cian to glide up and down Barkor's back as they rode out the last pleasurable spasms. They grunted together. Cian's orgasm was long and unending. Barkor, the big alpha male who bludgeoned his enemies, had submitted to him.

It's definitely too soon to say I love you.

He rolled off Barkor's back. "I don't have words."

"Hmmm, so good, so good," was all Barkor moaned, drunk with pleasure. Puddles of sweat ran down Barkor's back.

"Yes, so hot, thank you," Cian said, looking for a hand or something to hold. Barkor felt too far away from him as he lay next to him. He settled for pushing a hand under his hipbone, enjoying Barkor's weight on his hand and the feeling of his iliac crest.

"For what, for letting you fuck me?" Barkor asked into a pillow.

"No, for coming to me and giving us a chance. And now that I've had you, I won't let you go. Never. You're mine, and I'm yours. I waited for you and never knew how much I missed you, even if we hadn't met." Cian made a fist and bumped his chest area over his heart. "There was a pull between us, and I learned to ignore it, but I can't anymore. I honestly think I would die without you now that I've met and tasted you."

"You big brute, who would have thought you're such a mushy lover? Honestly, I've always known the others weren't like me. I've outlived and lost a lot of people I cared for. It sucked, and I told myself I would have reached the end of my purpose if Leo had been gone and I had my people safe. I never thought my life only started when you jumped to help me carry Leo onto the ship. Let's take it one sleep cycle at a time."

Cian's pager flickered with an orange light, signaling an incoming message. Cian scooted off the bed and got up to fetch it from the pocket of his uniform. "First, we must get the humans safely to Earth." He stopped speaking to read the message.

"What is it? You seem worried."

"It's news from Ish. He keeps sending me these weird messages. Look for the ships, but don't look. Six small Zelk ships are unaccounted for. But they won't be no more." Cian reread the message. It was as if Ish was rhyming in a secret spy language. "Motherfucking six ships, where have they been hiding them?" He looked at Barkor, who was already sitting up. "When all this is sorted, I promise we can do whatever people do for relaxation."

Cian threw the pager on his desk, held a hand out to Barkor, and pulled him up into a standing position. His big muscled body had Cian wondering if they could squeeze in another round.

“No, Cian,” Barkor said but sounded like he was wondering the same thing.

“Come, let’s go clean ourselves. You can join me in the bridge command. Would you like that?”

“Yes, please, I would,” Barkor answered as he was pulled into the bathroom. Once inside, neither couldn’t resist. Their mouths met, and they kissed under the running water between washing, groping, and smiling at each other.

Chapter Eighteen

"Good morning, new citizens of Phoenix.

It's now six a.m.

Did you know you can add a splash of fun with water floaties when you go swimming?

Floaties are definitely water essential if you enjoy some quiet time bobbing in the waves.

Visit your community news page to book swim lessons or space to take part in water activities and sports.

Breakfast is served until eight a.m.

Hope you have a kick-ass day!"

Ivan Romanov

95 A.T.

The Warship Horizon

Somewhere between Mars and Jupiter

Ivan pulled his puzzled and unsuspecting husband into the airlock chamber.

"What is this? What's going on, Ivan? Is someone hurt?" Eryn shot question after question but never resisted.

"Don't worry. This is for us. For you and me. It's going to be so much fun." Ivan coaxed Eryn inside, and the door shut behind him. Eryn looked bewildered at the door.

"Don't worry, my big Brawl, no one is going to hurt you," Ivan whispered and hit the button for the opposite door to open the zero-gravity training room. "We're going to fuck until neither one of us can come anymore. I've already told Cian not to expect us at the helm any time soon," Ivan said, ripping off his clothes and boots and sending them drifting. Eryn watched him. The puzzled look on his face was replaced by wonder and anticipation.

I need him now.

"Come here. You're a beautiful creature." Eryn flung his arms around Ivan's neck and kissed him until they needed to stop for air. "I missed you so much. I promised myself that when I enter you, it would be with my bare feet planted on Mother Earth. I want to smell mud and semen. Grass and water and..."

"Okay, big boy, I get the picture. Your frogging Brawl ass misses the earth, but I missed you, and I want to come at least three times now," Ivan demanded.

"Look around you. We're in a zero-gravity room. How will I be able to fuck you into the floor or up the wall? You'll fly to the opposite side as soon as I poke you with my finger." He pointed to a wall about fifty feet away from them.

"We just need to be creative," he said seductively, knowing Eryn would never say no to him. The big Brawl was wrapped around his pinky and his alone. "Come, let me help you."

He started to loosen his belt before pulling it through the loops and sending it floating behind him. Then he removed Eryn's pants. His big cock sprang free. Eryn had shrunk his cock to a more manageable size because having two cocks bothered him while walking around, and the two ten-inch cocks were fun when they experimented, but penetration by such big members had torn Ivan open when they were younger and stupid.

Eryn was more traumatized by the ordeal than Ivan. *They'd gone to Mika and Connor. Both fathers had recommended Eryn make his dicks shorter and smaller for Ivan. Both Eryn and Ivan had decided to have Eryn return to having only one dick, exactly like Ivan's. Eryn had asked Mika and Connor how big their cocks were and wanted to see them. Mika and Connor had handled the situation with tact and finesse and had shown Eryn their cocks. As their cocks were also not small, that was how they had ended up talking about recipes for lube.*

Ivan smiled thinking about it and remembered to pay attention.

"This isn't fair. I wanted..." Eryn protested lamely.

"Shh, let me show you how much I missed you." Ivan opened his mouth wide to insert the Brawl's cock into his mouth. Pulling the foreskin back, he rolled his tongue around the rough, sensitive edges of his cockhead, then set about teasing it with small licks and bites just the way he knew Eryn liked it. He suckled and worked it until he tasted his sweet pre-cum. Eryn swore in every language he knew, signaling to Ivan it was time to slowly push every bit of meat into his warm wet mouth and down his throat until his lips touched his hairless pubic area.

He looked up at Eryn, who stared back with a scorching hot look in his golden-green-slitted eyes. He knew he had successfully seduced and convinced Eryn. The hunger in his eyes and his throbbing ejaculating cock said so. Eryn grabbed Ivan by the hair and fucked his mouth hard several times.

"See what you have done? I'm already coming, fucking nymph," he said as he thrust. Ivan's eyes were tearing up, but the absence of a gag reflex gave Eryn the perfect hole to fuck until every last drop was in Ivan's stomach.

It thrilled Ivan by creating new unforgettable memories. To him, it felt like they christened their first love-making session, thus creating a new golden standard for future fucks.

Eryn pulled his long flaccid dick out of his esophagus, and Ivan vacuumed long, heaving breaths with a smile. "Delicious, just as I imagined it would taste and smell. I missed you like crazy," Ivan said between gulps of air.

Eryn ran the palm of his hand down Ivan's cheek. "Thank you, that was your best blow job ever. I missed you, too, very, very much, my beautiful Ivan," he said with tears in his eyes, stroking the line of his jaw with his thumb. They looked deeply into one another's eyes. Both their bodies glowed a light blue sheen. Their fevered gazes of desire turned into a predatory stare, and then they attacked each other with pent-up hunger, longing, and frustration, grabbing each other greedily to get as much and as deep as possible into and of each other.

Growls and moans filled the big space, and Eryn was rock-hard instantly. He pumped his cock, looking like he was about to devour Ivan. "Is this what you wanted? Did you want me to fuck you so hard that you feel it in your throat? I'm going to rip you open and put you back together again," Eryn snarled into Ivan's mouth.

"Yes, please," Ivan said like a needy slut, and Eryn's hands slipped around, cupping his backside to open him up for the intrusion.

"Go ahead. I'm ready for you," Ivan urged.

"Fucking frog balls, Ivan, you're already slick for me?"

"I am. I fucked my dildo and left lots of lube inside for us," Ivan said and flung his legs around Eryn's waist. The movement sent them drifting. Ivan didn't know where since his eyes were closed as he worked Eryn's cock head through his sphincter.

"Dear sweet lollipops! I forgot how good it feels," Eryn exclaimed, pushing deeper, panting deeply. "Oh, ah," he moaned with a deep baritone and croaked a long, bellowed holler of ecstasy Ivan had never heard before.

Eryn's eyes rolled back as he pushed and pulled Ivan by the hips up and down. Ivan held onto Eryn, enjoying the friction his cock received between their slick sweaty bodies. Small sparks of light escaped between their touching bodies, and Ivan opened his eyes to see the ribbons of blue and gold emanating from their union into the space around them. He loved seeing it, it meant they were making love, and the brighter it glowed, the deeper they were immersed in the act of giving and receiving.

Eryn laughed as if hearing his thoughts. The deep chuckles vibrated in his chest, and Ivan searched his face, noticing there was another source of his amusement.

"Why are you laughing? What's so funny?"

"Look at us," Eryn said, barely getting the words out.

Ivan was confused, he was mid-coital, and coitus interruptus was not on his schedule, especially not for a laughing fit. Eryn was hitting that spot he loved and he was one stroke away from ejaculating. He turned to the side where Eryn pointed to their reflection in the massive bay window. Frowning deeply, he saw it. In the darkness, their up-and-down movement looked like two glowworms in the bioluminescent caves below Phoenix.

"Okay, that is funny." They laughed and reached a climax together.

"This was fun, but I think sex in space, in zero-gravity, sounds better than it really is," Ivan said while swimming through the air to grab and collect their clothes to get dressed.

"Agreed, but anywhere is always good, as long as it's with you." Eryn kissed Ivan deeply, took his hand to pull, and pushed him forward to float back to the exit with his arms full of their clothes.

"Oh, I couldn't agree more," Ivan said.

A pager pinged somewhere in the heap of their clothes. Eryn scurried through it, looking for his pants pockets, and he looked at it. "It's a call from Cian." He pressed a button on the receiver. "Speak, brother."

"Ivan, Eryn, come to the helm. We need you. Bring your spear and sword," Cian said in an authoritative voice.

"What's our brother up to now?" Ivan asked.

Chapter Nineteen

"Good morning, new citizens of Phoenix.

It's now six a.m.

Did you know superheroes were so scarce in the days before Phoenix that Universities researched the science of these knights and dark knights to determine how the human body can be adapted to perform heroic acts and combat crime and criminal acts?

Did you also know these same scientists adapting the human bodies were criminals themselves? Because adapting and modifying someone against their knowledge or will is illegal.

Visit your community news page to book your seat for a popcorn movie line-up about human enhancements.

Lasitor is showcasing Ben the Robot, Robot Vegan Man, and Oops, was that a Robot?

Breakfast is served until eight a.m.

Hope you get the message today!"

Juandre

2014 A.D.

Disciples of the Anunnaki compound

Lexington, Kentucky

United States of America Chapter

Creepy Gregorian chanting woke Juandre. *We must be underground. It's humid, cold, and musty.* His thoughts rushed, trying to make sense of where he was. He thought he was in Rome for a moment, hearing the Latin plainsong he grew up with. Men dressed in black robes chanted the medieval musical notes on their knees, surrounding him. On his right side was an altar adorned with all kinds of relics and papyrus rolls. On his left was a small table and one chair. High on the wall behind them, tapestries hung. *It must be an underground church.* Embroidery of a white dove sat on a robed figure's shoulder as the man pointed his hands up to the sky, to the moon. A gigantic hand reached down; fingers open as if reaching to pick the figure up.

Juandre watched the leader, puzzled and afraid for his life. The leader wore a black robe with golden lapels on the back of his neck and draped over his shoulders. He'd been chanting Latin, then speaking in English with a Middle Eastern accent. As he continued, the men repeated what he said, sounding like a mindless cult.

Am I an offering? What the fuck do they want from me? He searched for clues. His gaze fell on that table to his right again. He squinted to see through the hazy fog. He knew they drugged him. Shaking his head to clear the cobwebs and sober up, he noticed upon clearer inspection of the apparatus *fucking torture devices!*

They looked ancient and rusted and designed to inflict maximum pain. He was panic-stricken. If they used that on him, and he wasn't dying of blood loss, he was definitely checking out with tetanus—spastic and never-ending seizures. The sight of them horrified him, and he screamed. A piece of cloth was in his mouth—so lots of hmmm-hmmm sounds and no words were emitted, but it didn't stop him from yelling.

The horrid chanting continued. Either they couldn't hear him, or they ignored him. A helmet with a lock, a weird corkscrew hand drilling thing for bones, pliers, and hammers had been laid out on the farthest end of the table. Juandre strained his neck to see. *Oh, and six-inch nails. Also rusted.*

Sweat beaded on Juandre's hairline and ran in rivulets down his temples. His groin itched and burned. It was damp and reeked of urine. *Must have happened when I was unconscious.* His eyes weren't covered. That was a bad sign. Around his head, they tied a cloth that kept the ball of material inside his mouth. They restrained him by tying his hands behind his back and his feet to the legs of a chair. He couldn't remember how he got into this situation. The last thing he remembered was climbing into bed, wanking, and falling asleep.

They must have broken into my house and abducted me without waking me up. They drugged me. My head feels woozy, like the time I'd taken that Extasy pill with Randy. No, that was the time I took the shrooms. Stop it, focus, Juandre. Yes, focus, even if everywhere I look is fuzzy around the e dges.

He recognized the *Dies Irae*. A chant dating back at least to the 13th century and maybe even older. The title referred to the "Day of Wrath."

"Dies irae, dies illa
Solvet saeclum in favilla
Teste David cum Sibylla
Quantus tremor est futurus
Quando Judex est venturus
Cuncta stricte discussurus!

Juandre translated it to English.

Will break up the world into ash
As testified by David and the Sybil
The day of wrath, the day of wrath, that day
Will break up the world into ash
The day of wrath, that day
Will break up the world into ash
As testified by David and the Sybil.
The day of wrath, the day of wrath, that day
Will break up the world into ash
Will break up the world into ash
As testified by David and the Sybil
The day of wrath, the day of wrath, the day of wrath
How much trembling there will be
When the judge comes
And strictly examines all things

The leader stepped forward and spoke. The others got up from their knees.

"My assumptions about the conflict in our organization will soon be clear to us. I have concluded that the next step to defer the chaos is crucial. We have waited a long time," he announced, and the others hummed in agreement.

He lifted his arms and spoke. "We achieved success by working hard, not just relying on our leaders," he boomed, his voice echoing in the cavernous hall. They hummed again.

Fuck this, Juandre decided. He needed to get out of what looked like an underground temple. He wiggled his wrists, looking for something sharp to cut the ties, but saw nothing.

The leader continued. "That which was preserved for us is why we are certain and wholly devout today. I assumed our leaders could lead us to create communities that would save us and let us live with our divine gods." He paused and looked over the crowd, then at Juandre, who stopped fidgeting with the loose ties.

Keep talking. As long as you're talking, you're not cutting me up. Juandre searched for escape routes. *Once free, I'm running and getting out of this place.* They'd forced the cloth deep into his mouth, and it was setting off his gag reflex. He hung his head low, forcing the vomit through his nasal cavity. He was on the verge of aspirating his vomit. Fearful of drowning, he strained to breathe through his nose.

Fuck, Andrew, please notice I'm gone. Please find me. Andrew said Tony could find anyone anywhere. *And if I died, would he ever find my body? Would he bury and mourn me? What will happen to Charlie?*

Juandre hoped Charlie was okay. He was at his mother's last night. Thank the fates for that.

"Our promise will be fulfilled when our communities come together. To live and walk among our true creators and divine beings. It will be a time of no trouble, and I promise you, our time of waiting has ended.

We will live exalted because we were the ones who carried the flame, the message to the chosen of humankind. We are a handful of scholars, but we are the chosen and gifted Disciples of the Anunnaki," he roared, and they clapped their hands. Their robes sounded like linen rattling in the wind.

They're all crazy. What the fuck, the Anunnaki?

"Yes, rejoice, scholars, for we are the people who nourish the future for life as everlasting as it should be."

"As it should be," they repeated like it was their mantra.

Juandre was in deep shit. At least his hands were loose now. He'd twisted and abraded the skin on his wrists, so the blood acted as lubrication to slip his hands out of their confinements. He kept them in place behind his back and hid them.

"Our purpose is practical, academic, intelligent, careful, intensive but straightforward, not to obscure and hide but operate under their watch."

"To operate under their watch," his audience chanted.

Oh, god, the leader's coming my way. Fuck!

"Juandre," he called his name as if he knew him.

Juandre couldn't see his face; it was darkened by the hood of his cloak.

My feet are still tied. He couldn't run. Tears streamed down his face, and he shook his head from side to side. The leader stepped closer.

"Juandre, do you see these?" He pointed to the altar, looking like a museum exhibition. "I translated and paraphrased these. They're scriptural passages written thousands of years ago. You are fortunate. Do you know why?"

Juandre shook his head. His ears zinged, and it felt like he was going to pass out. He gulped for oxygen through his nose and then heaved again, desperately trying not to inhale the vomit. He was about to remove the gag himself, but the man beat him to it with one tug.

Juandre gasped and coughed and vomited again. He was a mess. But he kept his loosened hands hidden. When he somewhat collected himself, he lifted his head and searched for a face he could identify later.

"I asked you a question. Do you know how lucky you are, Juandre?" he asked with a sickly smile.

His voice was pompously high, like a female voice, but not. As he spoke, he held his head high and stiffly spoke down his nose. As if he thought he was royalty and Juandre was a measly peasant. Juandre wouldn't be surprised if they were all castrated. The robes, the chanting, and the aloof high-pitched voices convinced him they were monks.

Yeah, come to think of it, they all sound a bit lacking in the testosterone department. Oh, my god, is that what the table with tools is for? Are they planning to cut my genitals off?

The man kicked at the foot of Juandre's chair. "Answer me!"

"Fuck no!" Juandre shouted on a wheeze. The hooded men in the background chuckled.

He walked over to the table, pointing to a flat big rock. "These tablets say how important your bloodline is. Your son will lead men and will take us all to the moon. Your son will be a Disciple." He walked back over to Juandre. A righteous aura of menace radiated off him.

Take us to the moon? Has he lost it? My Charlie is only ten years old.

"Your father has connections in Rome. You know that, don't you? We have been searching for you. It wasn't until your divorce and your wife changed your son's last name to her last name, Montgomery, that we found you. We have Rome's authorization to teach you good morals, approved by your father and ex-wife. Sign these papers and leave Charlie with his mother."

"What the fuck are you talking about? I never permitted her to change my Charlie's name. And what has my father to do with this? I haven't seen him in years," Juandre asked, looking at the papers on a small table.

The hooded men in the peanut gallery chuckled again.

"You obviously don't know how to fuck a woman, so I guess your father stepped in to help you."

Now it all made sense. He never slept with Chrissy. The paternity tests were incorrect, after all. The nucleotide markers could have suggested it was him, but they could also point to his father.

"Fuck this! Are you saying Charlie isn't even my son? He's my half-brother. But I love him. I raised him." Juandre's heart broke—*all the deceit.* "Where are they? I want to talk to them," he demanded, spittle flying.

"They are waiting for you to decide. Vanish from Charlie's life on your terms, or we indoctrinate you until you forget your perverted ways."

"What? So you want to castrate me? Cut off my balls, and you think being gay would disappear? Are you fucking hearing yourselves? You all sound like a bunch of schoolgirls! Are you even aware your fucking gonads excrete that testosterone? Cutting off someone's balls doesn't make him more male, you dumb fuck!"

"My name is Gordon Fincher," the leader said and removed his hood from over his head. He was okay in the looks department, but his evil intent made him terrifyingly ugly as a demon from the lowest level of hell.

"Perhaps you will be more accommodating to your family if you understand who's in charge here." He pointed to the others, who still hadn't removed their hoods. "Your father sends his regards, of course, no, father wants to see his son cleansed. After today, I believe you'll abandon your immoral lifestyle and raise Charlie with a backbone, laying a solid foundation for him and his new brothers."

"We haven't spoken to each other in years. I don't need his regards! And fuck my ex-wife!" Juandre yelled. His father was a rich asshole that cared more about what his friends would say than his son's happiness. And it seemed his ex-wife had his father's cock in hand. "Thank you. You just confirmed what I suspected all these years. They're two heads of one monster."

"Tsk-tsk," Gordon spat at him. He shook his head, trying to rid it of the foul spittle.

Juandre wanted to go home and face the two who forced him into his fake marriage. He made a life for himself, and maybe he needed his father's money to finish his education, but all these years, he needed him more than his money. His father left him and his mother all alone while he traveled the world and most probably fucked Chrissy. Juandre's stomach was churning. His worst fears were unfolding. He knew this was bad for him, especially if his father and ex-wife were involved.

"Please, Gordon. I have no clue what you're talking about and what my father and ex-wife have done. Are you the mafia or something? Do I have to pay for the sins of my father? Just please let me go, or let's contact my father so I can find out what's going on. Does he owe you money? Why are you taking my son?" Juandre asked in desperation, trying to make sense of this.

"No, not just mafia, but you're on the correct path. We have those traits. We comprise many of those groups. For example, I am LAZ. That's a Caucasian ethnic group originally from the Middle East. But we influence many regions and many religions in that area. We are from many parts of the world. Your father and I are good friends. We all consider you a friend, too. After all, you're Charles's father. All of us here want to be your friend."

Suppose I'll see my father again. I'm going to strangle him. What did he get himself into?

Gordon turned to his men. "What do you think, men, shall we begin with his cleansing?"

"It's getting late," a hooded man said, and Gordon looked at him with an evil grin on his face.

What are these crazy sons of bitches up to? Juandre wished he knew, and his answer came as if they heard him asking. They were all shedding their robes and standing naked in front of him.

Unsmiling, their lifeless eyes focused on him. They seemed to be of different ages. The youngest looked about twenty-five, and Juandre guessed Gordon was the oldest, about his father's age, if not older. Their bodies and cocks were also different sizes and shapes. Some seemed castrated, and others did not. Fear, like he had never felt before, assailed Juandre. He heaved breaths of air as his heart sped up at the sight of their mutilated bodies.

"What are you doing? What do you want with me?" Juandre asked no one in particular.

"You will know soon enough. We've arranged a special time for you," Gordon told him with a sickening, lustful smile on his face.

"Show him, turn him around, and untie him," Gordon ordered the youngest. He jumped to get something from their apparatus table, probably a knife, and that was when Juandre took his chance.

He reached up and grabbed Gordon's engorged cock and balls, and with all the strength he could muster, he twisted. As a trauma surgeon, he knew precisely how to rupture the tunica albuginea. Juandre heard a crackling, then a popping sound, and knew he was successful when Gordon screamed.

Juandre held on and twisted it in the opposite direction for good measure right before a fist connected with his jaw. Juandre and his chair fell to the side, skidding over the dirty tiled floor.

Gordon howled, and someone screamed, "No, don't touch it. We must take him to the hospital."

Another one said, "What will we tell them happened?"

Juandre couldn't focus. Everything was dull, and things swam in his field of vision. He had a concussion. The noise of men yelling sounded like he was underwater. He shook his head. Salty blood and spittle ran from his nose and mouth.

"I'll take him to the emergency room. Cover him in his robe. He won't be able to put pants on anyway." Juandre heard someone volunteer.

He let his head fall to the ground and closed his eyes as he prayed for Tony and Andrew to find him. His feet were tied, but his hands were free, Juandre remembered.

Opening his eyes, he scanned his surroundings.

It's time to run.

He slipped his feet from their confinements.

"Shit!"

Two of them grabbed him, hauled him into the air, and carried him to the back of the cavern. One struggled with his belt, but was too slow. The other men ripped his pants and pulled them down, then took off his underwear.

"You pissed yourself." They laughed.

"Put him in the swing and tie him up. I don't want to get hurt like Gordon," a deep voice to Juandre's left said.

"Stop!" Gordon ordered.

What? Gordon? Did he come back? Perhaps I never fractured his cock. Did he want to go first? Juandre's thoughts spun, trying to make sense of the chaos.

"He said stop," a voice much like Andrew's said. Then, like a flock of birds, they scattered as the sounds of a roaring madman spun around him and echoed off the walls. The unmistakable cracking of bones, dull thuds, and tearing flesh was accompanied by howls of pain and gasps.

Juandre saw a blur of motion. Men running and flying. He struggled to see what was happening, but he was pretty sure Andrew had come for him, and he was on a rampage. Only he could move like the wind. Screaming and begging, just like Juandre had just done, filled the cavern.

Snapping, cracking, breaking, and gurgling sounds filled the air. Ferocious growls and hisses emitted like a wildcat.

Juandre turned his head this and that way to see behind him and noticed Tony's friendly face. Tony covered his body with a robe and wrapped him inside it. It was a bloodbath around them. It seemed Andrew had broken their necks and ripped all their arms off. Naked male bodies, their heads at unnatural angles, were strewn like confetti. Juandre whimpered. His cries filled the sudden silence. Then Andrew stood in front of him.

"Dammit, I was too late. I'm so sorry, baby," he said repeatedly while rubbing and checking for broken bones. "Sick fucks!" Andrew's deep baritone echoed over the stench of death. He was drenched in blood. Even his face and Juandre had a fleeting thought that he used his teeth. *Most probably.*

"No, you came just in time. T—thank you, thank you," Juandre said through chattering teeth and sank towards the ground, relieved and exhausted.

"My love." Andrew caught him in midair. Strong arms enveloped him. "I'm taking you away from this place," he said and carried Juandre like he weighed nothing.

"Before you go, sir," Tony said. "Should I bring the relics?"

"Yes, please. Only bring the tablets and scrolls." Andrew sounded livid; Juandre could hear it in his voice. It comforted him. He felt protected.

"Tony, can you get someone in to clean up my mess and get rid of those bodies? Torch it all. We knew this day was coming. Follow the plan. Thanks. I'm taking him to the hospital," he said over his shoulder.

"Don't worry, baby, I'll take all this away and make you forget them. Do you want to remember or forget? It's your choice, whatever you need," Andrew asked as they exited the building.

The last yellow rays of the sun blinded Juandre as it sank behind the mountainous tree line. “I was gone for a whole day,” Juandre blubbered.

“I'm taking you to the hospital. Hold on. I'm so very sorry, so very sorry, my love,” Andrew said, and his voice broke. It sounded like he was crying.

“No, take me home. I'm okay. I don't want to go to the hospital. Everyone will recognize me.” Juandre objected in a moment of fearful clarity. And shame. His strength was draining. “I just want a bath and a bed. And then I want to forget this day.”

“What about testing and anti-virals? Are you—aren't you hurt?” Andrew asked, scooping Juandre into his blue *BMW* and buckling his seatbelt. Juandre noticed they held him at a secluded stone building as they drove off.

“No, you came just in time, just before...”

“Thank the fates!”

“You're full of blood. You can't go to the ER like that. Andrew. I want to lie in your arms, and you can help me forget this when I fall asleep tonight. Can you do that for me?” Juandre asked sleepily. The adrenalin was wearing off.

“Of course I can, and I will,” Andrew answered, stroking up and down his leg while he drove them home.

“They knew me. My Charlie, my father, and Chrissy,” Juandre said between sobs. “It was so confusing. They said Charlie isn't mine. He's my father and Chrissy's,” he cried. “Can you find out what's going on and why, Andrew? Do you think Tony can go get Charlie and keep him safe for tonight?”

“Yes, I will. We have the relics now. I will fix this—just rest. Close your eyes. You can sleep a bit.”

“Thank you for saving me. I must remember to thank Tony.” Juandre mumbled. “How did you know where to find me?” Juandre asked groggily without opening his eyes.

"Tony. He had a tracker on your car. It seems they packed a bag and took your phone and wanted to make it look like you were going somewhere. I started looking for you when I smelled them in the house. Otherwise, I would have thought you left."

"What? My car and phone were here? Weird. Do you think they wanted to kill me? Did my father and Chrissy ask for this? I knew they hated me, but this was extreme."

"Don't know. Tony and I will sort this out. You're safe now. Gordon was the leader of the American Disciples. I'll explain when you can listen better later. Tomorrow, okay? They can't hurt you anymore. Not you or Charlie."

"Hmmm." Juandre believed Andrew and drifted off into a peaceful sleep.

Chapter Twenty

"Good morning, new citizens of Phoenix.

It's now six a.m.

Did you know communication is usually defined as transmitting information from one place, person, or group to another?

Want to communicate better?

Visit our community news page for tips that will help you get your message across, avoid misunderstandings, and improve your relationships.

Breakfast is served until eight a.m.

Hope you get the message today!"

General Cian Romanov

95 A.T.

The Warship Horizon

Asteroid belt between Mars and Jupiter

Cian stood with his arms folded and a hand gripped tightly under each armpit. Barkor's back was to him, and to prevent himself from touching and groping his mate in front of his men, he squeezed tighter each time Barkor moved, and he got a whiff of his scent.

"Lasitor, are you scanning and recording?"

"Yes, I am, Cian," Lasitor answered.

"Please show us that area on the asteroid belt Ish identified," Cian said.

The big ten-by-five-foot monitor flickered and divulged what Cian hoped would reveal the Zelk waiting to ambush them. This mission would have been lost if it weren't for Lasitor. His attack on the Zelk mainframe regressed their system to a century before Doomsday. Thus, weakening their hive capability and obliterating their entire communication system.

These ships that Ish had discovered were a big problem. Cian suspected they were scouting droid ships hiding and had not recently been grounded. It was cumbersome and might mean that they were inactive and just waiting to be activated, or this was kept from him on purpose. Either way, he'd missed them and didn't do a thorough enough sweep of the Grayrak Zelk fleet. It could also mean they were a much bigger infestation in their solar system.

Cian had never attempted going further than Jupiter but realized now these scouting bots never needed restocking or refueling. He was sure the Horizon was the mother ship, but if he saw anything bigger than a scouting bot, he would have to take drastic steps to eliminate them.

He would do anything in his power to avoid a battle. Maneuvering through the asteroids was already risky. Even if Ish's preprogrammed route through the space rubble was unbelievably easy once Cian had installed the map through the maze and Lasitor knew precisely when to turn left, right, or up and down.

"That's it. There they are. The fuckers," Cian whispered.

"Divide and conquer them, sir," Lasitor said.

"Yes, Lasitor. But, for now, scan their composition. I want to know whether they are classes C, S, or M-typical asteroids," Cian said, noticing Barkor pulling a *what-the-fuck* face and shaking his head. Cian didn't wait for him to ask. He explained. "The C-type asteroids consist of clay and silicate rocks and are dark in appearance. They're among the most ancient objects in the solar system. They're easy to scan because anything not made of clay would show up on the scanners much easier because we know the Zelk are made of Tungsten. The S-types are made up of silicate materials and nickel-iron. They're thicker, but still scannable. Lastly, the M-types are metallic, with iron in the center. They're going to be difficult to accurately scan from one direction. And would be a good hiding spot for the Zelk, who are also metallic."

"I can't see them," Barkor said as he leaned back. Cian felt his body heat radiating through his shirt. Their bodies didn't touch, but if he leaned in one inch, he could press up against him. Maybe rub his nipples against him.

"How do you know it's them?" Barkor asked and stepped forward, squinting to see better. Cian immediately missed his closeness. He stepped to his side and stood next to the man who had him feeling like a love-sick puppy. From the corner of his eye, he watched Barkor grimacing, shaking his head slowly from side to side. His nose almost touched the monitor. "Sorry, the more I search, the less I see," he said, and Cian's heart melted into a puddle.

He's so bloody cute. He's going to be the death of me. He doesn't even know it.

"Sir, they're S-types. I confirm there are six of them. All six are smaller than a one-person craft."

A heavy weight lifted from Cian's shoulders. They were scouts, and he would assume that they were armed.

"Look at the size and positions of all the surrounding asteroids." Cian released his right hand from the vice grip under his left armpit and pointed to the asteroids that appeared as red dots on his screen.

"You see here and here. If you're looking for a ship, you'll only see asteroids, but look for the opposite. Look at the randomness of scattered spaces and asteroids and the space they don't occupy," he said and leaned a tiny inch closer while speaking to sniff Barkor's scent. He inhaled slowly and almost closed his eyes as the deliciousness washed over him.

"Oh, moon-god, where? How do you see it? Show me?" Barkor asked as if Cian were hiding them. He turned his head, inquisitive blue-green slitted pupils sparkling, his eyes almost catching Cian in the act.

Cian smiled inwardly and couldn't break his stare. *The man's stunning.* Dark blond curly hair framed his handsome face. Light blue-black stubble lined his firm jaw—thin, wide lips. Smooth pale skin. Low, thick eyebrows. A straight but flattened nose like Eryn. Now that Cian had seen Barkor more intimately, up close, he looked less like Eryn and more like the man he fucked a few hours before. Barkor locked gazes with him, and there they stood. Their gazes locked, and Cian couldn't move.

Someone coughed and cleared their throat. It sounded like Lasitor.

Fuck, I'm getting hard. Jesus Christ, it's not the time.

Cian moved one step away. *Breathe, dammit, and think of asteroids and Zelk and Bubblecars. Think engines, atom reactors, and gears turning.*

It seemed Barkor was also affected. He stepped back, raking his fingers through his wild curls while smiling naughtily at him.

Cian cleared his throat and dried the palms of his hands on his hips. Then he turned to the screen, hoping he didn't sound stupid because he was sure he'd forgotten what they were talking about. "Hmm, where was I? Yes, look closely at this spot. See how the asteroids almost form a shape if you connect the red dots?" He connected the dots on the touchscreen.

"Sorry, Cian, I still don't see it," Barkor said.

Cian used his thumb and forefinger, tipping the view about ninety degrees, and suddenly, the shapes of six weaponized scouting ships appeared.

"Oh, now I see them. It's because we're in space," Barkor said, smiling widely, exposing a beautiful set of teeth that sparkled.

I wonder if there were dentists on Grayrak? Cian was staring. *I'll ask Barkor once we're alone again.*

Forcing himself to look away, he said, "Exactly, our eyes are trained to look for up or down."

"Hmmm, so they hid by camouflaging themselves with asteroids?"

"Yes, smart, but not smart enough. And now that we know where they are, we should assume they know where we are. We need to act fast. I'm not sure if they're combative or whether they know we're escaping. They could recognize the Horizon as the mother ship, but because we deleted the Zelk programming in totality, only Lasitor remains, and they would immediately respond by attacking because Lasitor is a trojan virus to their mainframe. Lasitor and I have been planning scenarios and have several options. Our position as such needs fast and coordinated work between the Horizon, my brother, and his husband," Cian said, not taking his gaze off the screen.

"I don't understand half of what you are saying. Who's going to give themselves away first?"

"I want to shoot them into oblivion, but that's a fifty-fifty approach. We want to win and not lose one person by obtaining damage to the ship and losing our precious cargo. We're going to turn away—"

"What?"

"Yes, we're fleeing. We can't start a war that we can't win without casualties."

"Fleeing? They'll chase after us and attack from the back."

"Exactly," Cian said and laughed. *God, that felt good.*

Barkor stood with his hands on his hips and looked at him, baffled, as if Cian was crazy. "I don't want to say it, but you make no sense, and it sounds like you're a scared little boy who pissed himself."

Cian burst out laughing again. His men turned their heads in their direction. He swallowed his musings. They knew him, and they were stuck on the Horizon with him while he walked around like an irritated predator. Cian was smiling now, so it must be a strange concept for them. He quickly did a summation of the room. They seemed puzzled, but not antagonistic. Good, because Cian wouldn't hide his love for his mate a second longer.

"Why are you laughing?" Barkor scowled, and Cian stopped resisting the pull between them. He grabbed Barkor by the lapels of his jacket, pulled him closer, and kissed him. Barkor melted into the kiss. Cian gave him one deep sweep into his mouth and broke the kiss.

"You crazy, sexy freak, you—" Barkor said, wiping his lips dry with the back of his hand. He had an indignant expression, but the corners of his lips twitched for a smile.

Cian tipped his head back and continued laughing maniacally. "And you love that about me." He punched a bunch of numbers into the console and then grabbed the microphone. "I'll explain in a second," he told Barkor.

"Speak, brother." Eryn's voice boomed and sounded short of breath.

"Ivan, Eryn, come to the helm. We need you. Bring your spear and sword."

Barkor watched as Cian worked. Next, he called and assembled the troops. "Gunners, report at cannon ports. This is not a drill. Load the anti-grav torpedoes, and south ports load those bombs. Stand at the ready. I repeat, all gunners to their stations." Cian ended the transmission and turned all his attention on Barkor. He needed to explain. Barkor wasn't used to spaceships and technology.

"Barkor, I need you to go to your people and explain our plans after this meeting—" Cian was interrupted by a beep and a swoosh as Ivan and Eryn strutted into fleet command. Dressed in their tactical black body suits, hair up and tied away. Sword and spear over their shoulders with a swagger screaming they just fucked and were extremely happy with the results. Cheeks and necks flame red, lips swollen. Cian waited for the rush of jealousy and resentment at the sight of seeing them, but nothing happened. *Not anymore.*

He stepped forward to greet them. "Thank you for coming. We need to act fast." Cian met them halfway and gave each a quick handshake and a one-armed hug.

"Hello, brother. Is it time to rumble?" Eryn asked, and Cian laughed. He missed them. And he missed their younger days—their camaraderie when they bubble-wrapped Phoenix and saved it from total destruction. Eryn patted Cian on the shoulder, and Cian immediately felt better. *I missed him so much.* Cian realized it wasn't the sex he missed but their friendship. He straightened up, inviting Barkor to stand closer as he started to explain the plan.

"Ivan and Eryn, you must get to the lower bridge deck. I'll need you to each grab an escape pod—"

"What in the ever-loving fucking moondust?" Barkor exclaimed and interrupted Cian, pointing his finger at his chest. "We're fleeing, and now you're sending your family to safety in the escape pods. What the fuck? I didn't think you were one enormous family of pussies. Fuck this!" Barkor jumped to sit at Cian's command console.

But Cian was faster, and Barkor was out of the chair and on the floor in one swift movement. Sitting on Barkor's chest, he grabbed his swinging fists and pushed them under his knees, immobilizing a seething Barkor. Cian's crotch was inches from his mouth. *Fuck he's even more beautiful when he's angry.* Cian kissed him.

"Get off me, you boneless, spineless yellow ass."

"Yellow ass?" Cian chuckled as Barkor bucked underneath him, moving him forward, crotch definitely much closer to mouth. Erotic thoughts amused Cian, and he laughed playfully. Teasing Barkor was fun.

"Yes, you're a weak pussy."

"Listen, you're all big-muscled and wild, but I'll explain. Then we'll see whose ass is yellow and whose ass is red."

"Explain then!" Barkor fumed, and Cian's cock filled.

"Lie still and keep quiet for a change? You can't go pressing buttons, please, Barkor. Listen to me," Cian said, chuckling. Barkor stopped squirming and let his head fall back in defeat.

Eryn and Ivan laughed. "Oh my god, Cian, you have your hands, legs, and knees full of trouble."

Barkor turned red in the face. Eryn's comment must have infuriated him. He struggled underneath Cian and shouted, "Trouble? You all think I came all this way only to flee, and what then? Where do we go? This is supposed to be the last and final stand, and you want to tuck tail?" Barkor glared at Eryn and Ivan. He didn't like them laughing at his expense.

This time, Cian didn't kiss him. Barkor lifted his hips and kicked his knees into Cian's back. Cian couldn't grab hold of his legs, so he covered Barkor's mouth with his hands. They lay like two brawling men on the floor. It didn't seem to bother Barkor.

"Please stop this. We're wasting time. Stop and listen to me," Cian said and lowered his voice while looking deep into Barkor's bewildered eyes. Barkor's smoldering gaze promised death by mauling or clubbing. "You better not bite me," Cian said, shaking his head."Calm down, please. It's not what you think."

"Do you need help with your mate, Cian?" Eryn asked sarcastically. Cian wanted to plug Eryn's mouth with a fist. He was fueling the inferno below him. Between his legs. Under him. Rubbing on his erection.

"I got this, brother. Don't we, Barkor?" Cian exuded calmness while pinning his lover.

Barkor looked at Cian's lips, then a wet tongue licked his hand. Barkor enlarged his eyes. Cian smiled. Barkor smiled back, and then he lifted his eyebrows twice. As if to say, *hey there sexy, want to roll*? Cian shook his head. Barkor gave another nod. His eyes were dark and teasing.

Cian remembered they were in front of his men. He released Barkor, jumped to his feet, and pulled him upright in one smooth movement. Their hands glowed when touching. Eryn and Ivan chuckled, knowing it meant they wanted to fuck.

"Eryn and Ivan are to take the pods and escape. We will slow down, make ourselves known, and wait for the Zelk. Once they've taken the bait, we'll drop a mirror image of the Horizon while cloaking and making a three-sixty and then approach from behind. Once we're behind them, we'll go *pow-pow, boom-boom*," Cian said, smirking.

"Oh," Barkor said.

"Yes."

"Then why didn't you say so?"

"You never gave me a chance." Cian winked at Barkor.

"Okay, that sounds like half a plan. I mean, not all your bases are covered, brother. What about us floating around while bombs are flying?" Ivan asked.

"Actually, we're going to be your decoy," Cian said.

"Explain, please." Ivan rolled his hands at Cian, hinting to say more.

"Eryn, you and Ivan will create a light and sound particle energy field."

They frowned. Cian noticed all his personnel were standing and listening to them. They'd run all the scenarios with him for the past year, so they knew what he was planning.

"I want you to create a stream that swings back and forth."

"What are you talking about, brother?" Ivan asked, looking at him perplexed as if Cian was speaking another language. His eyebrows were skewed, awaiting something to make sense.

"I know you can do this. It would go faster if I were with you, but I must drive this tin can from behind. When the Zelk realize what's happening, I'll push them forward, driving them like cattle into the funnel. They'll want to turn but can't because they'll be packed tightly together. By the time they calculate to turn as one, it would be too late, and they'll be sucked into the maelstrom, and it will be impossible to reverse or escape. The Horizon will skim the top with lasers and drop torpedo bombs on them. That energy blast should create enough momentum to force the center to bend out and twist."

"Ahh," Ivan said, and Barkor stood blinking—looking adorable and unsure what was happening.

"Are you asking us to make a spout?" Eryn asked and seemed to grasp Cian's meaning immediately as he smiled.

"Yes. You can start with a few molecules, send them back and forth, and add to it until it's so big the blast will destabilize the current. Think about it, once you have the current going, when something enters it, the center will stretch and collapse, forming a vortex, and that's when you twist and snap. By the time the spout forms, their ships will already be moving in that direction while the front is being sucked into the funnel. Because the Zelk behaves in a hive, their ships are built and programmed to follow each other, so they won't be able to break formation and thus be sucked into the funnel."

"Where would they go?" Barkor asked.

"We don't know. But they won't be here anymore, and unless they can create the same force at the same spot wherever they are, they'll never be able to return," Cian explained. "Tada! See, it's a good plan," Cian said proudly, looking around only to see horror-struck faces.

"Actually, it's the worst plan ever in the history of horrible plans," a loud, abraded voice growled over the speaker system, reverberating through Cian and bouncing off the walls. Cian saw fine vibrations on the windows, computer screens, and the water's surface inside the staff's water tower.

"General, I'm picking up a signal from an unknown ship," Captain Bill Thornton said.

"Show me," Cian ordered and hastily jumped to see the monitors.

"It's hovering above us, sir."

"Who is this? Identify yourself," Cian said, worried because he was in a situation where the enemy could make demands and bomb them. Any spaceship commander worth his salt should know that was their weakest point.

"It is I, Ish." His voice boomed through the bridge command.

Cian straightened up but was happy it was Ish and not the enemy. "You have a ship?"

"Yes, I do, I do, I do, I do," Ish sing-songed, and then two distinct male voices started to sing *It's You, It's You, It's You* by Joe Dolan.

*

"It's You, It's You, It's You
The Only One I Want
The One I've Been Searching For
And If You Look At Me
You'll See A Lonely Man
Who's Been Too Long Without A Home
So Why Don't We Just Get Together
And Try To Live Our Lives As One
It's You, It's You, It's You
The Only One I Need
To Fill My Empty Heart."

*

"Ish, stop! Ish, for fuck's sake! Who's with you? Are you two drunk?"

"No, and yes. How do you think I traveled and searched for a new home? It's not a ship. It's a machine," he said.

A second man sang again, "And it is beautiful."

"Beautiful," Ish joined in, and they repeated the chorus, "Beautiful, beautiful, beautiful, beautiful!"

"Jesus, Joseph, and bloody Mary. Then why didn't you say so?" Cian asked with his hands on his hips.

"You never asked?" They chuckled like maniacs.

"Motherfucker!"

"Ha-ha-ha." Ish laughed, causing pens and other loose items to roll around on the desks generated by the vibrations. The mesh covering the speakers pulsated.

Cian feared they would blast the speaker system. "Please reduce the volume, Lasitor!"

"It's small. See, nothing worth mentioning." A golden ship with two passengers pulled up so close to the Horizon that Cian could see the crow's feet at the corners of Ish's eyes as he laughed. And next to him sat Doctor Peter von Leutzendorf, looking like he sniffed too many test tubes. His eyes weren't focusing, and he kept falling to the sides while struggling to sit up. His long blond hair curtained his face. He wiped it out of his eyes, and Cian saw the intoxication—the lack of coordination as he was laughing his ass off.

"Stop laughing at us," Cian ordered, stepping closer to the window and pointing his finger at Ish.

"I'm not! It's Peter."

"Yes, you're both fucking laughing at us!"

"Okay, I am. It's all Peter's fault," Ish said.

"Maybe a little. We're just having a little bit of fun," Peter said. "A little bit of fun, a little bit of fun," he sang again, the same melody as before.

For a long moment, no one spoke, just watching the show. What were the chances that two drunk off their asses Anunnaki lovers would appear out of thin air? In the middle of a war. Somewhere in space.

The ping-ping sounds coming from the console in front of Captain Thornton broke the silence.

"That's the most dangerous plan I've ever heard," Ish added long after the fact.

"I know it's creative, but I know we can do it."

"Cian, it is not safe to do," Ish said in a serious tone.

"Do you have a better idea?" Cian challenged him.

"Actually, we do. We want you to go home, and we'll handle the Zelk."

Cian blinked wordlessly. Then thought of Ish and his weird-ass casings that took care of problems that shouldn't be a problem. He'd seen them being used in the market the day they abducted Leo. He wondered if Ish could take care of the six Zelk ships hiding from them.

Ivan spoke first. "I think what Ish is trying to say is that we don't want to be negative or question your belief in us, but don't you think we would get sucked in, especially if the suction becomes so big and strong enough to disappear Zelk ships? Don't you think we would create a big hole we can't close? Then what if it sucks in us, asteroids, planets, the sun, and galaxies?" Ivan spoke louder and louder. "Do you want to create a big fucking bang?"

"Yes!" Cian answered, upset with his brother once again doubting him.

"No!"

"Yes!"

"No!"

Cian stepped closer to them, noticing Barkor watching him. "Yes, and I know if I help you, we can close it. Ivan, please trust me. You must trust me. This is the only way."

"Children," Ish interrupted.

"What the fuck?" *Did he just call us children?*

"I mean, don't go on like children."

Cian heard the comeback. Something weird was going on, and he couldn't put his finger on it. Okay, he was drunk or something. Maybe...he'd revisit that thought later.

"Ish, stay out of this. You two should go home with your itty-bitty ship. You're going to get all of us killed. We're about to attack the enemy," Cian said. He got more laughter for an answer. Cian was close to losing his shit. "Oh my god, Ish, stop laughing." Cian watched them wiping the tears from their eyes. Then, after seeing each other wiping their tears, another fit of laughter followed. Cian couldn't help but smile. They were ridiculous.

"Sorry, I can't remember when last I had so much fun," Ish said between hiccups and chuckles. Suddenly his ship flew straight for the Horizon's observation window. Men ducked, throwing hands over their heads; others turned their faces away from the impending crash, while some reflexively dove onto the floor. The golden two-person spacecraft stopped a few feet from colliding with the Horizon.

"Jesus fucking Christ!" Captain Thornton shouted while frantically dabbing and drying his spilled drink from his dashboard.

"It's a circus. Ish, this is so many shades of cray-cray!" Eryn laughed, not fazed by the danger of the situation. Shaking his head, he turned to Ivan, who blinked and said nothing, stupefied by the recklessness.

"Oops, that was close. Sorry, what, Eryn?" Ish asked, swallowing his hysterics.

"He said we are shades of gray crayons," Peter guffawed.

"You two motherfuckers are going to kill all of us! Get the fuck away from the Horizon. You're intoxicated!"

"Forgive me, I accidentally bumped into the forward throttle, and it's your fault. You're making me laugh." Ish poked Peter on the shoulder. Peter poked him back.

"Stop laughing! Stop joking around. I said get the fuck away from the Horizon!" Cian yelled and turned to Ivan's husband, hoping he would help him see reason. "Eryn, help me. This can work. We must separate ourselves from the pull as soon as the first of their fleet enters the spout. I calculated once the spout starts forming and the first ship enters, it will sustain itself, giving you enough time to get out of its way. By then, we would follow from behind and drop the anti-gravitational reactors behind the last ship. Plugging the hole and counteracting the pull to its center."

"That's just in theory, Cian," Ivan said. He pointed his sword at the jokers inside the ship, who had somewhat calmed down. Less with a scowl and more with a smile, Ivan said, "I think, considering what Ish suggests, would be wise." Then, tapping his sword on the palm of his hand, he said, "Give me a minute." He appeared to be thinking and compartmentalizing the problem away from the distractions.

Cian bit down a retort and waited for Ivan to do his mental calculations. His brother had always been an overthinker, but Cian knew the plan would work once he said he was in.

"I'm not a stupid child that needs input and guidance from all of you. I'm the bloody General Fleet Commander. Lasitor and I ran multiple possibilities and planned this while you worked at the factory," Cian said, getting nervous by the second because their window of opportunity was growing smaller.

"You meant a hospital, not a factory," Ivan said.

"He's correct, my love. It was a Zelk factory, using humans to make more Zelk. We worked the production line," Eryn said with a stern look.

Cian sighed. "We have to move. Do you think you can do it? Those two are off their rockers. I can't put the lives of all these people in their hands."

"Yes, whatever you decide," Eryn said, and it seemed he was having a silent conversation with Ivan.

Ivan nodded and turned to Cian. "Yes, brother. You decide. Show us where you want us positioned."

"General," the captain called.

"Yes, Captain. Speak!" Cian said shortly. His captain pointed to the screen on his dashboard.

"He's gone, sir. Ish is gone. I can't ping him. It's like their ship vanished." The captain pushed a few buttons, slapped a screen, and looked up. "Nope, not seeing them. Maybe he cloaked the ship?"

"I don't have time for this. I told him to go home, and maybe he did." Cian turned to Barkor, who'd been gaping, hands in front of his mouth at the spectacle. "He's your friend. Where do you think he's gone? He better not kamikaze the Zelk. He'll fuck up my plan, and we won't have another chance like this."

"My friend? No, Cian. He's your friend, not my friend."

"Yes, he is," Cian said, and Barkor shook his head. "Of course he's your friend. The day we landed and found you, didn't you trade Donali with him?"

"No, why would I do that? Donali said he would stay and learn from us. I sent no one with you. Why would I do that?"

"I don't know, maybe to represent you and tell our fathers how bad it is? It was a trade, wasn't it?" Cian looked to Eryn for answers.

Eryn shrugged. "Yes, I said so, but I think you misunderstood, brother."

"But isn't that why Donali stayed? I showed and told Ish everything, and he was supposed to tell you and Sarinka. If he wasn't with me, he was with you, Donali, and Sarinka. When we returned after our last provisions trip to Phoenix, he and Sarinka left with you."

"Yes, and Ish went back to you," Barkor said, and Cian sensed he was telling the truth.

"Ish never came back to me," Cian said.

"He's not from Grayrak, Cian. He's from Earth. I would know. I've been on the moon for many, many years." Barkor put his hand over his heart, showing he wasn't lying. Cian believed him.

"No, he's definitely not from Earth. He's from a place called Anzulla or something. Didn't he tell you the story about his destroyed home and how he searched for a new place to call home on the moon?"

"What? What are you talking about? No, as far as I know, the day you arrived, he arrived. And what the fuck is an Anzulla?" Barkor asked, and Cian's hackles rose.

"It's where his home is. I thought it was a neighborhood in Grayrak. I thought he was one of us and assumed, like Eryn, who's a King of the Brawl, his parents were king and queen on the moon. Maybe Anzulla is a planet?" Cian slapped his forehead, looking at Eryn, who brought Ish to them. Eryn only shook his head in disbelief.

"Brother, how did you not know that? His whole family is Anunnaki, and their home was destroyed. He said that more than once."

"I know, but we're also Anunnaki, aren't we? I really thought...You know what, leave it. The few times I'd spent time with him...how was I to know?"

Cian counted on his fingers and turned to Barkor. "So if he's not your friend and not from Grayrak, then he's Anunnaki with a golden ship. How stupid am I? He keeps sending me these weird messages on the communicator. Look here, Ish had given me this over a year ago." Cian took the pocket-sized device out of his body suit's back pocket. He switched it on and jumped to his first message, then read it out loud.

"Good travels. Reroute now, *89.339.4473.2333.5957* galactic one seven nine."

Eryn, Ivan and Barkor stepped closer. Captain Thornton pulled a chair closer and climbed on it to see over their towering shoulders. Eryn pushed him inside the circle. Looking at the screen, Cian read as he pressed the white button, flipping through the messages. Small purple letters and numbers flashed. "These came through randomly, and I followed them as best we could.

"Change your current position to these galactic coordinates, *895.44 4.55.3395.7281*.

"No, turn to Mars right now.

"Then, as we traveled each hour, the fucker had us changing direction. Ish explained he had re-plotted the course, and it was a more efficient route.

"Later, he said Zelk was destroyed and to turn back to Earth.

"Then he sends a message. There are Zelk unaccounted for. Stay on the route.

"Early this morning, he said six Zelk were hiding behind asteroids. Search for them. Don't engage.

"Then he said find the six and fuck them up. Checking a different AI, I can't discuss moving to the next point in time."

Then an orange light flickered while Cian was holding it in his hand. "This is a new message. In purple letters, a new message says; *Your plan stinks. Go home! Go home, go home, go home!*

"He's a bloody time traveler," Cian said, and Eryn gave him a look as if he didn't expect this kind of slowness from him.

"Brother," Ivan said, hands on his hips.

"No, wait! Please wait," Cian exclaimed and stopped all the madness. He lifted his hands, grabbing everyone's attention. They halted, focusing on him. "Please wait. Let me think for a second."

"Eryn, brother, please help me. If he's a time traveler, then he must know what's about to happen. If he says it's the worst plan ever, don't you think we should reassess?"

"I agree, Cian," Ivan said. "I respect you, and I will support what you decide. Stopping to think was never your forte. If you need us to do this—"

Barkor took a step closer. It meant everything to Cian. His heart warmed, and he took a deep breath. "Give him a second to think. Keep quiet," Barkor said in a no-nonsense, stern, and menacing voice, which Cian first heard when they abducted Leo.

"Yes, thank you," Cian agreed. He had a ship full of responsibilities. He couldn't just follow through after he was warned. Everyone on the fifty-by-fifty-foot command center was quiet. Cian looked at Barkor, then his brothers, and then said, "Captain, give Lasitor command of the ship."

The captain nodded, following Cian's orders without question.

Cian spoke up to get the AI's attention. "Lasitor, plans have changed. Slow the Horizon, and send the dummy mirror image to continue the due course. Increase its speed, five hours ahead of us."

The lights dimmed, all the computer screens blacked out, and silence fell over the flight control room. The four men sitting in front of the consoles pressed and turned the big red button on their keyboards, removed their hands by folding their arms, and sat back in their chairs while only keeping their gazes on the monitors.

"Autopilot initiated," Lasitor said, and Cian checked his watch.

"Lasitor, at current speed, how long before we enter Earth's atmosphere?"

"Sixteen hours and twenty-five minutes, General."

"Start counting down."

"Yes, General."

"Barkor, tell everyone we're on lockdown. Tell them to eat, drink, and use the washroom. They have an hour. They need to be buckled in and get prepared for impact. Captain, use the same frequency. I'll send one from this device, as well. Leave the following message and put it on repeat. He's been listening in, so I'm sure he'll hear me."

"Ready to record, General," the captain replied.

"This is Cian Romanov, General Fleet Commander of the Warship Horizon. Ish, we set due course for Earth following your direction. My man, you take care of that fucking Zelk. I know you and Peter can and will. We trust you. It makes sense to me now. You were right, my friend. You warned me many times about this moment."

Cian turned to Eryn, Ivan, and Barkor. "He sent me more voice messages a few months ago. One message was to watch out for six Zelk, but once I see them, to ignore them, he will find them, and I mustn't ignore him. Who the fuck talks that way? Obviously, he was drunk off his ass, but I thought he was talking about six Zelk on the moon."

"Are you sure about this, brother?" Ivan asked.

"One hundred percent sure!"

"Yes, brother, I agree. It sounds exactly like time-traveling idiots have messaged you from today—this time. I trust you. You've impressed me with your choices and how well you removed the humans without bloodshed and war. Let's do it," Eryn said and turned to Ivan, who looked relieved to avoid creating vortexes and causing big bangs. Ivan, Eryn, and Barkor's emotions were calm and supportive. It seemed to make sense to them, as well.

Barkor looked confused, but at least he seemed to stay at his side. Cian's men waited for his orders. "Lasitor, prepare a message for transmission to Phoenix."

*

To: General McCormick at Phoenix City.

From: General Cian Romanov, Fleet Commander, The Warship Horizon.

Subject: Prepare for re-entry.

"We're executing Plan B-fifty-three. Sir, we pinpointed the enemy and are going into radio silence. We will enter Earth's atmosphere within sixteen hours. May we all see each other on the other side.

"We Are Coming Home!"

Chapter Twenty-One

"Good morning, citizens of Phoenix.

It's now six a.m.

Did you know that before Phoenix Environmental Project One had been built, six thousand five hundred languages existed?

Although only English is primarily spoken, several other languages like Russian, Irish, and Spanish survived the Big Flood.

Leadership is preparing for an influx of humans who adopted Lunar pidgin, which means they have simplified their means of linguistic communication and constructed an impromptu, new native language.

These folks will have to learn English as a second language.

Visit your community news page to sign up for language tutoring and other ways you can help to make them feel welcome at Phoenix.

Breakfast is served until eight a.m.

It's all semantics, have a good day!"

Juandre

2014 A.D.

Lexington, Kentucky

United States of America

Juandre dragged Andrew out of their bedroom by the arm and into the kitchen and sat him down at the kitchen island. He thought he'd gone to bed early the previous night; after having a massive migraine since yesterday. He noticed he'd slept for almost twenty-four hours when checking his cell phone. His head throbbed in beat with his pulse, and he rubbed his eyes to relieve the pressure behind his eyeballs.

He was woken up by Andrew grunting and seemingly having a nightmare. Juandre had woken him up as gently as possible, and he was worried about him. Andrew was pale and sweaty, and the residual adrenaline from his nightmare needed to be worked out of his system. He put two glasses of milk into the microwave and watched it turn and turn while warming up. The microwave pinged, and Juandre handed him a glass.

"Thank you." Andrew rubbed his face, looking extremely troubled.

"Tell me, as a vampire, are you alive or dead now?" Juandre asked and pulled a chair out for himself. It was four o'clock in the afternoon. "I'd made up my mind, I want you to turn me into a vampire, but first, I need to know more about this. I don't want to end up saying you should have told me this before and then hate you. Tell me your honest story. How did you end up here today? Why do you have these nightmares? Is it because you drift between planes, and your soul can't rest? You're neither living nor dead. I heard you mumble something about being alive and dying and you seemed to cry and fight with dead people?"

Andrew chuckled cynically. "I'm glad you decided. I kind of already knew. As for killing people, I really can't answer that because I don't know what the dream was about. Lately, I've wanted to kill many people. I suppose it could be suppressed anger issues. As for being a vampire, I know it's not what you've read in books or seen on television. The word vampire is a made-up name from books. The person who gave me this gift did have fangs, only he wasn't a vampire. He was something else.

"My memory has been diluted by the passing years, and although I remember significant things like smiles and laughter, the hows and whys that took place before are getting convoluted as the years pass. That's why I have nightmares. They come to refresh my mind. For example, think about a beautiful full moon that you've seen. And then try to remember what you were doing that specific night. You can't because the full moon impacted you, so your brain deletes useless information to make space for more."

"Oh yes, that's true," Juandre said, thinking of Charlie's birthday and not remembering what he wore that day. He smiled at him lovingly. They always got each other the first time.

"Anyway, I would be an empty husk with a tortured mind if I had to recollect the scope of it all daily. I'll tell you the full story, and then I'll shelf it back under *open only in case of an emergency*, okay?"

"Maybe don't tell me if it will bother you like that," Juandre said and meant it. He didn't want to ask anything if it meant hurting Andrew.

"No, I have to tell you, we're planning to be together, so I have to tell you. If it's not now, it will have to be later, and I really want to tell you about myself and my friends. The things I've seen and the future I imagine coming to fruition sometimes scare me, and I need to share this with you, or my head will burst. They're memories of someone else, given to me to remind me of things to come." Andrew seemed tired, like the fate of mankind rested on his shoulders. Those eyes that once sparkled so intensely answered him with emptiness as Juandre sought to know what he saw in his mind.

"Surely, Juandre... I'm not dead. I've been given a choice like I gave you one, but I was also born a certain way. Something was forced onto me as a fetus and onto my mother. I was an experiment. Luckily, the choices I made and that I'm currently working on saved me from my family's clutches. I was made into this to enhance my ability to save others. And to save you."

***

André as relayed by Andrew to Juandre.

1968 A.D.

West Berlin, Germany

It was early nineteen sixty-eight when I'd been forever changed. The protests against the Vietnam War had stirred more worldwide unrest, now known as the nineteen sixty-eight generation. Faculty and students alike were flamed by the call for liberation of our own restrictive governments. I was out celebrating with fellow protestors as I had just earned my doctorate in chemical science and was just starting my tenured professorship.

I got swept up in the fray at the Opera House protests, then joined the celebrations of a successful march on solidarity and the abolition of national borders across Europe. It quickly turned into a night of loud music, dancing, and many shots of schnapps.

By midnight, I had to return to the apartment I shared with Peter, my best friend. He went home earlier, not liking crowds and preferring to finish packing. We had a train to catch at nine o'clock the next morning that would take us to Vienna, then Switzerland, and, ultimately, we'd catch a flight to America.

Our fathers were professors of physics and science at the Humboldt University of Berlin. Still, the wall between East and West Berlin didn't bar the organization's reach into the West.

We had inherited our features. Peter, with his white-as-snow hair and crystal blue eyes, and me, with blond hair and green eyes, from our fathers and a special bloodline that was bred from an ancient line of genetics. We were constantly measured and monitored, and being gay was punishable by death. Girls fell over their feet for us, but we were happy staying single as best friends.

We kept that a secret and maintained we were best friends and sometimes brothers. The university had offered each of us a position, and we knew we had to take the chance and escape their clutches the next morning before returning and serving the organization.

If we left, they would only miss us that coming Tuesday. We were frowned upon if we mixed with friends outside the organization. Even the apartment belonged to the university, which ultimately belonged to the organization. We planned to take our degrees and find work in America.

That night, I'd kept catching the eye of one oddly beautiful man. Each time our gazes locked, it was broken by some drunken patron passing between us.

Just before twelve, when my money was finished, and I drank my fill of schnapps, I said my goodbyes and headed for the washroom to relieve myself before making the short walk home. It smelled dank and old, like all the beer halls in Vienna. I walked up to the long trough, which reeked of urine, pulled my cock out, and sighed in relief as a strong stream came out.

A deep male voice over my shoulder startled me. "*Very nice!*" I was shocked to see the handsome man I'd been ogling standing beside me, staring at my junk. The schnapps must have dulled my senses because I hadn't heard his entry or approach. I didn't respond but continued draining myself into the enamel basin. I heard the unsnapping of buttons, and soon, his stream joined mine. I couldn't help glancing over to quickly see what he was packing.

He was standing much closer than was necessary. His dark cock was long and thick. I noticed he wore a golden ring of various sizes and designs on each of his long fingers because I watched intently as he relieved himself. He continually pulled his foreskin, retracting it and then pushing it forward over the large head. He never took his gaze off me. I was uncomfortable as fuck. Men did things like that to test you, and you ended up being battered to death in the alley. I stopped pissing and hastily tucked myself away to get out of there.

He purred at me, and his tone was minacious, accentuating the dark aura that emanated from him. "Why do you act so nervous? I'm sure there have been many men who compliment, perhaps even worship, such a fine cock as yours. It is made even more impressive by the body to which it is attached."

He was gorgeous, and everything about him screamed danger. Like a predator. A big predator. I estimated him to be an easy seven feet tall. His lips were full, and his skin was smooth and hairless. His dark complexion didn't match his weird big golden eyes. His deep baritone alone had my cock taking notice.

I lied and said, “I’m not nervous.” I was already seeing him pounding into me relentlessly. And I wasn’t sure if he wanted to fuck or kill me. “I’ve just stayed out later than I planned, and I have much to do,” I answered shakily and turned to leave.

Before I reached the door, I felt a hand on my shoulder, which turned into a grip. I was turned around, and my back was shoved into the wall. He brought his face to mine and forced me into a rough kiss. I pushed him back and tried going for the door. Once again, he grabbed me and slammed me against the wall.

He leered at me. “Why are you in such a hurry? I only want to have a little fun,” he hissed at me with a wanton look on his dark, angelically beautiful face. His voice was deeper than before. He must have been a fallen angel because he emanated immoral and shameless debauchery.

I begged, “Please, I just want to go home.” I’d never been so frightened.

Still holding me against the wall, he demanded, “What is your name, boy?”

I was no boy. I was in my thirties. He was obviously getting some delight from seeing the fear in my eyes.

“An...André, ”I stuttered.

He nodded slowly. “André,” he said. Then he took a shiny electronic device from his pocket and held it beside my face. I wondered why he asked and was worried our fathers sent him to collect us.

He put the device back in his pocket. “That is a very German name. You should change it when you reach America. You’re going to be very famous one day,” he said slowly.

Fuck, he knew about our plans. My system flooded with adrenaline, and I wished someone would enter the restroom so that I could flee. I focused on his eyes in the light, which had a sheen to them, like an animal. His irises were something I’d never seen before. They had rings of gold and black around the pupils.

I wasn't going to let him know how scared I was that he was right. "I'm a professor at West Berlin University. I'm not going to America. You must have me confused with someone else," I said, mesmerized by his otherworldly eyes and hoping to reason with him.

He continued looking at my face as if he'd memorized it and confirmed I was who he thought I was. "You are from my lover's city. It is a pity we did not travel to meet each other earlier. So we have to work with the time we have. Don't worry. We will have enough time to have a good time." He seemed to ooze out the last three words, then he smiled, revealing pointy white incisor teeth.

Still hoping to convince him to let me go, I asked, "I don't understand what you mean. Why would you have a lover and still want me? Won't he be jealous? I know I would be jealous. I really need to get on my way."

"But of course you do," he said as he tilted his head from side to side, his gaze never leaving me, lingering on my lips. I licked them involuntarily. My cock was achingly hard, and the big man overpowering me really turned me on. I was not small when compared to Peter, but in this man's presence, I was the itty-bitty mouse, and he was the lion.

"Yes, please," I answered, not knowing where our conversation was leading while certain it was not to a virtuous place.

He smiled at me and, with a serious look, said, "André, I am Ishtar, but you can call me Ish. I'm looking for a group that calls themselves the Disciples. You have heard of them, yes?" he asked and hissed through his lengthening incisors.

"How could I not have heard of them?" I stupidly answered truthfully. I took the opportunity to slide toward the door to get out of his reach because Peter and I came from big families that largely belonged to the stupid psychotic group. "I wish you a good night," I told him.

I mustered a smile and turned to the door when I heard his deep, authoritative voice. "I did not give you permission to leave."

My breath hitched. "I apologize. I thought our conversation was at an end. I didn't mean to be rude," I said calmly, while inside, I was feeling lightheaded and on the verge of panicking.

"André, I forgive you, but you must make it up to me," he responded. It sounded like a lisp as he spoke through the teeth hanging out the sides of his mouth. "Don't be scared," he said.

My fight-or-flight response betrayed me. I wanted to run or fall down and play dead, but instead, I stood shaking and it wasn't from fear. I was excited by the hunger in his eyes for me. I let my gaze fall on his impressive bulge.

"How...what do you mean? What do you plan to do to me?" I asked, not wanting to know and eager for an answer.

"Go through the door at the end of the hall. That will take you into an alley. I will be right behind you. Do not even think of running," he said as a purr. "I will catch you."

He gestured for me to leave, and I obeyed. I was scared his buddies were waiting, ready to bash my head in for being attracted to men. I had no choice, so I pushed the heavy door at the end of the hall open and walked out into the crisp night air.

The alley was completely empty except for cans of trash. A full moon peeked through the opening between the two buildings. The sounds of people, cars, and horns curtained us from the world outside, so close but still out of my reach. When I turned around, Ish leaned against the brick wall of the building we'd just exited. He stared at me, looking deep into my soul. A look only one man can give another, a look of lust and hunger that only a man could satisfy. A woman would cower under that gaze, and I was no woman.

"Don't be afraid, tell me now, do you want this or not?" he asked soothingly as he unbuttoned his green and gold crisp uniform coat. It looked aristocratic from another era. "I just want you to do what you so obviously enjoy doing with that pretty mouth."

"I don't know what you mean," I responded, knowing my lies were falling on deaf ears. And I liked it.

The smile left his face. "Over here in front of me now and on your knees, boy," he ordered me. I could see that he was serious and meant every word. I should have taken the opportunity and said no, and run. But my body betrayed me. My cock stirred at his command, and I knew I liked it. I walked up to him and sank to my knees.

"There now, be a good boy and take out my cock." Once again, he was speaking in his catlike purr with no signs of anger only authoritative dominance. I wanted to keep him purring, so I reached out and undid his belt buckle and methodically began unclasping the weird hooks of his pants' front.

"Ah, there's a good boy. Now reach in and pull it out."

Gingerly, I put my fingers through the opening of his underwear. I was surprised to find no hair at all. It was silky smooth. I caught the scent of male musk and felt the root of his cock, which was thickening even as I grasped it and pulled it into the open air, where it continued to respond to my eager manipulation. He was huge, and I shivered as I enjoyed doing what I was ordered.

"Put it in your mouth and suckle it, boy. Suck on my piss slit," he said through his abnormally long incisors.

I did as I was told. I opened my mouth wide and tried to cover my teeth with my lips. As his cock slid into my mouth, the thick foreskin was retracted from the sensitive head, and he gasped. I tasted the bitterness of unwashed cock and the sweetness of fluid leaking from his slit but didn't pull off. I swallowed eagerly.

"That's right, clean it. Wash it, pretty boy," he whispered and ran his hand through my hair, signaling his approval. I complied and hoped he wasn't working for the people we planned to run from in the morning. Maybe he was collecting intelligence against us. He knew about us and our plans.

Ish placed his hands behind my head and held me in place as he thrust into my mouth. Spit and pre-cum dripped out of my lips and down my chin. His thrusts became fast and frantic, jabbing down my throat. The bulbous head of his cock intruded past my tonsils, and I couldn't breathe.

No man had ever had such a spell over me. Grunting and pulling my hair, he held my head firmly in place. He pulled back for a minute, just long enough for me to get a breath of fresh air, and in the back of my mind, I found quietness, silence, and peace. With the new air entering my lungs, full consciousness returned.

Ish prolonged the delicious sinful act of one man sucking another off by pulling out and staving off ejaculation. With my head still held in place, I rolled my eyes up to see his grinning face looking down at me.

I thought I heard the door open and shut and saw another man beside Ish. I tried jumping up and away, startled at being caught.

"No! Don't stop," Ish ordered, holding me in place by my hair. "This is my lover, Peter." He introduced us as if I wasn't holding his cock warm in my mouth. "I'm sure Peter will want to enjoy you when I have finished. Peter is also from here. Tonight is a reunion of some sort. Am I correct, Peter?"

Peter smiled and seemed delighted to see me like that. He was also dressed in a style of clothes I'd never seen in Berlin. He wasn't nearly as tall as Ish, who must be more than seven feet tall. His long hair was white-as-snow, and he almost looked exactly like my roommate, Peter. Even the blue eyes were the same. This Peter's hair cascaded over his shoulders. My Peter had short hair—otherwise, I would have said it was the same person.

"I think that he likes being on his knees. Is he good at this, Ish?" Peter appraised me up and down, lingering on my swollen lips.

"He is superb. It took a little convincing, but I can assure you that he's done this before," Ish said with an amused sparkle in his predatory eyes, then returned his attention to me. "Get going, boy. I don't have all night. The sooner you finish me off, the sooner you can suck Peter."

I resumed my sucking on his fat cock head in all earnest. Peter stood to our side and watched me fellating his lover. Ish was soon back into rhythm, pumping my mouth fiercely as he moaned and held my head in place. Tears were streaming from my eyes as he fucked my mouth.

"Peter, take your cock out and get it ready for our young friend," Ish ordered his lover.

Peter laughed and undid his pants. His staff, already erect, was long and thin with a wicked curve to it. As he watched me, he manipulated his foreskin slowly...almost casually. From the corner of my eye, I could see the glint of liquid oozing from the yawning tip.

"As always, Ish, you like a good mouth fucking," Peter approvingly said as he looked at us.

"Peter, put your hand on my cock and feel it slide in and out of this boy's mouth and kiss me while he milks me." His voice was ragged with lustful urgency and without further hesitation, Peter placed a hand on Ish's shaft, where my lips would touch him whenever Ish's thick cock slammed into my throat.

At the same time, he bent his head toward Peter, who I noticed had normal human teeth. Ish became so excited by his lover's actions that I felt his balls rise against my chin as his cock swelled to almost unbearable thickness as it shot thick wads of cum against the back of my throat.

I was on the border of losing consciousness from lack of oxygen when Ish pulled out of my throat and wiped what remained of his ejaculate against the side of my face.

No sooner had he withdrawn before he grabbed the length of Peter's staff and guided it to my mouth. Peter gasped, moaned, laced his fingers in my hair, and shoved himself into me, hard and deep. His cock being slim, went down much further than Ish's into the distinct curvature of my already bruised throat. I gagged and coughed and tried to pull back, which resulted in Peter pulling his cock out of my mouth. Peter and Ish both laughed.

"Now suck it right and don't pull back, or I won't be so nice next time! You're doing great. You're such a good boy," Peter praised, sounding exactly like my Peter. The lack of oxygen and euphoria intensified my enjoyment of being used, and I ejaculated in my pants.

Now Ish grabbed Peter's length and held on to it as my mouth was assailed. Peter didn't last as long as Ish. In just a matter of minutes came the familiar swell and release of sperm. Unlike his lover, Peter didn't force himself further down my throat as he orgasmed. Instead, he pulled out and, holding my head in place, spent copious amounts of warm cum over my face and even into my eyes. When he'd finished, he pushed me over, knocking me on my back in the alley. I was dazed, and my mouth fucked senseless, not knowing what to expect next. Maybe a beating.

"Now, go home!" Ish ordered.

I struggled to my feet and looked back at them only once, still disorientated and coming down from my own orgasm and experience I didn't understand. I began to run as fast as my aching knees would allow me. I made it to Losberg Street, where many protestors I'd partied with dispersed. I shoved past them. Those who saw me coming jumped out of my way but must have noticed the spunk running down my face.

I didn't stop running until I reached our apartment. I tore through the door. And that was when my understanding of the world as I knew it shattered.

I crashed inside, calling for Peter, and fell over the suitcases he had packed.

He stumbled out of his bedroom with wide eyes and bed hair and helped me up. "André, what happened to you?" he asked, concerned and struggling to get me up from the floor. It wasn't an easy task since he was smaller than me in height and weight. "Why do you smell like..."

Ashamed, I watched as he assessed my hair that had been grabbed and pulled, my face smeared with cum, and my well-used mouth. "Wait, did you get attacked? I knew it. I told you we're not safe here!" He was referring to the Disciples sending men to punish us for being attracted to men instead of a woman.

I was scared of something totally different. I was mouth-fucked by strange men that were surely not human or from here and somehow made themselves look like us.

A deep rumble and chuckles of an unwelcome visitor woke me from my hysterics. "We thought you would never get here," Ish said from the direction of the living room.

I pushed Peter back. "Get out, Peter, run!" But he didn't move.

"These two forced me to suck them off in an alley... they... are here to kill us. They're fucking hunting us. They know about us leaving!" I heaved for air and frantically pulled Peter to push him out the door, willing him to leave. The apartment was dark. No lights were on, and yet I somehow knew they saw us.

"They want both of us, and they asked about the Disciples." I turned to look in their direction. "Leave my friend alone, and I'll tell you everything about the Disciples," I said.

Peter resisted and wasn't moving. My body was shaking, and as soon as he heard me mentioning the Disciples, he flung himself around.

"Those right-winged hooligans think we live in the dark ages. They use intimidation and fear to achieve their ends. We want out, you hear me! We don't want anything to do with them! I will tell you anything you want to know. Can you help us?" Peter asked.

"We know, and that's why we're here," the other Peter said and chuckled, and the light in the living room came on.

Peter froze as he was stunned by the two handsome but dangerous-looking strangers. Inside the apartment with its low-hanging ceiling,

Ish looked even bigger. Even though they'd just forced me to suck them, my cock stirred at the sight of them.

Other Peter chuckled. "No, I, we had enough for tonight, down, boy," he said as if reading my mind.

"You never said no. You enjoyed every minute of it," Ish said, and I wondered whether there was a time I could have said no. Yes, he did ask, only I'd never answered.

"We are here with a very important message and, of course, to help you," Ish said.

My Peter gasped, and he slammed both hands in disbelief over his mouth. "You, you, me, no. How can that be?" He pointed back and forth between himself and the other Peter. He must have thought it was him, and I stepped closer to really take him in. It was dark in the alley, so here, next to each other in the light, there wasn't any fucking doubt in my mind. It definitely was his double or a long-lost brother, I thought.

Then other Peter answered in the same voice and same Bavarian accent, "Yes, it's me, and no, I'm not your brother or any other relative. My name is Peter." He lifted his sleeves, showing his wrists, the same wrists my Peter had slashed a month before. I found him bleeding out and trying to die because he was gay.

Since then, we'd devised a plan to escape our fathers and the organization that had been ruling our families for generations.

"We know what you're planning with regard to getting on that train tomorrow, never to return. That train is going to be bombed by a right-winged communist. Only Peter will survive. You will never make it or escape to America. Let me help you, and..." Ish said, interrupted by my Peter hitting the floor passed out cold.

"Get a cold cloth, Ish," other Peter said and jumped to help as I scooped my Peter's head into my lap.

"Come on, be okay. I love you. I can't live without you," I cried, as the night's oppressive, disorientating emotions flooded my system and broke my resolve. Tears streamed down my face as I remembered how close to death I found him just a month before, and now pale as a sheet again, reminding me how fucked-up our lives were.

"Here you are." Ish handed me a cold, wet rag.

I wiped over my Peter's forehead, his cheeks, and down to the back of his neck. "That's it, open your eyes," I coaxed.

And other Peter said, "Don't worry, you're fine. We're not here to hurt you. We need your help as much as you need ours," he said, smiling gently at my Peter and me. Not at all the motherfuckers from the alley.

"Tie your hair away so I can see your face," I ordered him this time. He happily took his long blond locks and tied them with a leather string he produced from his pocket. Ish bent down to kiss other Peter, and my mouth hung open.

"*Donnerwetter,*" my Peter whispered in German and passed out again. I wiped his face again until crystal blue eyes opened and looked up at us. The same blue eyes in the face of the man I sucked off in the alley. I knew both pairs of eyes very well. The other Peter's eyes were maybe a few years older, but not much.

"How is this possible?" I asked, continuing to wipe my Peter's face to soothe him.

Ish came closer, bent to one knee, and scooped my Peter up. "Come, let's put him on the sofa," he said gently, and I trusted him for some inexplicable reason.

Once my Peter had woken fully, they explained who Ish was. He was the last of his kind and definitely not a vampire. He told us about a timeline he discovered and, so too, distant relatives and his lover, the other Peter. They knew about our fathers and the organization, the experimentation on us as fetuses, and explained that we were also distant relatives of Ish. His blood was the ancient bloodline of the Anunnaki who created humans and exited the earth at the fall of Babylonia, and it was they who left the gold cylinder engraved with the tree of life. Ish had been trying to rectify the demise of his planet and Earth, but the more he meddled, the worse it got. His family, the timeline the other Peter was from, had him swearing to stop fiddling and let it be. This was apparently our timeline. He could visit with us and promised not to change the timeline and how things were when he met the other Peter in the future.

* * *

Juandre

2014 A.D.

Lexington, Kentucky

United States of America

"Holy shit. My head is spinning," Juandre said with an effeminate lisp as he listened intently and tried to take it all in. "I fucking need something stronger than milk." He jumped up and rumbled around for anything and found a half-empty bottle of Lord Andrew and put down a tumbler for each of them. Then, he sat back down and sipped the strong liquid burning his throat, feeling instantly relaxed. Now he could continue listening.

Andrew continued. "But when they said alien, my Peter fucking lost it. He laughed and curled himself into a ball, rolling hysterically on the floor. It took my Peter and me a few hours to ask questions and listen to their adventures and explanations. The condensed version is that we were half relatives and needed to be given the gift, as Ish called it. He said the world was near ending as we knew it, and we had to be prepared. They handed us a list of things to collect and told us where to go store it for our future selves. The biggest and weirdest request was whiskey. Hence me owning a whole bloody distillery. Apparently, that will make a general and thousands of men very happy in the future. Peter is currently working undercover, we grew apart, and it wasn't until I met you that I truly felt something. It took me ten years to realize. But I'm here and only offering the bite if you truly want it."

"Tell me more. Why did they force you to suck them off in the alley?" Juandre asked.

"I don't know, they didn't really force me. I thought about it many times—and I think I didn't realize it was an S/m kink I have. When you picked me up and took me to the hotel in twenty-oh-four, I loved how you took control and the power-play we exchanged. They must have known the future me. They said they're from a time when only men walked the earth. When men were married, and sometimes there were not just two, but three, four, and even five men in a coupling. Their children are born without a living woman."

"No way!" Juandre said with disbelieving wonder.

"Yes, and I can't wait to see it! That's what Peter is doing now. He's out collecting and preparing eggs and technology to make it all possible."

"And the Disciples?" Juandre asked, never missing a beat.

"We have them sorted. They don't want us to interfere too much with the timeline. Things still need to happen as they did, and we can make it easier and better by not fiddling too much, and Ish keeps track of them. They are..." Andrew stopped mid-sentence and frowned, looking like he wasn't ready to divulge something, so Juandre didn't pry.

"So they traveled in time? How?" he asked, changing the subject to more exciting things.

"Apparently, it's always been possible for the royal family. Ish has a ship that can jump in time. He's the last member of the royal family of Anzulla. I have no clue where his planet is or if it's even in our Solar system. It sounds like he's some kind of time police or timekeeper."

"Really? A time-traveling alien, and not a vampire, but Anunnaki from Anzulla, is in love and traveling with your Peter?"

"They told us that night that I never would have made it to America and that Peter basically returned and continued with what he's working on now. That's why he had to go on doing his work and research. I was put on another train to escape the train crash, but my family believed I'd died in it because Peter told them I had run away and had taken that train destined to take me to America.

"When I arrived, I changed my name from André to Andrew, used my doctorate to create the perfect whiskey, and started Lord Andrew Distilleries. All the while, I monitored the organization's American chapter. I still talk to Peter occasionally. Unfortunately it's as if he's lost interest, and his work has become everything to him. I think he's just going through the motions while he's waiting for Ish."

Juandre jumped up. "Okay, I don't want to waste another bloody minute. Bite me, drink me, and then fill me up," he said with vigor and slammed his hand on the table, eager to get this ball rolling.

"Are you sure about this? Do you want me to bite you and spend the rest of your life with me?" Andrew asked.

Juandre put his hands on his hips and answered him with his smoldering gaze. Then, to be super sure, he nodded and smiled.

Andrew's fangs peeked over his bottom lip, and Juandre thought he was also falling in love with them, too. He looked adorable when they were extended. His eyes sparkled with a green sheen. Although he didn't like the word vampire, he was otherwise a stunning teddy bear. Juandre saw himself waking up beside his magnificent beauty and in those strong arms daily. *Easily*.

"Your place is equipped for protection, so I guess living there with you is the smart option, but it's a bit far from my work. Where would we live? Should I find a job closer to the distillery? And what about Charlie?"

Andrew jerked his head up and stared at him with an intense look, and Juandre forgot what he wanted to say. "Don't worry about those details now. That will sort itself out."

They didn't break eye contact as Juandre took his hand, led him to the sofa, sat him down, and climbed on his lap. Slowly he massaged his cock with the palm of his hand.

"If you suck me, I'll suck you," he pleaded with a promise.

"I'll suck you even if you don't suck me, but then you won't have a friend to spend eternity with," Juandre said seductively.

Andrew sighed, and it sounded like relief as he plopped his head back, and his breathing became faster.

"Do you need oxygen like everyone else? Why else would you breathe?" Juandre kept his voice low and teasing. The bulge beneath his hand grew in size and firmness. Juandre lowered his zipper slowly, freeing him, and kept leisurely rubbing his stiffness while kissing him hungrily. His shaft was a solid rod of flesh, and at the first hint of pre-cum, Juandre slipped his thumb over the slit, smearing it into his cock head.

He wanted to taste Andrew badly, so he released the kiss to slide down and sit back on his heels. Bending forward, he tasted the sweet taste of Andrew's arousal, and it was exquisite. Juandre wanted more.

He slid his lips over his cock, and then licked all around the head. Slipping his tongue into it, delving deep for more of his sweet nectar. Juandre relaxed his throat and swallowed him down to the root, so his pubs tickled his nose. Andrew's breath hitched, and he swore obscenities and grabbed hold of his hair, holding him in place. Juandre closed his eyes, enjoying the taste of him while he listened to Andrew panting and begging for more and not to stop.

To prolong his pleasure, Juandre drew back. "Baby, I haven't even started yet."

Andrew's dazed eyes popped open as he lifted his head. He stared down at him, his pupils blown, and it seemed like he forgot to speak. He opened and closed his mouth and plopped his head back again.

Juandre dug his fingers into the sides of Andrew's hips and squeezed hard.

"Lie down," he ordered, and Andrew hissed through his fangs but fell obediently to the side, surrendering. Juandre moved his hands to his tight, muscled butt and grabbed hold of the thick blanket of hair covering them.

"Close your eyes and only feel. I love your hairy body. You're built like a mountain man and move with the swagger of a lion. You're all man, my man, and you smell so fucking good."

Andrew rolled his head from side to side in answer to Juandre loving him with words and his hands, surrendering to his touch.

"I'm yours. Do with me as you please," Andrew whispered in a whine while lisping the *please*, begging him to do more to him.

Juandre sucked the head of his cock through his tight lips, knowing exactly how it felt, then swallowed him down again. Arching his back, Andrew hissed and groaned his pleasure. Juandre continued moving his mouth up and down, getting his cock as wet as possible. Andrew's eyes opened, and they glanced at each other. Again, he seemed to want to say something, thought better of it, and gave up. Juandre smiled around his thick cock and loved the solid feel in his mouth.

"I want to bite and fuck you," he slurred like a bear waking up from slumber.

Juandre scraped his teeth over his shaft and let his cock fall with a plop out of his mouth and tore his gaze away from the beautiful thing, and grinned at Andrew.

"Today is the first day of the rest of our existence together," he said and rubbed his face in the fuzziness of Andrew's lower belly and pubic hair and moved down to where his member lay, twitching for attention. Shudders coursed through Andrew, and it seemed he liked the soft sensual caresses just as much as the painful ones. Good to know because Juandre loved finding out new ways to pleasure him.

Sliding his tongue down, first the left and then the right side of his iliac furrows, Juandre reached behind to grab his buttocks, squeezing hard. His engorged cock leaked a drop of pre-cum, and Juandre suckled the tip, teasing him.

"Please, Juandre, for love of, just do something," he begged.

Juandre glanced up. "Something wrong, lover?"

Andrew gave him a mock death glare. In answer, Juandre flicked the head with his tongue. The heavy blood-filled organ twitched. Sweeping around the head in deliberate slow circles, Juandre asked, "Is that better?" Then, he kissed his way down along his shaft and grabbed Andrew's balls, pulling them and rolling them in the palm of his hand.

"Yes, just like that. Hmmm, that feels amazing," Andrew muttered.

"I think it's time," Juandre said. Like a predator taking notice of his prey, Andrew's eyes shot open, and he watched himself being climbed like a tree, never breaking eye contact.

"I'm going to ride you while you bite me. Is that okay?" Juandre asked because he wasn't sure if blood was going to get on his furniture or not.

Andrew swallowed audible gulps, his Adam's apple bobbing up and down, while Juandre removed the last of their clothes. "Are you going to drink me dead and turn me like the movies, slash your wrist, and let me suck on it?"

"No, it's not like the movies, and I'm not a vampire!" Andrew chuckled.

"Then what are you if not one? You have a sun allergy, fangs, drink blood, and sleep during the day. You're fast and strong, and you smell very good. You can read minds and plant ideas. Of course, you're a fucking vampire. What else would you be?"

"I'm a superhuman with Anunnaki DNA and was gifted these powers from a royal-blooded Anunnaki. And no, all I have to do is fuck you and then bite you, after which I inject whatever is in my venom into you. I only have enough for one bite. You'll have enough for one bite. After the sac is drained, it doesn't refill. That's what Ish told me."

"I wish I could meet your Ish. He sounds like...hmmm," Juandre moaned and rubbed lube all over his entrance and Andrew's cock and then ground his ass in tiny circles over his cock.

Andrew held his breath, his gaze pinned on Juandre as he sank until the head of his cock sat nestled inside him. Once he'd adjusted to the girth, he started moving his hips and began to pump. The erotic sounds coming from them were erratic and grew louder. Juandre smiled inwardly, knowing he was the one giving Andrew his pleasure and that he'd waited and wanted Juandre all this time. Warmth flooded through him. Juandre was very sure it was love. He wanted to spend an eternity with this man, with this vampire.

The euphoric feeling between them built, as the orgasm building wanted to explode. He yelled, "Oh fuck, I'm going to come!"

Then Andrew's teeth were over his jugular, biting. Scorching hot pain and pleasure shot through him as Andrew wrapped both arms around him, holding him in place. He couldn't move. Sparks flew before his eyes, but only his howls of pain and pleasure filled his living room. He felt weaker and sleepier, then it all went black as he passed out and lost consciousness.

Chapter Twenty-Two

"Good morning, citizens of Phoenix.

It's now six a.m.

Did you know people used to get married for purposes of accumulation?

Yes, together, they accumulated money, children, goats, land, and even cattle.

The upside was they had a timestamp of, give and take, fifty years on such a union.

Lasitor, can you imagine the heaps of children and livestock running around Phoenix if married couples never called it quits?

Visit your community news page to book your marriage and couple counseling sessions or to apply for the dissolution of such unions.

Breakfast is served until eight a.m.

May we all come together in the spirit of unification day!"

Andrew

2014 A.D.

Lexington, Kentucky

United States of America

Andrew stepped from the cloud of bellowing steam following him from the ensuite bathroom and tied his terry cloth belt loosely around his waist with twitchy fingers. He patted the side pocket to make sure his surprise was still there. The steam mixed and disappeared in the soft yellow light as it cut through it like sunlight would cut through the early morning mists of a rainforest. His gaze roamed over the scene and drank in the breathtaking sight before him.

"You know I've always dreamed of you waiting in our bed for me, but this sight before me, I could never have imagined, this is so much better," Andrew said.

Juandre lifted the red satin sheet off his body, pushing it aside and spreading his legs so Andrew could see his balls already pulled up and the dark silhouette of his cock straining against the white-laced briefs. Juandre reached slowly inside and freed his cock from its sexy confinement and palmed his erection—stroking it until a bead of pre-cum appeared at the tip.

Andrew's mouth watered. He wanted to lick it. His pointy incisors lengthened and pushed over the round bow of his bottom lip. His gaze wandered over Juandre's olive skin and drank in the perfect form of his body. The matching white lace top of his nightie softly draped over his well-defined pecs, and the dark, prominently pointed hard nubs of his nipples called to him to bite them. The lace ruffled over the chest hair that trailed down over the hills and valleys of his abdominal muscles and stopped right above the neatly trimmed dark bush surrounding his impressively thick eight-inch cock. Andrew didn't stop there. He trailed further down his long sexy thighs, ending at his beautifully pedicured red toes. He was stunning, even more so now that he'd taken his bite. Andrew had to remind himself to take a few deep breaths.

"Do you like it?" Juandre purred seductively and thrust up into his hand. His eyes were dark with lust, and self-confidence oozed while he rubbed the loose lace over his chest and abdomen.

"My dream has finally come true," Andrew muttered, moving closer. "Here you are in my bed, dressed in your sexy lace nighties, just for me, and so hungry for sex. And we're both vampires. I wished for this so many times. To make love and to be touched, without secrets between us." *He better get on with it*, he thought as his heart thundered in his chest. When he reached the bed, he dropped to one knee, took the surprise out of his pocket, and held up a small blue and silver-colored box, like an offering to Juandre.

Juandre was up and at the edge of the bed in an instant. Gripping the edge tightly, he swung his feet over to the floor. "Andrew, what is this?" he asked, eyes wide with amazement.

Andrew loved the effeminate lilt in his surprised voice. He loved everything about this man. He wanted to spend his eternity with him.

"Juandre, shh, please let me do this," Andrew urged him, their gazes locked.

Biting his lip, Juandre nodded.

"You know, I loved you from the moment I first saw you. When you stopped your red *Porsche* next to me on the I-seventy-five. My heart broke that instant because I was convinced you could never return my feelings. I thought you were happy, and you had your whole life planned out. You were on your way to becoming a doctor, and the longer we fucked that weekend, the more I wanted you. I played into your fantasy, never realizing that it was mine, too. Although we parted physically, my mind couldn't part ways with you. You stole my heart and soul, and the longer we spent time apart, the more your smile and face taunted me. Every day without you was filled with loneliness and bitterness. The hopeful joy I experienced when I found out you lived in the same town as I?" Andrew stroked his trembling fingers over Juandre's plump bottom lip. "I wasted so much time. I was such an idiot. For ten years, I suffered, not knowing you suffered, too."

Juandre reached out, took his hand, and held it. Squeezing as if to say, *I hear you, go on*.

"The company was never meant to see what I felt for you. I was determined to keep my private life and feelings locked away. I was afraid of losing my respectability and control over them. I built Lord Andrew from the ground up and saved it for a future that has yet to come. I was scared of losing you and the company. Never realizing it's bloody mine, together we're stronger, and no one can take it away from me. You opened my eyes and unlocked the cage I built for myself and hid inside. From love, from you, Juandre. I know all this has been a tornado of change for you. The way you handled it and accepted it still takes my breath away. You're so much more than I expected. I hope I'm worthy of you. Just being with you, how your mind works, and how you calculate every next step, amazes me. I want to be with you as much as I want to fuck you."

Juandre chuckled and leaned closer, his breath washing over Andrew's face. Juandre smiled and looked down at the box in Andrew's hand as he opened it, revealing the glowing blue band Ish had given him to give to his husband one day. "It was made from metal not yet discovered," Andrew said, and an intake of breath made him look at Juandre, who stared at the ring.

"It's a gift from my friends, I told you, the ones that visited me and turned me, you'll meet them in our future. It's a metal that glows blue at night, and apparently, they built spaceships from it. It's our secret. I love you and wanted to know if you would agree to marry me one day when it is legal. But until then, and after that, I will serve you and love you as best I can."

Juandre pulled him closer, tears in his eyes and smiling. "Are you putting the ring on my finger, or should I do it myself?" he asked.

"Don't be impatient. We have eons ahead of us." Happiness and excitement shot through Andrew as he pushed back his own tears of joy choking him. "Juandre, will you spend the rest of your life with me? Will you marry me as soon as we're able?"

Juandre wrapped his right hand around the back of Andrew's neck and offered his left hand for him to slip the ring onto his finger. Andrew realized he was still waiting for him and hurriedly took the glowing ring out of the box, threw the box somewhere over his shoulder, and slipped the ring onto a smiling Juandre's finger. His glistening white little fangs pushed down his bottom lip. He was still getting used to them, but he looked so cute with them.

His turning was easy and extremely erotic. Andrew penetrated him, and they made love through the whole ordeal, just like Ish had turned him all those years ago. Being a royal family member from Anzulla, each family member had a special gift, which could only be passed on to one special person. He gave his gift to Andrew because Peter didn't need it. Afterward, they handed him this ring and told him to search for his mate, make whiskey and save the earth and, ultimately, the universe one day. Yes, they did drink blood. But they also ate and drank everything they used to. The high protein globulin concentrations were what they needed from the blood to survive. The human liver and immune system made globulins. Those proteins were what their bodies needed to fight cell breakdown and infections. And that was why they drank blood.

"I'd like it if we could play a game tonight," he said with a lisp through his new incisors. His cock pointed at Andrew and bobbed a few times on its own. Like saying, *here I am, come get me*. "Hmmm, let Daddy make you feel good tonight," Juandre said as he took the bottle and applied a generous amount to two fingers. "Get on your hands and knees, boy," he ordered.

Andrew immediately switched to being submissive and unrobed, then did what he was told to do.

Juandre carefully rubbed lube around his entrance. "Hmmm, you feel ready for your Daddy tonight. You're such a good boy, aren't you?" he asked as he twisted and pumped slowly with one finger. He worked it in all the way, hitting Andrew's prostate. He knew exactly how to rub his pleasure button.

"You were so good, asking Daddy to marry you. I'm proud of you for showing courage and your love." He pulled back, and one finger was joined by many more. The discomfort was unexpected, but Andrew enjoyed it and wasn't going to ask or protest.

I'll let Daddy do whatever he wants to me. I trust him and can't wait to feel what else he sticks into me tonight.

"Ahh, Daddy, that feels so good! Thank you, Daddy," Andrew whined and sunk deeper into his role.

"You deserve everything I'm going to give you. Just enjoy this, my boy. Just enjoy," Juandre coaxed.

"Ahh," Andrew moaned, and his eyes rolled back in his head. For what seemed like a long time, Juandre worked his fingers around and in and out of him. He glided over his prostate with precision, and Andrew sucked in breath after breath. He moaned and rocked his ass back and forth for more.

Juandre pulled his fingers out. And the feeling of emptiness had him begging. "No, Daddy, please don't stop. I was so close. I need more, please, Daddy." He felt more lube drizzling over him. Juandre was doing an enthusiastic job of it and lubed him so good it dripped down his aching balls.

"I see you washed yourself out for Daddy, didn't you? You expected to be used well tonight?" Juandre gave his approval, revving Andrew's motor higher.

"Ah, yes, just for you. I wanted you, Daddy," he admitted because, yes, he did. Andrew felt what could only be something huge. It stretched him so wide he thought he was tearing open. *Must be a coned sex toy.*

"Daddy," he yelled in surprise.

"Take it. I know you can," Juandre said and moved the cold thing back. Andrew wanted to look, but he enjoyed the sensation too much. It drove his endorphin levels sky-high, and bliss washed over him.

Then he felt Juandre getting up from the bed, and the mattress dipped this and that way. He heard rummaging in the closet. Ripping and crunching of paper bags. "Wow, Daddy, are you getting more toys? You're going full throttle on my ass," Andrew said. He needed him to bring whatever he had and fuck him.

"Lift your chest," Juandre said, and Andrew did. Juandre lay three pillows in front of him. "Okay, lie down. Thank you, you're such a good boy, but I need you to just feel, no questions and no looking."

Andrew was delirious with happiness. He loved him so fucking much. "Yes, Daddy," he said and lay down, making himself comfortable.

Next, Juandre tied his hands to the bedpost and applied some kind of spreader to his ankles. He could probably break out of them, but the illusion made Juandre happy, and that made him happy.

"Oh, my fucking, shit!" he howled into the mattress. Juandre poured something extremely hot, no, not hot, it was cold. Also not cold. "What are you doing? You're burning my insides. I can't take it," Andrew exclaimed, and Juandre purred and massaged it deeper into him until his hand worked into his channel. Pumping it rhythmically back and forth while his other hand rubbed Andrew's balls and cock with the hot and cold lube. They were on fire! He was jelly.

"Feels good, doesn't it?"

"It burns."

"Are you sure you're burning?"

Andrew stopped and concentrated. *No, it wasn't burning, it was tingling!*

"You want your Daddy to stop?" Juandre asked him gently, putting a fat hand on his back.

"No, sorry, Daddy, I'm ridiculously stupid."

"That's okay. Daddy wanted that to happen, don't worry. Daddy will only do things that are safe for you. You can tell him to stop anytime."

"Okay, yes, please, Daddy," he said and felt Juandre removing his hand and moving in behind him. He heard something being sprayed out of a can, and then warm hands massaged it over his well-stretched hole.

"Hmmm, tastes so good," Juandre said, and Andrew relaxed. Whatever he doused him with smelled sweet. His vampire senses told him that he was busy with cream and chocolate.

When he was done, Andrew was a lump of relaxed, lustful flesh, just lying there enjoying it. Juandre lay down on top of his back.

"I've always wanted to lick cream and chocolate from your beautiful body," he said lovingly in his ear and thrust his cock inside him.

The pleasure was intense. "Daddy's cock's just right for hitting my good spot."

"Okay, baby boy. Daddy's going to fuck you. Daddy needs to get his cock deep inside you!" Juandre started power fucking him, harder than he'd ever remembered being fucked, and realized it was because he had vampire strength now. They reached their first orgasm fast and were cheering, satisfied, impressed grunts when their cocks swelled, and Juandre filled him again and again.

"Yes, Daddy, fill my hole!" Andrew begged.

Juandre obliged, and they orgasmed for the fourth time. They were a sticky mess. Drenched with sweat and totally sated when Juandre finally rolled off him.

Short of breath he heaved. "I should untie you and get you in the shower, boy."

Andrew didn't say a word. He was totally and inexplicably fucked. Marriage to Juandre was going to be awesome! He grunted and agreed. Juandre untied and rubbed life back into his wrists and arms.

"Can't wait to marry you. How do you feel about a honeymoon in South Africa?"

"I think I fucked you senseless. Why South Africa?"

"That's where I store the whiskey. I want to take you and Charlie on a safari and show you the big five in their natural habitat." Andrew looked into those sparkling chocolate brown eyes that looked so lovingly back at him.

"That sounds adventurous, and adventure is my middle name," Juandre said and kissed Andrew with deep affection.

Chapter Twenty-Three

"Good morning, citizens of Phoenix.

It's now six a.m.

Did you know the place and time of the invention of the wheel remained a mystery for thousands of years until recently when one of our own scientists discovered a Mesopotamian tablet with a figure handing another figure the wheel?

Another interesting fact about wheels is that they can mean many things. For example, if someone has one hand on the wheel, they're taking control, but if they have two hands on the wheel, they're giving pleasure to two men at one time.

Lasitor doesn't know if the Mesopotamians handed each other a wheel or cock.

Obviously, no one took control of the situation.

Visit your community news page for more facts about wheels.

Breakfast is served until eight a.m.

Have a just roll with it kind of day!"

General Cian Romanov

95 A.T.

Earth

Cian's fleet commander chair rattled so hard and fast his jaws vibrated and he had a fleeting thought of his passengers chipping teeth and that dental appointments were imminent once they landed. Behind him, his men sat wide-eyed, strapped in, and clutching their seats.

"Ready yourselves. Switching off all engines. We don't want to go kaboom. If we survive this, gas masks will not be removed until we determine the air is safe to breathe. Hold on! Here we go!" Cian's voice crackled over the speakers.

The blue water-covered planet came closer and closer until the ship entered the exosphere, and streaks of blue, white, and gray clouds flashed by, obscuring their view. The Horizon creaked and cracked. Loud whistling cut the droning noises of the thundering winds as they descended and cut through the gas clouds.

"All engines down," Lasitor announced.

"Bloody marvelous. This better work. We can't fuck it up now. We've come so far," Cian said, willing it to be miraculously so.

He checked the overhead security panels for Barkor. He was grabbing and handing the ropes and parachutes to the line of men working together.

"Who decided free-falling was a good idea?" Ivan asked rhetorically.

Eryn answered, "You and your brother."

Cian looked at them, Eryn seemed calm as usual, while Ivan was crushing the hand rests, and sweat beaded on his frowning pale forehead. The noise was deafening. Cian worried the ship would light a spark if they re-entered the atmosphere too fast. The air thinned. The pressure increased. Breathing became difficult. He sucked air through his pursed lips and worried about the humans who must all be experiencing labored breathing.

Suddenly momentum forced them back in their seats, and Cian knew Barkor and the men successfully deployed the parachutes. The noise died down. The rumbling reduced. He checked the air pressure and oxygen levels, confirming it stabilized as he breathed easier.

"Something's wrong." Cian watched the security feed. Barkor and the men were struggling to release the last crate with parachutes. "They need help, Eryn. Something's happening. They can't get it out the fucking door. They're pushing and pulling. It's not moving! Come on," Cian muttered through clenched teeth. "Release the parachutes. Release the 'chutes now!"

"They need help, brother," Eryn shouted, already up and making his way outside.

"No point in trying to steer and fly now. We're falling too fast." Cian released his seat belt and joined Ivan and Eryn. The ship was tilted, so they had to pull themselves on the handrails up the walkways. Eryn jumped ahead, propelling himself like a tree frog off the sides to the back of the ship as fast as possible.

Angst-ridden faces of passengers glanced at them. Children cried. Mothers and fathers consoled and protected them by keeping their heads braced as they were told.

Some uneasily murmured and peered out the port windows at the fast-approaching blue speckles and sparkling sunlight on the water below.

Just as Cian and Ivan managed to reach the loading bay, Eryn, Barkor, and the men pushed with no success. Eryn stuck his spear underneath the crate, closed his eyes briefly, and the crate popped out of the track and burst open. Parachutes deployed, and the men jumped to hold on. Momentum thrust the ship back and forth as it stabilized horizontally. Bodies and anything not tied down were being tossed around them like projectile objects.

"You're hitting the water in ten, nine, eight, seven, six. Brace yourselves, four, three, two!" Lasitor counted down.

"Hold on!" Cian jumped for Barkor's hand just as he dove for a man flying through the air on his way out the open door.

Loud crashing followed the pandemonium. His neck flipped backward from the momentum, while he held onto Barkor.

Suddenly all was quiet, and they were airborne. He looked around frantically, checking where to help next. Then the silence was filled with humans screaming.

Airborne. Anything not tied down was in animated suspension—ropes, shattered plexiglass, children's toys, crates, weapons, and people.

"Zero-gravity?" Barkor loudly asked, as if he was used to screaming. "Is it over?"

Crackling noises came from the speaker system. "Welcome home, sirs. The engines shut down, and we re-entered safely through the flammable gas clouds." Lasitor's voice was raspy and echoed through the cargo area, announcing the obvious too late. "Please remain seated. Do not remove your masks and safety harnesses until announced that it is safe to do so," Lasitor added.

"Welcome home," Cian said with a big smile. He needed to kiss Barkor. "I guess we made it. And all in one piece." Ripping his mask off his head, he pulled Barkor closer and removed his mask for him, and then he kissed him. Barkor hesitated, the onslaught of lips and tongue momentarily stiffly received, but then he relaxed, lips softened, and tongues glided as he kissed him back.

Voices of people reminded Cian they weren't alone. "Come, let's go help the humans," Cian said, as some of them had already moved to the open back end of the ship where the loading bay gaped open revealing crystal blue waters.

Bemused, the people looked dumbfounded at each other. Some yelled, astonished as the anti-gravitational system deactivated, and everything fell to the floor as gently as a feather. In the commotion, Lasitor had opened the opposite side doors of the loading bay. Loud mechanical gears click-clucked as it mechanically hoisted the doors up, revealing blinding sunlit waters. Scared children cried and pointed to the outside while shielding their eyes. Once again, it was chaotic topsy-turvydom. Some seemed to realize it was normal, while others ran to hide, grabbing children and ducking for cover from the sun.

Cian laughed. "Thank fuck, no big smashes or flames."

Barkor stopped in his tracks. "Wait a fucking minute? What is that?" he asked, pointing to a big bird in the sky. Barkor's face filled with the joyous realization. "That must be a bird. I saw a bird first!" He shouted and hopped on the balls of his feet. It flew by, squawking. "That's a bird, isn't it?" he asked.

The rest of the humans righted themselves before standing closer and watching in awe. Some peeked out the doors, windows, and loading bays.

"No, that's not a bird, that's an... honestly, I don't know what the fuck that is, but it's not a bird. I would know," Cian said.

Eryn and Ivan joined them. "I agree. I've never seen a bird that size. It looks like a giant pelican," Ivan said.

As the ship hovered over the ocean water, the flaps of the open loading bay doors filled with people. The masses of humans pushed and shoved to get a look. Some fell into the water, pushed from the back, and some jumped into it. They laughed and jubilated. Some must have remembered Lasitor's lessons on floaties because they hung on crates, and others just took their clothes off, jumping in naked.

A boy clinging to his mother's side exclaimed, "Mamma, look at all the water!"

"Look at them. No one knows how to swim," Eryn remarked, frowning, and Cian felt the worry emanating from him.

"I agree this is going to end in a tragedy, brother. You better hang onto something, or you'll sink!" Cian harrumphed at the sight of the happy people realizing they couldn't swim who were now drowning.

"Surely, they wouldn't drown now that they're safely home. Someone, please throw something that floats for those idiots—" Cian pointed, smiling as he grabbed a thick rope and threw it so they could pull themselves to the sides.

His smile was quickly wiped from his face as he watched in horror as the strange bird dove out of the sky straight toward the splashing humans.

"Oh fuck!" Eryn screamed. He saw it, too, and jumped into action.

"Out of the water, get out of the water!" Cian yelled.

But no one heard. The bird opened its beak, gulped a woman up in its mouth, and disappeared into the dark blue depths. Now the humans moved, climbing over and onto each other to get to safety.

Eryn jumped, leaped, and dove over them with his spear in hand down into the ocean's depths.

Cian and Ivan frantically helped the eager swimmers back into the Horizon, and Barkor disappeared into the fray of disorganized humans.

When everyone was safely out of the water, Eryn appeared soaking wet with the drowned woman under his arm.

Cian ran to help. Ivan yelled, "Put her down. We can try C.P.R." Eryn gently laid her down, and Ivan started chest compressions. A circle of people formed around them, wet and crying. Cian pushed her chin up to open her airways and started puffing air into her lungs.

A man pushed through the ring of spectators and rushed for the woman they worked on. "Sophia! Sophia," he cried, shocked, wet, and trembling.

After ten minutes of unsuccessful cardiopulmonary resuscitation, Ivan stopped and said, "It looks like she's passed."

"May I try something?" Eryn asked softly. He spoke calmly, touching the man's shoulder. He stopped crying. "May I try something?"

"What? She's dead. He said she passed. What do you want to do?"

"I know, sir, but sometimes when the blood is still warm, I can make it flow again," Eryn said with reassuring empathy.

"Yes, yes, of course, try whatever you can," he said, wiping his snot on his sleeve.

Cian knew Eryn had extraordinary abilities. "Do you need me and Ivan to help?"

"I don't know. Let me see if I can help her." He closed his eyes and placed one hand on her forehead and the other on the center of her chest. The hull of the ship fell silent.

"Look, he's glowing, Mom," a little boy said. His mom pushed him back as if protecting him.

"Yes, Mommy sees," she said.

Another woman said, "Let's be quiet and watch them." She picked her child up from the floor and sat him on her hip.

Although it was a bright sunny day, the blue and gold waves emanating from them danced like flames blinking in and out of sight in the sunlight. Cian looked up and saw Barkor walking through the tumult of people watching. Their gazes met, and Cian nodded a thank you. This was what Cian loved about him. He didn't ask what was happening. He watched, assessed, drew conclusions, and then knowingly affirmed the situation by nodding his head. Barkor joined him, holding onto Cian's shoulder, supporting and letting him know he was there for him.

"Don't be scared. They're helping her. She swallowed too much water," Barkor told them. Cian hoped they didn't all turn and run screaming.

Each hummed their separate songs. Cian concentrated on feeling hope and life and looked at Barkor. Then he felt love and goodness. His brother, Ivan, hummed peace and the knowledge of wisdom, and Eryn hummed creativity and calmness.

Silence fell over more than two thousand people witnessing a miracle. The gods they went searching for on the moon and had been traveling through the stars to bring them back home were here with them on Earth.

"It's the prophecy. The prophecy has come true," one woman said.

"Our saviors," a male voice said, and then a little boy began to laugh, pointing at the tiny spirals of blue and gold rays of light escaping the circle where the four singing demi-gods worked.

"Look, the promised prince, Mom. He really is our prince!"

Light streaks surrounded and drifted over the crowd of onlookers.

The woman coughed and convulsed, expelling frothy seawater. She opened her eyes and sat up, vomiting more water.

"Jesus, how much water did she swallow?" Cian asked.

The man on his knees beside her reached for her. Shocked and thankful, he kissed her face all over. The crowd of humans murmured. Some began babbling and dancing. Ecstatic with happiness, people threw their canes to the side, hands in the air they all danced.

"What the fuck?"

In the background, Cian heard Lasitor attempting to get their attention.

"Excuse me, excuse me!" Lasitor called louder than the thumping and whooping horde.

"Shh," Cian said while waving his hands. They settled down as Cian pointed to his ear and the speaker.

Silence.

"Lasitor, go ahead," Cian said, shaking his head at the craziness.

"Your fathers want to speak to you."

A beep-beep sound behind him caught his attention. He spun around and looked. Men were exiting Bubblecars and climbing onto the loading platform of his ship.

"You know how to make an entrance, don't you? Welcome home, everyone," Brad said, arms stretched wide in a welcome gesture.

Cian did a double take. No, not Brad, or maybe it was? *It sounded like him, but something was different about him.* It was the manner in which he spoke and how he sounded. Cian couldn't put his finger on it for the second time today.

"Son, so glad to see you," Connor greeted and enveloped him. Again, *something was off.* Cian stepped back. From head to toe, he looked them up and down, Connor, Mika, and Brad. They looked different. It was their clothes—they were dressed in silver-colored mesh suits and weird flip-flops. No, not flip-flops. There was nothing through the toes. It was a thin sliver strap over the bridge of the foot. They looked like space-age hippies. *Where are the black bodysuits and boots?*

"Hello, handsome," a voice from his past greeted him. A man stepped closer. His big friendly eyes and chunky body reminded Cian of someone long ago. He was the friendliest teddy bear of a man, always hugging and laughing. He had braided, long dark blond hair and the sparkliest green eyes. Next to him stood another man who reminded Cian of his partner.

"Can it be? Juan and Drew, is that really you?"

"Yes, who did you think I was? Whatever you've been snorting up there, I want some, too," Juan said in his familiar effeminate lilt. His body suit was purple, and a bright yellow bowtie was around his neck.

What the fuck? Cian looked at his perplexed brothers. They looked as baffled as he felt. Juan crossed his arms and tapped his foot, waiting. Cian dropped his head back and screamed into the blue earth sky.

"Ish, you motherfucking time-traveling son of a motherfucking meddling alien! What have you done?"

* * *

Barkor, the Promised Prince

95 A.T.

Alternate Timeline

Earth

Barkor just blinked and listened as Cian and his big family rambled. It was a lot to digest, and Cian kept saying that this was not possible, and yet, they all stood in a city underwater, breathing fresh, clean air under lights as bright as the sun but cool as a breeze of cold air. Cian never left his side. The sexy big bombastic fleet commander held his left hand tightly, and although he didn't crush his hand, it might as well have been glued to his. For Barkor, it was a sign that he was wanted, and it was an endearing thing.

As he was introduced to Cian's people—all male and looking eager to meet him, he heard how long and hard Cian had driven them to the point of insanity to build a Spacecar. Over his shoulder, Cian kept saying these weren't his people and that he would explain later.

Firstly, Barkor's flock needed to get settled and moved in. The Phoenicians were prepared to house the new citizens and make them comfortable. Schedules were posted for them, and the talking community news page, which they grew accustomed to on the ship, would show them where to go, to eat, sleep, and explore. Each received a talking wristband connected to Lasitor, the talking computer—not Zelk.

Over two thousand rooms, which they called apartments in the old Earth language, were built, fully stocked, and furnished if a person chose to move in. Barkor's people preferred to stay together. He read their fearful faces and their clingy bewilderment and had just said the words to Cian, and Cian organized beds and mattresses to be carried into what he called the Athletics Dome.

Men and boys of all ages jumped to get it done for them. Their friendly enthusiasm was creepy. Barkor figured it would take them many sleep cycles, at least five hundred of them, before Grayrak's people would be used to living in this sparkly clean and happy place underwater.

Luckily he had Cian, and they had him, so he guessed his people would acclimate with time. Barkor was worried about the women and children, especially Talali and her friends. He had only the frame of reference of his upbringing, and he worried that the Phoenicians would take them and use them as the Disciples did. But no matter their age or gender, they were treated like they mattered and were all as precious as newly discovered jewels, with dignity and sympathetic care. Something they were not accustomed to, and as odd as it felt, he encouraged them to trust their hosts because he trusted Cian. He was Barkor's pillar, strength, and hope, as Barkor was to the Grayrakians.

Cian's song was all around him, from the moon's surface to underneath the earth's waters. It was an invisible force. An intense yet gentle vehemence that pulled and bonded yet encouraged. It energized, and Barkor figured it was the seed of hope for new beginnings.

Just then, Ish and a man Barkor had seen inside the golden spaceship stepped closer. He was much shorter than Ish, with long platinum-blond hair and bright blue eyes. He looked friendly and offered a hand to shake, which Barkor shook with his free hand.

Later, the two other men that greeted Cian earlier stepped closer. One with dark hair and dark eyes, dressed in all purple—the only one dressed like that—looking sexy, dangerous, and chirpy, accompanied by another bigger muscled man with blond braided hair and green, friendly eyes. The happy one pulled Barkor and Cian in for another hug. He had zero personal space issues, and Barkor thought anyone could jump in his arms; he wouldn't mind. Cian growled at him. And he flapped his hands like Cian was an irritating fly. Either he had no respect, or he was familiar with Cian.

"Hello, my name is Juan," he said, pinning Cian with a stare while greeting Barkor. "Stop sounding like you're warning me or something. I changed your bloody diapers and will smack you if you try something, boy."

Cian looked irritated and amused. "Juan, the last time I saw you alive, I was a boy, so that must have been a slip of your tongue," Cian said, holding his free arm out. Juan fell into the embrace.

"*Pfft*, no slipping of tongues just yet," Juan said and cackled. His eyes glinted with a strange sparkly sheen. "Can we go sit and talk somewhere?" Juan clapped and asked the crowd that'd been droning around them. As soon as they landed, Barkor was swept up in the fray and introduced left and right. He couldn't remember anyone's name. It was as if everyone knew Cian and his brothers, and they all spoke with him, with them, and with each other. It was exhausting. The chaotic pace had continued for over twenty-four hours, so sitting down sounded good to Barkor.

They made their way down long corridors. The color of the light surrounding them changed as translucent roofs and walls displayed the sea life outside. They ended up in what they called the leadership conference room. It was a big room with one long table and chairs enough to sit about fifty men. Behind those were more rows of chairs, making it an area where over five hundred people could sit.

Cian pulled Barkor over to the table, where they found a spot. He pulled a chair out for Barkor and sat beside him. Barkor noticed other couples doing it, so it must have been an Earth thing. Barkor decided to keep quiet and observe because he felt out of place and held onto Cian's hand, where he found the strength to hold on for dear life.

"Can one of you explain why we returned to a place that's the same but not the same? For example, you wore black when we left, and now you wear silver. Juan and Drew are alive while we buried them almost one hundred years ago." For once, it seemed Cian was the only person who spoke.

From the opposite side of the long table, their leader got up. He carried himself as if he was in charge. Although he didn't interrupt or ask to be heard as if his word was more important than the others. Next to him sat his husband. If Barkor remembered correctly, he was the medical doctor who walked through and checked who needed immediate medical attention. Cian called it triaging. As the leader smiled warmly at Barkor, he nodded with a nonverbal acknowledgment to Barkor, then looked at Cian as if he was proud of him.

"Cian, firstly, and may I repeat myself, good job! You have planned and executed a flawless escape plan and impressively landed a warship without the engines running." He pointed to Ish. "That man has to tell you what is going on." He nodded, then sat down. It seemed everyone around the table agreed that Ish had some explaining to do.

Cian stood and said, "I agree, Ish. You better explain, or I'll wrap my bare hands around your throat and—"

Ivan interrupted, "Brother, no!"

"Well, get on with it," Cian added and sat down. Barkor wanted to jump and grind on Cian.

Ish got up, removed his sunglasses, and spoke. He was not the tallest, but he was definitely the biggest muscled. His dark skin and gold and black-ringed eyes were an obvious contrast to the mostly pale-skinned earthlings.

"Cian, your plan of creating a vortex and sending the vermin, I mean the Zelk, into it was good. I was tasked to disintegrate them. Make the entity go away, rather than move them from one plane to another. The universe is much bigger than you could ever imagine. And if I start moving problems around, instead of doing my job, I'd get us all into deep trouble. When I was given my time machine, I was told to wait for you and your Bubblecar, and then help you. In my solitude and waiting, my only entertainment for decades was drinking and watching them." Ish pointed to Barkor. "I kind of developed an addiction while drinking intoxicated Disciple blood."

Peter jumped up. "I can vouch that the stuff is highly intoxicating. I had one sip, and we almost crashed into the Horizon." Peter chuckled, and Cian snorted.

"Yes, it's funny now, but you could have killed us all," Ivan added.

"We know, and we're sorry." Ish placed his hand over his heart, apologizing sincerely. He swept his gaze over the audience. Silence followed.

Smiling shyly, he shook his head. "Anyway, I remembered if I used my powers, I always have to do it for unselfish reasons and was allowed to give two things, I mean change two things. I wanted to give you and your people so much more back."

Ish lifted his arms and explained animatedly. "You have to understand. Before all this happened. I searched uncountable realities, and yours was the only one I missed. I realized I missed it because of what Eryn had told me. He said I'm not living it, only watching. This was true, but he meant the one I'm going to live in would be the one I experience and not travel." He pointed and smiled at Eryn. Eryn gave one affirming nod. "He's a smart man. He'd spoken of this timeline. The one I'm supposed to live in. I realized I traveled all the time in timelines of other people's histories—not my own. I was physically put here and given a job to do.

"Once I realized I needed to lock those doors and come home, I wanted to bring back something for your leader and asked him. If he could have done two things differently, anything at all, what would it be, he said, *have more fucking whiskey and not have Juan and Drew killed."* The room erupted in laughs and giggles. Brad joined the laughter but soon put up his hands to quiet the men down so Ish could continue his story.

"Thank you, everyone. Ish, please, continue. I want to hear it."

"Oh, I love how you can laugh at each other's expense and not find it belittling. You're all such a fresh bunch of humans. I'm honored to join you."

"Yes, yes, tell your story, and we'll decide who joins who," Connor said with a scowl.

Ish cleared his throat and made eye contact with Peter, seemingly searching for approval. Peter mouthed, *I love you. You can do this.*

Ish shifted from one foot to the other. "After I got to know Peter, he told me how good you were for him. I made a point of it to get to know Brad and the parents who raised these beautiful boys. I'm not talking about the outsides. I'm talking about the insides. The purity and unselfishness they spread like an infection. For once, I could see the fates would unfold in front of my eyes. I decided to help you as best I could, using the tools I was given. But I couldn't do it alone."

Ish bent down to kiss Peter on his head and continued. "The day I came to meet your people, I saw Peter. And it was the vision of him that somehow jogged a memory. A fluttering feeling instantly bloomed in the pit of my stomach. An infatuated-in-love connection clicked into place. It was as if I knew him. Like his essence and my essence sang a song."

"Hmmm, we heard that before. We grew quite accustomed to the singing and glowing," Brad interrupted sarcastically. Peter giggled shyly.

"When we met, he reacted the same. I realized he was the key to everything, to my existence. Once we'd spoken, he'd told me about himself and how he'd waited for me."

All attention zoomed in on Ish as the screeching of chairs—seats being pulled closer—filled the room.

This story is important.

Peter gave Ish another approving nod and pushed a glass of water closer for him. Ish took a sip, put the glass down, and spoke in his weird deep baritone.

"We met in nineteen-sixty-eight, but I also appeared with his older self that night. That was the night and point in time the switch started." He pointed to Drew. "Andrew, better known as André, is Peter's best friend and brother. I determined Juan, Drew, and Peter to be key factors and jumped back and forth, realizing the man who shot Juan and Drew was Juan's son. He shot them because he hated his father and was a Disciple. I decided to check why he hated his father and dug deeper—"

Cian interrupted Ish. "Bloody damn, you're like an investigator and a fixer." Juan and Drew chuckled and agreed. Ish smiled, burrowed into his black shirt's neckline, and pulled a big clock watch on a chain underneath his shirt.

"I am the master timekeeper. That is my gift bestowed onto me. My father used me. I was supposed to watch and manage it, so he could continue like I will continue living here with you.

"It's a blessing that they're not here with me. They would have discarded Brad and killed all of you, who seemed to be a threat to him and take it all for himself. We Anunnaki are the fathers and mothers of everything here, past and coming."

A chorus of coughs and throats clearing came from around the table.

Ish lifted his hand, indicating they were to wait. "That's what we thought. And it's not true. We are but another cog in the big wheel of existence. You're not in danger. For thousands of years, I searched for this timeline, this one where everything reset naturally. As I said, it was hidden because I willed it. I locked us out. No one can travel inside or outside this loop because I am here with Peter and my bloodline. We are now able to restart from this point forward. That is why, when I returned to Anzulla, it was crumbled and desolated."

Ish sat down, and Peter got up. He spoke with a strange, nasal accent. Skittishly he continued.

"I could never tell you anything, and it drove me to madness. Now that it's all over…" Peter paused to wipe tears from his eyes and sniffled. "You know I'm one of the original products who survived Hitler's scientists in the Jewish prisoner camps. I don't have many details, but I suspect it was horrific as women were mutilated, and babies were made, tested, and discarded until our Aryan line was singled out. We were treated well, but—" He let his head fall, shaking it lightly.

No one said a word and waited for him to compose himself. He lifted his head, wiped his red tear-filled eyes with quick, controlled movements, and cleared his throat. Everyone watched him and waited in silence. Barkor sensed no judgment or animosity—only empathy. The places and times Peter spoke about were interesting, and he soaked up the history of the Disciples and their sick creations. This was his history, as well.

"I have or have had many brothers, but at this stage, it's safe to say it's only André, sorry, Drew, and myself who survived." He pointed a hand over to Drew and Juan. And Drew got up.

"Yes, I would have died if Ish and Peter didn't come to save me. Peter and I were friends. We grew up together. Our fathers were scientists and friends at Humboldt University when the wall went up. The four of us were transferred to the western side. It was renamed New Berlin University. We were the lucky ones. The others had stayed behind." He turned to Eryn. "I suspect this is where your father was raised." Eryn crossed his arms and gave a slight nod. "We knew it was only a matter of time before we got split up and punished for being *der homosexuelle*. The organization was set on continuing our bloodline, and as you know, artificial insemination was not an option in the nineteen-sixties, and our partners were chosen for us."

"Motherfucking sick fucks," Mika, Cian's father, who had been quiet in the background, interrupted and coughed. "Sorry, Drew," he said, holding his hands up in apology.

"Yes, Mika," Drew agreed. "The first successfully performed test-tube baby was performed in nineteen-seventy-eight. We were Aryan and gay. One way or the other, they needed our sperm, and they wanted the next generation of super babies. We knew we had to flee to survive and had our suitcases packed and ready for the Americas the next morning. That was when Ish and older Peter appeared and explained it all to us. The train would have crashed, and I would have died, and Peter would have transferred back to East Berlin. Ish gave us a choice, but with older Peter there, we knew what the answer would be," Drew said.

"Mika, Connor," Peter said to get their attention. "Somehow, your bloodlines were meant to come together. Ish and I can't figure out whether it was by design or miracle, but your bloodlines plus the string code I sew into the zygote formed the missing link Ish and his family waited for to continue their species. Pieces of Anunnaki are in each of us. We are all ultimately created by them.

"Let me start by explaining it as if we spoke of Ish's Anunnaki Monarchy. Eryn is King, Ivan, Cian, and Barkor are the princes, and Drew, Juan, and I are knights," Peter said and shrugged.

Eryn shook his head, he didn't want to be the King, and everyone knew that because Barkor had heard him say that at least twice in this short time.

Juan jumped up. "Tell them, my bear, tell them. Show them. You guys are going to shit your pants," he said excitedly. Lifting his knees high, he pretended to run in place. *Wait, he was running.* So fast it looked like he stood still. The air moved around him. Drew walked over as if this was an everyday occurrence, and he was used to seeing Juan running as fast as the wind in the same spot. He grabbed Juan's arm and pulled him closer. Juan came to a dead halt. The flutter of air seized.

"Juan and I have a burning secret. Can we share this with them now?" He looked at Ish, who smiled, exposing thin, longer-than-usual incisors. Juan rolled his top lip back while Drew opened his mouth wide to show his long fangs.

"No fucking way!" Cian exclaimed, still holding Barkor's hand.

"Yes, fucking way!" Juan answered and giggled. "This is how we survived and lived so long."

"How, tell us?" Ivan and his husband exclaimed at the same time.

Ish stepped forward and cleared his throat. "Well, Brad said he wanted whiskey, and Drew is Lord Andrew. He stocked whiskey for miles high inside the mineshaft marked with a blue tower in South Africa," Ish said proudly, hands on his hips and smiling wide, exposing all his white teeth. Juan and Drew bowed as if to say you're welcome. Cian and his brothers gasped, looking baffled. He gave Barkor a side eyed look, shaking his head in disbelief.

Barkor moved closer to whisper in Cian's ear. He wanted to ask him why, but Ish spoke. "I gave Drew my bite, and he'd given his bite to Juan," Ish said. "It's meant to bond partners to the monarchy in Anzulla. I was already mated to Peter by blood, so I could give it away without the fear of outliving my partner or bonding with Drew."

"Yes, Juan told me, vampires, but not vampires. I'm getting thirsty. I suspect there are more stories. I can see where this is going. Who ambushed and killed them in your timeline?" Brad asked.

"Charles Montgomery killed them," Cian said, and his brothers agreed.

Juan explained, "Well, this sexy vampire built a whole distillery, Lord Andrew Distilleries. When I divorced Charles's mom, Andrew showed up, and we got married in South Africa. I took Charles with us. If I had left the marriage and sent Charles to his mother, he would have joined the Disciples. But instead—" He stopped, looking strangely out of character and uncomfortable. "Andrew killed the whole American chapter." Drew hugged Juan, and they sat down.

"We can tell you the details another day," Drew said, his face seriously somber, and the men around the table respectfully stayed silent. Impressing Barkor.

"We were abducted but never ambushed?" Cian asked Ivan and Eryn, who looked puzzled at Brad.

"We went to rescue you, Ivan, and my boys from the mines. Killed Eryn's brothers and brought back crates of whiskey after we sent a rocket we found in the mineshaft to the moon," Brad said.

"They were never killed because Charles never shot them," Ish added. "This was where the timeline had shifted."

Barkor chuckled, thinking of Cian calling Ish's eyes *honeybee ass* eyes. He'd never seen one, and Cian showed him earlier on the computer screen what it was. Ish pointed to Cian. "When you sang your song for the moon, you put into motion a timeline shift." Ish laughed and clapped his hands. "See how awesome you all are?" He was very impressed with himself and his big reveal.

Cian looked questioningly at Ish. "Yes, it's the song of creation. You sang it. You willed it."

"No way!" Cian said, looking around. Barkor pulled his shoulders up. This was news to him.

"What did you think you were doing?"

"I sowed the seeds and sang my heart's song as if I was singing it to Barkor." He turned to Barkor and blushed. Cian lifted the hand he'd been clamping the whole time and kissed it. Barkor's heart melted even more for him. He was such a softy. A softy that could tell seeds to grow.

"Then I scattered the seed bombs. I willed them to sprout and grow."

"Yes, go on," Ish encouraged.

"I imagined colorful gardens and beautiful butterflies, dragonflies, and bees to pollinate the flowers. I imagined water and fruit trees. Okay, I see. I may have created a garden, so what?" Cian asked, not seeing it.

Ivan tapped him on the shoulder. "Brother, none of us can create gardens, insects, and anything nearly like that. You have a green thumb, and you created a garden of Eden on the moon."

"But they sent seeds and seed bombs. All I did was sing to them."

"Probably to let nature take care of it in time. We never thought you would do that," Brad said as Ivan and Eryn came to hug their mystified brother. Cian never let go of Barkor's hand. All this history of life before Barkor was born intrigued him.

"Okay, so explain what happened after Brad killed Charles Montgomery," Eryn said.

Brad frowned. "I never killed Charles. He's Juan's boy. Why would I kill him?"

"Somebody, please fucking make sense to me. I'm getting a headache," Cian said, rubbing the nape of his neck.

Ish put his hand up. "Juan and Drew were shot and killed in your reality. The moment Juan and Drew met, thanks to my Billboard ads, they naturally changed their own course of their lives. All I had to do was find a position in time to cross and swap—" He waved his hands, one crossing the other. "It all worked out. All is now as it should be."

"Wait, I have a few more questions!" Mika's husband said with an accent Barkor recognized as Irish.

"That cylinder, the ancient golden cylinder that was originally the shape of an apple. Mika assembled and disassembled it and figured out that if broken into several pieces and then rebuilt, the golden apple was its original form. Someone was smart enough to crack it open like a puzzle box and then reassemble it as a capsule instead of it being a cylinder and rolling it in ink, so it printed out the string codes and star maps. The codex for genome mapping was just a tiny bit of the information embedded on the inside. Peter and the rest of our gifted ones are the direct results of its message. Who knows what the fuck else could have happened if someone accidentally rebuilt it into the cylinder form Mika had discovered. Also, those stone tablets, maps, and hieroglyphs, who planted that? Because there was freaky foreboding shit on it," Connor asked and turned to Mika, pulling him up by the elbow to stand. "*Gille-toine*, tell them what you think happened."

Mika's chair loudly scratched the floor. A long low sound—a thing of finality. He pointed two fingers at Ish. "He's the motherfucker who started all this shit! Ish, hand over the keys to your ship, and, Brad, take his time keeping compass away from him. We must destroy it!"

"I assure you my intentions go beyond the way of living in this reality. We have a common enemy. I saw firsthand the horrors of the malevolence. I escaped alive but was forever changed. You are the resurgence, the gift of the light. A product of goodness. Call it the last card or the last fight that has destroyed the ultimate dark enemy. The moon was once my precise position that I was told to wait and take no action until the ball-shaped ship appeared. It was pre-programmed into my ship. I was only allowed to jump for one person and change only two things, but I kind of fucked it up. I thought I did do it intentionally, maybe subconsciously. I realized I will never remember the pattern I followed, or interrupted, so I ended up leaving messages for myself, until Peter suggested I revisit Phoenix, record the original history by uploading your news broadcaster. I assure you, nothing was lost."

"Ta-da!" Lasitors' voice surprised all of them. A round of laughter broke out in the room, breaking the tension.

Ish pointed to every man around the table and then to himself by thumbing his chest. "To be fair. I was led here.To today. I was given these keys to the locks of time and told to use them wisely. So was the plan, and I could foretell you never knew it. Look what you have. You have integrity. You have knowledge, and you wield it without knowing it. You have life-everlasting. Somehow you succeeded. And you don't see it. You *are* the plan."

"Yes, and which plan is that?" Brad asked.

"It is the plan that worked."

"How many plans did you try?" Cian asked.

"I don't know. I never counted," Ish said, letting his head fall in defeat.

"You were intoxicated, weren't you?" Cian asked.

"Hey. Don't you like it when the plan just comes together? Look at you. You're successful, you all have love, and you all have partners. Look at this building. It's miraculous. You live underwater. You have ships in the shape of balls. These people are looking up at you. They are following you," Ish said, smiling as if he saw a light at the end of a dark tunnel.

"You are true gods. In the end, that's all that matters," Ish said to the astonished men listening and bowled over by the statement.

"In the end?" Cian asked.

"Yes, the end."

"Yet you say this is the new beginning."

"Yes, that it is."

The End.

To be continued in According to Ish.

About the Author

Kashel Char Logo

Kashel Char means Castle Black. Chosen for the apparent reason that Kashel is a Game Of Thrones fan.

"I found it surprisingly beautiful. In a brutal, horribly uncomfortable sort of way."——Tyrion Lannister to Janos Slynt.

Kashel is a Canadian speculative Male/Male Sci-Fi Fantasy and Paranormal Romance writer, currently residing in the Rocky Mountains of beautiful British Columbia, Canada.

Kashel loves bubblegumming questions about our existence as humans with fantasy, folklore, and conspiracy theories featuring hot, powerful godly men. Their stories are unpredictable, sickly twisted with a dash of humor, centered around gay characters. Kashel's wild imagination will have you question your existence among these worlds and make you wish you could escape to these places peppered with taboo subjects and foul-mouthed heroes who struggle and strive to save humankind while experiencing a life filled with pleasure, freedom, and love.

Pronoun: They/Them I/We She/Her He/Him Gender Non-conforming, Gender Fluid.

Love to all Creatures.

Kashel Char.

Website: https://KashelChar.com

Milton Keynes UK
Ingram Content Group UK Ltd.
UKHW010651250923
429338UK00001B/69